Jasper Wild

a novel by George Mercer

Library and Archives Canada Cataloguing in Publication

Mercer, George, 1957-, author

    Jasper wild / George Mercer.

(Dyed in the green ; 3)

Issued in print and electronic formats.

ISBN 978-0-9879754-4-7 (softcover).--ISBN 978-0-9879754-5-4 (PDF)

    I. Title.

PS8626.E743J37 2017   C813'.6   C2017-900067-5

                            C2017-900068-3

FSC
www.fsc.org
MIX
Paper from
responsible sources
FSC® C016245

Cover art and design: Dan Stiles

Editing: Kate Scallion

Typeset in Bell at SpicaBookDesign

Printed in Canada by Friesens on 100% recycled FSC-
certified paper.

For Jill and Basil

DYED IN THE GREEN – THE SERIES

Book One – Dyed In The Green (2015)
Book Two – Wood Buffalo (2016)
Book Three – Jasper Wild (2017)

PLANNED FUTURE RELEASES

Fiction

Book Four – Fat Cats (2018)
Book Five – Dyed And Gone To Heaven (2019)
Book Six – The Rhino's Horn (2020)

Non-Fiction

Six Parks (2020)

PROLOGUE

STANDING ON THE lip of the canyon wall, Malcolm Seawell did a last minute check of his harness, then leaned back over the edge, letting the climbing ropes take the strain as gravity fought for control of his body.

This was always one of his favourite moments in any climbing adventure, second only to the triumph of a successful ascent that would invariably see him resting for some time at the top, drinking tea and savouring the moment as he surveyed the landscape below stretching off to the horizon.

In stark contrast to the effort of getting to the top, the descent was gravy, usually a quick and methodical series of rappels that would take him to the bottom in a fraction of the time it took to climb to the top.

Light and agile, Malcolm relished the efficiency of heading back down, feeling almost weightless as the rope fed through the figure 8 in his left hand, his right hand held tightly against his waist, maintaining an even strain on the rope as he effortlessly hopped from ledge to ledge, braking ever so slightly to lessen the impact of each touchdown.

As he was about to go over the edge, Malcolm smiled to himself as he remembered his climbing partners ribbing him about his slight frame and wiry build.

"One hundred and forty pounds, soaking wet," they would say.

"Carried packs almost as heavy," they'd add with a laugh.

"I suppose you did," Malcolm would reply.

There was no lack of bravado or ego in the climbing community, he thought. Everyone was all about me.

But over the years he'd been lucky. He had a long list of former climbing partners who shared some of his greatest climbing achievements, men and women both, who had finally given up as age, injuries or more serious mishaps caught up to them.

Remarkably, Malcolm had climbed for more than forty years, most of it injury free. He'd avoided major mishaps, but like everyone in the climbing community, he knew many who hadn't been so lucky.

Climbing had taken its toll, so much so, that his wife still couldn't fathom why he continued to do it when a number of his best friends were now gone.

She just didn't get it.

For as long as they'd been together, Marion had never really taken to climbing.So while Malcolm packed ropes, harnesses and hardware and headed out for a day of climbing, Marion often took the canoe and went exploring.

Together they amassed an almost encyclopedic knowledge of one passion they shared: Jasper National Park.

But increasingly they were concerned about the park's future, doggedly following up on any rumours of a new development or expanded human use, convinced these were eroding the very principles national parks were based on and eating away at wilderness.

Together they'd become a burr in the side of Parks management, unwilling to concede one more inch of the park to developers or the latest fad, and always on the lookout for something amiss in Jasper.

Even earlier in the week, it had happened again: while Marion was away visiting their daughter, Malcolm had come across flagging tape in the Maligne Valley. Following it he was surprised to find what he thought was a survey stake, but its location made no sense, practically sitting in the middle of nowhere, some distance from the Maligne road, and not near any of the trails in the area.

A quick call to the park's office had done nothing to satisfy his curiosity and once again he'd been handed off to a junior park planner, who told Malcolm he'd check into it and get back to him.

Brushed off yet again, Malcolm thought.

And when he went back to check, the tape was gone. Despite spending several hours searching, he was unable to find the stake again.

To jog his own memory to investigate further, Malcolm left a note of sorts stuck to the refrigerator, a cryptic scribble typical of his many notes to himself, which he often had to reread multiple times to decipher his own words.

He was getting older, after all.

The thought brought another smile to his face as Malcolm angled out from the ledge, leaning back and stepping down the rock wall until the rope settled against the edge.

Flexing his knees and pushing off, he hung in midair for a split second before dropping down the wall, taking his time to ensure the descent was smooth, trying to avoid rubbing the top rope against the rock's abrasive surfaces.

Ever the miser, today he was using some of his old equipment, wringing the last pitches from some old ropes before cutting them into shorter lengths for canoe tie downs or tent ropes, whatever he needed.

As he lowered himself Malcolm sensed movement on the rope and paused for a moment to look skyward. Seeing nothing at the top of the ledge, he looked past the canopy of fir into the bands of clouds sliding quickly across the afternoon sky, then relaxed his grip and continued his descent.

But once again, Malcolm sensed something wasn't right.

Ever so subtly his grip tightened.

Suddenly he brought up with a lurch, suspended above the canyon floor as the weight of his body swung him toward the wall.

Just as quickly he heard a sharp crack from above and instinctively lowered his head and braced for impact.

The falling rock caught him on the edge of his helmet, glancing off the hard plastic and plummeting to the canyon floor.

Momentarily stunned, Malcolm's grip loosened as a small torrent of stone shards dislodged by the larger rock stabbed into the back of his bare hands, sending the climbing rope speeding through the figure 8.

Reacting more than thinking, Malcolm clawed the air for purchase, but to no avail. With a muffled cry he plummeted to the bottom of the rock wall, landing with a sickening thud on the canyon floor.

CHAPTER 1

BEN MATTHEWS AND Kate Jones peered through the windshield of their small pickup truck as the heavy, thick snowflakes coated the highway.

"Typical spring weather," said Ben, as he took a drink from his water bottle.

"It won't last," said Kate. "We'll run out of it as we head south."

Ben looked at Kate with raised eyebrows, as the snowflakes got even larger. Ever since leaving Fort Smith for Jasper, the weather had been variable and they'd taken their time driving, stopping at a few of the points of interest they hadn't been able to get to in their short stint North of 60.

After an all-night party hosted by Wood Buffalo's chief park warden and his wife, and a late breakfast of home-cooked bannock, they'd finally piled into the new truck, purchased in Hay River just a few days before, and pulled out of Fort Smith. Now as they passed the turnoff to Hay River and headed south toward Enterprise, the fact they were leaving the Northwest Territories was suddenly sinking in.

At the territorial border, they pulled into the small campground and spent the night huddled in their tent, bemoaning the fact it was all ending too soon.

"This sure wasn't how I wanted it to end," said Ben as he snuggled into Kate.

"No. We were just getting our feet wet. I was really starting to like the place." She turned and looked into Ben's eyes. "But who knows? Maybe we'll get a chance to come back North someday."

"I hope so. This was just a tease."

After a sleepless night of fitful dreams Ben lay motionless staring at the frosted roof of their small tent, thinking about the conversation they had before Kate was finally pulled away into a deep sleep.

We were just getting our feet wet, he thought. *But we had to take a stand on the bison issue, even if it meant putting our jobs on the line.*

Ben sighed and looked at Kate. Thankfully they were both on the same page when it came to dealing with what happened in Wood Buffalo. Luckily they were able to move on and get an offer from Jasper National Park. It was unfortunate they had to leave the North so soon but they made their own bed and now they had to sleep in it. Maybe someday they would get back but for the next while, Jasper would be their new home.

Looking at his watch, Ben realized it was time to get up and carefully pulled himself out of his sleeping bag. Trying not to wake Kate he quietly unzipped the tent and crawled out into the dull light of morning, stood up and stretched.

The world around him was coated with a thin layer of snow, a reminder that in the North, the transition to spring could sometimes take a step backward.

Ben closed his eyes and for a moment he was back in Terra Nova National Park in Newfoundland, standing on the wharf at the park's headquarters. He was lost in thought until a subtle stirring brought him back to the frosty reality of springtime camping in the Northwest Territories.

"Should I send out a search party?" Kate said as she wrapped her arms around him.

Ben smiled. "Yeah."

"Where should I send them this time? Sweetgrass? The Highlands?"

"Newman Sound," said Ben. "In Terra Nova."

Kate shook her head and looked into his eyes.

"It was the light," Ben continued. "Heavy cloud, the hint of snow." He looked around. "Well more than a hint." He paused and looked past Kate. "During spring, when most of the inner sound was still ice-covered, I used to spend hours watching ducks feeding in the few small patches of open water they could find. Every so often an eagle would try to take one, but they weren't always successful. For the duck, it only took one wrong move and it was game over."

"Kind of like what we used to say about the poachers in Cape Breton," said Kate. "They could come into the park every night and take a deer, but we only had to catch them once."

Ben nodded. "Kind of like that. Only for the ducks, the stakes were higher." Ben's last words caught in his throat and he broke out of Kate's arms.

She walked up behind him and moved in close, leaning into his body. "You've got to let it go. I should never have mentioned Cape Breton."

"It's not your fault," said Ben, looking off into space. He turned and looked in Kate's eyes. "I don't think about it as much anymore, but every now and then, I'm back there. Cape Breton was special, but it was tough. Terra Nova is my escape, before things got complicated."

Ben looked up as a flurry of fresh snow descended on them. "We should get going. The roads will probably be slippery. It'll be nice to head toward some warmer weather."

Breaking camp and packing up, they pulled back onto the highway and continued south past the small town of High Level, deciding it was too early to stop for gas and a break.

"We'll try and make Peace River," said Ben. "And put some distance behind us while the going is good."

The farther south they went, Ben and Kate were struck by the gradual transition from Jack pine to aspen and poplar as the newly budding trees morphed into a full canopy of green foliage lining both sides of the highway.

"I don't think we saw a vehicle from Enterprise to the border and only a couple before we got to High Level," Kate commented, as a large pickup towing a trailer with two all-terrain vehicles flew past headed north.

"And now it's bumper to bumper." Ben laughed as they both looked at the long stretch of empty asphalt snaking its way south.

Kate smiled and shook her head.

"You know," Ben added. "Margaret, the postmistress in Fort Smith, was funny when I told her we were leaving."

"How so?"

"Well, I guess I must have seemed kind of excited about the notion of a move. When I asked her for some change of address cards, she looked up from what she was doing and asked where we were going. When I told her we were moving to Jasper, she just put her head down, tossed a few cards across the counter to me and said 'Welcome to the rat race.'"

Kate's eyes opened wide and her jaw dropped. "Seriously?"

Ben looked at her and nodded just as another large pickup blew past them, headed south, the driver leaning on the horn as he swerved in front of them and raised a finger.

"God, what's his problem?" said Kate.

"I was probably going too slow for him," said Ben, pushing the accelerator a little to emphasize his point.

"He should get a life before he kills someone."

"Whoa, girl." Ben laughed. "Let it go. They probably don't get a lot of sightseers on this road."

As they crested a slight hill, Ben and Kate caught their first glimpses of the Peace River Valley, the aspen forest opening up into broad expanses of rolling grassland dipping down to the river.

"Beautiful," said Kate.

Ben nodded.

"So where's the dam?" asked Kate.

"The Bennett Dam?" said Ben. "It's still a long ways upstream."

"Hard to think something so far away could be having such an impact in Wood Buffalo," said Kate, pulling out a roadmap and tracing the line of the Peace River toward Hudson's Hope and the Williston Reservoir.

"It is hard to fathom," Ben agreed, "but the scale of everything is so much bigger up here. Imagine controlling flows on a river that large," Ben added, sweeping his hand in front of him. "It has to make a difference to everything downstream."

"I guess we saw it firsthand," said Kate. "I mean the overflow we ran into going to Sweetgrass."

"Yeah. It makes river travel tougher for the folks who rely on it, but we probably don't even understand the full effects on a system this large."

"Isn't that dam supposed to be one of the largest in the world?" said Kate.

"Apparently," said Ben. "I couldn't imagine what it would do to places downstream, if it ever failed."

"Could that happen?"

Ben shrugged. "It's an earthen dam. You never know."

"Wow," said Kate, shaking her head. "After seeing the flood in the delta, I have a better appreciation of how massive an event it could be."

Pulling into Peace River for fuel, food and a pee break, Ben and Kate found a small gas station and café.

"If you want to get a table, I'll gas up," said Ben. "I'll only be a few minutes."

Kate nodded and got out, then disappeared inside.

As Ben began to fill up their truck, a large pickup rumbled into the gas station and took up the stall on the opposite side of the pumps. The driver, a husky man wearing a TruNorth Drilling ballcap, slid down from the cab and grabbed the other nozzle.

"If you can't drive any faster than you were going, you should get off the road."

Ben looked around into the grizzled face of the pickup driver, the roadmap of lines and grooves covering the leathered face suggesting someone who'd been around.

"Sorry?" said Ben, caught off guard by the comment and turned off by the stench of diesel wafting over him.

"You heard me," said the man as he glared at the canoe perched on top of Ben and Kate's truck then turned his head back to the nozzle. "Damn environmentalists."

Ben bit his tongue and ignored the comment. He finished filling up then parked on the side of the café, nodding at the other driver as he walked inside. Kate had already ordered tea and as soon as Ben sat down, the waitress was hovering over him with a fresh pot of coffee.

"Thanks," said Ben, sliding his cup toward the waitress while looking at Kate. "Did you order?" he asked, running a finger down the menu.

"Not yet."

"I'll give you a minute," said the waitress.

Ben nodded and looked out the window as the heavy duty pickup pulled away from the gas station.

On the road again after a quick meal, quiet prevailed as Ben and Kate sat back for the next leg of their drive.

"We turn here," said Ben pointing to the sign for Grande Prairie. "We'll head toward Grande Cache and then we hook up to the Yellowhead into Jasper."

Travelling south along the Grande Cache Highway, the rolling topography of the foothills and Eastern Slopes gave way to the grey outline of the Rockies in the distance, the peaks lost in a heavy cover of cloud.

"Pretty nice," said Kate, as the road wound closer to the mountains. "Other than one trip to Jasper for training at the Palisades, I've never really seen it from this perspective."

"Yeah, my two trips to the training centre were a bit of a blur," said Ben. "Met some great folks, but never got to see much of the park. Coming at it from this direction should give us a nice taste of what it offers."

As they followed the road south, they took in the endless landscape of evergreen forests interspersed with forestry cut-blocks and seismic lines, bordered to the west by a series of mountains seeming to flow uninterrupted toward the opposite skyline.

At one point, Ben and Kate were both surprised to see a small group of woodland caribou picking their way through a cutblock before disappearing again into the forest.

"Funny," said Kate. "I never really thought of this as caribou country."

Ben was about to reply when they drove around a curve and spotted two more caribou, standing in the middle of the road. Slowing down, they approached the animals to within a few metres just as a large truck suddenly appeared behind them, blasting its horn and sending the two caribou into a frantic attempt to escape as they clawed for traction, stumbling on the asphalt. As it sped past, Ben and Kate recognized the truck, the driver once again giving them the one-finger salute in his rearview mirror.

"What the hell?" said Ben, as he glared down the road then turned his attention back to the caribou. The animals regained their footing and bolted for cover, leaping into the ditch and crashing through the buffer strip of young pine that separated the cutblock from the highway.

"What an asshole," said Kate. "He could have killed them both."

"Not to mention us," said Ben. He pulled the truck over to the shoulder and turned off the key.

"What's that guy's problem anyway?" said Kate.

"Beats me. Back in Peace River he called me 'an environmentalist.' A 'damned environmentalist' to be exact." Ben laughed. "I think the canoe spooked him."

"I didn't realize you saw him there," said Kate.

"Aw, it was nothing," said Ben, regaining his composure and starting the truck. "He's just a hothead." He pulled the truck back on the road. "We'll probably never see him again."

CHAPTER 2

AFTER THE EPISODE with the caribou, the drive south was relatively uneventful as Ben and Kate made their way toward the Yellowhead Highway. Closer to Hinton, Highway 40 dipped toward the Athabasca River, its headwater still almost two hundred kilometres upstream.

"Wow," said Kate as they crossed the large bridge over the river. "I wasn't expecting this."

"The Athabasca?" said Ben.

"Yeah. I completely forgot it runs through Jasper."

"And ends up in Wood Buffalo."

Kate nodded. "It's pretty amazing, really." She paused. "Think about it. This river connects both parks, ecologically and physically. It's kind of cool."

"Yeah, that is cool," said Ben. "The river starts in the Icefields as glacial melt, travels more than a thousand kilometres and settles out in the delta and Lake Athabasca. I wonder if anyone ever considers that."

"And on the way, it's going past cutovers, farms, mines, the tar sands ..."

"And towns that pull water from it every day and probably pump their shit back in it every night," said Ben. "On the downstream side."

"Treated sewage," said Kate.

"Yeah," said Ben. "Right."

"We all do it," said Kate.

"I know," said Ben. "But now that we've seen the end of the pipe, so to speak, don't you think about it a little differently?"

Kate nodded as they pulled to a stop at the intersection with the Yellowhead Highway. As they pulled onto the Yellowhead and headed west, the heavy cloud cover that seemed to travel with them all day cleared a little, revealing hints of blue sky and sunshine that lit up parts of the foothills and front ranges of the Rockies. In the distance, the sharp face of a massive mountain stood out above the green slopes.

"I think that's around Pocahontas," said Kate, rifling through a map unfolded across her lap. "The mountain's Roche Miette," she added as her finger landed on the name.

"The park gate is just down the hill," said Ben as they descended past a large sign for the Overlander Lodge and turned a corner.

As they pulled up to the gate, a young woman in a Parks uniform leaned out the window and looked down at their licence plate.

"I love the polar bear plate," she said as Ben rolled down his window. "Will you be visiting the park or travelling through?"

"I think we're staying for awhile," said Ben, looking over at Kate, who smiled.

"How many days exactly?" said the park attendant. "If it's more than fourteen it's cheaper to buy an annual pass."

"We're thinking years," said Ben. He and Kate laughed.

"You're moving to Jasper?" said the park attendant.

"Yeah," said Ben. "We work for Parks." He reached out a hand. "I'm Ben Matthews and this is Kate Jones."

"Pleased to meet you," said the young woman. She looked across the truck at Kate. "I'm Patsy. Welcome to the park." She handed Ben a small bundle of papers. "You can pick up a resident's pass when you get settled. Here are a few brochures and a park map to help you get oriented."

"Thanks," said Ben as a large truck pulled up behind them.

"I'd love to chat," said the attendant smiling, "but duty calls."

Ben leaned out and looked back at the line of traffic making its way down the hill toward the gate.

"Just a heads up," Patsy added before Ben rolled up his window and drove away. "There are lots of sheep on the road ahead near Disaster Point and we've got reports of elk at Talbot Lake. Drive carefully."

Ben acknowledged the advice with a wave and handed the brochures to Kate who immediately began thumbing through them, reading aloud as they made their way into the park.

"Fiddle River, cool name," said Kate as they drove across the first of several bridges they would encounter on their way to the town of Jasper. "And Miette Hot Springs," she added as they passed the Pocahontas bungalows. "Now there's a place I want to check out."

Driving past a series of flooded wetlands Kate said were referred to locally as the "Poco Ponds," she pointed out flocks of geese and ducks as a pair of Mallards glided down in front of them and settled in the water.

"Disaster Point's coming up," she said, motioning to a large rocky promontory sticking out into the highway. "Some say," she read, "the name 'Disaster Point' refers to an incident in which packhorses fell off the trail along the cliffs and landed in the river." She laughed as she silently read the remainder of the explanation.

"What's so funny?" said Ben.

"Well it says the real 'disaster' was when Sandford Fleming broke his whiskey flask on a rock just east of Roche Miette."

Ben laughed.

"He was the chief surveyor for the Canadian Pacific Railway," said Kate.

"When?"

"1892," said Kate, checking the write-up.

"That's a while ago," said Ben.

As they neared Disaster Point, Kate pointed at a small group of bighorn sheep standing in the middle of the road. "Patsy was right."

"Licking salt by the looks of it," said Ben as he pulled onto the shoulder to get past a large ram with massive horns slowly making its way across the highway.

"Wow," said Kate. "Impressive."

"As long as they don't get run over," said Ben. He motioned toward a large transport truck approaching from the opposite direction, the whoosh of its air brakes echoing off the cliff face as the driver slowed down for the sheep.

The driver gave several short blasts of his horn to try and get the sheep moving, but to no avail. Slowly, he pulled the truck over to the opposite shoulder and geared down. He raised a hand to Ben and Kate as he worked his way past the sheep and continued eastward, just as a pickup, the *same* pickup, barrelled up from behind and fishtailed through the group of sheep, narrowly avoiding the big ram as the driver once again leaned on the horn and sped away.

"Unbelievable," said Ben. He pushed the accelerator to the floor and sped after the pickup as it disappeared around a curve. "Let's see if we can get a licence plate number."

"Let it go," said Kate as their little pickup tore down the highway. "You'll never catch him."

Ben was about to reply when he noticed an approaching RCMP vehicle do a quick U-turn on the road ahead, its red and blue emergency lights flashing.

"Maybe there is a god," said Ben as the police car sped down the highway after the pickup truck.

A little farther along, Ben and Kate watched as the pickup and patrol car pulled over to the side of the road. As the RCMP officer got out and approached the pickup, Ben pulled in behind the two vehicles.

"What are you doing?" said Kate. "Let it go."

Ben sat silently staring ahead until the officer began walking back to his car with the driver's papers. As Ben started to get out of the truck the officer motioned for him to stay in his vehicle, walking back to Ben's side of the pickup and motioning for him to roll down his window.

"Can I help you?" the Mountie asked, looking down at Ben with a frown on his face.

"I'm just glad you stopped that guy," said Ben. "He barrelled past us at Disaster Point and just about killed a bunch of sheep. He's passed us twice already today. He's been driving like a maniac."

16

The Mountie bent down and glanced across the truck at Kate, then back at Ben, looking somewhat skeptical.

"Is that how it happened?" he asked Kate.

"Pretty much," said Kate. "He nearly hit some caribou on Highway 40 as well."

"Where are you folks coming from?"

"The Northwest Territories," said Kate.

"We're wardens with Parks," said Ben. "We're moving to Jasper from Wood Buffalo."

The Mountie nodded and straightened up as he thumbed through the driver's papers. "Well, let me deal with this guy. You folks can make your way to town. If I need more information, I'll track you down. Jasper's a small place."

With that, the Mountie returned to his vehicle and Ben and Kate continued on their way to Jasper.

Kate yawned as Ben pulled the truck back onto the highway.

"It's been a long day," said Ben. He looked at the truck's odometer. "Almost a thousand clicks."

Kate continued to thumb through the park pamphlets as they came upon a large lake on their left. "Talbot Lake," she said. "This is where the attendant said the elk were."

"Like that one?" said Ben, motioning to a large bull elk feeding in the grass by the side of the highway, its newly forming antlers covered in a layer of velvet. Kate pointed to a second animal feeding at the base of a sandy ridge on the opposite side of the highway.

"Are those sand dunes?" said Ben.

Kate nodded as she read. "Yeah, they seem to run along here for several kilometres."

At breaks in the dunes, they could see a large expanse of sand off to their right. "Jasper Lake," said Kate.

"A lake?" said Ben. "Seriously?"

"Apparently it fills in the summer, but for the most part, it drains in the winter."

"Sounds backwards," said Ben.

"But I guess it makes sense," said Kate. "The Athabasca is primarily glacier fed here in the park and as temperatures heat up in summer, there's more runoff from the glaciers."

"Make sense," said Ben. "Kinda neat just the same."

Finally crossing the main bridge over the Athabasca River, the highway took a sharp turn toward the south.

"Now that's impressive," said Kate, pointing to a massive rock wall on their left and an equally spectacular sheer cliff on their right that buttressed the main river valley. "The Colin Range," Kate gestured to her left.

"And the Palisades," said Ben, excitedly, nodding to the rock wall on their right. "I remember this from recruit training. We never got to see much of the park, but it was hard not to be impressed by the Palisades."

As they watched, blue sky and sunshine emerged from the heavy clouds and the valley was lit up with warm colours as evening began to settle in around them. Turning off the highway and into town, they looked at each other and smiled.

"We made it," said Kate. "Now to find a place for the night."

"It's early in the season," said Ben. "Shouldn't be a problem."

Driving down the main drag, they reconnoitered the array of lodges and hotels, rubber-necking as Kate pointed out Signal Mountain, the Whistlers and Mount Edith Cavell before backtracking and pulling in to the Sawridge Inn as a train slowly worked its way into the massive rail yard on the opposite side of the road.

"This looks fine," said Kate.

"Huhuh," said Ben. He yawned and looked at Kate. "Just give me a bed. I don't care about anything else right now. We can touch base with the Parks folks in the morning."

As they crawled out of the truck and stretched, the truck that had been playing leapfrog with them all day rumbled past and disappeared farther into town.

CHAPTER 3

ZANE RITTER PUSHED the TruNorth ballcap back on his head and looked around the smoky bar. Shuffling his way inside the Bear's Den, he pulled out a stool and sat down, then nodded to the bartender, a lean young man wearing a North Face toque pulled low around his brow.

"Gimme a draft," Ritter ordered, shoving a crumpled twenty-dollar bill along the scarred wooden bar with a callused hand that had seen its share of fights.

The bartender started listing the types of beer on tap, but Ritter held up a hand. "Your cheapest draft," he said, making no effort to hide the disgust in his voice.

Zane Ritter didn't like coming into Jasper.

Despite the cross section of people that called the town home, everyone from railroaders and ski bums to multi-millionaires, he always felt people were looking down at him, and he resented it. Having outfitted for a time in Jasper, he knew the town and the park probably as well as anyone, but he knew the eastern part of the park and the neighbouring foothills north and south of Hinton even better. He felt comfortable there, in his element, and always had a hard time rationalizing the differences on either side of the park boundary.

Being stopped by the cop at the east end of the park only added to his frustration.

Seventy friggin' kilometres an hour in wildlife zones. What a bunch'a horseshit. Ya won't be able to stop if an animal darts out on the road.

He laughed and looked at his mirror image behind the bar.

I can stop. Stop'em dead. Dead in their tracks.

He looked around the bar at the toques hauled down over long hair, the Mountain Equipment Co-op jackets and Patagonia pants, and shook his head. *These deadbeats wouldn't know the first thing about survivin' out there.*

"Another draft," he said to the bartender. He drained the glass and pushed it back toward the bartender, just as a hand grabbed the shoulder of his jacket.

"Boo," said the voice behind him.

Ritter barely turned his head. "Make that a jug instead," he commanded, looking over his shoulder at the huge body behind him. "And bring it over to the table," he added, finally turning around to confront the man. "You're a little late."

"Got away late," said the other man. "How was the drive south?"

"Okay, I guess. Had a few other stops to make so turned on the afterburners to get here." Sliding off the stool, Ritter motioned to a table in the corner and the two men silently picked their way across the room. Nothing else was said until after the bartender delivered two clean glasses and a jug of draft, sitting it on the table between them.

"Did you bring it?" said the other man.

Ritter poured himself a glass of beer. "Course," he said, pushing the jug across the table. "You got the cash?"

The other man nodded and poured, then raised his glass and chugged back the beer.

After downing the second beer, Ritter motioned to the door. "Let's go."

The other man pulled a twenty-dollar bill from his pocket and tossed it on the table, then followed Ritter outside.

"This is too easy," said Ritter.

"Tell me about it," said the other man as they walked across the deserted main street to another oversized pickup parked next to Ritter's behemoth.

Both men pulled the tailgates down on their respective trucks.

"It's heavier than snot," Ritter said as he jumped into the back of his truck and opened a massive job box. Reaching inside, he manhandled a large bundle wrapped in thick plastic and rolled it out onto the tailgate with a thud.

As he slid out of the truck, the second man began unwrapping the bundle.

"Whoa there," said Ritter, as a park warden truck edged its way down the main street, slowing down as it passed the parking lot. Ritter stood against the tailgate with the other man, blocking the package from view. After the truck passed by and turned up a side road, Ritter quickly pulled back enough of the plastic wrap to reveal a large bison head.

"Nice," said the other man.

"It was the best of the lot. Had two others I dropped off on the way here."

"It'll make a great mount," said the other man, quickly inspecting the head then rewrapping the package. With Ritter's help, he slid it into the second pickup and closed the tailgate. "Where'd it come from?"

"Up north," said Ritter.

"From that big park up there? What's it called? Wood Buffalo?"

"Outside the park," said Ritter.

The other man regarded Ritter suspiciously. "I didn't know there were buffalo outside of the park."

"Don't worry about it," said Ritter, casting his eyes down the main street. "Let's just finish this so we can both get outta here."

As Ritter waited, the man reached into his jacket and hauled out a sealed envelope. "It's all there," he said, as Ritter pulled out a small skinning knife and was about to open the envelope.

"Sure it is." Ritter smoothly slid the razor-sharp knife into one end of the envelope and ran it down its length. Looking inside, he fanned the bills with his thumb, then closed the knife and pocketed it along with the cash. "Let me know if you need anything else: sheep, bear, buffalo, I can get whatever ya want."

"Good to know," said the other man, motioning toward another park warden truck slowly cruising toward them along the main road. "I'll be in touch."

Ritter nodded and shook hands then walked around to his truck. "You head out first."

"Will do." The other man climbed into his truck and started the engine. Pulling out of the parking lot, he drove across the divided main street and turned west toward the warden truck, which now appeared to be slowing down.

Is he going to pull a u-ey and chase 'im? Ritter wondered, as the warden truck got closer. Quickly, he started his vehicle, pushed the stick shift in reverse and popped the clutch. The huge vehicle lurched backwards with a squeal of rubber and stalled. Smiling to himself, Ritter watched the warden truck turn off the main street and pull into the far end of the parking lot, slowly making its way toward him.

That's it. Come'n get me.

Restarting the truck, he popped it into gear and began to drive away. He laughed to himself as the warden truck's emergency lights came on, the red and blue strobes washing across the storefronts lining the main street, just as the taillights of the other truck disappeared toward the opposite end of town.

CHAPTER 4

AS HE MADE the return trip down Connaught Avenue, Jimmy Rand was second-guessing himself about which of the two vehicles he should try to pull over. When he'd gone by a few moments earlier, he thought he recognized one of the trucks as belonging to Zane Ritter, a former park outfitter turned oil worker, and wondered what Ritter might be doing in town.

This time he considered stopping the second vehicle to find out who the driver was, but the jerky movements of the other truck as the driver attempted to back out of the parking lot across from the local bar drew Jimmy's attention.

He might be drunk, Jimmy thought as he turned on his emergency lights and pulled in behind the larger truck and placed a call to dispatch.

"Hey, Trav," he said, when the voice of Jasper's dispatcher came over the park radio. "Just checking a pickup downtown on a possible 10-55. Alberta licence Whiskey Tango Foxtrot 666." He smirked at the vanity plate's lettering and wondered how the provincial motor vehicle folks had missed the obvious meaning of WTF. "I think I know the driver," he added, speaking into his portable radio as he got out of the warden truck. "I'll be back in a minute."

"Ten-four," came the response from the dispatcher.

As Jimmy approached the truck, he stood on his tiptoes to look into the back, then made his way toward the driver's window. Reaching up and tapping on the side window, he waited for the driver to roll it down completely before saying anything.

"Thought it was you, Zane," Jimmy said as Ritter leaned his head outside and looked down at the park warden.

"Evenin', Jimmy. Whassup?"

"Not too much, Zane. What's up with you?"

"Nothin'. Just came to town to meet an ol' buddy. Had a couple o'beers and now I'm headin' home."

Jimmy knew from experience Zane could pound back the booze without any obvious signs of intoxication, but he wanted to make sure he didn't send an impaired driver out on the highway. "Mind getting out of the truck?"

"No problem." Ritter opened the door and slid onto the ground, the stench from inside the vehicle wafting into Jimmy's nostrils.

"You been livin' in this thing?" Jimmy chuckled as he shone his flashlight along the floor and behind the seats.

"Pretty much. Been workin' up north in the patch. But they just put on the spring road closures, so I came south until they're lifted."

"You goin' north again?" Jimmy Rand asked as he walked to the back of the truck and opened the tailgate.

"Prob'ly, when things harden up," said Ritter, following the warden. "TruNorth expects t'be puttin' in more wells, so I don't see why not. But I also got some work down this way, helping a survey crew at the new mine. So I'll be around for awhile."

Jimmy shone his flashlight into the back of the truck, illuminating the detritus of Rand's latest journeys: beer cans, plastic oil jugs and a waterlogged cardboard box of soiled rags. Running his hand along the base of the tailgate he put a finger to his nose and sniffed.

"Been huntin' lately?"

"Not since last fall."

"Cleaned your truck lately?" Jimmy's voice was tinged with sarcasm.

"Not since ..."

"Last fall?" Jimmy finished the sentence as he lifted the tailgate. Leaning in with his shoulder, he pushed until he heard it latch.

"Yeah," said Ritter.

Jimmy turned and shone his flashlight directly at Zane Ritter, taking care to avoid shining it into his eyes. "So, you've been drinking?"

"Had a couple beers."

Jimmy watched Ritter's every movement but saw nothing to suggest he was impaired.

"Okay, Zane. You caught my eye when you popped the clutch, so I figured I should check you out. Take it easy on the way home."

"That's the only way I take it." Ritter laughed and lightly punched Jimmy on the shoulder. "You take care now, Mr. Warden. I'll keep an eye out for ya. Make sure everyone sticks to the law."

Jimmy grinned and watched as Ritter climbed in behind the steering wheel. "Where did you say your buddy was from?"

"I didn't," said Ritter, his voice taking on a harder tone as an RCMP cruiser pulled in behind Jimmy's warden truck.

"So where *is* your buddy from?" said Jimmy as a Mountie emerged from the cruiser.

"Lala Land," said Ritter, pointing toward the west end of town.

"B.C.?" said Jimmy.

"That's what I said. Lala Land." Ritter started the truck and was about to drive away just as the officer walked up to them.

"Everything okay, Jimmy?" said the Mountie, shining his flashlight over Ritter's pickup.

Zane Ritter glared at the police officer.

"Yeah," said Jimmy. He nodded to Ritter then waited until he was out of the parking lot and headed east on the main street. "Just doing a spot check."

"You know that guy?" The Mountie pulled out his notebook and thumbed through the pages. "I pulled him over today, out east."

"Yeah," said Jimmy. "He used to be an outfitter here. We go back a ways."

"The 10-29 I ran earlier came back negative," said the Mountie, "but he's got a long list of priors."

"Yeah," said Jimmy. "He was a bad cat in his day. I'm hoping he's cleaned up his act. Otherwise I'd be concerned that he's back around the park."

"Why's that?"

"He's, how would you say it, an *avid hunter*," said Jimmy, his eyes still on Ritter's truck as it moved slowly down the main street headed toward the highway.

"Poacher?" said the Mountie.

Jimmy nodded. "The worst kind."

CHAPTER 5

MARION SEAWELL CLOSED the office door and locked it, then turned to face the mountains. Shutting her eyes, she pulled a deep breath of cool air into her nostrils, filling her lungs. She held it for a moment then exhaled and looked up at the night sky.

It had been a long day.

Pouring over the pile of development proposals facing the national park, Marion wondered how it was possible for Jasper's management team to entertain some of the ideas being put forward by businesspeople and developers when the park's primary role was to protect wildlife and their habitat.

She was tired and now that Malcolm was no longer with her, the work for Jasper Wild, the local environmental group, seemed endless. There was no way to stay on top of everything.

Malcolm's death the previous autumn had been devastating and there was still something about the climbing accident that nagged at Marion. Truth be told, she was surprised something hadn't happened to him sooner considering the amount of time he spent tied into a climbing rope. But it was the cryptic note he'd left behind that bothered Marion most about his death, and she questioned the coincidence of it all.

Malcolm had found something in the Maligne Valley, which his note suggested needed further investigation. Then, within a day or so of scribbling the message, he was dead.

Marion had been challenged to decipher Malcolm's note, but managed to figure out he had found some flagging in the Maligne that warranted a second or third look.

It may not have been anything of consequence, Marion thought. After all, they found areas with flagging tape all the time and

27

usually deduced it was someone's route to a favourite climbing location or just someone trying to ensure they were able to get back to the road after a day spent exploring.

But if that was the case, it seemed odd for Malcolm to leave a note about it. And his reference to a survey stake—now that was unusual.

His note suggested a single stake with an inscription, and although Marion couldn't decode his notation, it looked like a set of initials, but she had no idea what the letters were or what they stood for. And, despite her best efforts, Marion was unable to find the location Malcolm had vaguely referred to in his note.

Although she had no reason to suspect foul play, Marion was convinced that Malcolm's death and the note were somehow related, but whenever she broached the subject with close friends, they were unwilling to consider her suspicions, certain luck and time had finally run out on her husband.

Now, with Malcolm gone, and a seemingly endless workload as new development proposals were put forth, Marion felt like a lone voice in the wilderness. And with a proposed new mine on the park's eastern boundary, Marion felt overwhelmed by the weight of it all.

She and Malcolm had been the stalwarts of Jasper Wild, tackling the bigger development projects proposed for the park and surrounding areas. Together they tag-teamed most of the workload, with Malcolm insisting that while Marion was a whirlwind of unfettered energy, as persistent as a dog on a bone, he provided the sober second thought, a more reasoned alternative to Marion's aggressive approach.

Good cop, bad cop, as Malcolm liked to say.

She smiled to herself, as she thought about how Malcolm was really the one who displayed dogged determination when dealing with the bureaucracy of Parks management or any developer unlucky enough to find themselves caught in his crosshairs.

Appearing cool and collected compared to her vociferous and passionate outbursts, Malcolm was a bit of an enigma whose underlying mantra always echoed in her brain; *nil bastardo carborundum*—don't let the bastards wear you down.

Smiling at the memory, Marion looked back up at the night sky then started down the sidewalk toward home just as a large pickup rumbled past, one of its massive roof-mounted side lights illuminating Marion for a brief second as it passed. Blinded by the glare of the lights, Marion stumbled slightly but caught herself and turned around in time to see the truck's taillights disappear into the night.

Finally making her way home, Marion made a pot of tea and settled into the sofa then turned on the television to watch the day's news. The lead story was about the proposed open pit coalmine on the borders of Jasper National Park, the third in a series of mines butting up against the park boundary.

Marion was disgusted by the thought of more development.

This is daunting, she thought as she listened to the piece, her attention drawn to a reference to an international mining company apparently behind the latest mine proposal.

Great, she thought. *They destroy their own country then come here and destroy ours. More people should be standing up against these types of developments.*

CHAPTER 6

WHEN THEY WOKE up the next day, Kate and Ben had breakfast at the inn then slowly made their way to the warden office for a scheduled meeting with Jasper's chief park warden. Their old boss in Wood Buffalo had filled them in on his counterpart in Jasper, but his description was short on details.

"Make up your own mind," Francois Masse had said. "He can be tough but if you're one of his wardens, he'll always have your back. And he agreed to give you guys a chance for a fresh start after all you've been through here."

Ben and Kate had been in the outfit long enough to know Francois was right not to tell them too much about what to expect. They were keen to finally meet the man who had given them the opportunity to turn a new page and let the stories of their exploits in Wood Buffalo fade from the memories of Parks' senior managers.

They *would* make up their own minds.

*****

Lou Walker sat at his desk, wondering what file to tackle next: the latest version of a draft report about arming national park wardens, or a preliminary notice from the Alberta government about a new coalmine application along Jasper's eastern boundary.

Lou wasn't one to waste his time on noble aspirations. He knew a decision on arming national park wardens was long overdue, but doubted the new director-general for Parks would side with the wardens, even after the murder of a park warden in Cape Breton a few years earlier.

Maxime Bolduc, or the Snake, as people had come to call

him, was one of the new breed of senior managers, politically picked by the government to do their bidding and tasked with making the minister look good. He was quickly making a name for himself by ignoring the best advice of experienced park superintendents and those in Ottawa who had worked their way up through the national park system.

Lou Walker wasn't afraid to get into a shit fight with him, and had a run in with him once before during the short time Bolduc had spent in Jasper. But that was before Bolduc leapfrogged into a senior management position in another department then used it as a steppingstone to come back to an even higher position with Parks.

Being a pain in Bolduc's ass again could be fun, but, being a practical person, Lou figured the coalmine was a more pressing issue for the park right now than getting his jollies pissing off the outfit's top bureaucrat.

Lou was on the phone discussing the mine with Francois Masse, someone he had come to trust over the years, when his office door opened and Colleen, his fifty-something front desk clerk, escorted Ben and Kate inside. Quickly introducing them, Colleen mumbled something, then ran out to tackle another task, leaving Jasper's newest park wardens standing wide-eyed, like deer caught in the headlights.

"Yeah, I think they just walked in," said Lou, speaking into the phone and waving Ben and Kate toward a couple of chairs sitting against the wall. "I'll call you back later," he said, putting the phone down as he sized up his new wardens.

Before he had finally decided to bring Ben and Kate to Jasper, Lou had made it clear he wanted them working on some of the larger issues facing the park. He didn't want them sucked into the black hole of operations. The phone call with them had been short and sweet, but long enough for Lou Walker to figure out he liked what he was getting, and the timing was perfect.

Ben and Kate had just been involved in the big environmental review in Wood Buffalo, so they'd bring experience the park could use if the proposed mine were to go ahead. Even though it was outside of the park boundary, it would add to the impacts of everything else happening along the Eastern Slopes.

And for landscape level species like grizzly bears that didn't recognize political boundaries and roamed in and out of the park at will, the mine would be one more thing bears had to contend with.

In Lou's opinion, another mine made no sense at all since there was a glut of coal on the market and already three mines in the area. Still, if it went to an environmental review, Lou wanted the park to be able to put forth its best argument as to why the mine shouldn't proceed, or if it did, how it could be done in such a way as to minimize impacts on grizzlies and other species.

So when Francois Masse called to say he was looking for a home for two park wardens who had gotten themselves in a little trouble with the bison disease issue, Lou knew they were the type of people he wanted to recruit to Jasper.

With Ben and Kate now sitting across the desk from him, Lou hoped his instincts had been correct. These two definitely weren't cowboy and cowgirl stock, but they had just taken on the outfit in what could have been one of the biggest fuck-ups Parks had ever been a part of. That had to take some balls.

Getting up from behind his desk, Lou introduced himself to his two new charges.

"How was the trip south?"

"Great," said Kate.

"Other than playing leapfrog with some moron in a jacked-up pickup," said Ben, as Lou sat on the edge of his desk, deriving first impressions.

"And how were things up north? Francois the same as ever?"

The trio continued to exchange a few pleasantries about Parks and people they had in common while Lou observed Ben and Kate closely as they shared their stories.

"Francois told me you were in deep on the bison issue?" said Lou.

"Yeah," said Ben.

"It was pretty intense," said Kate, "especially when the outfit decided not to present the information we'd been working months to prepare for the review panel."

"So, what'd you do?" Lou had heard through the grapevine about the internal revolt and how someone had gone to the media, but he was keen to hear Ben and Kate's version of events.

The pair looked at each other before responding.

"We took matters into our own hands," said Ben, explaining how they had used a contact in the media to let the public know what was going on.

"You could screw yourself if you tried that kind of stuff around here," said Lou.

"Public support was critical," Kate added.

"Even so," said Lou. "Jasper and Banff are in the spotlight compared to parks up North. If you embarrass senior management here, you can kiss your jobs goodbye."

"But ..." Ben started to protest.

"But nothing," said Lou.

Right off the bat, Lou thought Ben seemed a little too rammy and impatient, but he kind of liked the balance Kate brought to the table. Not unlike his partnership with his wife, Lou could sense that the sum of the parts was likely a potent combination he could make good use of. They still had a lot to learn, but he'd dealt with young colts before and had a reputation for being able to break them in.

"I brought you here to tackle some of the issues we've been letting slide for way too long. Big picture stuff that'll get us talking to our neighbours with the Alberta and B.C. governments."

"Such as?" said Ben.

"Grizzly bears and caribou, mostly," said Lou. "Landscape-level species that use the park for part of the year and the provincial lands on our borders for the rest of it. The latest issue is the coalmine I told you about on the phone." He paused and looked out his office window as a warden truck hauling a horse trailer pulled into the parking lot. "And I should warn you. You might not get a lot of help on these issues. You'll run into some folks who might make you want to pull your hair out. Some might even be fellow park wardens." Lou watched as a park warden got out of the pickup and made his way toward the office. "But not him," he added when he realized Ben and Kate had been following his gaze. "He's one of the good guys."

Ben and Kate looked at each other and smiled.

"That's okay," said Ben. "We've been there before."

"Seems to come with the job," said Kate.

"Yeah, well this might be different. Now don't get me wrong. I'll put our wardens up against any in the country. But they can be a tough lot sometimes. Kinda like grizzly bears. They'll eat their own."

Ben smiled at the expression.

"I'm not kiddin'," said Lou. "And it's not like I'm talking behind their backs. I'm one of them. You start your career here in the mountains and it's a catfight from the get go. Some of these folks have been seasonal wardens for ten years or more, clawing and scratching for a permanent number. You have to understand it's not easy getting into the outfit here in the mountain parks."

"Why don't they leave?" asked Kate. "Try out east or up north, or somewhere else in the system."

"Some do," said Lou. "Some take a crack at the North just to get a permanent position, but they head south as soon as they get the chance."

Ben and Kate nodded in unison but said nothing.

"A few have ventured to the East Coast. But too many of them worry they'll never get back."

"So?" said Ben. "There're lots of great parks in the country beside the mountains. Hell, we're even keen on doing something internationally. Africa perhaps. Just to get experience we can't get here."

"Agreed," said Lou. "I always encourage young wardens to leave and broaden their horizons. If they're good at their job, they don't need to worry about getting back."

"So is it a self-confidence thing?" Kate challenged.

Lou Walker laughed at the comment. "You both know self-confidence isn't an issue for park wardens. Most are loners and just as happy to do things their own way. An old-time warden once told me park wardens would never follow each other, unless it was uphill, through four feet of snow." He laughed again. "That's pretty much how it is."

"So people are just reluctant to leave?" said Kate.

"Yup," said Lou. "But once you've had a chance to see the park for yourselves, you might understand why."

"We're looking forward to it," said Kate.

"In the meantime," said Lou, "I'll get someone to show you around and introduce you to the crew. As soon as I can break away from the paper jungle, maybe I'll get you out on a horse trip to show you some of the country, especially along the east side of the park near the proposed mine.

"Things are booming out there right now. With oil and gas moving in, along with the mining and forestry that's already happening, the Eastern Slopes are getting hammered. If a person hasn't seen it for a while, they wouldn't even recognize the place."

"Sounds rough," said Ben. "Is everyone on board with all of the development?"

"Most folks support new industry," said Lou. "But there are a few brave souls on the other side saying there's already too much happening out there." Lou chuckled to himself. "Environmentalists are almost as rare in this province as hen's teeth," he added, almost as an afterthought. "But we've got one of our own that will give any of the industry folks a run for their money."

"And who's that?" said Kate.

"Marion Seawell," said Lou. "Probably the toughest old gal you'll ever meet. She's a thorn in the side of Parks, but sometimes you need a little burr under the saddle to get you to sit up and take notice. Marion does that in spades."

"She lives in Jasper?"

"Since Christ was a cowboy," said Lou. "She and her husband started Jasper Wild, the local environmental group. The name pretty much says it all. But her husband's not around anymore. Malcolm died last year in a climbing accident." Lou paused as if collecting his thoughts. "Kind of odd circumstances."

"How so?" Ben fished for more information, but Lou brushed him off.

"That's a story for another day." He flipped through an agenda on his desk and stood up. "So we'll have to find you some housing," he said, bringing the discussion around to the immediate priorities. "Things are a little tight right now, but something will open up. In the meantime, I was thinking you could hole up at Poco Warden Station. If you're going to be working on stuff along the eastern boundary, it'll be easier for you travelling back and forth. But if you want to be in town, we can probably squeeze you in to one of the shared duplexes."

Ben shot a quick glance at Kate. "We might just look around for our own place," said Ben. "We kinda did the transient thing, you know, been there, done that. I'm thinking it's time to find our own place."

"You mean buy a house?" said Lou. "Well good luck with that. A teardown here in Jasper will set you back a quarter million. There's not much decent stuff for under a half million."

Kate's eyes opened wide. "A half million ... dollars?"

"Yup," said Lou. "That's why park housing is at a premium. Now if you were married with kids," Lou hesitated for a moment, "I could probably get you bumped up on the list."

"Ah, yeah," said Ben, looking sheepishly at Kate. "Well that's not in the cards right now."

"No," Kate confirmed, scrambling to add her two cents. "So I guess we'll check out our options. Poco is it?"

"Yeah," said Lou. "Pocahontas. You passed it on you way here."

"I remember it," said Kate.

"We've got other spots too," Lou continued, rhyming off the list of warden stations, "Cavell, Athabasca Falls, Decoigne, Sunwapta, Maligne, but I think the only thing open is Poco."

"It's a house, right?" said Ben.

"Hell no," said Lou. "The station warden's in there. You can stay in the trailer."

Ben and Kate looked at each other apprehensively.

"Oh it isn't so bad," said Lou. "It's not vintage 1950 or some ATCO shit box. It's actually pretty nice and places you a little higher on the pecking order than plain old trailer trash." He laughed. "You can hang your hats there until something nicer comes along. Just watch out for the park warden who lives in the house. He can be an ornery son of a bitch at the best of times."

Ben laughed. "I think we're getting pretty good at dealing with those types."

"Hell, you might even know him," said Lou. "I believe he's originally from out east. His name's John Haffcut."

CHAPTER 7

THE RETURN DRIVE toward Pocahontas gave Ben and Kate a different perspective on the Athabasca Valley and the eastern side of the park. Even the weather seemed to change as they left Jasper in blazing sunshine and headed toward a band of ominous dark clouds moving in from the east.

"What are the odds?" said Ben as he took in the changing weather.

"Of John Haffcut being here in Jasper?"

"Yeah. I'm surprised we never heard anything about that before we moved here."

"It's a little funny actually." Kate looked and Ben and smiled. "Like we're following him around."

Ben didn't smile at the suggestion. "Not sure if that's a good thing."

"Oh, it'll be fine. We really don't know much about him other than he worked in Cape Breton Highlands before we got there."

"I guess," said Ben. "Just seems like things were in a bit of a mess after he left and we had to clean it up."

"Stop worrying. "It'll be fine." Kate smiled and took in the scenery. "It's kind of funny, eh?" she said, trying to change the subject. "How the same landscape can look so different coming at it from the opposite direction."

"Yeah," said Ben. "The light on the mountains isn't the same as when we drove into the park yesterday."

"I imagine it's different every day," Kate offered. She pointed out the subtle shades of green that draped themselves over the base of the mountains lining both sides of the valley and the various colours of the mountains themselves, ever-changing shades of grey as banks of cloud cast the mountains into the shadows only to have their faces, angles and spires revealed by the next opening of blue sky and sunshine. Pulses of rain showers moving through the valley added to the kaleidoscope of colours as the refracted rays of sunshine gave birth to intermittent rainbows only to have them dissolve against the limestone backdrop of the Front Ranges.

As they crossed the main bridge over the Athabasca and picked their way eastward along the edge of Jasper Lake, Roche Miette stood out over all the other peaks, its massive north face and shear vertical drop dominating the skyline on the south side of the valley.

Turning off the highway at the Pocahontas Warden Station, Ben pulled into the driveway past the warden residence and garage, and parked in front of the antiquated trailer that would serve as their new home for the time being.

"I guess this is it." They exited the truck and climbed the steps to the door.

Kate tried the key Lou had given them, but the door was already unlocked. She pushed it open and walked inside, surveying the dated furniture as Ben walked in behind her and plopped himself down on the flowered sofa.

"It'll do in a pinch," he said, looking around.

"Yeah," said Kate as she ran a hand across the kitchen counter top. "It's not so bad."

"But maybe we'll still take a look at properties outside the park," said Ben. "I'd still like to get our own place. Build some equity."

Kate laughed. "Build some equity, eh?" She walked to the sofa and pulled Ben to his feet. "Thinking of a more permanent arrangement?" she added, wrapping her arms around him.

"Perhaps," said Ben, smiling mischievously.

Just then a park warden truck pulled up in front of the garage.

Ben and Kate watched as the driver got out and slammed the door. Grabbing a pack out of the back of the truck, he slung it over his shoulder in one motion and began to walk toward the house. He stopped for a moment, noticing their vehicle for the first time, then carried on, stomping up the wooden stairs and throwing the screen door open with a crash before pushing his way inside the house and disappearing.

"He's in a good mood," Kate observed.

"Maybe we'll give him some time to settle down before we introduce ourselves," said Ben.

"I don't think we have the option." Kate pointed to the man as he made his way back down the stairs and turned toward the trailer.

Ben heaved a sigh. "Okay, let's get this over with, but let's not get into anything about Cape Breton. That's for another time."

"Agreed," said Kate.

They walked to the door just as the man was about to knock.

Ben opened the door and smiled but the facial expression and body language of the man in front of him suggested he was more than a little put out that Ben and Kate had parachuted into his space. Still wearing his park warden uniform, his shirt was unbuttoned to his chest and the sweat marks on his t-shirt stood out like coffee stains on a white tablecloth. What appeared to be dried blood or shit—Ben couldn't determine which—was caked on the knees of his pants, the cuffs of which rode above his partially laced work boots. Topping off his lanky six-foot-plus build was a dirty blond crew cut inflected with spots of grey. A few days' worth of stubble growing on his face gave him the look of an old salt just back from crossing the ocean.

"Hey, I hope you don't mind, we kind of took over this place," said Ben. He held out a hand. "Ben Matthews."

Kate followed suit. "Kate Jones."

Their introductions got barely a stir from the man, his first response being to take a step inside and look around the trailer.

"John Haffcut," he mumbled, taking a step back as if to better assess his new neighbours. "But I guess you already know that," he added gruffly. "I've got a bunch of my stuff in one of the bedrooms. I should clean it out before you set up house."

"No worries," said Kate. "It's fine for now. We can give you a hand when you're ready, but there's no rush. We don't have much of our own furniture."

"Almost none, in fact," said Ben.

John Haffcut barely acknowledged the comment then turned back toward the house. "I've had a long day, a long week in fact. We can sort things out later."

As he walked back to the house, Ben and Kate looked at each other and shrugged their shoulders.

"Mr. Friendly," said Ben. "Maybe we don't bring up Cape Breton at all."

"He's just tired," said Kate. "He looks bagged."

"I hope that's all it is. We might be holed up in this place for a while."

They were about to get back to the task of sorting things out when another warden truck pulled into the driveway. Ben and Kate were surprised to see Megan Weaver jump out and make a beeline for the trailer. They'd met Megan in Wood Buffalo when she came to help her father collar bison, and took an instant liking to her, but weren't sure how much they'd see of Megan in Jasper.

"Hey," she said, throwing her arms around Kate and Ben as they met her at the door. "Welcome to Jasper."

"Thanks," said Kate. "This is a nice surprise."

"Did you meet Grumpy yet?" Megan winced.

"Kind of," said Ben.

"He didn't exactly tell us his life story," said Kate.

Megan laughed. "Give him a chance. He's had a rough couple of days."

"Cat got his tongue?" said Ben.

Kate glared at Ben and shook her head.

"They had to put a grizzly down yesterday and were dealing with some of the fallout today," said Megan. "John's bummed about it."

"I would be too," said Kate. "What happened?"

"The park has been trying to deal with waste management," Megan began. "If everyone isn't on side, it defeats the whole purpose. One of the restaurants in town has been slow cleaning up their shit. They left some pails of grease in the back alley and a bear got into them. The bear got into more trouble later at one of the lodges up back of town. John and one of the other wardens tried to snare it so they could relocate it to the backcountry. But it didn't end well."

"What about the restaurant owner?" Kate asked. "Will they be charged?"

"Or shut down?" Ben added.

Megan laughed at the last comment. "Hey, it's Jasper. Businesses don't get shut down. And they're rarely charged. The superintendent would like to be able to do something to enforce things, but she's been told to work with businesses to get them onside. She's made a lot of headway, but there are some that just don't seem to get it. And as the wildlife guy, John's at the end of his rope. He's ready to string someone up, but unfortunately he's been taking it out on Anne."

"The superintendent?" said Kate.

Megan nodded. "Yeah, Anne Winters. She's great and she's had some good support from the folks in Ottawa, but things get political here pretty quickly. Jasper is in the public eye more than most parks. It's even worse in Banff. People are politically connected and don't mind going over the head of the local managers to get their way. Anne is already on the bad side of a couple of the local businesses that have an in with the director-general in Ottawa. She has to watch herself or her job will be on the line."

"Great," said Ben. "To be replaced by some 'yes man' no doubt."

"Hopefully not," said Megan. "Anyway, we don't need to get into this now. I just stopped by to say welcome and see if you wanted to come for supper tonight. I was going to get a few folks in so you could meet some of the crew."

"Thanks for the offer," said Kate. She looked at Ben. "We'd love to."

"I might even see if Grumpy wants to come," Megan smiled and nodded toward the house. "But I'm reluctant to poke the bear, if you know what I mean."

Ben and Kate laughed.

"Maybe we can give him some time to cool down and ask him later?" Kate offered.

"Would you mind?"

"Not at all." Kate looked at Ben who nodded.

"Sure," he said. "But we'll approach carefully. Do you have any bear spray in case he attacks?"

Kate hit Ben's shoulder forcefully.

"Hey," he said. "What was that for?"

Megan laughed and started to leave. "I'll let you two sort it out. I can give you directions to my place, but John knows the way."

"What if he decides not to come?"

"Anne will be there," Megan said. "He'll come." She smiled but then her face took on a more serious tone. "John's wife's passed away a while back and it's taking some time for him to get over it. But, he'll do pretty much anything to get out of cooking." She smiled again. "You can use that to your advantage whenever he's a little ornery. Which is often."

CHAPTER 8

"PULL IN HERE." John Haffcut pointed to a small duplex and Ben turned into the driveway.

Not much had been said on the drive to Megan's house and although John hadn't apologized for his earlier behaviour, Ben and Kate didn't press the issue. They'd also chosen wisely to leave any reference to Cape Breton out of what little discussion there was. Rumours in the outfit had a bad way of festering over time and often weren't based on anything close to the truth.

All Ben and Kate really knew was John Haffcut had preceded them in Cape Breton and something had led to his early departure, but whenever the topic came up, people clammed up and the discussion turned to something else.

Getting out of the truck, the trio walked to Megan's door. John knocked, but entered without waiting for the door to be answered. Kate and Ben followed along behind.

As Kate tried to determine the number of voices in the house, Megan popped her head around the corner.

"Hi again," John gave her a quick embrace. "Are Marion and Anne already here?"

Megan nodded.

"Great," John said under his breath. "Let's not get into what happened." He looked to Megan for confirmation then walked past her into the living room.

"Come on in," Megan said to Ben and Kate, stepping into the entrance wearing an ankle-length, side-split printed dress. The First Nations motif accentuated Megan's sharp looks and angular features.

"Wow," said Ben, his reaction a little unexpected by Kate who added her own look of surprise.

"Yeah, wow," she said, slightly embarrassed as she noticed her own reflection in a small mirror hanging on the wall next to a coat rack. *My cleanest T-shirt and jeans might not fit the bill tonight.*

"Hey sorry," said Megan. "I didn't mean to throw you off by dressing up. But every now and then a girl's got to ditch the uniform and feel alive again."

Kate laughed as Megan's comment took the edge off the situation. "Isn't that the truth," she said, running a hand along Megan's shoulder. "The material's got a beautiful feel to it."

"Thanks," said Megan. "It's Navajo inspired. Kind of fits with my Dene roots."

"How so?" Ben queried.

"Our people were all connected at one point," said Megan. "Dene and Navajo share linguistic roots. Some of the folks I know from Fort Smith have even travelled to the American southwest and said they were surprised they were able to talk with the Navajo people they met in their own language, with no problem."

"Very interesting," said Kate.

"Anyway," Megan continued, "come in and meet everyone." With a whisper she added, "They're not all *parkies,* thank god."

Kate and Ben smiled and walked into the small gathering as Megan began introductions with a middle-aged couple dressed in western shirts and jeans, helping Kate feel a little more at ease with her choice of clothing.

"This is Jimmy and Shirley Rand. Jimmy's one of Jasper's longest serving wardens. Shirley's the unofficial park historian. There isn't a thing about the history of this place she couldn't tell you."

John Haffcut popped his head between the couple and added, "And he's a mean shot. Most days." He nudged Jimmy and laughed, then backed out of their faces and returned to the others in the room.

Jimmy smiled and lowered his head, toeing the carpet as Shirley filled in the gaps.

"John's just lucky Jimmy still likes him," she said. "Otherwise he might have let that bear have a chew before Jimmy finished him off. The bear, I mean," she added with a laugh.

"You'll have to fill us in," said Kate, shaking hands and smiling as Megan motioned them to the next couple.

"This is Sherry Allan and Bert Gosse," she said. "One of them is a railroad engineer, but I bet you can't guess which one?"

Ben and Kate laughed, a little caught off guard by the challenge, but Kate immediately noticed the difference as they shook hands. Bert's hadn't seen much in the way of hard work for a long time while Sherry's grip was strong and firm.

"I'm going with Sherry," Kate said and a sparkle emerged from the young woman's eyes while Bert laughed.

"Railroaded again," he said, looking at Ben.

"No doubt," said Ben, shaking hands with the pair. "Just to be different though, I'll take my chances and say you're with the railroad."

Megan laughed. "Well you're both right, but I should have been more explicit. Sherry's a railroad engineer. Bert's one of the managers with CN."

"I'm really just a paper pusher," said Bert. "Nothing more. Sherry actually runs the trains."

"I'm pretty new though," said Sherry. "We'll see if I can make it in a man's world." The confidence she exuded left Kate with no doubt she was just kidding around, but they shared a look of mutual understanding before Megan led them away for the next introductions.

"And this is Jasper's superintendent, Anne Winters." Megan turned to a woman Kate guessed to be in her early fifties. Anne was wearing a western skirt and jacket. Anne's dark hair and eyes and tanned features suggested Italian ancestry, but she had a country air about her that softened the somewhat rigid posture and aura of supreme confidence she exuded into the room.

"Our top dog," said John, once again poking his face into the middle of the introductions then pulling back, but only after taking a quick elbow to the ribs from the superintendent, who proffered an innocent smile that caused Ben and Kate to look at each other with slightly raised eyebrows.

Anne Winters turned back to Ben and Kate and shook hands. "So pleased to meet you both. Lou has been looking forward to your arrival and I know Bert Melnyk speaks of you both in glowing terms."

"Bert was a great superintendent to work for," said Ben.

Anne turned to Kate. "It's too bad you had to leave Wood Buffalo so soon."

"Yes," Kate agreed. "We were definitely hoping to stay longer."

"Oh well," said Anne. "Things have a way of working out. And their loss is our gain."

Ben and Kate both smiled as Megan turned them toward the last person in the room who was busy bending John Haffcut's ear.

"Did you really have to shoot the bear?" Kate overheard the woman ask John.

"Well it was probably the bear or me, ..." John started to explain but before he could finish, Megan shushed him to the side and touched the elderly lady lightly on the arm. "Marion, I'd like you to meet our newest park wardens, Kate Jones and Ben Matthews."

Marion Seawell's eyes lit up as she turned to face them, displaying a youthful enthusiasm that contrasted sharply with the facial lines of someone who had lived a full life. "Marion Seawell," she said, shaking hands with Ben and Kate.

"Marion is the backbone of Jasper Wild," said Megan, with more than a hint of pride in her voice.

"Well, somebody has to give this place *some* backbone," said Marion, her strong English accent contrasting with her cheeky grin.

Megan laughed. "She and Malcolm started the group many years ago. It's still the voice of reason when it comes to development proposals in the park."

"They've put everything into standing up for this place," Shirley Rand chimed in, "to make sure it doesn't turn into another Banff."

"Hmphh," Marion muttered. "Now don't make me sound like Joan of Arc. It's not like I intend to be a martyr for Parks. Not when you have so much high-priced help sitting in management."

"I heard that," said Anne, sidling into the conversation with a frown directed at Marion.

"Oh, I wasn't referring to you, Anne," said Marion. "Goodness, you've been like a breath of fresh air here in Jasper. Although I'm inclined to say I don't have the same feelings for your director-general."

"You mean the Snake?" said Megan. "Didn't you give him that nickname?"

"Only because he deserves it," said Marion with a laugh. "Actually it's probably an insult to the reptilian line."

Everyone laughed.

"Thank god we've got someone here who will stand up to him," Marion added, putting her arm around Anne. "Although I do wish," Marion continued, "you'd tell us what you know about this new coalmine. Goodness, I can't believe there's any coal left out there. Why would anyone propose to put another mine on the Eastern Slopes?" She shot a glance at Anne, but the park superintendent offered no comeback.

"Okay, everyone," said Megan, projecting her voice over the banter. "Dinner's ready. It's buffet-style so dig in and find a place to sit."

"We should have brought something to contribute," said Kate.

"Next time," said Megan. "You just got here. It's not quite like Fort Potluck in the North," she added, referring to Kate's favourite nickname for Fort Smith, "but we get together quite a bit."

Kate smiled, reflecting on Wood Buffalo, but looking forward to making friends in their new home. With any luck, they'd be able to put down some roots and stay in Jasper for a while. Who knew, maybe she and Ben would even get married.

CHAPTER 9

LEAVING MEGAN'S, BEN, Kate and John piled into the cab of the pickup and drove out of town, headed east to Pocahontas Warden Station.

The night was crystal clear and the sky was a blanket of stars spanning the Athabasca Valley. Making their way slowly along the highway, John pointed out small groups of female elk and calves in the main valley and single bulls bedded down in the grass as they passed Talbot and Jasper Lakes. As they approached Pocahontas, John motioned for Ben to keep driving past the station.

"What's up?" said Kate.

"I just want to show you something," said John. His earlier edge seemed to have disappeared and he was more relaxed. A little ways past Pocahontas, John asked Ben to pull over on the shoulder. "Swing the headlights toward that small wetland," he instructed.

Ben pulled the truck slightly off the road.

"Do you seem them?" said John as the truck's headlights cut a swath across the small pond.

"The eyes?" said Kate.

"Yeah," said John, watching as the shape of a bull moose gradually distinguished itself from the surrounding clumps of wolf willow and alder. "He's been around here for the past few nights. Every year I see a few moose around here. But every year they get whacked."

"Poached?" said Ben.

"No. Hit on the highway. Usually at night and usually by a semi."

"That's too bad," said Kate. "Is there no way to stop it?"

"Yeah. Get rid of the highway." John snickered. "As if that's gonna happen. Instead we have thousands of vehicles barrelling through here at all hours of the day and night, killing deer, elk, sheep, moose, bears, you name it. We lose between one and two hundred large mammals a year."

"That's staggering," said Ben.

"Yeah," said John. "It kills me we've been unable to solve the wildlife-vehicle issue. The highway and the railway take a huge toll on wildlife in the park. It's so predictable."

"That's a tough challenge," said Kate. "Both are important travel routes between Alberta and B.C. What do you think the options are?"

"Slow everyone down for one thing," said John. "And mix things up a little. Instead of static wildlife speed zones that never change from one season to the next, we need to move them around to reflect changes in wildlife movement throughout the year. I won't see any moose here for months, but for a few weeks every year, they're here in the valley bottom. We need to be able to respond to those types of realities."

"What about the railway?" Kate asked.

"The problem there is grain spills that attract bears," said John. "A lot of the rail cars are old and some of the hoppers leak constantly. Sherry and Bert tell stories of cars leaving Saskatchewan and being empty by the time they get to Vancouver."

"But surely that can be dealt with?"

"It can and it is," said John. "Bert Gosse has been making some noise to his bosses and CN is working to repair cars and clean up their act, but it takes time. And money. Until they replace all the old cars or fix the ones with defective hoppers, bears and other animals will continue to get killed on the tracks."

"What about this guy?" said Ben as they watched the moose work its way along the edge of the wetland and disappear into the forest.

John sighed and looked across the cab at Ben and Kate. "He'll be dead in a few days."

"You're pretty matter of fact about it," Ben said.

"I wish I was wrong, but I'll put money on it," John affirmed as a string of semis passed, pushing a wave of wind that rocked the small truck. "Anyway. Let's head back to Poco. No point belabouring things sitting out here."

Ben nodded and pulled the truck back onto the shoulder. When the last semi passed, he did a quick U-turn and headed to Pocahontas.

As they pulled into the driveway and parked, John slid out of the cab and turned to Ben and Kate.

"It's still early. Come in for a nightcap," he said.

Ben and Kate looked at each other. "Sure," Kate agreed.

Inside John's house, their host opened an almost empty refrigerator and offered Ben and Kate a beer, then grabbed one for himself. Leading them into the living room, John collapsed into a large recliner and pointed his beer bottle toward an old couch along the wall. "Have a seat."

As Ben and Kate sat down and took in the sparse furnishings, John answered their first question without them even asking.

"I know it's pretty barebones here." He took a long drink of his beer and wiped his mouth with the back of his hand. "After Peggy died, I never felt like much of a homemaker."

"Sorry to hear that," said Kate. "How long were you married?"

"Twenty-five years." John's face contorted as he rolled his lips under his nose and sniffed. He grabbed a tissue from a box on an end table, clamped it around his nose and blew. "She died of cancer two years ago and it seems I've been living in a fog ever since."

"Where're you from originally?" said Kate.

John laughed. "God knows. My father was in the Forces so we were all over. I think I was conceived in an air force base in Germany and born in another one in the States, but the first place I really remember was Cold Lake, Alberta. Aptly named, I might add." He chuckled. "I think I saw ten different schools in ten years, which qualifies me for the Airforce Brat title."

"Was Peggy with you in Cape Breton?"

"Yeah. We met on the West Coast and stayed there for a while. Then once the kids were done school and spreading their wings, we started to pop around the country with Parks. Those were good years, for the most part."

"How many kids?" Kate asked.

"Two. Our son is in the States doing a wildlife degree and our daughter is a marine biologist on the West Coast. When Peggy was alive, they'd be back at least a couple of times a year. But since Peggy died, I don't see them as much anymore." He paused and blew his nose again. "We're all good; it's just they're busier now, what with partners and all."

"Makes sense," said Ben. "Life's busy."

John nodded and looked at Kate. "You started to ask about Cape Breton?"

"Yeah," said Kate. "I'm not sure where I was going with that."

"You probably heard," said John.

"We heard almost nothing," said Ben.

"We knew you were there before us, but that's about it," said Kate.

"That's a bit of a surprise," said John. He looked sharply at Ben and Kate.

"Kate's right," said Ben. "I know you were in the Cheticamp position before I took over, but that's it."

"Whenever your name came up, you could hear a pin drop," said Kate.

"Did something happen?" said Ben.

John raised his eyebrows. "You might say that."

"Want to talk about it?"

"Only if you want to," Kate injected quickly and frowned at Ben.

"Of course," said Ben. "Only if you want to."

John sighed heavily and sat back in the chair. "Where do I start?"

For the next hour, he kept Ben and Kate glued to their seats as he shared his stories from Cape Breton, relating similar tales to their own about battles with the Moores, as well as the park superintendent.

"Dickson wasn't a fan," said John. "He thought I ruffled too many feathers trying to clamp down on the poaching."

"Sounds familiar," said Kate. She looked at Ben.

"So was John Donald Moores always a bad ass?" Ben took a swig of beer and peered at John.

"Always. He thrived on intimidating the community and poaching whatever and whenever he wanted. I always wondered why Dickson was scared of him, but I guess you two figured that out."

"In a manner of speaking," said Ben. "But why did Dickson want to run you out of the park?"

"I think I was getting close to figuring out the hold John Donald had on him, but I couldn't prove anything. So he pulled in some favours to get rid of me. Promoted me out of there, as they seem to do when they want to get rid of someone."

"Where'd you go?" said Ben.

"Churchill," said John. "I think management figured it was the gulag, but actually it was great, incredibly exciting and challenging. There's a small staff of park wardens there, so they made me the chief. But I'm not cut out for paperwork and a desk job, so I started working on polar bears and made myself the wildlife guy. No one was really checking up on me, and with Peggy sick and all, they knew better than to bother me."

"When did you come to Jasper?" said Kate.

"Just after Peggy died. I think Lou took pity on me and brought me in from the cold. I'd run into him a few years ago at a national meeting for chief park wardens." John laughed and nodded toward his guests. "I guess he's a sucker for rebels."

Ben laughed at the reference.

"So you've moved around a lot," said Kate. "And fairly quickly. Not unlike us."

"Seems like there's two breeds in the Warden Service," said John. "Some, like us, seem to have a short half-life in whatever park we're in. Others, like Jimmy Rand, end up staying in one park for their whole career." He paused. "I'm not sayin' one is any better than the other, but I always wonder how the lifers manage to do it."

"Maybe they don't rock the boat?" said Ben.

John shook his head. "Nah. It's not that. And I don't want to take anything away from guys like Jimmy. He might seem like a pushover, but he's far from it. I've seen him stand up to the director for the mountain parks at a meeting and quite honestly, I was surprised *he* didn't end up in Churchill." He laughed. "Some guys just seem to have a way of doing things without pissing off management."

"Now there's a trait I know someone could use." Kate elbowed Ben with a gentle smile.

"Others haven't got much tact," John added.

Kate nudged Ben again, but this time he pushed back.

"A friend once told me," John continued, "tact is the ability to tell someone to go to hell, and watch them go merrily on their way."

"Yeah, I definitely don't have that ability," said Ben.

"Me either," said John.

"Maybe it comes with maturity," Kate suggested with a grin, drawing sharp looks from both men.

"Which side of the coin do you land on," said John, directing his question to Kate.

"I don't know. Somewhere in between, I guess."

Ben laughed. "She seems to have an innate ability to always pick the right side of the coin."

"I do not."

"Hmhmmm. Do so." Ben turned to John. "I've got to watch her like a hawk." He laughed. "She can charm the old guys like nobody's business."

"I do not," said Kate. "I just like to listen to their stories. You can learn a lot from them. And they like to be listened to." She looked at John. His cheeks had a noticeable reddish hue.

"See what I mean," said Ben. "You don't even know she's doing it and then she's got you under her spell."

They all laughed.

"Women can be like that," said John.

"So is there another woman in your life?" said Ben. He quickly turned away from Kate's glare.

"It's okay, Kate," said John, raising a hand to her. "I get it all the time."

"So?" Ben pried. "I kind of thought the supe was eyeing you up tonight."

"Ben!" Kate glowered at him again.

"You don't miss much do you, son?" John sat back and took a long swig of beer. "Yeah, she's great. And what's not to like? She doesn't put on airs about her position and to her, she's no more important than one of the park's truck drivers. In her eyes, everyone has a job to do and they all have to get done for the park to run efficiently."

"I like that," said Kate.

Sitting upright, John placed the empty beer bottle on the end table and pulled himself from the chair. "Well, I hate to be a party pooper, but I've got an early rise in the morning. I have to track down a couple of caribou collars in the Maligne and Tonquin. If you two want to come along, there's room."

"Absolutely, we're in." Ben was quick to accept the offer before it could be rescinded.

"What do we need to bring?" said Kate.

"Just a lunch and a good stomach for flying," said John. "Although I expect it'll be pretty tame. Clay is one of the best pilots you'll ever fly with, as long as he wasn't on a bender tonight."

CHAPTER 10

MARION SEAWELL MADE her way home under a star-filled sky, smiling to herself about the new wardens she'd met at the party. Kate and Ben seemed nice, but she wondered if they would be around long enough to make a difference. Over the years she'd seen park wardens come and go, but few seemed to take the time to dig into the real issues affecting the park. And some of those who remained seemed more entrenched in the lifestyle than making a difference. Yet there were those like Jimmy and Shirley Rand who'd been around almost as long as she and Malcolm, and who wore their hearts on their sleeves.

There was no doubting Jimmy and Shirley's commitment, especially Shirley's. Women, and wives in particular, were the unsung heroes of the Warden Service, the so-called silent partners. In days past, they were the glue that held things together in the warden districts, raising their families and doing the many mundane tasks that kept the districts running while the men patrolled, performed rescues, conducted surveys and whatever else was required of them.

While the men stood in the limelight, women took a back seat. Or so it seemed to those who only read the headlines. Truth be told, many of the women were the push the men needed to speak up about some of the travesties happening in the national parks.

Marion recalled the battle over predator control, the killing of large carnivores such as grizzly and black bears, cougars and wolves. It had taken a long time to convince park managers these apex carnivores were critical to maintaining ungulate populations. Otherwise, elk and deer ate themselves out of house and home, leading to winter die-offs in some years that raised the ire of an uninformed public who thought the park should be feeding these animals to save them from the ravages of a particularly harsh winter.

Those misconceptions took time to change, but eventually Parks came around to the notion of a more balanced approach to resource management.

Still, old attitudes die slowly and were hard to eliminate completely. With the province still allowing and promoting grizzly bear hunting and wolf and cougar trapping, protecting those species in the park remained a challenge, despite efforts to educate the public about the role of large predators in natural systems.

Shirley Rand had been a driving force behind changing the park's policy around how it managed garbage and other attractants that brought bears into town. Some of the first female park wardens in Jasper and the other mountain national parks were also on the front lines of these battles. Marion thought the park could use a few more like them. It was those women who had inspired Marion to become more vocal when it came to matters affecting the park and the species it was meant to protect.

It had been easy enough to bring Malcolm along on that journey. An avid climber, he was already deeply committed to protecting wilderness and the mountain parks guarded some of the best wilderness areas remaining in the west. Yet, every climb not only brought him to new heights, it also gave him a view of what was going on in the valleys below, both inside and outside the park; he always had stories to tell Marion.

Every time he climbed a mountain outside of the park or near the park boundary, he contrasted what he saw on one side of the boundary with that on the other. Inside the park, he also saw the subtle markers of progress as rail lines, pipelines, roads and a major highway bisected the Athabasca Valley, turning west at the town of Jasper and heading toward Yellowhead Pass and the Fraser River.

From the top of Roche Bonhomme or Pyramid Mountain or any of the other peaks bordering the valley, it was easy to see how transportation corridors were compromising the prime wildlife habitat of the valley bottom, the montane. Wildlife trying to cross those corridors not only had to contend with increasing numbers of vehicles at all hours of the day and night, but also with trains that seemed to get longer every year.

Malcolm wondered how it could be sustainable.

Marion was convinced it wasn't.

And so she fought. Or rather, they fought.

Their previous battles with Parks' bureaucracy and local developers had been hostile at times, but they had managed to walk a line that allowed them to continue living in the community without alienating or becoming alienated by people with different views from their own. There had been a degree of mutual respect in their past dealings with developers, but that seemed to have gradually changed.

Increasingly, development proposals were being put forward that appeared on the surface to be the efforts of local entrepreneurs, but were in fact owned by foreign multinational corporations trying to get a piece of a fast disappearing commodity: wilderness.

As Marion and Malcolm researched these companies, digging into their activities in other countries, the stakes seemed to get higher. Somewhere along the way, they had turned a corner, literally immersing themselves in a world of global connections that were dubious at best and quite likely criminal in nature. It had been new ground for them and they had to tread lightly.

Marion couldn't put her finger on it, but for some reason had a gut feeling she should be more concerned than normal with her personal safety. It was a feeling she couldn't shake, no doubt aggravated by the fact her soul mate and confidant of more than half a century was no longer there to provide a touchstone of reason and understanding. Malcolm's death had left her reeling, especially considering the circumstances. Despite being a proficient climber, he was on a relatively easy climb in a narrow slot canyon in the Maligne Valley when he'd fallen. Seeing his vehicle still parked by the side of the road late in the day, Jimmy Rand had investigated and found Malcolm's body tangled in his own ropes near the bottom of the technically uncomplicated pitch.

The circumstances befuddled the RCMP officers who investigated Malcolm's death, but they classified it as an accident—unfortunate—but an accident nonetheless.

Marion had misgivings about the official findings, but in the end, it didn't change things. Malcolm was dead. She was on her own and had to approach things differently.

The carefree attitude to exploring the park had been replaced by an almost compulsive need to have a plan, and a back-up plan, for everything she did. Lunch and extra water in a small day-pack were no longer enough to sustain her forays into uncharted territory. Increasingly, she harboured a nervousness about travelling alone off the beaten path, ensuring she always brought extra clothing, enough food to get her through a night in the backcountry, matches and a flashlight, all packed into a dry bag that went with her everywhere.

Their daughter Susan had also noticed the shift and suggested Marion stick to the park's many well-marked trails. Realizing her mother was unlikely to follow her advice, she implored Marion to leave a detailed itinerary of where she planned to go, so others would know where to look for her in the event something happened and she was unable to make it back to her car.

Marion finally conceded but there was no stopping her almost insatiable desire to get into the park, a desire she felt more now than ever before. She especially enjoyed the solitude of paddling alone on a small lake. Sometimes she would take her daughter's advice and find a paddling partner, often one of the young women who worked for the park who she'd taken under her wing and put a roof over their head.

Finding a renter who she could mother was easy enough in a town where rental accommodation was at a premium, despite many people having sectioned their houses off into small rental units to maximize profits or to simply make ends meet in what was fast becoming an expensive resort town.

Living in Jasper wasn't cheap.

Her most recent renter, Megan Weaver, had been a godsend, a woman after her own heart, and Marion had mixed feelings when Megan finally got into government housing, happy for Megan, but sad to be losing a kindred spirit.

Going home to an empty house just wasn't the same.

Marion didn't think she was getting paranoid, but she seemed more sensitized now than ever before. She heard everything, her ears perking up with every creak and groan of the old house. Her daughter dismissed her concerns, but that did nothing to appease Marion's unease about the constant rumours swirling around town: rumours of the new mine along the park's boundary that now seemed likely to happen, or another new development in the park that would go against everything the park stood for, and most unsettling of all, rumours that some of the park staff who stood up against all of these pressures might be transferred.

Thankfully they had Anne Winters.

For as much as the rumours about new developments concerned her, Marion knew Anne had faced similar threats before, stared them down and snuffed them out before they had a chance to materialize. Hopefully she wasn't going anywhere soon. A new superintendent might deal with these same issues differently. Without Anne at the helm, Marion worried about her own stamina to keep up the fight, especially now that Malcolm was gone.

Turning down her street, she walked to her gate and lifted the latch, thankful she had left the outside light on over the backdoor. As she unlocked the door, she could hear her phone ringing and quickly went inside, surprised someone would be calling at this late hour.

"Hello?" she said, apprehensively waiting for a reply. "Oh, it's you, Megan. Yes thanks, I got home fine. Thanks so much for checking in on me." She paused and listened to Megan as she looked out the kitchen window. Only half concentrating on the conversation, Marion squinted her eyes, trying to decipher the outline just beyond the reach of the streetlight's beam.

Was there someone or something there?

She could have sworn she'd heard footsteps behind her on the way home.

Thanking Megan again for inviting her to the party, Marion hung up the phone then turned her gaze back to the empty street. Shaking her head, she locked the back door, turned off the lights and walked down the hallway to her bedroom.

CHAPTER 11

TIRED FROM HIS flight from Berlin to Ottawa, Helmut Stenger followed the commissionaire through the Langevin Block to the Office of the Prime Minister, smiling to himself at the ease with which he could access the highest office in the Canadian government.

It paid to nurture connections with the top.

The diminutive German businessman was about to enter the office when the door opened and Arnold Grimes, the minister for the environment, walked out, almost running into Stenger, pushing him slightly off-balance by the sudden encounter.

"Mr. Stenger?" said the minister. "We weren't expecting you until this afternoon."

"Why hello, Arnold." Helmut Stenger held out his hand. "So good to see you. Yes, I had planned on taking a domestic flight, but decided to come by private jet instead. You know how frustrating having to stop in Toronto can be. It's a difficult place to get out of, even with good weather."

"I know only too well," said Arnold, leading Stenger by the elbow to one side of the large hallway away from the entrance to the prime minister's office. He cleared his throat and looked down at the tiny figure in the Armani suit.

"Our meeting with the prime minister is on schedule?" said Helmut.

"Yes, er, well, it has been delayed," Arnold stammered. "A minor change of plans." He spoke quietly and quickly. "The prime minister has been called back to Centre Block and won't be able to meet with you today." Arnold shot a glance back toward the door of the prime minister's office. Gently placing a hand on Stenger's elbow, he led the German businessman farther down the hall and around a corner. "Your proposal is meeting with some opposition, Mr. Stenger. Since it's in the prime minister's home province, it's a sensitive issue. I'm sure you understand."

"But I will be meeting with him?"

"Yes, yes, arrangements have been made. There is a private dinner scheduled for tomorrow evening. You will have an opportunity to meet with him there, out of the limelight, so to speak. In the meantime, his role in this must not be made public. It would put him in a very awkward position."

Helmut Stenger nodded. His face tightened into a grimace as he studied the minister. "The arrangements for tomorrow?"

"I will have a car pick you up at your hotel at six o'olock. In the meantime, I have other business to attend to." Arnold fidgeted waiting for Helmut Stenger to depart.

Instead, Stenger put his hand to his chin, flexing his fingers as he seemed to ponder the new circumstances. "Very well, Arnold. Changes of plan are a matter of course. But I should remind you, we have an agreement." He paused to let his words sink in. "I will be expecting to speak with the prime minister tomorrow evening. No later."

The minister took a deep breath and nodded. "Yes, of course." His voice sounded resigned. "My driver will be at your hotel tomorrow evening at six o'clock. Please be ready."

"I will be ready," Stenger replied firmly. Giving a final nod, he turned and made his way down the vast hallway and disappeared.

Arnold waited until the German businessman was out of sight then quickly made his way back to the prime minister's office.

*****

Helmut Stenger looked at his Rolex and sighed. It was well past six o'clock and his ride had not materialized. Stepping past the doorman, he peered down the street just as a black Cadillac pulled up in front of the hotel. The driver quickly got out and walked around the car, motioning Helmut toward the rear door

When the driver opened the door, Helmut was surprised to see Arnold Grimes sitting in the rear seat.

"Arnold, you didn't have to come yourself. Just your driver would have been fine."

There was a look of concern on the minister's face as he motioned for Stenger to get in. "Something has come up," he said as Helmut slid into the car and the driver closed the door. Grimes waited until the driver pulled the Cadillac onto the busy street then turned to Helmut. "The prime minister won't be able to see you this evening," he said as the limousine headed east. "He's asked me to look after this matter."

"Then where are we going?" said Stenger, looking less than amused.

"For a short drive." The car travelled east for a few blocks and then turned south. "Your proposal will be very contentious in Jasper."

Stenger nodded.

"It will attract a great deal of media attention," Arnold continued. "The prime minister absolutely cannot afford to be seen to be involved."

Helmut Stenger placed his hand on Arnold's arm to get his attention. "I understand completely," he said, his face turning very serious. "But let me take care of those concerns."

"And how do you propose to do that?"

"That's nothing you need to concern yourself with," said Stenger, "but people will be too busy worrying about other issues to pay much attention to our little project." Arnold was about to interject, but Helmut Stenger squeezed his arm. "Let me worry about how to direct people's interests to other issues. *You* should focus on taking whatever steps are necessary at your end to ensure this project proceeds." Stenger took off his glasses and wiped them with a clean handkerchief. "I don't have to remind you what's at stake."

"I understand," said Arnold as he motioned for the driver to turn west along an empty street.

"And in the near term, I need two things from you," Stenger continued.

"They are?"

"A reintroduction to Jasper," said Stenger. "I have to visit the park and meet with my people on the ground. While I'm there, I would also like to see the lake again."

"I'll arrange it," Arnold said as the car turned north. "And the second item?"

"My contacts in Jasper suggest there will be some resistance locally, especially on the part of the park superintendent. I'm not sure she will be amenable to our plans."

"Not to worry," said Arnold. "I've spoken with the director-general for national parks and he understands the situation."

As the car turned east again, the driver pulled up in front of Stenger's hotel and was about to get out of the car when Helmut raised a hand to him. "It's okay. I can get the door." The German businessman slid out of the Cadillac, then turned back to the minister. "I will be in touch to make sure everything is proceeding as planned. Please don't let me down, Arnold. In the meantime, I'll be in Jasper over the next few days." He turned away before Arnold Grimes could acknowledge his comment and walked into his hotel.

CHAPTER 12

THE THREE MEN occupied a corner booth in the hotel restaurant, opting to speak English to avoid drawing any more attention than necessary. As the waitress took their orders, Helmut Stenger assessed the two men opposite him, wondering if they were up to the task at hand.

Gunter and Jakob were German ex-pats who had come to Canada in their early twenties and stayed, working in hunting camps in the Yukon and Northwest Territories until they bought out an operator in British Columbia's Pink Mountains and began guiding on their own. Helmut had tracked them down through an acquaintance who had come to Canada to bag a Dall sheep, adding another trophy to his list.

There was something about the man's story that made Helmut question the legitimacy of the hunt. When pressed, the man finally conceded the sheep had been taken illegally from within Nahanni National Park in the Northwest Territories. He'd indicated the two guides were meticulous in their handling of the operation, including dealing with the pilot who flew them across the boundary into the national park, and the paperwork necessary to clear customs with the sheep's head and cape.

Used to working with hired guns, so to speak, Helmut decided to follow up. In his business dealings in Africa, Helmut often hired quasi-paramilitary operatives, but he had his own criteria for assessing their work. He rarely took on someone who hadn't personally proven themselves to him in some way.

But that was Africa, where the law of the jungle applied, literally. And there he had the services of a man he could trust to do what was needed, no matter how brutal the task. Helmut knew he would never be able to get away with what he'd been

67

able to do there in Canada. He would have to tread carefully as he propositioned politicians, bureaucrats and businesspeople to get past the more rigorous hurdles he would face here.

But Helmut also knew that no matter where he invested his time and fortune, there were universal human traits that served him well: greed and ambition.

Money talked and power could be bought. It was that simple. It could be masked by pretense and posturing, but in the end, greed and ambition were unwavering forces that made his work easier, giving him easy access to the most influential people in governments around the world, including Ottawa and Edmonton.

Still, he needed people on the ground to do his dirty work. Helmut was convinced it was necessary to have options in case things didn't work out the way he hoped they would. And invariably there were challenges.

"Are you sure you won't have anything sir?" the waitress asked Stenger.

"Thank you, but no." Stenger waved the waitress off and waited for her to get out of earshot before questioning the two men.

"You are familiarizing yourselves with the area?"

"Ja, er, yes," said Gunter, the largest of the pair, catching himself as a cloud of cigarette smoke protected him from the piercing eyes of the German businessman. "We drove here in our own Land Cruiser. We've been checking out the border areas along the boundary of the park."

"Good sheep country," said Jakob. "With lots of bear sign as well."

Helmut Stenger shook his head and glowered. "That's not why I hired you," he scowled. "Your job is to lay the groundwork for the mine and deflect any opposition I might encounter with my other project. Do not let your *extracurricular* activities distract you from the task at hand. There can be no mistakes. Understood?"

Gunter nodded in agreement but said nothing.

"Have you made any contacts?" Stenger continued.

"Yes," said Jakob. "One of our associates in B.C. told us about someone from the area who might be able to help us. We met him a few days ago." He pulled a piece of paper from his pocket. "His name ..."

Stenger quickly held up a hand and looked around the restaurant. "I don't need to know." He looked hard at both men. "The fewer people involved, the better. I want no direct connection with any of this. Understood?"

Gunter and Jakob nodded.

"And he will take on this kind of work?" said Stenger. "Is he trustworthy?"

Gunter smiled, deviously. "I think he will be perfect."

"As long as he gets the job done," said Stenger. "Whatever happens, he must not be tied back to you, *or me*. This is an extremely sensitive undertaking. The consequences will be severe if any mistakes are made."

The two men looked at each other then back at Stenger.

"But, I am willing to make it worth your while to ensure there are no mistakes." Stenger reached into an inside pocket of his jacket and handed each man an envelope. "Fifty percent now and fifty percent when I am satisfied you've done what I've asked." He reached into his pocket again and handed the larger of the two men another envelope. "This is for expenses, for the man you've hired, or any other costs you incur."

Gunter checked the envelope and showed the contents to his partner. "Very well. How do we contact you in the future?"

"You don't," said Stenger. "I will contact you. If anyone asks, I am a client looking to set up a hunt in Alberta and you are working with a local outfitter to assess the options." He paused. "As well, you should know I have a contact inside the national park. At some point he may need your services or the services of the man you hire. I will expect you to do whatever is necessary to accommodate him."

"Who is he?" Gunter asked.

"You will know when you need to know."

As the waitress returned to their table, Stenger waited until she had given the men their orders and gone back to the kitchen, then stood to leave.

He nodded, "I will be in touch."

CHAPTER 13

THE FOLLOWING MORNING was sunny and clear as Ben and Kate piled into John Haffcut's warden truck and headed for the park compound in Jasper.

"I hope you two have everything you need for the day," said John, "I hate going into the office if I don't have to. Once you go in there, someone's always after you to do one thing or the other." He pointed to the Bell 206 sitting on the helipad. "It's way easier to just jump in the chopper and get the hell outta town."

"We're good to go," Kate assured him.

As they pulled up to the helipad, the pilot, Clayton Kelvin, climbed out of the helicopter. Middle aged, he sported an ancient leather jacket bearing the wings insignia for the Royal Canadian Air Force. A pair of mirrored aviator sunglasses hung from his breast pocket.

"Hard night, Clay?" said John. "Your eyes look like two piss-holes in the snow." He walked past Clay and tossed his pack into the helicopter.

He didn't condone Clay's after-hours behaviour, but it was hard to argue with the fact Clayton Kelvin was the best pilot he'd ever flown with, bar none.

Watching Clay and his net-gunner capture caribou always amazed John. They could spot a small group of animals, isolate their target, usually an adult female, and have it down in the snow in a matter of seconds. John had actually seen "Tiny," Clay's oversized assistant, leap from the machine as it hovered a few feet above a netted animal and have it hobbled faster than a cowboy wrestling steers at the Calgary Stampede. When the two men were zoned in and doing wildlife work, they were like

71

poetry in motion, even if their true characters were probably a better fit in some sort of action flick.

As the three park wardens climbed into the helicopter with John riding shotgun, Clay flipped switches and checked instruments, then powered up the machine. "Where to this morning?" he asked, wincing as he peered through bloodshot eyes.

"Hmphh," John muttered. "A bit hung over?"

"Just a tiny bit." Clay tried to manage a smile but the effect was lost on John.

John shook his head and pulled out a set of maps. Thumbing through the stack he picked two and handed them to Kate and Ben in the backseat.

"We're looking for a couple of collars," John said over his shoulder. "One in the Maligne and a second one in the Tonquin. We'll follow the Maligne River up to Medicine and Maligne Lakes, then flip over into the Tonquin. That way you can get to see a bit of the backcountry." He turned to Clay. "You got that?"

Clay nodded then flipped on the intercom. "Everyone ready?"

"Ten-four," Ben and Kate said in unison.

John Haffcut nodded to the affirmative and watched Clay's every move as he pulled the machine off the ground and hovered above the helipad. Turning toward the sun, Clay let the machine drop down toward the Athabasca River, picking up speed as it slid into the valley bottom.

"That's Jasper Park Lodge and the golf course," said John, as he pointed to a large collection of log buildings and broad expanses of manicured turf nestled in a forest of lodgepole pine and Douglas fir. "Signal Mountain's behind it. It used to have a fire lookout on top, back in the day."

Ben and Kate were busy looking at the landscape as Clay followed the Athabasca to the confluence with the Maligne River, where he took a sharp right turn and flew directly over Maligne Canyon as John pointed out other landmarks to the two new park wardens.

"Back on our left is the horse range," said John, throwing a thumb over his shoulder toward the horse corrals and barn. "In the past we've had fifty or more horses in the backcountry program here in Jasper, but every year it's getting whittled down a little further."

"Why's that?" asked Kate.

"Time's are changing," said John. "The park had district wardens who spent their summers patrolling the backcountry on horseback, but there's less and less use back there every year. Most of our wardens are gobbled up by the townsite and campgrounds, doing ops and dealing with all of the visitors who come to the park. I bet now we don't get fifty people on the north or south boundary in a year. Everyone wants the quick fix, a short hike to a lookoff with a cool view. Then it's off to the next photo op. Like I said, times are changing."

"That's too bad," said Ben.

"It is what it is", said John, "but I wouldn't be surprised if it comes around again, you know, people wanting to get back to nature so to speak."

"I hope so," said Kate, admiring the towering peaks on either side of the helicopter as they flew up the valley. "It'd be a shame for people not to know what we've got here."

"To a point," said John.

"How's that?" said Ben.

"Well, we're kind of loving this park to death," said John. "Too many people in my opinion. I've been trying to tell the managers we don't manage ecosystems, or wildlife for that matter. The best we can do for this place is to manage ourselves. Humans."

"Interesting," said Kate. "How does that go over?"

"Like a lead balloon usually," said John. "But it could be really simple. Put the right number of people in the right place at the right time doing the right thing. It sounds kind of corny but I call it 'RP squared, RT squared'."

Clay shook his head but said nothing.

"I saw that," said John.

Clay looked straight ahead. "Hey, you're preaching to the converted. I've only heard this sermon, what, two, three hundred times?"

"He's bullshitting," said John. He looked over his shoulder at Ben and Kate and laughed. "Can't be any more than a hundred."

"But it kind of makes sense," said Kate.

"See," said John, lightly elbowing Clay. "I'm serious. It could work."

"And how have your bosses taken to it?" said Clay, looking across at John as they approached Medicine Lake.

"Not so well," he admitted. He shook his head and peered out at the lake. "Along with some of the folks in town who don't want to give up anything they've got, most managers think I'm angling to shut out human use in some parts of the park. I'm kind of tired of listening to them whine."

"Now who's whining?" said Clay.

"I'm serious," said John. "Even the last superintendent couldn't get it into his thick head. Thank god he moved on and they promoted Anne into the position. She and Marion are the only two who really get it."

"So is this Medicine Lake?" said Kate, inserting herself into the conversation.

"Yeah," said John, still flustered. "It's very neat actually. It drains in the winter and fills again during the summer."

"Like Jasper Lake?"

"Kind of, but Medicine is more unique," said John.

"How's that," said Ben, looking out at the large mudflats extending most of the length of the lake.

"Sinkholes," said John. "You had those in Wood Buffalo, too. But here they serve to drain the lake after it fills up with glacier and snowmelt. During the summer, the sinkholes can't handle the volume, so the lake fills and spills into the lower section of the Maligne River. In the winter when there's less water coming into Medicine Lake, it drains and empties. Then the cycle repeats itself come springtime."

Continuing south, they flew over a small delta where the Maligne River emptied into Medicine Lake.

John pointed to a small group of caribou feeding in the delta. "Those are some of the animals in the Maligne herd." He pulled a small leather case into his lap and opened the lid, revealing an instrument with a series of switches and knobs. Attaching a thin black cable to the instrument he turned the unit on and listened. "This scanner has all the frequencies of our radio-collared caribou loaded into it."

As they listened on their headsets, they could hear a light pinging sound.

"One of them is collared," said John, looking over his shoulder as Clay circled the group of animals. "I think it's that bull." He pointed to the largest animal in the group. "But we don't need to get any closer. He's not what we're looking for today and there's no point disturbing them." He motioned for Clay to continue upstream, listening to the scanner as they followed the river.

"How is the caribou population doing in the park?" Kate asked.

"Not so well," said John. "It's declining."

"Why's that?"

"We're not entirely sure if there's any one factor," said John. "South Jasper doesn't have the greatest habitat to start with. Add predation by bears, wolves and cougars, and caribou have a lot of things working against them. A warmer climate doesn't seem to help either."

"Is there anything we can do to help them?" asked Ben.

"Absolutely," said John. "To start with, we need to make sure our own activities don't tip the scales further against caribou."

"Your idea of managing human use?" said Kate.

"Exactly," said John. "There are some simple things we could do. Like that road down there." He pointed to the paved road snaking toward Maligne Lake. "Every winter we plow the road to the lake and pretty well any day of the week I can show you wolf tracks going up the road. They use it to access the lake and then use the backcountry ski trails to access the sub-alpine and alpine. Like I said, it's not rocket science."

"So we're helping wolves get to the caribou during winter?" said Kate, "When they're most vulnerable."

"Yeah," said John.

"Has there ever been any thought given to closing the road?" said Ben.

"Oh yeah," John said with a sigh. "But it never went anywhere. That's why we'd hate to see any more winter use in places like the Maligne or Tonquin. Once it starts, it's hard to scale back. Before you know it, we've got populations like these caribou that are on the brink of being extirpated from the park."

"I'm playing devil's advocate," said Kate. "But it's not all a function of human use. You said so yourself."

"Agreed," said John. "But it's really the only thing we can manage, unless we want to do what the province is doing and begin shooting wolves."

"I wouldn't go for that," said Ben.

"Me either," said Kate.

"If we don't try to manage our own activities, these caribou don't stand much of a chance," said John as Clay piloted the helicopter over the last small rise before Maligne Lake. "And once they're gone we'll probably never get them back."

"Wow," said Kate, as they caught their first glimpses down the lake.

"Impressive, eh?" said John.

Ben and Kate nodded in unison.

"What's this below us?" said Kate, pointing to a number of buildings at the headwaters of the Maligne River.

"The summer boat tour operation," said John. "They take folks down the lake to Spirit Island."

"Spirit Island," said Ben. "I've heard of it and seen pictures but I've never been there."

"Well, we'll be flying right over it," said Clay.

"Does it get busy on the lake?" Kate asked as Clay circled the north end of the lake.

"Busier than snot in July and August," said John.

"Is that a warden station?" said Ben, pointing to a house and small barn on the edge of the lake.

"Yeah," said John. "That's Jimmy Rand's place."

"Sweet," said Kate. "Paid to live in Paradise."

"Ten-four," said John. "Someone's gotta do it."

John motioned for Clay to keep going south as they continued to monitor the scanner. "I think we'll find the collar somewhere near Maligne Pass. Let's pick up some altitude and see if we can hear it."

As Clay piloted the helicopter higher above the subalpine forests, they crested several rolling hills of blackened snags.

"An old burn," said John as they made a beeline for Maligne Pass.

"Lightning strike?" said Ben.

"Most likely," said John, "but we get a few careless campers too, although back here, more than likely it was lightning ..."

Before John could finish, Clay raised a finger to his mouth. A rapid pulsing sound could be heard over the headsets.

"Mortality signal," said John. He checked the frequency on the scanner. "It's the collar we're looking for."

As the signal increased in strength, John and Clay worked together to determine where the signal was coming from, finally pointing to a small drainage coming out of Maligne Pass. As they approached a creek flowing through a maze of willow, John pointed to the remains of a caribou.

"Damn. I was hoping for a dropped collar and not a dead animal," he said as Clay brought the machine in to land. "Looks like a winter kill. Wolves most likely."

"There are wolves way back here in winter?" said Ben. "We're a long way from the road."

"Some years they're back this far," said John. "If the snow's not too deep. Or if we get a mid-winter thaw followed by a freeze, they can walk on top of it and go wherever they damn well please." He sighed as Clay put the machine down next to the carcass. "But that's the way it goes, I suppose. Wolves seem to focus primarily on moose around the lake, but incidentally take a caribou or two if they run into them." He pulled off his headset, opened the door then dropped to the ground as Clay went through the motions of shutting the machine down.

"Walk around to the front," Clay said to Ben and Kate as they exited the back seat. "Stay away from the tail rotor."

Following Clay's instructions, Ben and Kate joined John, who didn't wait for the rotors to stop spinning before investigating the carcass, essentially pieces of skin and bone loosely connected by a partial series of vertebrae to the remains of the skull and antlers.

"Pretty sure it was wolves," said John. "This animal died before the grizzlies emerged from their dens a few weeks back. We were getting a mortality signal on our last fixed wing flight, but obviously couldn't get in here without a helicopter."

"There's not much left," said Kate as Clay joined the trio.

"Never is," said John. "I'm actually surprised there's this much. They didn't even chew apart the collar." He took a small wrench from his pocket and undid the lock nuts on the collar. Grabbing one end of the webbing, he slid the collar out from under the carcass, quickly inspected it for damage then placed it in his pack.

"Pretty much picked clean," said Clay.

John nodded and looked around at the broad expanses of alpine meadow sloping off toward the nearby ridgelines. "But if you had to die," he said, "this wouldn't be a bad place to do it."

"Says you," said Clay with a grin.

"Better than flattened like a pancake when your helicopter pile drives into one of those mountain faces," said John.

"Great image," said Ben.

"And we still have some flying to do," said Kate.

The four laughed and climbed back into the machine.

"Where to now, boss?" said Clay.

"Let's see if we can find the other collar in the Tonquin," said John, "and show these two just how amazing this park really is. Once they see the Ramparts, they'll never want to leave."

"What we've seen so far isn't too shabby," said Ben.

"You haven't seen anything yet," said John.

CHAPTER 14

AFTER THE FLIGHT to the Maligne and Tonquin valleys, John invited Ben and Kate back to the office to check the data from the GPS collars they'd recovered. He was keen to know if the collars had been working properly right up until they switched to mortality mode when the animals had died.

Ben and Kate were surprised by the state of John's office and the stench of field gear drying on a makeshift rack.

Megan Weaver sat at a small corner desk glued to her computer screen. "Good flight?" she said, barely looking up from her work. "Sorry," she added, flipping back and forth between the computer as she ran a finger down several pages of numbers on her desk. "I just need to finish checking this list."

"It was amazing," said Kate as she walked up behind Megan and looked over her shoulder. "Especially the Tonquin."

"Yeah. That place is pretty special." Megan made a notation next to the list of numbers and finally turned to face the others. "Sorry for the mess." She grimaced looking around the office. "And the smell."

John's desk was piled with papers and reports. Even the desk chair was toppling with another load of papers. John picked them up and looked around for another spot to set them down.

Megan just shook her head.

"Organized chaos," John muttered. "I know it looks terrible but everything's in its place."

"And there's a place for everything," Megan grabbed the pile from John and placed it on top of the piles already on the desk.

"Kind of reminds me of Gordie's collection of radio collars and other gear," said Ben.

Megan laughed.

"Goes with the territory," said John.

"Huh oh, here comes the story," said Megan. She laughed and looked at Ben and Kate as if to say "wait for it."

John smirked and sat on the edge of his desk. "Hey, what can I say, people like the story."

"So let's hear it," said Kate.

"Oh, it was nothing really," said John. "The Snake came in here one day and saw the mess and just about had a coronary." John spread his arms around. "All this stuff drove him nuts."

"The Snake?" said Kate. "What was he when he was here, assistant superintendent or something?"

"Yeah." John was trying to keep it together. "The only Frenchman I never liked. Anyway, he came in here and got all red-faced and in his heavy French accent said to me, 'Haffcut, a messy desk is the sign of a messy mind.' So I looked at him and said, 'So, what is *your empty desk* a sign of?'" John buckled over laughing. "I thought he was gonna fire me right there on the spot. Or die. I'da been happy with either right about then."

Megan shook her head. "You crazy fool."

"Anyway," John continued. "The Snake was speechless. His little frog body went into all sorts of contortions and his face turned beet red. He didn't know what to say, in either official language. He just hurtled on out of here, jumped in his car and never came back. Literally. He never stepped a foot in my office again. Before we knew it, he took a promotion with another department. Wouldn't you know it, now he's the friggin' director-general for Parks." John shook his head and looked at Megan. "We were hoping we'd never see him again."

Megan looked at Kate and Ben. "See what you're in for, working with this guy?"

"Oh, Megan," said John. "You love it."

"Sure." Megan rolled. "Anyway, you were going to give these two the tour."

"Yeah," said John. "Well, it's all here." He looked around the room then walked over to a series of shelves. "VHF collars, GPS collars, receivers, scanners, antennae, trail counters, remote cameras including video and still, the whole shootin' match." He picked up a camera and handed it to Ben. "These film cameras were the first puppies I used." He handed another newer camera to Kate. "But we're just starting to use these digital cameras now. It's amazing how far the technology has come in such a short time. And you saw these on the flight," he said, passing a newer GPS collar to Ben and Kate. "Now that we can schedule them to drop off the animal, we don't have to do recaptures all the time. Unless of course we want to put a collar back on."

"Slick," said Ben, taking a closer look at the collar.

"Yeah," said John. "The boys in Banff didn't think these units would work up here. Said the valleys were too tight and the satellite coverage wouldn't be up to snuff. But they worked like a hot damn and the first caribou data we pulled off opened a lot of eyes."

He pointed to a map on the wall. "These are all the caribou locations collected using the collars, including places the caribou are using that a lot of the older outfitters never figured was good habitat. Ultimately, the data tell us caribou use pretty much all of the habitat available to them. Not all at once maybe, but at different times of the year, different parts of the park are important to them. It probably depends a lot on things like snowpack, weather, wolves, the whole nine yards. And it probably varies from year to year." He placed the collar back on the shelf. "Now the wildlife guys in Banff have more collars out than you can shake a stick at. They're learning lots, but I sure wish they'd leave some of the animals alone. I don't think the tourists can get a picture of a bear or wolf down there without it having a friggin' collar on its neck." John paused and looked at the map again.

"And truth be told, if we don't start using the data to *inform decision-making*, as they say, I'd just as soon we didn't collar another animal."

"Shades of Wood Buffalo," said Ben.

"Yeah," said John. "Megan told me the outfit didn't use any of the data her dad wanted to show the bison review panel. It's almost criminal considering every time you capture an animal, you run the risk of it getting injured, or killed." John raised his eyebrows and looked at the trio.

"Yeah, they tried to deep six it," said Ben, "but we managed to find a way around all that." He paused and peered at the map. "Hopefully things will be different here."

"Well, so far so good," said John. "Anne's been pretty supportive of using any information we can provide her to ward off the folks who want more development in the park. There are a lot of outfits with their eye on turning a buck in our parks and it seems like there's only so much the folks in Ottawa can do to fend them off."

"Thank god we usually have the public on our side," said Megan.

"Yeah, but there's only so much they can do," said John. "Money talks and you can bet there are more than a few greased palms in the halls of Parliament."

"Still, the public is huge," said Megan "And that translates into votes."

"We saw that in Wood Buffalo as well," said Kate. "The public really went to bat for us and wrote hundreds of letters to the government."

"It also helped that we had a connection to the media," said Ben. "I'm not sure where we'd have been otherwise."

"Getting in bed with the media?" said John with raised eyebrows. "I'm not so sure that's always a good idea."

"I didn't say get into bed with them," said Ben, suddenly turning red. "But we would never have gotten our messages out without them."

Kate chuckled as she watched Ben backpedal out of the hole he was digging for himself.

"Am I missing something?" said John.

"You had to be there," said Kate, placing the camera back on the shelf and picking up a scanner. "This looks more sophisticated than the one Gordie used in Wood Buffalo."

"Aw, probably not much different," said John. "Maybe just a different manufacturer. They all pretty much work the same. Program in the frequencies you want to scan for, then let her roll. I usually keep the list of frequencies tucked in here." He slid a finger between the scanner and its leather case and pulled out a laminated list of numbers. "Don't tell anyone, but if for some reason you need to use this baby, you know where the list is. It's not a big deal, but prying eyes might like to have it and you never know these days. If someone wanted to track down one of our animals for some nefarious reason, this list would be a goldmine."

Megan laughed. "C'mon John. You're thinking conspiracy theory again."

John smiled. "You're probably right. But the list also includes some of the collared bears in the province. The Fish and Wildlife biologists sure wouldn't want that to fall into the wrong hands." He hesitated for a moment as he ran a finger down the list. "And Hope's frequency is here as well, don't forget."

"Hope?" said Kate.

"A little sow grizzly John and Clay collared near Rocky Pass," Megan explained. "She's come as far west as the Maligne Valley, but now that she's got cubs, she spends most of her time outside of the park around the mines and along Highway 40."

"The mining companies love her," said John, "because she's showing us grizzlies can live side by side with bulldozers and ore trucks."

"She's the poster child for industry in the province," said Megan. "I bet her picture has been on every newspaper in

Alberta." She was about to go on when Jimmy Rand walked into the office, a serious look on his face. "Something wrong Jimmy?"

"Yeah. I just got off the phone with Fish and Wildlife. One of their officers called to say some bears were shot out near the Cardinal Divide. Probably came out of the park."

"Grizzlies?" said John.

Jimmy nodded. "A sow and cub. It's a few days old, but he wondered if we wanted to come and take a look at them."

"Jesus," said John. "It better not be Hope." He shook his head and sighed heavily.

"Man, that's three bears this week. The population around here can't sustain these kinds of losses." He looked around at the group. "Well, we've still got a machine sitting outside if Clay hasn't already left. We can fly to the Divide and check it out."

"Sure," said Ben. "Let's do it."

"Did they catch who did it?" John turned back to Jimmy, his eyes on fire.

Jimmy shook his head. "Fish and Wildlife have their ideas but they have next to nothing to go on."

"How'd they find them?" John continued his interrogation.

"Research folks flying for collared bears saw them in the pass."

"But these weren't collared bears?"

"I never asked." Jimmy paused. "But I'm pretty sure these were new bears."

John Haffcut smiled at the comment. "*New* bears."

"Hell, you know what I mean," said Jimmy.

John nodded and patted Jimmy on the back. "Yeah. Thankfully there's still bears out there we don't know about and haven't put a friggin' collar on." He stopped as if thinking about what he'd just said. "Or *were* out there, I should say. The bastard poachers are going to drive me to drink." He looked at Jimmy. "You should come with us. We can squeeze you into the backseat."

"Sure," said Jimmy. "It's been awhile since I've been to Rocky Pass."

CHAPTER 15

UNLIKE THE CARIBOU flight, the trip to Rocky Pass was direct and fast. As they approached the pass, John pointed to the two provincial Fish and Wildlife officers making their way toward the helicopter.

"No other machines around," said Clay. "They must've been dropped off earlier." He set the helicopter down in a patch of bearberry and raised a thumb to John.

"You wanna come?" said John.

Clay considered the offer. "Not sure if I want to see a poached bear, especially if it's a few days old. It can be pretty nasty. Think I'll just shut down and sit here. Besides, I've got a trouble light showing there," he said, pointing to a blinking red light in an array of lights and switches above his head, "so I might just figure out what that's all about then take this puppy for a test drive."

"Your call," said John. "We won't be long." He opened the door and joined Ben, Kate and Jimmy as they got out of the back seat. Keeping their heads low, they walked outside of the rotor's reach and made their way toward the two provincial officers, who stood waiting for them in the middle of the pass.

"The biggest guy is Brent Rideout," said Jimmy, before they were in earshot of the provincial wildlife officers. He turned to Ben. "I think his family's originally from the Rock. Not a guy you want to be on the wrong side of."

"Who's the other guy?" asked Kate.

"Not sure," said Jimmy. "But I guess we'll find out."

"Hey, Jimmy," said Brent Rideout, extending a hand. "Thanks for coming."

"No worries, Brent. Just wish the circumstances were different."

"This is Dale Weychuck," said Brent, motioning to the other officer. "He's new here, so I thought I'd show him what we're up against."

Jimmy shook the other officer's hand then introduced Kate and Ben.

"So where are they?" John asked.

"Over this way." Brent led the others to the south side of the pass and scrambled up the rocks toward the body of the first animal. As they approached the remains, two ravens lifted off and set down again on a large boulder a few metres away, squawking their displeasure.

"It's a little ripe," said Brent as a foul odour enveloped the group. "It'd be worse, but the cool weather helps preserve the carcasses."

"What a friggin' waste," said John as he knelt down by the sow and checked over the body. "At least she wasn't nursing," he added, pulling the fur back from the teats.

"But she had cubs," said Dale. "One at least." He pointed across the slope. "We found it a little ways over there. Same deal, paws cut off and the gallbladder removed."

"What a waste," said Kate.

"Any ideas who might be responsible?" said Ben.

Brent and Dale shared glances.

"We have our hunches," said Brent. "I was just telling Dale before you folks got here, Ritter is back in the area. I wouldn't put this past him."

"Zane Ritter," Jimmy said to Ben and Kate. "A local poacher that gives these guys no end of trouble."

"And he's not to be taken lightly," said Brent. He has a special hate on for the feds, but we don't rank a helluva lot higher in their books."

"What's his deal?" said Ben.

"Wildlife trafficking," said Dale. "Zane's been running back and forth from up North and the word is he's trafficking wildlife parts from all over the province."

"Zane works in the oil patch," said Brent, "but used to work for the coalmines until our guys nailed him for poaching bears. The mines wanted no part of him. They have enough on their plates without having to deal with some employee out poaching near their mine sites. It's bad for business."

"So he was fired?" said Ben.

Brent nodded. "Yup. And told specifically to stay off the mine's property, otherwise they'd nail him for trespassing. Even got a court order to back it up."

"That would probably set him off," said John.

"For sure," said Brent. "They don't call him 'Inzane' for nothing."

"Shades of John Donald Moores," Kate said to Ben.

John nodded. "Huhuh." He looked at Kate. "Remember, I was there too." He got up and headed across the slope. "Show us the other bear, Brent."

Ben and Kate followed the others to the body of the bear cub as the two officers walked ahead with John and Jimmy.

"Last year's cub for sure, judging by the size," said John. "A little female."

"How long would she stay with the sow?" said Kate.

"A few years," said John. He wiped a hand across his forehead. "Boy, it's tough to see bears wasted like this."

"Especially females," said Jimmy.

"Yeah," said John. "And she likely had at least one other cub with her. Its chances of surviving are a lot less now with the mother gone."

"If that's the case," said Dale, "whoever did this essentially killed three bears."

While the others focused on the cub, Ben and Kate stood looking around the area, trying to size up the scene when the poaching happened.

"What do you think, Brent?" Kate asked. "Where were these animals shot from?"

Brent pointed to a patch of willow downslope, in the bottom of the pass. "Dale and I figured whoever did it came in by ATV."

"They likely drove their truck to the Divide and came as far as they could down the old cut lines," Brent continued. "From there they would have made it to treeline, then ditched the ATV and hiked to the pass. There's no other way to get here other than horseback or flying, and we didn't see any sign of horses."

"And flying's not in the cards for most poachers," said Jimmy, rejoining the group. He pointed to the helicopter sitting in the pass. "That's part of the reason they hate us so much. They figure only government types can afford to waste taxpayer's money using helicopters to fly them around."

"What do you think?" Ben directed his question to Jimmy. "After looking at those bears, do you have any ideas?"

"Well," said John. "This is different from most of the poaching we're used to seeing. If they only took the paws and gallbladders, they weren't after a trophy or anything like that. That suggests trafficking."

"And that brings us back to Ritter," said Brent. "But if it's him, he obviously has some connections to get rid of the stuff. He wouldn't want this stuff lying around attracting attention, so he'd have to have a way to dispose of the parts."

"Where would he get rid of it?" Kate asked.

"Through a middleman most likely," said Dale. "Usually someone with a connection to Asia."

"And the most likely route from here would be through B.C.," said Brent. "There are direct flights from Vancouver to China every day."

"So does Zane Ritter fit the bill to do something like this?" said Kate

Brent laughed. "Absolutely. He's just bad ass, no matter how you cut it."

"And dangerous?" said Kate.

"If caught in the wrong place at the wrong time," said Brent. "I wouldn't trust him as far as I can throw him."

"Well," said John. "I hate to say this, but I'm glad the sow isn't Hope." He turned to Brent Rideout. "So how's our girl doing anyway?"

"Great," said Brent.

"I kinda worry about her always being near the road," said John. "She'd be easy pickin'."

"I don't think you have to worry," said Brent. "She's become the darling of everyone around here, including the mines. She's a good news story as far as they're concerned. Anyone who goes after her will also have the wrath of the miners to deal with."

"And me too," said John.

CHAPTER 16

AS SHE SAT in the tiny Byward Market wine bar, Anne Winters couldn't help but think the man sitting across from her was the one person who hadn't given in.

Over the years, Anne had relied heavily on the advice of Jeremy Large, the most senior bureaucrat in Parks headquarters. He had risen through the ranks and now occupied the seat next to the recently appointed director-general for Parks, Maxime Bolduc. But even Jeremy seemed at a loss to figure out a way to stifle the latest attempts to push development in the national parks.

"You know, I've wanted to tell you this for some time," Anne said as she ran her finger along the rim of her wine glass. "I've always been impressed by the fact you've never compromised your values. You've always stood for what's right."

Jeremy sat back in the booth, his face a little flushed from the comment.

"I don't think there's many people like you left in headquarters," Anne added.

Jeremy sat upright and ran a finger inside his collar then grabbed the knot of his tie and pulled it a little looser. "That's not true," he said as he extricated himself from the noose and undid the top button of his dress shirt. He folded his hands on the wooden tabletop and looked Anne squarely in the eyes. "There are a lot of us but you get worn down." Jeremy sighed. "And with this government you have to very careful what you say. It feels like we're all walking around on eggshells. You keep your head down and do your best, but even then you can get canned for no apparent reason."

"Hmmm," Anne murmured. "I know what you mean."

Jeremy looked around the wine bar and lowered his voice. "The new government totally sold a different agenda during the election."

"Well I know they promised to limit development in national parks," said Anne. "But they're obviously pro-development."

"Obviously. And appointing Maxime Bolduc doesn't help things."

"That has to be frustrating," said Anne.

"Tell me about it," said Jeremy. "You work your whole life rising through the ranks and then they parachute some yes-man in above you to run the outfit. He has almost no experience working for Parks."

"He's obviously connected," said Anne. "He did a short stint in Jasper before jumping to another department and now he's back as the most senior bureaucrat in Parks next to the deputy minister." Anne paused. "Is it true what I hear that he doesn't bother dealing with the DM but goes directly to the minister whenever he wants something?"

Jeremy raised his eyebrows and shrugged.

"Well, with any luck," Anne continued, "this will just be a stepping stone for him and he'll be gone before we know it. Then maybe you'll get your chance. You're next in line after all."

"Don't get your hopes up," said Jeremy. "Or mine. He's open to doing whatever it takes to make Parks a money-making organization."

"It's crazy," said Anne. "Everything outside our boundaries is getting eaten up with industrial development and now we have a government that wants to eat into what's inside our parks as well."

"We'll be Disney North if Maxime has his way," said Jeremy. "And with the watered down environmental assessment process the government wants to bring in, new proposed developments will only get a cursory review. It'll be all about approving development at the expense of what the parks are meant to protect."

"Getting to 'yes', as they say?"

Jeremy nodded. "Pretty much."

"What about projects outside parks like the mine proposal near Jasper? Is it a case of getting to yes?"

"Pretty much," said Jeremy. "Although it's really a provincial decision.""True," said Anne, "but I think we need to have a line in the sand. Parks can't keep letting the province develop right up to our boundary."

Jeremy laughed. "It's not like the feds have a lot of sway in provincial matters, especially in Alberta."

"True, but it's tough enough dealing with all of the development proposals put forward for inside Jasper, let alone the ones along our borders. The pressure to develop seems unending."

"Welcome to my world," said Jeremy. "It's no different for Parks people here in Ottawa. Worse perhaps, because they aren't just seeing the proposals for Jasper. They're seeing the development proposals for all of the parks. It's demoralizing to say the least." He refilled their wineglasses. "At least at the end of the day in Jasper, you can go for a hike or horse ride, or just sit back and look at the mountains."

Anne smiled. "If only it was that easy. The reality is when you're closer to the action, you also have to deal with the folks who come in off the street and berate you for even considering another development."

"You mean Marion and the folks with Jasper Wild?" Jeremy laughed. "Marion hasn't changed since I was a junior manager in Jasper. She has a way of putting it all on your shoulders, of making you feel like a failure if you don't come through."

"Exactly," said Anne. "I feel like my hands are tied when senior management doesn't stay true to the intent of the management plan. And it just feeds the flames for the folks in town who want to see more development."

"You're caught between a rock and a hard place," said Jeremy.

"In a way," said Anne. "I'd have no problem dealing with the pro-development camp if I knew I wasn't going to be undermined by some political decision at the top. But it's hard to defend our position when the folks with Jasper Wild hold our feet to the fire."

"Maybe it's time you moved?"

"But then I feel like I'm letting so many people down." Anne let out a heavy sigh.

"I know exactly how you feel, Anne. But after putting in a full career battling for Parks, you deserve to think about yourself. Don't fall on a sword and be a martyr. After all, you only have a few years left before you retire. Don't jeopardize everything you've worked for."

Anne closed her eyes and ran a hand through her hair. "That sounds like the easy way out. I'm not sure that's my style."

"I know it's not, but it may be the sane thing to do."

"And give up without a fight? Marion and the others would be so disappointed."

"That's not your worry. They aren't going anywhere and will still be battling this."

"But I should be there to support them, fighting alongside them. It seems so wrong to me that we rely on volunteer organizations to hold us accountable, to ensure we uphold our own mandate."

"Keep fighting and you might not have a job. It's that simple."

"But where would I go?" Anne sighed again.

"There are always opportunities," said Jeremy. "I hear they might be looking for someone to help move the park establishment process ahead on the West coast."

Anne looked at the empty bottle and Jeremy's matching stare. She put a hand on his and squeezed it until he looked up at her. "I'll think about it," she said. "In the meantime, keep me informed about what you're hearing here in Ottawa."

"As for the mine," Anne continued, "there's no way we can avoid it. We just picked up two new people from Wood Buffalo, who'll probably be very good at dealing with that sort of thing. I think Lou Walker is already getting them up to speed."

There was a pause in the conversation.

"What time do you meet with Maxime tomorrow?" said Jeremy.

"Maxime?" said Anne. "You're on a first-name basis with the Snake?"

"C'mon, Anne. He's my boss."

Anne shrugged. "Sorry, I didn't mean anything by it. I'm meeting him first thing in the morning. Won't you be there?"

Jeremy shook his head. "I don't get called into these meetings anymore. He likes to play his cards close to his chest. He has a few loyal servants he relies on, but I'm not one of them."

"That's too bad," said Anne. "He's losing out on an experienced voice."

"Right," Jeremy muttered. "But I'll be interested to know who's at the meeting with you. I expect Tom Erickson will be there. He seems to be walking a fine line between siding with the rest of us and doing the director-general's bidding. I'm not sure what he's up to, but I think he's gunning for my job. My only advice to you is the same thing I tell my son when he plays hockey: keep your head up." Jeremy's expression looked serious. "These days, nothing is ever as it seems."

CHAPTER 17

KONRAD VINCENT-BLAIS SAT outside the office of the director-general, still smarting from the colossal backfire in Wood Buffalo that had left him a diminished figure in the eyes of his superiors. Intent on making up time and climbing back up the ladder, he had been like a prisoner on good behaviour as he dealt expeditiously with all the duties of his northern assignment, doing whatever Tom Erickson asked of him.

Climbing back up the ladder. Konrad snickered at the thought. *More like clawing your way to the top.*

For a moment he recalled the primary "life lesson" his father had provided. Survival of the fittest, he'd say, emphasizing each word as he poked his finger into Konrad's forehead.

Swim, or sink.

Kondrad was certain he would have drowned if not for his mother.

One would think empathy was a trait he'd have picked up from her. But instead, he seemed hardwired to follow in his father's footsteps, demonstrating a penchant for getting the job done using whatever means necessary. That trait, plus the acquisition of some political savvy along the way, helped him turn a potentially long-term sentence in Inuvik into one of just a few short months.

In truth, he was surprised Tom and the director-general had given him a reprieve.

And the offer to go to Jasper was almost too good to be true.

Assuming the trust in him was somewhat restored, Konrad was determined not to make the same mistakes again. He was chomping at the bit to make amends.

But he would never forget the people who threw his career off the rails in Wood Buffalo.

He'd heard through the grapevine Ben Matthews and Kate Jones had also been transferred to Jasper and relished the thought of putting them in their place, especially Matthews. He was certain the young park warden had spilled his guts to the media, and one journalist in particular: Kalina Strong. He wouldn't forget that name anytime soon.

As Konrad sat stewing outside the director-general's office, he was on tenterhooks. When the door finally opened and the young assistant ushered him in, Konrad brushed past her.

He was surprised by the reception he received.

"Konrad, good to see you." Tom Erickson stood and welcomed Konrad with a firm handshake and pat on the back. Despite their convoluted history with the Wood Buffalo issue, Tom seemed intent on letting bygones be bygones as he turned to the director-general, who sat stern-faced waiting for the formalities to be over.

"This is our new director-general, Maxime Bolduc."

"Pleased to meet you," said Konrad as Bolduc dismissed his assistant and got up to shake Konrad's hand.

"I trust your time in the North was time well spent," said Bolduc, his face displaying no hint of emotion. Not waiting for a response, he offered the two men a seat and returned to his chair behind the large desk. "Tom has apprised me of what happened in Wood Buffalo. This time, there can be no mistakes." He directed his comment at Tom Erickson, but followed it up with a glance at Konrad.

Both men nodded.

"Jasper is facing several challenges," said Bolduc, "including a new mine along its eastern boundary. It has the potential for significant impacts on the park and will be the focus of our efforts." He paused for a moment to make sure he had both men's attention. "There is also a proposal for a backcountry lodge."

"A what?" said Tom Erickson. "A lodge?"

The director-general nodded.

"But that's never even been discussed in any management plan," Tom protested.

"Yes, I understand that," said Bolduc, glowering at Tom. "It has the potential to be very controversial."

"To say the least," Tom muttered.

The director-general raised his hand. "As of yet, it's not a formal proposal. Still, it has the potential to be politically sensitive. I need you both to deflect any attention away from the minister's office and the PMO. You must avoid any inference this is a politically influenced process. Understood?"

"Understood." Tom Erickson responded for them both.

"Vincent-Blais, you will be dealing directly with the proponent," said the director-general. "He is a German businessman, Helmut Stenger."

Konrad nodded.

"He is not to be taken lightly," Bolduc continued. "He's politically connected and very influential at the highest levels of government. His proposal must be viewed as entirely keeping with the guidance provided by the park's management plan." He smiled. "Of course there is enough ambiguity in the document to allow us flexibility when it comes to deciding on permissible activities, but we need to show this is well within the development parameters specified in the park's plan."

"The park's superintendent will go ballistic over this," said Tom. "You realize that of course."

"Yes," said Bolduc. "We haven't told her about the lodge, yet. In fact, the three of us are the only people in Parks who know about it. For now, that's how it will remain. When it's time to tell Ms. Winters, I expect she'll be very resistant to the idea. So we need a Plan B."

"A Plan B?" said Tom.

"Reassigning her," said Bolduc.

"You mean getting rid of her?" Tom Erickson winced at the notion.

"In a manner of speaking," Maxime said as he thumbed through a large file on his desk. "From this earlier correspondence, I can see she's resisted any proposals of further development in Jasper."

"That's true," said Tom. "But in a sense, I agree with her." He was about to continue but the director-general held up a hand.

"I'd like you to convince her she's the type of person we need on the coast," said Bolduc. "To help lay the groundwork for establishing a new national park. We all know those types of initiatives take years. By then she'll have retired."

"Based on her track record, if she didn't support past development proposals put forward for Jasper, she especially won't like the notion of a lodge in one of the premier backcountry valleys in the park. But she has too many years in to put her pension in jeopardy and she'd be crazy to leave Parks. The move to the coast gives her an out."

"This is dangerous territory," Tom advised. "The locals will see through that strategy."

"Well we'll only go that route if absolutely necessary. We'll give Anne an option to work with us. In the meantime, I expect you, Konrad, to be our eyes and ears in Jasper. Your position as assistant superintendent is temporary. Essentially you are on probation. Play your cards right, and you may be able to take on the superintendent position if we move Anne Winters. Play them wrong, and you *will* be looking for work."

CHAPTER 18

ANNE FELT A little like she was starting all over again, being asked by the young receptionist to wait outside the director-general's office as headquarters staff arrived to start their day. She wanted to remind the bottle blonde with the pouty French accent she had a scheduled early morning meeting, but chose to take it as an opportunity to get a feel for the Ottawa office.

Today I'll be a fly on the wall, she thought, paying close attention to the receptionist, who rifled through the mornings newspapers while seemingly keeping a tally on staff as they arrived for work. Anne took note of the lack of "good mornings" and the absence of smiles as employees dutifully made their way past the receptionist.

With each arrival, she appeared to record something in a ledger, then returned to the newspapers, speaking under her breath as she cut out articles with a pair of scissors and placed them in a manila folder.

Anne smiled to herself as she caught the occasional heavy sigh accompanied by a comment in French.

She had once worked for a park superintendent who spent hours holed up in his office, reading what the local media had to say about issues relevant to the park. He was a total control freak. Anne felt he would have been better off dealing with people directly instead of worrying about what the papers were saying. She had used the experience to refine her own approach to management and rarely worried about the media, opting instead to put the park's position out there for public consumption rather than waiting for someone else's interpretation of it, which, she figured, was usually wrong.

As she reflected back on her evening with Jeremy Large, she wondered how much more patience she had to deal with the changes happening in the outfit. The option of an easy exit had some appeal.

Looking up, she saw Jeremy enter the office and shoot a glance her way before disappearing into the bowels of open cubicles and shuttered offices. Anne wondered who else she might be meeting with and when they might arrive to wait with her. She was surprised when the receptionist got up, straightened out her tight-fitting blouse and skirt, and made her way over to where Anne was sitting.

"The director-general will see you now," she said, waiting for Anne to get up before knocking on the door and ushering her inside.

Anne was surprised to find three men already in the director-general's office: the director-general, Maxime Bolduc, Tom Erickson, who had recently been promoted from the Winnipeg office, and a third man she didn't recognize.

At a nod from the director-general, Tom Erickson was on his feet.

"Good morning, Anne. How was your flight from Edmonton?"

"Fine, fine. Toronto was a pain as usual, but at least my return flight is direct from Ottawa."

"Anne, you've met Maxime previously."

"Yes," Anne replied. "Good morning."

Bolduc nodded before Tom continued with the introductions.

"But I don't think you two have met before." Tom turned to Konrad. "Konrad Vincent-Blais, Anne Winters."

"Pleased to meet you," said Anne as Vincent-Blais barely rose from his seat to shake hands before sitting down again. Konrad's name was vaguely familiar, but Anne wasn't able to put her finger on exactly where she'd heard it. His apparent lack of manners was already making an impression on her.

With his back to the director-general, Tom bit his lip and glowered at Vincent-Blais, before taking a deep breath and turning to Anne. "Please have a seat." He smiled and held the chair as Anne sat down, then returned to his own chair at the corner of the director-general's desk.

"Well let's get right to it," said Bolduc.

Tom Erickson nodded and turned back to Anne.

"Anne, we know Jasper is facing a number of important issues and we want to make sure you have the capacity to deal with everything that's landing on your plate."

"We have been stretched pretty thin," Anne conceded.

"Now it appears there is another proposal, quite literally on your doorstep, that may stretch you even further," Tom added. "So we'd like to offer you some help."

"You mean the mine?" Anne didn't bother wasting time, even though she couldn't fathom why another mine on the park boundary would ever be considered.

"The mine indeed," Tom confirmed. "An open pit coalmine. We've been notified by the province they've given the coal company tentative approval to proceed with their proposal."

"Don't they need to do an environmental review first?" said Anne, shaking her head. "Or at least some consultation?"

"Yes," said Tom. "We have it on good authority there will be. a federal-provincial review."

Anne shrugged. "Just what we need." She knew such a review could tax a number of her staff and they were already swamped with other proposed projects. "Along with everything else on our plate, we'll be challenged to deal with this."

"But we'll have to," said Tom. "The minister will expect us to be a player in the review process."

"If the province even accepts a joint review," said Anne.

"Well, that's obviously a different matter," Tom offered. "But it's on provincial land and they are the regulatory body. Still, you may be expected to play a part in seeing a joint review does take place, considering Jasper is the closest federal land to the proposed mine."

"That hardly seems to be my role," said Anne. "Surely senior management should be dealing with it."

"Typically we would," said Tom. "But headquarters staff are as strapped as you are. And input from Ottawa, well, the province is not likely to be keen on that. Being in Alberta, you may be able to have more influence with your provincial counterparts."

Anne burst into laughter. "You can't be serious?" she said when she had regained her composure.

"Deadly serious," said Tom.

"Tom, you know how these things go. It would take a lot on our part to provide a response to a joint review panel, if the province even accepted a joint review. You know how obstinate they are when it comes to the feds trying to influence what they see as a provincial matter. And to expect the park to force the issue with the province, they'd laugh us out of the room."

"We're talking about a mine that would butt up against your boundary," said Tom. "You'll have concerns, especially about shared species, like grizzly bears. So we need to be prepared."

Anne sighed. "You think *I* don't know that?"

"We're prepared to help," Tom added.

"How exactly?"

"We've decided to fill your vacant assistant superintendent position," said Tom.

"You have?" Anne sensed there was more to this than met the eye. "I thought the plan was to remove the position altogether, to flat line our management?"

Tom smiled. "It was, but the timing isn't good. And you need help. So for now, we've decided to let you keep it."

"Do I get a chance to put it out there to see if I can attract a good candidate?" Anne's eyes opened wide with the possibilities of bringing in extra help.

"Not quite," said Tom. He turned to the director-general.

"I've assigned Konrad the position on a temporary basis," said Bolduc. "He's had experience with the most recent review panel in Wood Buffalo and can help shoulder some of the weight going forward."

Anne smiled inwardly at the *going forward* comment but refrained from saying anything. These expressions seemed to be part of the new regime's look and feel, as if *going backward* had been the approach of earlier management. More worrying, though, was the notion Konrad would be her second in command. The Wood Buffalo reference reminded her of where she'd heard his name before. He'd been actively involved in the bison issue in Wood Buffalo, which was, by all accounts, a disaster. She worried he might bring the same management style to Jasper.

"That might turn a few heads," said Anne, "considering Jasper is a sought-after park and these positions don't come up often. I expect there are a lot of qualified people who would be disappointed." She turned to Konrad. "No offence intended, but I'm not sure your experience in Wood Buffalo would really be considered an asset considering how well that turned out."

Tom Erickson winced at Anne and lowered his head as the director-general stood up from behind his desk before she could continue.

"Ms. Winters, I should remind you, I'm responsible for deciding what is and isn't in the best interests of the park. I'm tired of established managers second-guessing my decisions to bring in a fresh face and a different perspective."

"Sorry," said Anne, stumbling a little over Bolduc's reaction. "As I said, I didn't mean to offend anyone. But I'm also looking out for the park's best interests. After all, I'm the senior manager on the ground in Jasper. It's a complex park with many competing interests."

Anne was about to continue when Tom Erickson interrupted.

"The decision has already been made, Anne. There's no point discussing it further. You, Konrad and I will meet later to discuss his role." He paused to let his point sink in. "And yours."

Anne took a deep breath and exhaled heavily. "Very well. We can get into the nitty-gritty later." She looked at the director-general. "Is that all?"

Bolduc nodded and pressed a button on his phone.

The receptionist's voice crackled in the air. "Sir?"

"Can you please escort Ms. Winters to the meeting room?" He looked at Anne as he spoke. "She will wait there for her next meeting."

"Yes, sir."

In a moment the door opened and Anne was escorted outside and down the hallway. As the receptionist led her to a small meeting room, Anne noticed Jeremy Large seated at a desk, engaged in a heated debate with a younger man. Jeremy barely noticed Anne as she walked by, leaving her to wonder about their conversation the night before.

CHAPTER 19

ANNE WAS PACING the floor of the small room, waiting for her next meeting and wondering what Maxime Bolduc and Tom Erickson had up their sleeves, when the door opened and Jeremy Large looked in.

"How'd it go?" he said, stepping inside and pulling the door to.

"I don't know," said Anne. "But they're going to parachute one of their yes-men into Jasper. To keep an eye on me no doubt."

Jeremy opened the door a crack and looked out into the hall before turning back to Anne. "Who are they sending?"

"Konrad Vincent-Blais," said Anne. She was curious to see how Jeremy would respond but his body language revealed nothing untoward.

"I've heard the name," said Jeremy, shaking his head and checking the hallway once again. "But I don't know him."

"He was in Wood Buffalo," said Anne.

"God, that's right," said Jeremy, pounding his fist against an open hand. "I don't know the whole story, but I thought the former director-general turfed him after the bison issue blew up in his face. They've kind of kept me out of the loop on some of those things."

"Well, I guess he's redeemed himself," said Anne. "Makes me wonder what he had to do to regain his stripes."

"These day?" said Jeremy. "It could have been anything."

He took one last look down the hall before turning back to Anne. "I should be going. I just saw you come in here so I thought I'd see how it went."

"Well, I was told to come here for another meeting with Tom and Konrad. I expect they'll give me my marching orders."

"Good luck," said Jeremy. He smiled at Anne, slid past the door and pulled it shut.

Anne had resumed pacing when the door opened again and Tom and Konrad walked in.

"I'll keep this short." Tom closed the door and looked sternly at Jasper's superintendent. "Anne, what I'm about to tell you must be kept completely confidential. Is that understood?"

Anne nodded.

"The mine proponent is politically connected," Tom started. "It's in our best interests to cooperate with him. We want to ensure Parks is in a position to get the best deal possible if the mine gets past the environmental review and is approved by the province."

"Which means what?" said Anne.

"Play the game," said Tom. "Maxime has agreed to let the park host the proponent for a day or two in exchange for future considerations."

"What exactly do you mean by future considerations?"

"Concessions, possibly," said Tom. "The province has us over a barrel and if they want to play tough, they could approve the mine without considering the park's interests. Remember, we have a shared boundary and shared species, grizzly bears and the like."

"What do you want me to do?"

"Just accommodate the man," said Tom. "We promised to show him around. Take him on a flight of the boundary area and give him an opportunity to see the park. It's the best way to demonstrate why we're concerned about major industrial development along our park boundaries."

"Sounds simple enough," said Anne, trying to keep the wariness out of her voice.

"I'm glad you see it that way, Anne. Maxime seems to think you haven't always been a team player on these matters and wanted me to impress upon you the importance of not making waves on this issue."

"Actually," said Anne, "I know there's not much we can really do about a mine outside the park, but if something is happening inside the park . . . that's a problem."

"What have you heard?" Tom's eyebrows shot up at Anne's words.

"Nothing." She let her word hang for a moment. "But with this government and with Maxime at the helm, anything is possible."

Tom sighed. "As I said before, Anne, he feels you haven't always been a team player on these matters. To some extent, you've lost his confidence."

"*I've* lost *his* confidence, by sticking up for the park and what Parks are supposed to stand for? Is that why *he* is being assigned to the park." Anne shot a glance at Konrad who stood silently to the side. "To keep an eye on me?"

"Anne!" Tom's exasperation was beginning to show. "Don't blow this out of proportion. Jasper is under a lot of pressure. Konrad is being sent there to help you."

Konrad nodded, but said nothing.

"He can serve as your go-to guy for the mine discussions," Tom added. "And he can show the proponent around."

Anne turned to Vincent-Blais, "Have you ever been to Jasper?"

"That's irrelevant." Tom Erickson jumped in before Konrad could answer. "He'll get up to speed along with the proponent. One of your staff can show them around."

"Fine," said Anne, not wanting to prolong the discussion. "I'll send them out with our wildlife specialist since most of our concerns will be wildlife related."

Tom shook his head. "Not John Haffcut. You know how Maxime feels about John." He looked at Konrad. "Let's just say they have some history."

"Very well then," said Anne. "If I can't use John, it will have to be Lou Walker." She knew her chief park warden would be almost as unpalatable to the director-general as John Haffcut.

"Fine," Tom acquiesced. "You seem to have a lot of *characters* in your park."

"I wouldn't have it any other way," said Anne. "I'm trying my best to keep Jasper from becoming Banff North."

"As you wish. In any event, Konrad will take on his new role in a month, but we're sending him there within a week or so to meet with the mine's proponent and show him around. He'll introduce you both, but please let Konrad deal with the man while he's in your park."

"Fine, but I will remind you, I'm the superintendent; he's the assistant. I have worked in Parks my entire career. I will not be told how to do my job by someone who is being parachuted in by HQ, especially one with *his* record in joint reviews," Anne warned. She opened the door and was about to leave when she turned back to Tom Erickson. "You know, not all of us have sold out to the highest bidder; in fact, some of us still care about these parks and what they're intended to protect and provide."

Anne Winters was about to storm out of the office but turned to Konrad. "I'll see you in the park. Check in with me before you do anything on your own." With that Anne walked out, moving briskly past the receptionist.

CHAPTER 20

Ben and Kate looked around the room as they walked into Lou Walker's office. The gathering had been called by Anne Winters, who sat at the small table surrounded by Lou, John Haffcut, Megan Weaver and Jimmy Rand.

"Pull up a stump and get cozy," said Lou, shuffling his chair to one side to give Ben and Kate room to sit down.

After giving everyone time to get comfortable, Anne looked around the table at the group. "I thought it was important to have everyone in one room and talk about the mine that's being proposed along our boundary. As you probably know, I've just come back from Ottawa and to make a long story short, I received my marching orders regarding dealing with the mine and the mine's proponent."

She paused for a moment before continuing.

"Ben and Kate, Lou tells me you're ready to get up to speed if this thing goes to an environmental review. And John, because the primary issue we'll be concerned with is grizzly bear management and the potential implications of another mine on the landscape, I want you and Megan involved." Turning to Jimmy Rand she added, "Finally, Jimmy, you're more familiar with that part of the park than anyone else, so I'd like your input as well."

"Happy to oblige," said Jimmy.

"I don't have a lot of details," Anne continued, "but I've spoken to Lou and told him that we will have some help from Ottawa on this one."

Lou snickered but remained silent as Anne continued.

"A fellow by the name of Konrad Vincent-Blais has been given the job as assistant superintendent, with the express purpose of stickhandling this project through the review process."

Kate looked at Ben with raised eyebrows as Anne turned to them both. "You dealt with him in Wood Buffalo?"

"Huhuh," said Kate.

"He's a piece of work," said Ben.

"I had the same first impression," said Anne. "Anyway, we don't need to get into that right now."

"Just be on your toes," said Ben. He looked around the group.

"Exactly," said Anne. "He'll show up here next week and I want Lou to be his first point of contact."

"Seriously?" said Lou, with a questioning glance at Anne. "How about I let Ben and Kate show him around."

Anne laughed but her expression was serious. "You're not getting out of this one, Lou. Ben and Kate have just arrived and are only just learning the park themselves. Besides they have some history with Konrad."

"What about John then," said Lou, testing Anne's patience.

"I want you to show him around Lou. You're a good judge of character. And when the mine proponent shows up, I want you to show him around as well. I'm curious what you think of both of them."

Lou shook his head in disgust, then turned to Ben and Kate. "You two better get up to speed pronto." Turning back to Anne, he added, "So have you met the mine proponent?"

"No. But word is, he's politically connected."

Lou snickered again. "What else is new?"

Anne glared at Lou. "They want us to show him around and get a sense of what his plans are. It will put us in a better position to figure out what an environmental review will involve. And you'll be able to let him know the concerns we have with another mine on the boundary."

"Then maybe John and Megan should be involved to talk about grizzly bears in the regional ecosystem," said Lou.

"No," Anne said bluntly. She turned to John and Megan. "Your main job will be to provide Ben and Kate with information you feel is pertinent to a review of the proposed mine. Of course that includes grizzly bears but there are other ecological issues as well."

She turned back to Jimmy. "And as I said, you know this country better than anyone, so I want you to provide any information you feel we're missing."

"Understood," said Jimmy.

Anne looked at her watch then back at the group. "So that's it. Any questions?"

"Nah," said Lou. "We're good." He grudgingly acknowledged Anne's direction then looked to Ben and Kate. "I want you both ready to deal with this. It might be a good idea if we take a trip down Highway 40 so we can show you the mines that are currently there and give you an idea what the country looks like."

"A horse trip from Maligne through to Rocky Pass might also be a good way for them to get a feel for that part of the park," said Jimmy.

"Yeah, that's an even better idea," said Lou. "I don't get to spend enough time in the backcountry and there's no better way to indoctrinate these two into Jasper." Turning to Anne, he added. "Can't wait to meet your new assistant superintendent so I can tell you what I think of him." He looked around the group. "Even though I probably already know."

CHAPTER 21

THE FOUR RIDERS slowly worked their horses along the hardscrabble slope, each footstep carefully placed as the river rushed past below them.

Lou and Jimmy Rand were taking Ben and Kate on a short backcountry trip that would put them on the park boundary near the proposed mine site. They spent the first day making their way to Rocky Forks from the Maligne Valley and stayed overnight at the old district warden cabin. Today's plan was to make it to the boundary and get picked up by vehicle, so Ben and Kate could get a feel for the east side of the park and see the mines and forestry operations already occurring in the foothills adjacent to Jasper.

As they picked their way along the narrow trail above the river, Jimmy took the lead, riding his favourite horse, Sarge.

Jimmy had ridden this trail many times before in all kinds of weather; today was not much different than the others, meaning it was the usual mix of constantly changing Rocky Mountain weather. It started off with a heavy fog hanging in the valley at Rocky Forks, but soon burned off as the morning sun made its way above the mountains. It clouded over an hour into the ride toward Medicine Tent, and now there was a hint of snow in the air as they climbed their way up and out of the valley toward Rocky Pass. By the time they reached the pass, Jimmy fully expected a snowstorm as the upslope winds pushed in from the east.

If you gave the horses their head, they knew what to do. They'd been on these trails most of their lives. But there was always one horse that seemed to be out of sorts with the others, and today it was Champ's turn.

Jimmy watched as Lou lost his patience with the young stallion while Kate and Ben seemed to be doing a good job on their two horses, Twister and Ace, staying calm and riding between the two more experienced horsemen.

Champ seemed to think he needed to be in front and whenever the trail widened even a dog's hair, he butted up against Jimmy's horse, but Sarge would have none of it, sending a quick one-legged kick backwards at his nemesis. Luckily his kicks missed the mark and Champ was brought back in line, if only for a short time.

As the quartet neared the top of the switchbacks, the trail turned away from the river, drawing the riders back into the forest of subalpine fir and Engelmann spruce.

Jimmy heaved a sigh of relief as the four horses gathered in the trees. "Everyone okay?" he asked between chews of tobacco. He leaned to the side and spit on the ground.

Ben and Kate nodded.

"I'd like to shoot this fucking horse," said Lou as he rammed his heels into Champ's sides. "What a place to decide he wanted to be a leader." He motioned back toward the cliff.

Jimmy smiled and spit again. "You did well, boss. Handled it like a pro."

Lou returned a skeptical glance.

"I'm serious," said Jimmy. He reached inside his slicker, pulled out a tin of tobacco and popped a pinch in his mouth. "Not kissin' ass. Besides, I don't need to. I already have the best job in the park." He turned to Ben and Kate. "Can't beat being a backcountry warden, even if the outfit is trying to get rid of us."

"Not so much tryin' to get rid of you," said Lou. "Especially you, you've been around. Just tryin' to get some of the others to realize there's more to the job than patrolling the backcountry." Lou turned to Ben and Kate. "There's still a place for horses and backcountry wardens, but we need to integrate them more with the resource management program. That's where we need to be going."

"Makes sense," said Kate.

"I hear you too." Jimmy nodded. "As long as management realizes it takes time just to do the upkeep on our cabins and trails. But I agree. There's no reason why we can't be contributing to grizzly bear management or whatever other projects are on the books." He turned his horse upslope and the others fell in behind.

As they broke out of the trees again, they caught a quick glimpse of a wide mountain pass spreading out in front of them. Just then the snow hit, the sharp wind cutting into their faces as the four riders pulled the collars of their slickers tightly around their necks.

"Rocky Pass by horseback this time," said Jimmy, turning to speak to Kate and yelling above the wind, as the horses lowered their heads and picked their way along the well-worn trail, gradually making their way along the pass.

In places where the trail braided, Lou rode up alongside Ben and Kate. "Everything okay?" he asked as he arm-wrestled with Champ.

"Yeah," said Kate.

"Ten-four," said Ben.

"You two are doin' fine," said Lou. "It's not always the most efficient way to get around," he added as he gave a hard jerk on Champ's reins to keep him from bolting ahead, "but it's one of the best ways to really see the park."

"This is great," said Kate. "I can see how someone like Jimmy wouldn't want to give it up."

"I wouldn't want to either, most of the time," said Lou, as Champ stopped abruptly, lowering his head to try and drink from a small creek crossing the trail and almost pulling Lou out of the saddle. Digging his feet into the stirrups, Lou's cheeks flushed as he pulled back on the reins with both hands, finally getting Champ pointed in the right direction before giving him another kick to catch up to Ben and Kate. "Next time, we'll take a helicopter," he sighed, forcing a smile as Ben and Kate watched with obvious amusement.

Leading the way across Rocky Pass, Jimmy brought the group to a halt before the trail dropped into the Cardinal River valley. Just then, the sun broke through the clouds and the last of the snow flurries settled on the ground.

"Classic mountain weather," said Jimmy. "Even in July, I pack winter gloves and a toque."

"Yeah, it's good to be prepared," said Kate.

"I wear my red long johns most of the year," said Lou. "Especially in the backcountry."

Jimmy laughed. "Now there's an image that'll be hard to shake."

Ben and Kate smiled and looked at each other.

"Don't say it," said Ben.

"What?" said Kate. "You mean you and *your* long red underwear at Sweetgrass?

Ben put a finger to his lips.

"What are you two gettin' on with?" said Lou.

"Inside joke from Wood Buffalo," said Kate, eyeing Ben. "You had to be there."

As the sky cleared, the four riders dropped down into the valley and made their way across the Cardinal River, following an old cutline eastward.

"We must be out of the park now?" said Ben as he pointed to ATV tracks sculpted into the ground.

"Yeah," said Jimmy. "The height of the land back in the pass is actually the park boundary. The park signs often get knocked off, or shot off the posts. It's hard to keep up with it all."

"What's with the cutline?" said Kate.

"Probably an old seismic line at one time," said Lou. "It's mostly used by ATVers and hunters now. But the whole Eastern Slopes are logged, drilled or mined. There's a lot of use out here."

"Does some of it come into the park?" said Ben.

"Some," said Lou. "There's the odd poacher who tries to take a sheep on our side of the pass. But they're few and far between.

Not like the constant poaching you saw in Cape Breton. The issue out here is mostly about human use."

"Still, there was that sow and cub," said Kate.

"Yeah," said Lou. "But that really was an exception. It's the last thing the mining and forestry companies want to see happen here. They know how volatile the grizzly bear hunting and poaching issue is; they don't want or need the bad PR. The mining companies have been especially strict and all of their active properties are off limits to hunting. And they've been all over the little sow John collared in the park."

"Hope?" said Kate.

"Yeah."

"But whoever's doing the poaching doesn't give a rat's ass about the mine," said Jimmy. "When it comes down to it, a couple of bad apples can really spoil it for the mines."

"Pretty much," said Lou. "And we kinda have an idea who those bad apples are."

At the end of the cutline, the riders turned onto a narrow gravel road and trotted the horses to the top of the rise.

"This here is what you call an industrial landscape," said Lou. He pointed to a series of clear-cuts in the distance. "It's all been logged pretty much and big chunks of it have been mined. Oil and gas is the new kid on the block and they're punching in well sites everywhere. Add in the seismic lines and access roads and it's a spider web of activity."

"You'll see it all on the way back," said Jimmy as a one-ton truck hauling a horse trailer rumbled up to meet them. "We drive right through the big mines and there's lots of forestry happening."

"This is what I wanted you to see," said Lou. Sliding off Champ and leading him to the horse trailer, he motioned for the others to follow suit. "We'll be driving back through the mine properties and a bunch of the forestry cutblocks. If we're lucky, we might actually catch a glimpse of Hope."

CHAPTER 22

THE RIDE BACK to Jasper was eye-opening for Ben and Kate as the narrow dirt road leading from the Cardinal Divide wound out of the alpine and through subalpine forests clinging to the hardscrabble slopes above the McLeod River. Passing through Mountain Park, the only visible sign of the early-twentieth-century coalmining town was a small cemetery, its white picket fence as out of place as the small groves of alder and birch pushing out of old tailings piles that dotted the landscape. Beyond Mountain Park, the road crossed Whitehorse Creek and passed a large limestone quarry eating away at the face of a small mountain.

Wedged into the club cab, Lou and Jimmy pointed out features to Ben and Kate while Megan carefully navigated her way toward Cadomin hauling the six horse trailer.

"Whitehorse Creek is another way of getting to the park boundary," said Lou, pointing out the turn-off into the provincial recreation area.

"I'll take you guys up there sometime and show you Poacher's Basin," said Jimmy.

"A great place for sheep," Lou added. "I counted thirty rams there on one trip."

"We should do our own trip," Megan said, motioning to Kate. "We can mix it up and go some place different. Maybe up along the North Boundary."

"I'd be keen," said Kate as they entered the small village of Cadomin.

"How about we pull in to the Hole In The Wall Cafe?" Lou suggested, pointing to a small gas station and restaurant proudly displaying a large sign that said 'Eat Here And Get Gas.' "Best burgers in Alberta," he drooled. "If not the world."

Jimmy laughed and motioned to keep going, but Megan had other ideas.

"Could use some gas for the trip back," she said. "I'd hate to be stuck on the highway with a load of horses."

"And this horse needs to take a piss," said Lou, grimacing and looking at Megan and Kate. "Sorry about that. I keep forgetting we're in mixed company."

"As if that ever stopped you," said Jimmy.

As they pulled into the pumps, Lou slid out of the cab and made his way to the restaurant. Just then a Land Cruiser drove up and parked in front and two men wearing camouflage gear jumped out and followed Lou inside.

"Getting ready for hunting season?" said Ben, pointing to the pair. "Kind of early isn't it?"

"Well, there is a spring bear hunt," said Jimmy. "But maybe they're just scoping out places for the fall."

"But they've got B.C. plates," said Kate, noting the licence on their vehicle.

"Hmpph," Jimmy muttered. "We always see a few non-resident hunters. But they have to have a local guide."

Just as he spoke, a pickup with a lift kit pulled up to the restaurant and Jimmy did a double take. "Well, will you look at that?" They watched as the rough-looking driver dropped out of the pickup and went into the restaurant just as Lou was coming out.

Ben nudged Kate. "Is that who I think it is?"

"Yeah, if you're thinking Zane Ritter," Jimmy confirmed.

Ben rolled his eyes at Kate and slid across the seat as Lou climbed back into the truck.

"Notice our friend as you were coming out?" said Jimmy.

"What?" said Lou looking back at the restaurant. "No. Who?"

"Zane Ritter just went in there. I wonder what he's up to?"

Lou shrugged. "Don't know, don't care, as long as he stays out of the park. I was more curious about the two hunters who came in after me."

"What about 'em?"

"Pretty sure they're Germans," said Lou.

"But their truck has B.C. plates," said Kate, pointing out their vehicle to Lou.

"Yeah, that'd be about right," said Lou. "The place is crawling with Krauts."

CHAPTER 23

WITH THEIR FIRST horse trip under their belt, Ben and Kate made their way down Highway 40 toward the Cardinal Divide, armed with a small pile of maps and provincial reports about coalmining along the Eastern Slopes. As the highway literally passed through the two mines already operating along Jasper's eastern boundary, Kate pointed to several small groups of bighorn sheep feeding on the reclaimed slopes as the noonday sun topped a cloudless sky.

"You know, from a layman's perspective, it all looks pretty good," said Ben as they scanned the graded slopes with their dips and valleys butting up against sheer rock faces that provided escape terrain for the sheep. "The reclaimed pits and re-vegetated slopes make for good sheep habitat."

"Yeah," said Kate as they passed by one of the mine's processing plants and saw a trainload of coal move slowly northward while large trucks and shovels worked the depths of the open pits. "But it seems crazy that it can be cost-effective to move that much rock around just to get at the coal seams. And now they're going to put in a third mine?"

Parking on the side of the road for a moment they watched the scene immediately in front of them. Beyond the mines, the landscape reverted to a mosaic of subalpine forests and alpine meadows wrapping themselves around the base of the Front Ranges. "It's not quite grizzly bear country anymore," Kate added, "but I wonder if the bears come out of the mountains from time to time and try to pick off some of these sheep."

"I don't doubt they would," said Ben. "The sheep are probably easy picking."

Turning off Highway 40 and onto the Grave Flats Road, Ben and Kate kept heading south looking for any sign of activity to suggest a new mine was in the works. Driving past the old abandoned mine site at Mountain Park they continued along the narrow dirt track to a parking lot near the Cardinal Divide.

"There sure doesn't seem to be much happening down this way," said Ben as they parked and looked around.

"No," said Kate as she scanned one of the maps. "But at least we're getting a better idea of the country around here. According to this, there's an old trail to the top of the Divide. We should go take a look."

"That must be it," said Ben, nodding toward a path leading into a swale of subalpine fir, exiting on the other side and climbing to the top of a rocky ridge.

"C'mon." Kate jumped out of the truck, slid the maps into her daypack and started off for the swale.

As the trail picked its way through the rocks and scattered trees, Ben pointed to a series of tracks baked into the dry mud. "Grizzly," he said, noting the claw prints sitting well in front of the toe prints.

"Did you bring the bear spray?" Kate asked, looking around as the trail led into a thicket of shrubs.

"It's back in the truck," said Ben. "But the tracks look old, so I wouldn't worry about it."

"Famous last words," said Kate as they emerged from the thicket and headed for the ridge.

Standing on the top, they looked down into the valley of the McLeod River, impressed by the view.

"Wow," said Kate. "It's stunning."

"Too bad it's going to be mined," said Ben.

Kate sat down on a large slab of rock and pulled several thick reports from her pack. "Funny thing that. It just doesn't seem to jive with what these reports suggest. Most of the coal that's easy to access along this part of the Eastern Slopes is already being mined. Getting at the coal around here sounds like an expensive proposition."

"The other thing I find odd," said Ben, "is that this whole area is supposed to be zoned as a provincial ecological reserve. The Divide is literally the dividing line for water draining to the Arctic Ocean on one side and to Hudson Bay on the other."

"Yeah," said Kate. "It would be a shame to see this country dug up and turned into sheep habitat." She got up and scanned the subalpine forests and bare ridges extending out in all directions from their bird's-eye viewpoint.

"Maybe this guy knows something we don't," said Ben as he pointed to a lone hiker picking his way up the scree slope toward their position. As the man got closer he appeared to be quite old, yet seemed agile for his age. His clothing and pack suggested someone who kept up with the latest trends in outdoor wear and equipment.

"G'day," said the old-timer as he walked briskly to the edge of the ridge and stood between Ben and Kate. He paused to wipe a bead of sweat from his forehead then pulled a water bottle from his pack and took a long swig. "Pretty nice view, eh?"

"It is," said Kate. "There can't be many places where you can drive into the alpine and see something like this."

"No, you can be sure of that," said the man.

"Too bad it's going to be mined," said Ben.

The old-timer laughed and shook his head. "Where in God's name did you hear that, son?"

"That's the word," said Kate. "We're down here trying to find out as much as we can about the new coalmine that's proposed for this area."

The man laughed again. "They could mine rock I suppose, 'cause that's about all that's left here."

"Really?" said Ben.

The man nodded. "I grew up in the coal branch and worked my whole life in the mines. If they can make money haulin'

123

coal out of here, I'd be very surprised. Sure, there's coal buried everywhere along the foothills, but they'd have to haul forty tons of rock to get a ton of coal out of this country. All the easy coal has been mined out."

"You don't say?" said Ben. He looked at Kate curiously.

"I do say." The man nodded to the pair and threw his day-pack over his shoulder. "Goin' for a ridge hike," he said. "Nice meetin' ya."

"Same here," said Ben. "Thanks for the information."

"There's something not right about all of this," Kate said as they watched the man make his way along the ridge.

"Maybe we should pick Marion's brain a little on this one," said Ben. "She seems to have a good handle on what's been going on outside the park."

Kate agreed and they made their way back to the truck. They took their time driving down from the Divide, checking out any signs of recent activity, including a freshly blazed survey line angling off the road. They hadn't noticed the line driving south from the other direction, but when they checked it out it seemed to disappear after a few metres.

"Seems odd," said Ben as they followed the line to its endpoint.

"Huhuh," said Kate. "Fresh flagging and there is this one survey stake" She toed a pile of freshly cut boughs and uncovered a wooden stake hiding underneath.

"What's it say," said Ben, kneeling down to inspect the markings.

"Looks freshly painted," said Kate, as she regarded the smudged lettering. "It just looks like a set of initials, D.M.I." She took out a camera and took a picture of the survey stake and a close-up of the initials. "I wonder what they stand for?"

"Beats me," said Ben. "Let's see what else we can find."

They returned to the truck and slowly made their way north-ward, finding two other flagged survey lines seemingly going nowhere, each with an occasional survey stake stuck in the ground bearing the same markings.

Farther along the road they were surprised to see a familiar pickup parked on the shoulder with its tailgate down and the back open to plain view. A small pile of freshly painted survey stakes sat on the tailgate but there was no one to be seen.

Ben and Kate looked at each other.

Pulling up to the truck they peered down another cutline and noticed a man walking toward them, stopping periodically to tie fluorescent orange flagging tape to the trees.

"Looks like our friend," said Kate.

"It does," said Ben. "But I don't want to stick around to find out."

"Fair enough. Let's keep going."

Pulling past the pickup, they continued down the road and around the next turn.Suddenly Kate pointed to the side of the road. "Ben, pull over."

Ambling through the open forest of spruce and fir adjacent to the road, a small grizzly bear was weaving its way across the slope, metres from Ben and Kate. From time to time, she would stop and root into old stumps, pulling them apart with ease and shoving her snout into the rotting mass of wood. A few more metres upslope, two small cubs chased each other through the undergrowth of willow and buffalo berry, obviously more concerned with playing than feeding on the ants and grubs preoccupying their mother.

"I wonder if that's Hope?" Kate finally said, breaking the silence as she and Ben stared in awe of the trio.

"What's the story on her again?" said Ben, as his eyes followed the bears along the sidehill.

"John and Clay caught her somewhere in the park," Kate explained. "But she's been spending most of her time out here on provincial land. John says she's kind of the poster child for the mines, demonstrating that industry and bears can coexist."

"That's encouraging," said Ben as they watched the grizzly sow and her cubs disappear into the forest. "But I wonder how she'll do if another mine gets added to the landscape."

"Yeah. I would wonder about that as well," said Kate. "But she's collared, so between John and the provincial Fish and Wildlife guys, they'll probably get a good idea of how she's navigating the landscape and staying out of trouble."

"Speaking of which," said Ben, as the large pickup they'd just passed rolled down the hill toward them, slowing down as it passed by on the narrow road. The driver was craning his neck to look past Ben and Kate toward the slope above their truck.

Kate's gaze followed the pickup and saw its brake lights come on for a moment before the truck rounded a turn and went out of sight. "Our friend again."

"Yeah," said Ben. "Ritter seems to be everywhere."

"I wonder if he saw the bears?"

"Let's hope not."

CHAPTER 24

"CURIOUS," SAID MARION, when Kate and Ben stopped by on the evening after their trip to the Cardinal Divide. "Although I'd be inclined to agree with the old fellow you met."

"Really?" said Kate.

"Yes," said Marion. "Oh, I understand it comes down to the price of coal they can fetch from the Japanese, but most of the coal branch has been mined pretty extensively. That's why I find the idea of a new mine a little surprising."

"So what about the survey lines we found?"

Marion shrugged.

"And the survey stakes," said Ben. "Do the initials D.M.I. ring any bells?"

"None," said Marion, pulling her laptop off the counter. "But let's see what we can find. Let's assume the 'M' stands for Mines or Mining." She typed in the initials and pondered the results. "Mmm?"

"What does it say?" said Kate, looking over Marion's shoulder.

"Not a lot. Looks like D.M.I. is a mining company with properties around the world."

"Based out of where?" said Ben.

"Germany," Marion replied as she scrolled through the list of search results. "But active in Africa, with other interests in the U.S. and Canada."

"Does it say anything about the area around Jasper?" Kate said as she peered down the list.

"No," said Marion. "But the information looks dated. There's nothing recent."

"Hmm," said Kate. "Well it's a starting point. We can do some more digging around to see what we can find out."

"It's going to be hard to prepare for a review if we can't find more than this," said Ben.

"We've only just begun," said Kate. "Give it a chance."

"Well if it's helpful," said Marion, I'll reach out to some contacts and let you know what I can find." She sighed and wrung her hands. "This is where I wish Malcolm was still around. He was more familiar with researching these types of things than I am."

"But you've already helped," said Kate. "It's a start. And I have some other ideas." She looked at Ben. "Lou has a coalmining background. He might be able to offer some insight. And the other thing I've been thinking about is how they'll ship the coal from down there. We saw a train at one of the mines. If they were going to extend the railway to a third mine, they would have to be talking to the railway early in their planning."

"Yes," said Marion. "That makes sense. "If you want I can ask Sherry Allan and Bert Gosse."

"The railroad folks we met at Megan's?"

Marion nodded. "Yes. They'll know if the railway has been involved."

"By the way," said Ben. "We also saw that Ritter guy down there. It seemed like he was the one putting in the survey stakes."

"Really?" said Marion, surprised by this revelation.

"Why?" said Kate. "What do you know about him?"

"Good god, nothing really. Only that he's a notorious poacher."

"But he's worked for the mines in the past, hasn't he?"

"Yes, but they got rid of him when he poached a grizzly on one of the mine sites. The word is he was bad for their business."

"So why would he be involved with a mining company now?" Ben asked.

"No idea," said Marion.

*****

After Ben and Kate left, Marion boiled the kettle and made a pot of tea then sat in her living room scouring the internet for any information about D.M.I. as well as mining in the coal branch area outside Jasper's boundary.

Out of curiosity, she fired off a short email to a young woman she'd met the previous summer from Germany, who was on a cross-Canada trip with her boyfriend. Marion had taken to Erika immediately and offered her and Mikael a room for their short stay in Jasper, which the young couple had graciously accepted. Over the course of their time with Marion and Malcolm, they realized their shared interests and told the Seawells they were both active with a German conservation group similar to Jasper Wild, also dedicated to protecting nature.

In her email, Marion inquired as to whether Erika or Mikael had any information about D.M.I., noting a possible Canadian connection with a new mine on the edge of Jasper National Park.

Because of the eight-hour time difference, Marion determined it was early in the morning in Germany so she was very surprised to receive a response almost immediately, albeit a brief one.

"Dear Marion," the email read, "Yes, I am familiar with D.M.I.—Deutsche Mining International. I will check with Mikael and our group to see if we can find out what interests D.M.I. might have around Jasper. We will be in touch again soon."

CHAPTER 25

AS THE HELICOPTER approached Rocky Pass, Konrad Vincent-Blais tapped the shoulder of the man riding shotgun and motioned to his headset.

Lou Walker barely acknowledged Vincent-Blais with a sideways glance. He was beyond pissed at Anne Winters for delegating him as the tour guide for Konrad and his German friend, especially for a tour of the mines along Jasper's border.

"Why not get John Haffcut to show them around? He lives at that end of the park. Better yet, give this to Ben Matthews or Kate Jones, or both of them."

"Really, Lou? After dealing with Konrad in Wood Buffalo, putting them with him now wouldn't be fair."

"Maybe they could drop him out of the helicopter some-where," Lou countered. "Our problems would be solved."

"Not going to happen Lou. I put John's name forward but got vetoed. You're the man." Despite his protests, Anne stuck to her guns. "Keep your ears open," she instructed. "Let me know what they say about the mine, or anything else. There has got to be more to this than meets the eye."

Still, the flight had been interesting so far and it was proba-bly a good thing that Lou was getting back out into the province to see the amount of development along the park's boundary.

Way too much happening, he thought, thinking about how the landscape had changed over the last few years. Still, it was encouraging to have seen Hope, and surprisingly it was Helmut Stenger who spotted her first.

"Is that a bear down there?" he'd asked when they were scop-ing out the proposed mine area not too far from Whitehorse Creek.

"Indeed it is," said Clay, bringing the helicopter around for a better view. "And she has cubs by the look of it."

"What kind of bear?" said Konrad as he leaned into the curve of the helicopter's side window and peered down.

"Grizzly," said Lou.

"I think it's Hope," Clay said when the bear stopped and gazed up at the helicopter.

"Hope?" said Helmut Stenger.

"Yeah." Lou turned in his seat to try and face the German businessman. "She's a little sow grizzly that our wildlife guy, John Haffcut, and Clay here, captured in the Maligne Valley. Since then, she's been spending most of her time outside of the park."

"John wanted to call her Hope to represent our hope for the wilderness areas animals like her need to survive," Clay added.

"How touching," Konrad espoused sarcastically, drawing glances from the others.

Clay ignored the comment. "It's really interesting how much time she's spending outside of the park."

"Yeah," said Lou. "The mining and forestry companies love her since she kind of shows us all how species like grizzlies can live inside the park and outside as well."

"So maybe we don't need parks at all," said Konrad. Once again his comment brought stares from the other three. "I'm just playing Devil's advocate," said Konrad, matter-of-factly.

"Oh we need 'em," said Lou, pointedly. "She's doing okay for now, but the real story is how she'll be doing in one, two, five or ten years from now."

"If she doesn't get shot first," said Clay.

"Exactly," said Lou. "I wouldn't exactly call this wilderness anymore." He pointed to the maze of cutovers and mining activity in the distance. "I think all Hope is telling us is that she's smarter than we give her kind credit for." He turned to Konrad. "You should know some of this, considering your new position as assistant superintendent."

Konrad looked at Helmut Stenger whose nod and raised eyebrows suggested he agreed with Lou's comment.

Biting his lip, Konrad sat back and silently looked out the window as they watched Hope disappear into the forest.

Continuing their flight along the Eastern Slopes, Lou picked up where they left off, pointing out existing mines and other activity before asking Clay to turn back toward Rocky Pass and Jasper National Park.

As the helicopter passed over the Rocky Forks warden cabin on their way back to the Parks office, Vincent-Blais tapped Lou on the shoulder again. Lou reluctantly adjusted the volume on his own headset and pulled the mouthpiece to his lips. "What's up?"

"I asked you for a tour of the rest of the park for our guest," Konrad almost spat into the headset with frustration.

"Oh, sorry," said Lou, disingenuously. "I thought you were only interested in the boundary and the mine area."

"We *were* interested in seeing those, but I'm sure Mr. Stenger would also like to know about other parts of the park." He looked over at the older gentleman sitting next to him.

Helmut Stenger adjusted the volume on his headset and spoke. "I would, Mr. Walker," he said. "If you don't mind," he added. "It's been many years since I climbed here and I'm afraid my memory isn't as good as it used to be."

"You climbed in Jasper?" Lou craned his neck to look at the German businessman.

"Yes," said Stenger. "Most of the smaller accessible peaks, but also Cavell and Athabasca. We never did get into the Maligne, other than to drive up the road and do some day hikes around the Opal Hills and Bald Hills, if you could even call it a road." He laughed.

"When was that?" Lou asked, motioning for Clay to steer a course toward the Maligne Valley.

"Oh my, back in the 60s," said Stenger as the rotor's steady throb reverberated through the machine, jostling the passengers as Clay steered the helicopter westward. "By then there'd been many first ascents and Jasper was getting a name for great climbing. I came for several summers in a row, before business interests drew me away to Africa."

As they crossed into the next valley and Maligne Lake opened up below them, Clay manouevered the helicopter into a slow loop of the north end of the lake, speaking into his headset while his hands and feet worked the controls. "What exactly would you like to see in the Maligne?"

Before Stenger could reply, Konrad motioned to him and pointed to the area below them. "I believe this is what you wanted to see."

"Yes," Stenger nodded. "Yes, yes, very nice. This is exactly how I remember it. So beautiful."

"What exactly are we looking for?" Lou asked.

"Nothing in particular," Konrad quickly replied before darting a look at Stenger.

Helmut Stenger smiled. "Would it be possible to fly down the lake?"

With barely a movement of his body, Clay subtly slipped the helicopter into a shallow dive, picking up speed as the water of Maligne Lake rippled below. As the lake narrowed and its water morphed from deep blue to emerald green, Lou pointed to a tour boat landing at Spirit Island.

"I guess we'll be seeing more of them in the future," he said, to no one in particular. "What with the push to cram more people into the park."

Clay looked over at Lou and feigned a smile, but said nothing.

"It's not about cramming more people into the park," said Konrad, again eyeing Stenger. "It's about allowing more people to benefit from these places, to enjoy our parks. They belong to everyone after all."

"Everyone with money," Lou countered. "More and more often, we're taking places that were free to visit and making people pay for the privilege. It's really about the bottom line, isn't it?" He looked over his shoulder at Konrad and waited for a response.

"That's a discussion for another time. Don't complicate things today."

The last statement sounded more like a threat than a comment. Lou didn't appreciate being threatened. But he knew there was a time and a place and this wasn't it. Besides, Anne would be pissed if he made a mess of today's tour.

As Konrad's face flushed, Helmut Stenger touched him on the knee to get his attention and shook his head. "Tell me, Mr. Walker," Stenger maintained eye contact with Konrad but spoke into his headset. "Are you a climber?"

"Not so much anymore," said Lou.

"But when you were younger?"

"Yeah. When I first started with the outfit. But I saw too many wrecks and dragged too many young bodies off these mountains. I kinda got away from it."

"But you enjoyed it? For a time?"

"Yeah. I was hooked. Couldn't get enough of it."

"I know the feeling," said Stenger. "We'll have to compare notes sometime. Perhaps over a nice glass of German beer."

"I'd like that," said Walker. "You people make great beer." He laughed and looked back over his shoulder at Stenger, barely catching the look the older German was giving to Konrad, before quickly turning around again.

He's working me, Lou thought. "*Damn Nazi*," he mouthed the words as he pushed his mouthpiece away from his face and glared at Clay.

Clay quickly reached forward and switched off the intercom system as the helicopter sped toward the far reaches of the lake and the towering face of Monkhead Mountain.

Looking out the side window, Lou spotted a small group of caribou along the edge of the lake. Ignoring their passengers, he motioned to Clay. "Those some of John's animals?"

"Probably." Clay reached down between his legs and pulled a leather case from under his seat. "Do you want to try scanning for radio collars? John leaves one scanner with me just in case he's not with me and wants me to try and track down an animal for him."

"That's a good idea," said Lou. He took the scanner from Clay.

"The list of frequencies is tucked inside," said Clay, pointing to a narrow seam between the instrument and the case.

Sliding a finger into the opening Lou pulled out the edge of the laminated list.

"What is that exactly?" Konrad leaned forward as much as the seatbelt would allow and peered over their shoulders. When there was no response, he tapped on Lou's shoulder.

Noticing him, Clay flipped the intercom switch back on.

"What is that?" Konrad repeated

"What?" said Lou.

"That?" Konrad pointed to the scanner as Lou pushed the list back into the case and closed the leather cover. He handed the case to Clay, who tucked it back under the seat. Looking over his shoulder at Konrad, he said, "Nothing you need to worry about, just warden stuff." He glared at Konrad. "If I told you I'd have to kill you."

After their flight, Lou watched as Konrad and Helmut Stenger headed out together, after Lou and Clay declined Stenger's offer to buy them a drink.

"I don't like either of those two," he said to Clay as the pilot secured the helicopter and walked with Lou back to the park compound.

"No kidding? You could've fooled me."

"Was it that obvious?" said Lou.

"Kind of," said Clay. "But if it makes you feel any better, I didn't like them either. I wouldn't trust them as far as I could throw them."

"What'd you think they were up to? It sure didn't seem to me like Stenger was doing a recon for a new mine."

"I didn't think so either," said Clay. "Truth be told, I don't get the impression anyone's thinking about putting another mine out there. I fly that country all the time with clients from forestry, oil and gas and even mining. Most think talk of a new mine is some kind of joke."

"Hmm," said Lou, scratching his head. "So why is Anne getting her chain yanked to put staff on this project, and being told to prepare for a big environmental review?"

"Beats me," said Clay. "What about the provincial folks you deal with? They must know something?"

"Sounds like all they've been told is there's a proposal on the table," said Lou, "but not a lot more. I'll have to dig a little deeper and see what the real scuttlebutt is. If I had to put money on it, I'd say Stenger was more interested in the park's backcountry than anything we saw outside the park."

*****

"Thank you for the flight," Helmut Stenger said as Konrad dropped him off at his hotel on Jasper's main street. "Would you care to join me for a drink?"

"Sure," said Konrad, eager to find out more about Stenger. It was always good to stay on the right side of those who were politically connected, Konrad thought as he followed the German businessman into the hotel lobby.

"Would you mind waiting here?" said Stenger. "I just need to check my messages and will be right back down. The young lady at the front desk tells me there is a nice pub just down the street. We can have a drink there."

While he waited for Stenger to return, Konrad stood by the large windows at the front of the hotel lobby and pondered his lot. Jasper was a sought after location and the notion of taking over the superintendent's position at some point had some appeal.

If I play my cards right, this could be mine.

He was lost in his thoughts and didn't notice Stenger return until the last moment.

"Thank you for waiting." Stenger led Konrad outside and the pair walked along Jasper's main street. Stopping under a large wooden sign for the Bear's Den Pub, Stenger turned to Konrad. "This is it." He pulled open the door and walked in behind Konrad.

Both men sat down and waited as the waitress took their orders.

"Your finest red wine," said Stenger.

"Whatever's on tap," said Konrad.

When the waitress returned with their drinks, Stenger raised his glass. "To good health."

Konrad lifted his glass and tapped Stenger's before taking a drink.

The German businessman took a sip of his wine and swirled it in his mouth before swallowing. "I appreciate your help," he said, placing his glass on the table and rolling the stem between his thumb and forefinger.

"Glad to be of service," said Konrad, curious to see where the conversation might go. He sensed that Helmut Stenger had another motivation for speaking with him besides wanting to show his appreciation for the helicopter flight.

"You know I often have to enlist other help when trying to get some of my projects approved," said Stenger. "Mining can be controversial." He hesitated and looked at Konrad. "Especially near a national park."

"I appreciate that," said Konrad.

"I don't have the luxury of spending a lot of time here anymore." Stenger paused to look out the window of the pub. "Although I would certainly like to."

"You said you spent a lot of time climbing in Jasper?"

"Yes, I came every year for many years," said Stenger. "This was one of my favourite places to climb." He paused and looked at Konrad. "You like to climb?"

The way Stenger asked made the question sound almost rhetorical to Konrad.

"Mountain climb, I mean," Stenger added. He took another sip of wine and focused on Konrad. "Of course, we all like to climb in our position in life, do we not?"

Konrad nodded and took a sip of his beer.

"And what are your aspirations, Konrad?"

Before Konrad could answer, Stenger continued, "By the way, is your name of Germanic origin?" Again, before Konrad could say anything, Stenger added, "I believe it is, Proto-Germanic to be exact. In fact I think it means 'bold advisor.'"

Slightly taken aback, Konrad said nothing as Helmut Stenger continued.

"I'm so lucky to have been assigned a bold advisor," he said. "I need brave people around me, people willing to take risks. But calculated risks. And someone who can provide good advice." Stenger took another sip of wine and continued. "But maybe it wasn't luck? Maybe you were assigned because your superiors already recognize those strengths in you."

Konrad liked what he was hearing, but he waited for Stenger to get to the point Konrad knew was coming.

"I need someone like you on the ground here in Jasper," Stenger continued. "To oversee things for me. Details I don't have time to deal with myself."

"But I know nothing about mining."

"I have others to deal with that," said Stenger.

"Then what do you need help with?"

Stenger leaned forward and whispered something, then sat back in his chair.

"I have men, operatives on the ground, who can deal with things I need done quickly, to move the mine forward. But the other project is more sensitive. It needs to be handled cautiously. I can't trust it to the men I've hired to advance the mine. Although they could also be put at your disposal should the need arise." Helmut's gaze cut into Konrad, giving the younger man pause. "Ultimately though, I need someone in your position and with your skills."

"To do what exactly?"

"To, how do you say it in Canada, to stickhandle this issue for me." Stenger paused only briefly before continuing. "And I know you might be asking …"

"What's in it for me?" Konrad cut in.

Stenger smiled wryly. "Exactly why I like you. You're a practical man."

"And your answer is?" said Konrad.

"I can help you get to where you want to go," said Stenger. "I have connections at the highest levels of your government."

"Higher than the director-general of Parks?"

"Yes, much higher."

CHAPTER 26

STANDING IN FRONT of her refrigerator, Marion pondered Malcolm's note, and wondered if she was missing something. His death continued to bother her and she was convinced the note was a key piece of the puzzle. But all she really knew was the note referred to a survey stake Malcolm found somewhere in the Maligne Valley, nothing more. And despite her best efforts, she'd been unable to find it.

By the power of deduction, she concluded the location was close to Maligne Lake because she knew it was one of her husband's favourite areas to explore. Also, since there was no infrastructure of consequence until you got to the park warden station and tour boat operation at the end of the Maligne Lake road, Marion figured it made the most sense if Malcolm was referring to somewhere in that area.

Determined not to give up on the search, she set out again for the lake.

Driving up the Maligne Valley, Marion kept her eye out for wildlife and was encouraged to see a small group of woodland caribou feeding in a small patch of vegetation on the Medicine Lake delta.

They're hanging on, she thought as she pulled over for a moment to watch them with her binoculars, *but only barely*.

Jasper Wild had been advocating for increased protection for the remaining animals by shutting down the Maligne Lake Road in winter to reduce the opportunities for wolves to gain access to the upper valley. But the group's efforts had fallen on deaf ears, incensing Marion and Malcolm, who argued wolves frequently followed the plowed road to the lake then used ski trails to penetrate the remaining pockets of habitat critical to caribou survival.

Anne Winters had been receptive to the idea of a closure, and John Haffcut's caribou monitoring program corroborated the anecdotal information about wolves using the road, but the idea had been quickly stymied by the director-general, who some suggested had been pressured politically to keep the road open.

Marion shook her head as she recalled the heated debates in town over trying to take any steps to control the levels of human use in the park. Increasingly, she felt Parks was losing sight of its primary mandate to protect wild places and the species that live there, but she wasn't willing to give up without a fight.

As she drove past the delta and followed the road higher into the subalpine forest, she was passed by an oversized pickup truck headed in the same direction. There was something familiar about the truck, but before she could figure out what it was, a sport utility vehicle speeding past distracted her.

"Hmphh," Marion muttered as she watched it disappear around a hairpin turn.

Slow down and live.

As Marion drove into the parking lot at the north end of Maligne Lake she noticed the pickup truck and the SUV, parked side by side. The pickup seemed to be empty but the SUV's driver was sitting inside his vehicle, apparently preoccupied.

Out of curiosity, Marion pulled into the opposite end of the parking lot, taking note of the company logo emblazoned on the driver's door of the SUV: three letters, M.P.D., with the M a stylized mountain.

Marion waited until the driver exited the vehicle and watched as he disappeared into a band of trees on the uphill side of the parking lot, seemingly focused on a handheld device to guide him away from the lakeshore.

A GPS, Marion figured. *I wonder what he's looking for?*

Getting out of her car, Marion walked over to the sport utility vehicle and peered inside. Seeing nothing of consequence she returned to her vehicle and grabbed her daypack. She was about to begin her search when she noticed the SUV driver walk out of the woods and stand at the edge of the road with a small camera, taking a series of photos and writing in a notebook after each shot.

Whatever he was looking for, he wasn't gone long, Marion thought as she watched the man pace back and forth along the road before returning to his vehicle. As he backed out and turned to leave, Marion slid along the side of her car to avoid being noticed, then watched as the SUV drove out of sight down the Maligne Lake road.

Walking over to where the man exited the forest, Marion noticed a small piece of pink flagging tape tied to a buffalo berry bush just at the edge of the trees.

Curious, she thought. *Malcolm's note mentioned pink flagging tape as well.*

Marion stepped off the roadside to take a closer look. The flagging tape looked old and when she scanned the forest for more, there was none to be seen.

Maybe this is some of the flagging Malcolm had referred to and whoever took it down missed this piece.

Marion stood still and focused on the forest sloping uphill in front of her.

He must have been somewhere up there.

Marion took a step forward and then another. Closing her eyes for a moment she imagined someone making their way up the slope. When she opened her eyes she was convinced she could see the subtle signs of a trail leading away from the road; a bent branch here, some crushed twigs on the ground where someone had stepped, a snapped branch stub broken as someone walked by.

Slowly, Marion made her way through the trees, stopping frequently to refocus.

Instinctively she let herself be pulled along, gradually picking up the pace as something drew her deeper into the forest.

With her head down, she carried on, searching for clues until suddenly she stumbled slightly and walked straight into a massive spider's web.

"Arghhh," she muttered as she swept her hands across her face and pulled the sticky mass out of her hair, spitting strands of webbing out of her mouth.

Regaining her composure, Marion stood and collected her thoughts, smiling as she recalled the old trick Malcolm had shown her when she was learning how to track wildlife. An intact spider's web meant nothing had passed by recently.

Obviously he didn't walk this way.

Looking around, Marion was unable to see any other sign that someone had walked through the area. Backtracking a short distance, she thought she could see other things suggesting the route the man had taken, but in the end, they all led nowhere.

Unable to go any further, Marion pulled her own small GPS unit from her pack and recorded a waypoint.

For future reference, she thought.

As she made her way back to the road, Marion realized how much elevation she'd gained over the short distance she'd walked. At an opening in the forest she paused to take in the view down Maligne Lake.

What a beautiful vantage point.

Closing her eyes she listened to a morning chorus of songbirds, trying to tease apart one species from another. But somewhere in the mix a branch broke and Marion suddenly turned around. Straining, Marion listened and watched for movement in the forest, but heard and saw nothing.

Continuing back to the road, she had the feeling someone or something was watching her. Deliberately, she picked up her pace.

As she walked into the parking lot, she noticed the pickup truck was still there and once again thought there was something familiar about it. Then she noticed the heavy roof rack and sidelights and recalled the night walking home from the Jasper Wild office, and being caught in the glare of the powerful beam.

A cold shiver went down her back and Marion pulled her fleece tight around her body as she inspected the vehicle, standing on her tiptoes to try and look in the back.

"What the hell are you looking at, lady?"

The voice startled Marion and she stumbled.

"Nothing," she said as she caught herself and peered into the bloodshot eyes of a thickset man dressed in a camouflaged Carhart jacket, his faded jeans rolled up over the tops of his work boots.

"Well get your nose out of where it don't belong." Without missing a beat, the man pulled himself up into the large truck and started the engine. Rolling down the driver's side window he glared at Marion as he popped the clutch and shot backward, turning the wheel quickly so that it almost brushed Marion as she jumped to the side.

Shaken, Marion stood and watched as the truck roared out of the parking lot and sped back down the Maligne Lake road.

CHAPTER 27

"MARION!" MEGAN BEGAN to berate the older woman after being told about her sleuthing at Maligne Lake.

"Calm down, Megan," said John. "Marion didn't call us over here to give her a hard time." John looked at Marion. "Why *did* you ask us to come over?"

Marion held up a hand as Ben and Kate knocked at the back door before walking into her kitchen. "Let me tell everyone at the same time."

Ben and Kate looked perplexed as they assessed the trio sitting in the kitchen.

"What's up?" Ben asked.

"Marion's got something to tell us," said Megan. "But she wanted to wait until we were all here."

The four park wardens looked to Marion.

Marion was about to say something then paused and retrieved Malcolm's note from the refrigerator. "This note has been bugging me ever since Malcolm's accident, so I decided to do some looking on my own." She sat back down at the table and related her story about the two men she saw at Maligne Lake and the piece of flagging tape she found. "I don't know if any of it is significant, but I'm not a big believer in coincidence."

Kate looked at Ben then back at Marion.

"I believe the flagging tape and the man in the SUV are somehow tied together," Marion continued.

"The second man sounds like Zane Ritter," said Megan.

"But were they there together?" Ben asked.

"On first appearances, it may not seem that way," said Marion. "But yes, I believe they were."

"So what were they up to?" said John.

Marion shrugged. "I tried to research the logo on the SUV, but came up with nothing. I didn't see the two men together, but something tells me they were meeting there or were there for a similar purpose."

"Which was?" said Megan.

"I have no idea," said Marion. "But there's something else." She turned to her laptop and opened an email. "After chatting with Ben and Kate about the survey stake they found, and its inscription, I sent an email to a friend in Germany. She and her partner Mikael belong to a nature conservation group." Marion scanned through the email as she spoke. "Erika replied that she was familiar with the mining company Deutsche Mining International or D.M.I. as it was commonly referred to internationally, but would check with Mikael and others in their group to find out what she could about any interests the company might have outside Jasper."

"When I got back from the lake, Erika had sent me a second email." Marion turned her laptop toward the group and listened as John paraphrased the email.

"D.M.I is a German-based, multinational mining company with major interests in Africa, notably the D.R.C."

"D.R.C?" Kate leaned in closer to the laptop.

"The Democratic Republic of Congo," said John. "But the company also has ties to diamond mines in South Africa." He looked at the others. "Erika finishes the email by saying D.M.I. doesn't have the best reputation."

"Meaning what?" said Ben.

"She doesn't say. But she promises to get back to Marion as soon as she has other information."

"So back to Ritter," said Ben. "What would he be up to in the Maligne?"

"Not sure," said John. "But I believe Jimmy Rand knows his background pretty well. Maybe we should talk with Jimmy?"

"Now I really want to know what it was Malcolm found," said Marion. "I'm going back to check."

"No way," said John.

"Ben and I will go," said Kate, looking at Ben for agreement.

"Yeah," said Ben, turning to Marion. "There's something fishy about Kate and I seeing Zane Ritter around the proposed mine site and you running into him in the Maligne Valley. Something doesn't add up."

CHAPTER 28

ARMED WITH THE GPS location Marion had collected, Ben and Kate made their way to Maligne Lake the following morning. They were back in town by lunchtime, reconvening at Marion's house with John and Megan.

"That was fast," said John, as Ben and Kate walked into Marion's kitchen.

"Yeah," said Ben. "It went faster than I thought it might."

"Shithouse luck," said Kate.

"You find anything?" Megan asked.

"Something very interesting," said Kate. "A survey marker."

"An old survey marker?" said Marion. "Maybe that's what Malcolm discovered. It's probably from the lodge proposal put forward years ago. It never got off the ground, thank goodness, but Malcolm and I were still finding old markers and bits and pieces of flagging for years after."

"Ah," said Kate, "this isn't that old." She reached into her pack and pulled out a wooden survey marker and laid it on the table.

"I don't understand," said John. He picked up the marker and looked at its inscription, three letters: D.M.I.

"It's the same as the survey markers we found near the proposed mine."

"What?" said John.

"That was our reaction as well," said Kate. "We have no idea what it means."

"Why would a survey marker for a mine on Jasper's boundary end up in the middle of a national park?" Marion asked the question on everyone's mind. She was about to continue, but noticed a new message on her laptop.

"What is it Marion," John asked as Marion stared slack-jawed at the screen.

"Another email from Erika and Mikael."

"With more information about D.M.I.?" said John.

Marion turned the computer so John could read the message.

"It repeats some of the information they told us previously," said John, "but adds some new information about the owner of D.M.I."

"What's it say?" said Ben.

"It says the owner has a mixed reputation."

"Which means . . .?" Megan prompted.

John shrugged but continued to read. "He's also known to be politically connected both in Germany and here in Canada."

"Who's the owner?" said Ben.

John scanned the details of the email. "A man by the name of Helmut Stenger."

"Incredible," said Marion, attracting everyone's attention. "I can't believe it."

"You know of him?" said Megan.

Marion nodded but held up a hand. "Keep reading."

"He has interests in the Jasper area," said John, reading further into the email then looking at Marion.

"In Jasper?" said Kate.

"Yes," said Marion.

"How do you know him?" Megan asked.

"Malcolm met Helmut Stenger sometime during the 60s," said Marion.

"Seriously?" said Ben.

Marion nodded. "Stenger became a proficient mountain climber and Jasper became one of his favourite destinations. He and Malcolm often climbed together. By the time I came along, Malcolm was climbing less frequently with Helmut but I met him on several occasions. Then they stopped climbing with each other altogether.

"Malcolm said they had a falling out, something about their different perspectives on …" Marion hesitated. "On pretty much everything I guess. Helmut was a budding industrialist and Malcolm was an avid environmentalist. He never spoke much of Helmut again and I haven't heard of him in years."

Marion got up and left the room, returning with a small pile of notebooks, which she placed on the table. "Malcolm was diligent about keeping field notes. These are some of the ones from his early years in Jasper. I've been devouring them since his *accident*."

"Very detailed," Kate said as she thumbed through one of the books.

"Yes," said Marion. "They're indexed and cross-referenced." She opened one of the other books then turned to the middle pages and handed it to Kate. "These are some of his notes about his climbs with Helmut Stenger."

"Hmm," said Kate as she scanned the pages. "So the company proposing a new mine next to the park is owned by a man known to you, or more specifically well known to Malcolm? Interesting."

"What else do you know about him?" said Ben.

"Not so much about him," said Marion, pulling the laptop back in front of her. "But Erika said there is a lot of information about his mining company, Deutsche Mining International.

"And," she added, "Erika said Mikael wanted to make sure she told me to be careful dealing with Stenger. His company has been tied to atrocities in Africa and he has been accused of hiring paramilitary fighters to do his dirty work." Marion looked at the group. "Erika finished her email by saying 'Please, be very careful.'"

"Lou was supposed to be meeting the mine proponent and taking him on a flight of the mine area," said John.

"When was that supposed to happen?" said Ben.

"I believe it already has," said Megan. "Lou really wanted John and I to be involved, but Anne insisted Lou do it alone. It was supposed to be confidential."

"It's odd that Kate and I were assigned the mine project," said Ben, "but not given the opportunity to meet the proponent."

"Who else went with them?" said Kate.

"Konrad, I think," said Megan.

"Figures," said Ben. He got up and started for the door, motioning for Kate to come along.

"Where are you going?" John asked.

"To see the boss," said Ben.

CHAPTER 29

BEN AND KATE found Lou in his office poring over paperwork.

"Do you have a few minutes?" Kate asked as they knocked on his open door and walked in.

Lou looked up and nodded toward two chairs sitting in front of his desk. "Take a seat," he said just as Ben was about to say something. "I've been wanting to talk to you." He waved a hand at the overflowing in-basket. "I'm trying to keep too many balls in the air."

"When were you going to tell us about Helmut Stenger?" Ben blurted out as he sat on the edge of the chair and leaned into Lou's desk. Almost immediately Kate kicked him hard in the shins and shook her head.

"What?" said Ben, wincing as he fired a hard look at his partner.

"Don't get your shorts in a knot young man." Lou pushed the paperwork to the side and leaned back in his chair. "I've been busier than snot and the mine is only one of the fires I have to deal with right now."

"Sorry for barging in," said Kate. "We just figured you should be the first to know what we've found out about Helmut Stenger."

"What?" said Lou. "That he's a wealthy Kraut who's greasing the palms of some of our top politicians?"

"You know that?" said Kate.

"No. Not for certain. But it's not every day I'm told to show some foreign fat cat around in a helicopter."

"So where did you take him?"

"Where we went on our horse trip," said Lou, nodding to Ben and Kate. "Out through the Rocky and around the proposed mine site."

"And that was it?" said Ben, finally composed enough to ask a question.

"No. He also wanted to see some of the backcountry."

"Like the Maligne Valley?" said Ben.

"Yeah?" Lou looked questioningly at the pair. "Why, what's up?"

"Get this," Kate began, before launching into their explorations around the proposed mine, Marion's sleuthing in the Maligne Valley, including her run-in with Zane Ritter, and their own discovery in the Maligne Valley that morning. She also related the contents of the emails Marion had received from her friends in Germany.

"No shit?" said Lou, looking bewildered as he heard the details.

"But we don't know what it all means," said Ben.

"I don't either," said Lou. "But I smell a fuckin' rat."

Lou got up from his desk and pulled on his jacket.

"Where are you going?" Ben asked.

"I need to speak to the superintendent. You two keep this under wraps for now and tell John, Megan and Marion to do the same." He shook his head at his last words. "There's no friggin' way Marion will stay quiet about this. But somehow you have to convince her that it's in the park's best interest if she lets us deal with this." He turned back to Ben and Kate before walking out the door. "You need to find out as much as you can about Stenger, D.M.I., Ritter, the goings-on at Maligne, all of it. But you need to keep Marion Seawell out of it. I don't want to see her get hurt."

CHAPTER 30

"TOM, WHAT'S UP with Helmut Stenger?" Anne Winters sat in her office leaning into the phone's speaker, waiting for Tom Erickson's response, furious after Lou had filled her in on the details dug up by Ben, Kate, Marion and the others.

"What are you talking about, Anne? There's nothing *up* with Stenger."

"I don't buy it, Tom. There's more to this than a mine proposal. And whatever it is, I also have no doubt your little gopher Konrad Vincent-Blais is in on it."

"Anne, Anne, please don't rock the boat on this one."

"Rock the boat? Tom, I haven't even started."

"Anne, this is a very sensitive issue."

"So sensitive that the park superintendent is left out of the loop?"

"Well, you haven't always been too open to any discussion of development in Jasper. Maxime thought it was in the best interests of ..."

"Best interests?" Anne fought to control her emotions. "Maxime Bolduc has only ever had his own interests in mind."

"Anne, I should remind you, he is our director-general. Flaunting his authority is tantamount to insubordination."

"Don't play that game with me, Tom. I know what I'm doing. But what I want to know is what you people in Ottawa are doing? What is going on here? I know we aren't just talking about Stenger's interest in a mine on Jasper's boundary. What else is he up to?"

"I can't speak to that, Anne."

"Who can?"

"Only the director-general. I'm sure you know that."

"I'm not sure what I know anymore. But in any case, put him on."

"Maxime? Anne you can't be serious. He's a busy man. He doesn't just drop things to take calls from the field."

"Too focused on the *big picture*, right?"

"Exactly, he ...," Tom started but Anne cut him off.

"I was being facetious, Tom. You need to stop and smell the coffee. And you better tell Bolduc we need to speak. I need to know what's going on here before Marion Seawell and Jasper Wild blow the top off of whatever it is you aren't telling me."

"Anne, I think you'll need to come in to Headquarters."

"What?"

"This isn't something Maxime is going to talk with you about over the phone."

"You want *me* to come back to Ottawa?"

"Yes. As soon as possible."

"But I just can't drop everything whenever you want to meet. My plate is full."

"I realize that, but some things take priority."

"And who sets those priorities?

"I think you know the answer to that Anne. I'll try to buy you a little time but Maxime is going to want to speak with you, soon." Tom Erickson paused. "And, Anne, you are going to have to think about your options."

"What are you talking about, Tom?"

"Maxime is going to want someone in Jasper who can follow his direction. If you can't or won't, you'll have to think about that."

Anne was quiet for a moment. "You mean my position in Jasper is on the line?"

"Possibly your career."

CHAPTER 31

ANNE WAS STARING at a shelf of pasta in the grocery store, lost in thought and hadn't realized someone was speaking to her. When she finally turned around she almost walked into Marion.

"Oh, hi, Marion," Anne said. "I must have been daydreaming."

"Too many things on your mind, perhaps." Marion reached past Anne for a jar of tomato sauce. "I just asked how things went in Ottawa during your last trip there? I know it was a while ago but I haven't seen you for some time."

"Oh fine, I guess. You know, it's Ottawa. It seems every time I go there I come back with more work."

"Sounds like you should avoid the place." Marion placed a second bottle of sauce in the plastic grocery basket. "But at least now you're getting some help."

Anne shot a questioning look at the older lady.

"Your new assistant," said Marion. She winked at Anne and smiled. "I should think you'll need it with all the talk about the new mine on the border of the park. First it seemed like just another unsubstantiated rumour, but now it seems as if it's actually on the table. God, another mine right up against the park boundary. You know our group won't take that sort of thing lying down."

"I wouldn't expect you to, Marion. But as it stands right now, any proposed mine adjacent to us would be subject to a joint federal-provincial review panel." Before the words were out of her mouth, Anne regretted saying them.

"You do realize we live in Alberta?" said Marion, sarcastically.

"How could I ever forget," said Anne. "It's a great province, but its politics are driving me …"

"Away?" said Marion.

God, can she read my mind? Anne thought. "I was going to say crazy." She gave Marion a puzzled look and wondered what other kinds of rumours were floating around town. "But if that's what people are saying, they shouldn't get their hopes up." Anne tried to laugh casually, suddenly aware of people slowly moving past them in the aisle, as if they were eavesdropping. "Because *I* don't have any plans to leave."

"That's good to hear," said Marion, the sound of her voice seeming to carry the length of the store. "We need a strong voice like yours in the park." Looking around, Marion stepped a little closer and whispered. "I assume someone told you about the goings-on at Maligne Lake. I'm wondering if your bosses in Ottawa are finally giving in to some of the pressure to build a lodge up there? You do recall there was a proposal at one time?"

Once again Anne did a double-take and wondered how Marion could be voicing the very concern she herself had about the information Lou passed on to her.

God, can she read me like a book?

"And now with the Snake in charge …?" Marion grimaced.

The last comment threw Anne for a loop, but she maintained her composure and didn't bite. "I really should get going," she said, scanning her grocery list.

"Very good," said Marion. "But you should come by for a visit, or for supper. I'd love to spend some time with you. And I promise," Marion added, crossing her heart, "no park talk."

"Oh Marion, I'd love to, but I'm afraid I have to …," she sighed, "I'm afraid I have to go back to Ottawa in the next little while."

"What? So soon after you last trip. God, they're going to wear you down."

Don't I know it. Anne wanted to say yes to the supper invitation, to spend more time with Marion, skip the trip to Ottawa and avoid everything else she had to do, but knew she couldn't.

"I'm trying to push it off for a few weeks," she offered. "I've got a ton of work to catch up on and don't really have time to be traipsing back and forth to Ottawa. But duty calls."

"Well, you take care and travel safely. We can get together whenever you have time."

"I'm sure we will," said Anne. She stood watching as Marion made her way down the aisle toward the back of the store. When she had turned the corner, Anne made a beeline for the checkouts.

CHAPTER 32

SITTING IN THE trailer at Pocahontas, Kate laid out all the pieces of the puzzle they'd discussed with Lou. "So what do *we* do?" she asked.

"What Lou told us," said Ben. "But I'd also like to dig into this a bit more."

"What are you thinking?"

"I'm not sure, but there's still a couple of things we need to follow up on."

"Like?"

"Remember Marion mentioned a sport utility vehicle parked next to Ritter's truck?"

"Yeah, and a man who was probably looking for the same thing we were."

"Exactly," said Ben.

"You're wondering who it was?"

Ben nodded. "I think Marion said his vehicle had a logo with three letters in a stylized mountain design. M.P.D. I believe it was."

"Marion said she tried to find out what it stood for but hadn't made any headway."

"I know," said Ben. "But there is someone who might be able to help us." He pulled a business card from his wallet and thumbed the embossed lettering. The business number had been crossed out but he was still able to decipher it.

"Kallie?" said Kate. "I don't know if that's a good idea."

"Well she does work in the energy industry," said Ben. "She might also be able to use her contacts to find out something about Stenger and his company. But those initials on the guy's vehicle are what I'm most curious about."

"True," said Kate. "But …"

"C'mon, let me give it a try," he pleaded.

"Fine," said Kate. "We probably should divvy up the work-load anyway and try to get out in front of whatever it is Stenger and Ritter are up to."

"Good idea," said Ben.

"When we get the chance I want to take Megan up on her offer of a horse trip," Kate added. "I'd like to go back out to the boundary and do some more poking around. You could concentrate on the Maligne and see what else you can find. Maybe Kallie will come through for us again." Kate bit her lip and walked down the hall into the bedroom.

Ben could tell she wasn't totally enamoured with the idea of involving Kallie.

But what the hell. He dialed the number.

"Strong Media." The voice sounded professional and confident.

"Hello, Kallie. It's Ben."

Her hesitation left Ben wondering if Kallie remembered, but his doubts were quickly erased.

"Ben Matthews, oh my god. How are you? I haven't heard from you in ages. Where are you?"

"Whoa there, Cowgirl." The name came out of nowhere and Ben looked down the hall to see if Kate was within earshot.

Ben smiled to himself at the thought of Kallie and her pink saddlebags. The chance encounter with the media specialist on a flight to Edmonton had turned out to be a lucky break when he and Kate were working on the bison issue in Wood Buffalo; Kallie was the straw that broke the camel's back.

"Are you in town?" Kallie's voice sounded hopeful.

"Calgary?" said Ben. "No. I'm in Jasper. I just thought I'd call and say hi."

"Well, how have you been? How was the move from Wood Buffalo? And Kate? How is Kate?"

"Fine, fine and fine. Everything's fine."

"Well it's so nice to hear your voice."

"Same here," said Ben. "It's been too long."

Kallie laughed. "And you still have a job, I assume?"

"Yeah. But to be honest, we're back into a similar situation as Wood Buffalo."

"How's that?" said Kallie. "I can't imagine anything quite like a buffalo slaughter happening in Jasper."

"Well, not quite," said Ben. "But in some ways it's even worse." He went on to give Kallie the essential details about what they were dealing with, filling her in on Helmut Stenger, D.M.I., and the mystery of the survey stake. "If you don't mind, I'd like to ask you a favour." Ben paused. "Another favour. I really shouldn't be bothering you but …"

"Bother me," Kallie said. "I'm intrigued. You can't just call out of the blue, tell me all of this juicy stuff, and then expect me to blow it off."

"Okay, okay," said Ben, smiling to himself at Kallie's unbridled enthusiasm. "But all I have are three letters: M.P.D."

CHAPTER 33

SUMMER SLIPPED BY quickly as Ben and Kate continued to find out as much as they could about the proposed mine, and the area along Jasper's eastern boundary. Kallie had been busy with her own work but promised Ben she'd get back to them when she had a chance to dig into things a little further. In the meantime hunting season was already beginning and Jasper's park wardens were ramping up boundary patrols to help keep hunters honest.

Finally able to do the backcountry trip they'd been planning for weeks now, Megan and Kate rode their horses silently through the clearing to Whitehorse Cabin and stopped in front of the hitching rail.

"You did well," said Megan. She let the lead rope of her packhorse fall to the ground and slid off Ash before looping the reins over the railing.

"Thanks," said Kate, following Megan's lead. "That was probably a pretty tame ride compared to some of the places you could've taken me. And Whiskey was great." She stroked the mare's neck and whispered into her ear. "Weren't you, girl?"

Megan smiled, untied the leather rifle scabbard and stood the Winchester against a post. "You can have the biggest wrecks on the easiest trails," she said as she loosened Ash's girth. "These ponies can blow up over the simplest thing." She laughed. "Sometimes getting past a bench on a trail is the biggest ordeal for some of these horses. You'd think they were trying to tiptoe around a bomb, but all the time, you know, the bomb is actually under your ass."

Finished with her own horse, she began unloading the pack horses then walked Kate through the motions, showing her the tack shed and barrels of feed. "The ponies deserve an extra helping of oats after that ride. It's a bit of a slog up the Fiddle River Valley. We could have stayed at the Fiddle cabin another night, but I wanted to get up here so we could do some exploring. There's a horse camp on the provincial side and the proposed mine isn't far from there. We can ride out there tomorrow and check things out. It's always good to see who's around, especially with hunting season starting."

"It was a good ride," said Kate. "Although I have to admit, my butt's a little sore."

"Goes with the territory," said Megan. "But hours in the saddle are what count if you want to be a good horsewoman."

With the horses fed and watered, Megan hobbled her mare and pulled off its halter. "Pull the halters off the others and these ponies will be good for the night," she told Kate.

"There's no need to hobble them all?"

"Nope. The others'll stick close to Ash." Megan strapped a bell around Ash's neck and gave her a light smack on the rear end. "If they do wander, you'll find them in the morning when you jingle them."

Kate gave Megan a sideways glance. "You want me to find them in the morning?"

Megan nodded. "Jingling's part of the training. If you ..."

"... want to become a good horsewoman," finished Kate.

"Exactly," said Megan. "Sorry if I'm being repetitive."

"No worries," said Kate. "Experience is the best teacher."

The two wardens hauled their gear into the cabin and unpacked then set about preparing supper.

"I hope you like stirfry," said Megan, placing all the ingredients on the counter and opening the packages.

"Sure," said Kate. "But I was kind of expecting canned beans and a loaf of white bread." She laughed.

"If you were travelling with Jimmy Rand, that's probably what you'd be eating, but I can't do that stuff anymore. Besides, on a short trip like this, we can pack fresh food and it'll last."

"I'm not complaining," said Kate.

The two women made quick work of supper preparations and were soon sitting down at the rudimentary wooden table with their plates loaded with rice and topped with stir-fried chicken and vegetables. When Kate poured them each a cup of wine, Megan lifted hers in a toast. "To a great trip and hopefully the first of many."

"Hear, hear," said Kate, raising her cup and touching it against Megan's. "This looks great," she added, digging into the meal.

"Everything tastes so much better in the backcountry," said Megan.

"You got that right," said Kate. "Still my favourite part of the job."

Megan smiled. "Same here."

Kate sighed happily.

"So what about Ben?" said Megan. "You figure he'll like it here in the mountains?"

"Yeah." Kate looked out the window at the horses. "He's pretty adaptable. I know he would have liked to stay in the North longer, but you never know, maybe we'll get back there someday. We're also both pretty keen on Nahanni or Kluane, and we've even talked about an exchange to Africa some day."

"Africa? Seriously?" said Megan. "I don't know if that's for me, although Nahanni or Kluane would definitely be on my list as well. But I'm in no hurry to leave Jasper. Some folks call it the 'jewel in the system.' The more I see of it, the more I agree. The town gets too many tourists for my liking, but the backcountry is to die for."

"I've been impressed so far," said Kate.

"The big challenge in most parks seems to be finding and keeping a relationship going," said Megan. "I kind of envy what you and Ben have."

Kate nodded. "I know. And it seems like it's doubly hard for a woman in this outfit. So far we've been making it work, working together and all, but it's got its challenges."

"Tell me about it," said Megan, topping up their cups and sitting back.

Sensing there was something Megan wanted to get off her chest, Kate sat back and waited as Megan looked out the window, seemingly lost in thought.

"Gordie didn't exactly set the best example," Megan continued, "but I get it. Relationships take a lot of work and sometimes things just don't pan out. I was pretty choked when he ended up with Abi. She's almost twenty years younger than him. But once I got to know her, I realized she was probably just what he needed. She kept him in line and seemed to really care for him. At first I thought Mom was going to shoot him, but she kept it together and now she's seeing someone else as well. So I guess it's working out."

"What about you?" asked Kate. "Is there anyone special in your life?"

Megan shook her head. "Not at the moment. I think women wardens scare some guys off and the ones that aren't scared off, well, I wouldn't want anything to do with them anyway. Maybe I'm just too picky."

"Picky's good," said Kate. "Unless you're just looking for a one night stand."

"Even then I'd argue it's good to be picky," said Megan. "But I'm not really into that. Maybe when I was younger, but you know what they say, the clock is ticking."

"Yeah," said Kate. "Makes it even tougher for a woman to find her way in this line of work, especially if you ever want to have kids."

"Is that in your future? Having kids, I mean?

"Not right away, but yeah, we've talked about it."

"And marriage?"

Kate nodded. "I think so." She paused. "Yeah, no, for sure, we'll get married. God, I don't sound very convincing do I?" She swirled the dregs of wine and stared into the bottom of her cup.

Megan laughed then reached across the table and placed her hand around Kate's, steadying the cup and sitting it on the table.

"Sorry, I didn't mean to put you on the spot. But if it's worth anything, I think you two make a great couple. You both seem to have your heads screwed on right."

Kate looked Megan in the eyes and grasped her hand. "Thanks. That means a lot."

"Just keep your eye on the tramps who come through here during summer," said Megan. "Bagging a warden seems to be on all of their bucket lists." She laughed. "Mind you, some of them are interested in a female warden as much as they are a guy. So when you hear the term guy, remember, it's gender neutral. There are *guy* guys and *girl* guys."

"I'll keep that in mind," said Kate.

Suddenly she sat upright. "Hear that?"

Megan shook her head.

Kate held a finger to her mouth.

Somewhere in the distance a mournful wail echoed through the valley.

"Elk bugling," said Megan.

"Really?"

Megan nodded.

"For a moment I thought it was the horses," said Kate. She got up and went to the door, followed by Megan. Unlatching the door and swinging it open, they were greeted by a brilliant moon, bathing the slopes as if it was daylight. Not far from the cabin, the four horses were standing still, their ears held erect, anticipating another elk call.

The silence was quickly broken by a series of competing elk bugles, the calls seeming to come from all around them.

"Dueling banjos," said Megan.

"So cool," said Kate.

They waited for the next round but nothing else came.

"Hmphh," said Megan. "Odd. I figured they'd keep going."

"Something else has them spooked," said Kate, as the horses slowly made their way back toward the cabin, walking at first then breaking into a slow trot with Ash two-stepping and hopping to keep up with the trio of un-hobbled ponies.

"Maybe there's a bear rumbling around out there," said Megan.

While Kate waited on the cabin step, Megan walked down to the horses and spoke softly to her mare. "Whoa girl. It's all right," she whispered, running her hand down Ash's neck and along her side. Walking back to the cabin she stopped at the hitching rail. "Better take the bear spray with you in the morning when you jingle the ponies. Unless you're packin'?" Megan smiled and walked past Kate into the cabin.

"You mean carrying a handgun?"

"Yeah," said Megan. "Lots of the guys have them."

"Yeah. No. Ben and I never have, although most wardens in Cape Breton did." Kate closed the cabin door behind her.

"Truthfully, I haven't either," said Megan, picking up the wine bottle and holding it to the light. "The Winchester's enough for me. But there are times I wish we did have sidearms considering some of the assholes we run into." She offered the bottle to Kate. "More wine?"

"I think I've had enough," said Kate. "I should hit the hay. Early rise you know."

Megan emptied the bottle into her cup as the horses whinnied outside. She pressed her face against the window.

"Something's still giving them the jitters," she said as Kate undressed and slid into her sleeping bag. "Be on your toes in the morning."

CHAPTER 34

STANDING OUTSIDE IN her bare feet, Kate wrapped a blanket around herself and surveyed the horses as the last rays of moonlight illuminated the mountains. She thought she would have slept like a baby after yesterday's long ride, but she tossed and turned all night while Megan seemed to be out like a light in the upper bunk.

The horses had been on the move all night, stomping and whinnying so much Kate finally slid out of bed and checked them.

Wow, this is stunning, she thought as the moon slid below the mountains and cast everything into darkness, save for the broad expanse of stars pinpointing the heavens.

Unable to figure out what was making the horses so jittery, and unwilling to venture further from the cabin, Kate finally went inside and climbed into bed.

Lying awake, she watched the hour hand on the vintage alarm clock ticking away on the shelf above the table, moving almost imperceptibly toward five o'clock. Finally resigned to the fact she wasn't going to get back to sleep, she pulled on her uniform pants and shirt and stoked the stove, then checked to see if Megan showed any signs of life.

Her partner was cocooned in her sleeping bag sound asleep, a broad smile creasing her face as she slowly rolled her body toward the back of the bunk bed.

I could still be lying there, toasty warm, Kate thought.

Pulling on her fleece and boots, Kate walked outside, purposefully closing the door with a loud thud as she started out to jingle the horses. Much to Kate's surprise, the clear night skies had transformed into a soupy fog clinging to the slopes.

I can barely see the trail, let alone the horses.

Grabbing a halter and lead rope, Kate fumbled her way off the step and walked in the direction of where she'd last seen the horses, calling out to Ash before stopping to listen for any hint of their presence. The thick fog seemed to amplify her every breath, but she could hear nothing that would suggest the horses were anywhere close by.

Reaching the edge of the trees, Kate stopped and listened. Somewhere to her left she thought she heard the tinny clang of metal and turned to follow it, sticking to the edge of the forest to keep her bearings.

There it is again. But now it's off to my right. And it seems farther away.

Disoriented, Kate turned again to follow the sound but stumbled over a broken branch and fell headlong into the bushes, her hands and face thrashed by the branches as she reached forward to break her fall.

Damn.

Clambering back to her feet, she brushed herself off and listened, straining to hear the horses and more determined than ever to find them and get this part of the morning's chores over with.

The next time she heard the clang of the bell, she beat a straight path toward it and didn't stop until the silhouette of the horses could be seen through the fog.

"Hey, girl," she said in a low voice, slowly making her way to Ash and slipping the halter rope around the horse's neck. Reaching up, she pulled the halter up and over Ash's ears, then cinched the strap under the mare's chin. Bending down, she removed the hobbles and looped them over her shoulder and looked around to make sure the other three horses were with her.

Satisfied they were all together, she began to lead the mare back to the cabin, coming up short as she walked out the length of the lead rope and tried to get Ash moving in the same direction.

Stubbornly, the mare stood her ground and gave Kate a look that sent shivers down her back.

"C'mon, Ash, time for breakfast." Agitated, Kate tugged on the rope but Ash stood statue-still and whinnied, looking past Kate at some point deep in the forest.

"C'mon, girl, for god's sake. What's wrong with you?" Walking back to the horse, Kate stroked her mane and tried again to get her to move, but to no avail.

Slowly Ash pulled her head around, as if regarding the other horses, testing Kate's patience as she dug her hooves into the ground.

Suddenly a branch snapped and Kate swung around, just in time to see the outline of a person disappearing into the thick fog.

"Megan?" Kate called out. "Megan? Is that you?" She stood waiting for an answer, the hair on the back of her neck standing up as a cold draft shot down her back. "Megan," she shouted one last time.

Standing still, Kate strained to hear movement in the bush, but the only noise was the measured breathing of the horses, waiting patiently for Kate to lead them back to the cabin.

Tired of the tug of war and wary of who might be walking through the bush at this hour of the morning, Kate draped her arms over Ash's back. Flexing her knees, she did a little hop and pulled herself onto the mare, sliding her belly toward the far side as she draped one leg around Ash's rear end and sat upright.

Allowing Ash to take the lead, Kate was surprised as the mare turned around and headed in what Kate thought was the opposite direction from the cabin.

"Whoa, Ash, where are you taking us?" Kate said. She pulled on the lead rope to try and steer the horse just as the low cloud began to clear and a small piece of blue sky opened up above them. Slowly Kate realized she had been totally turned around and had been trying to lead the horses farther away from the cabin.

"So you do know where you're going. I should have trusted you to begin with." Kate leaned forward and stroked Ash's neck as the mare led the quartet out of the forest and into the meadow below the cabin. Riding up to the hitching rail, she slid off and let the lead rope fall to the ground just as the cabin door opened and Megan walked out holding two steaming cups of coffee.

"Where've you been?" she asked, unable to hide the worried look.

"On a little adventure," said Kate, as she walked up the step, suspiciously wondering if Megan was the person she'd seen in the fog.

Megan handed her the coffee. "An adventure?"

"Yeah. The horses had gone back down the trail a little ways and I was trying to get them back. You didn't hear me call your name?"

"No, not really. I was just about to get up and thought I heard something, but when I came outside, there was no one around. You okay?"

Kate peered over her coffee. Her hand trembled slightly as she motioned toward the forest. "There was someone out there."

"What? No way." Megan turned and followed Kate's stare toward the edge of the forest.

"I saw him, them, whoever it was, I don't know. I saw some-one and they had to have seen me. I thought it was you and I called out, but whoever it was vanished into the forest."

"Christ, Kate, now you're getting me worried. Who'd be out here at this hour of the morning?"

Kate shook her head. "You'd have a better idea than me. A hunter perhaps?"

"Were they carrying a gun?"

"I could barely see the person. It was pea-soup fog out there when I got up. I guess I got totally disoriented. I didn't have a clue where I was until the sky cleared a bit. Ash figured it out and led us back here. Otherwise I'd probably still be looking for this place."

"Always trust your horse," said Megan. "They know the way back home."

"I'm realizing that now," said Kate. "It's just that whoever I saw threw me off a bit."

"I wonder if that's why the horses were spooked last night?"

"Maybe."

"Come with me," said Megan. She placed her coffee cup on the cabin step and started off down the trail toward the pass. "The horses will be fine. We'll only be a few minutes."

"Where are you going?" Kate called, running to catch up.

"I just want to check something," said Megan, walking briskly into the forest. A few hundred metres from the cabin, she stopped and crouched down, peering intently at the trail in front of her feet.

"What is it?" asked Kate, finally catching up to her partner.

"Fresh tracks," said Megan, pointing to the partial imprint of a boot heel. "Whoever it is has been trying to stay to the side of the trail, using rocks where they can, to avoid leaving a footprint in the mud."

"What would they be up to?" asked Kate.

"Checking the cabin to see if any wardens were there. The boundary's not far away and the elk bugling probably got their attention. Likely trying to push an elk or a sheep toward the park boundary and across the line."

Megan turned back toward the cabin.

"Shouldn't we follow them?" said Kate.

"No. We'll go back and get geared up. We'll have a good vantage point at the pass. Whoever it was knows we're out and about anyway, so the element of surprise is lost."

CHAPTER 35

AT FIRST, ZANE Ritter brushed off his new employers' suggestion to show them the sheep and elk country around Jasper's boundary, but the two Germans had been persistent and he'd finally given in. While they had other work to do for their boss, whose name they never mentioned, the Germans said they had time on their hands and could possibly line up some future outfitting trips into Alberta with Ritter's assistance. Making a little extra on the side, while also on someone else's payroll was like gravy, and not something anyone else had to know about.

For his part, Ritter was pretty sure the Germans' business was as questionable as his own, but he was willing to do pretty much anything to attract more clients willing to buy skins, heads, antlers, horns or anything else that would make him a few bucks. And if he could line up some outfitting work for himself, well that was even better.

Considering his history, going into the Whitehorse Creek area, as close as it was to the mine he used to work for and the new mine he was doing survey work for, was taking a bit of a chance, but Ritter lived for taking chances.

He was even willing to take another crack at a grizzly, if the opportunity presented itself, but when the Germans' raised the idea with him, he'd convinced them to try for a bear somewhere north of Hinton, away from the mines.

He'd show them elk and sheep country, and that was it. Taking ATVs up Whitehorse Creek was as close to the park boundary as he dared to go with them for now. When he suggested going the rest of the way on foot and crossing into the national park, they balked.

In the end, Zane was able to convince the Germans to look for elk or sheep sign outside of the park, while he snuck inside the boundary to see what he could find. He wouldn't shoot anything, but he wanted to check the warden cabin at Fiddle Pass to see if anyone was there. If there wasn't, he'd probably try to push an animal out of the park and across the boundary.

Getting up well before dawn, the trio drove the ATVs as far as they could before setting out on foot. Close to the park boundary, Ritter sent the Germans on their way, while he headed to Fiddle Pass, picking his way up the horse trail, guided only by the scant rays of moonlight filtering through the canopy of lodgepole pine. Crossing into the park and approaching the cabin, Zane was certain he could hear horses but an early morning fog rolling in around the mountains muffled any sounds.

Disappearing into the trees and staying off the trail, he made his way toward the cabin. Off to his left, he could hear horses whinnying and a cabin door open and close, the sound of hinges squeaking carrying across the stillness of the morning as a thick cold fog settled over the forest. Making his way to the edge of the forest just below the warden cabin, Ritter was surprised to see a woman standing on the cabin porch wrapped in a blanket. As he stood partially hidden behind a large fir, he rubbed his eyes and shook his head and looked again, just as the woman disappeared inside the cabin.

Gonna' have some fun with this bitch, he thought, as he picked his way along the edge of the trees, following the sound of the horses down the trail past the cabin, until he was sure they were close by. Moving off the trail, he grunted and huffed like an old boar grizzly, moving the horses farther and farther away from the cabin while looking over his shoulder through the fog to make sure no one was coming his way.

They were several hundred metres from the cabin when Ritter heard the cabin door slam and a female voice calling "Ash." Stepping away from the horses, he hid behind a tree and waited as the voice slowly came closer. He grinned when he heard the woman fall and curse, then waited until she'd discovered the horses before he made his next move.

As the woman put a halter on the lead horse and removed its hobbles, Ritter moved closer, but he was almost caught off guard when the woman turned and tried to lead the horses away from the cabin.

"What the ..." he said to himself as she pulled the horse's lead rope and backed up to where he could literally reach out and touch her. Ritter held his breath and tried to escape the piercing look of the horse as the woman pleaded to get it moving. As she finally walked up to the mare, Ritter cautiously inched his way back. He was almost out of sight when he stepped on a branch, his heavy weight snapping the wood. Turning quickly, he bolted through the trees and disappeared up the trail.

CHAPTER 36

BACK AT THE cabin, Megan and Kate fed the horses and ate a quick breakfast before pulling together the gear they'd need for the day: binoculars, scope, a thermos of coffee and some lunch.

Leaving the two packhorses behind, Megan and Kate rode the narrow trail toward Fiddle Pass and dismounted.

"We'll walk from here," said Megan. "Loop the reins around a tree. We won't be long. The horses will be fine till we get back."

Shouldering their packs, they scrambled along the talus slope and picked a vantage point that gave them a clear view of the boundary.

While Megan set up the scope, Kate peered at the ridgeline and the valley on the provincial side of the boundary with her binoculars.

"Whitehorse Creek is that way," said Megan, pointing southeast. "The campground there is set up for horse outfitters, but every year there's more and more ATV use. Hunters typically base out of there and hunt the open slopes along the boundary."

"What are they after usually?" Kate asked.

"Sheep and elk mostly, but the odd hunter who was lucky enough to get a tag might be looking for grizzlies."

"That's legal?"

"Yeah," said Megan. "The province is under a lot of pressure to abandon the grizzly bear season, but so far they haven't bowed to the pressure. The hunting lobby is pretty strong, especially up and down the Foothills. Ranchers in particular want the option to be able to shoot any bears that kill their cattle and so far they've been able to get their way."

"So the bears better stay in the mountains?" said Kate "If they know what's good for them."

"It's kind of like that," said Megan, "even though grizzlies were a Plains species before we killed them off."

"Really?"

"Yeah, historically they ranged from Mexico to the Arctic. In the heyday of the big buffalo herds on the Prairies, bears were their main predator."

"I had no clue," said Kate. "Growing up on the East Coast, I always think of grizzlies as living solely in the mountains and foothills."

"Only because it's the last decent habitat left for them," said Megan. "If they could even venture as far as the Prairies, which is unlikely, they'd be sitting ducks. And with the buffalo gone, cattle become their target; that pisses the ranchers off big time."

Kate was about to say something when Megan raised a finger to her lips and pointed down the boundary.

Kate scanned the slopes with her binoculars while Megan focused in with the scope. They watched a pair of hunters wearing blaze orange hats pick their way along the ridgeline, staying just outside the park boundary markers.

"They're toeing the line pretty closely," said Megan as the men stopped by a boundary sign and glassed the slopes, looking north toward the wardens.

"Let's duck in behind these boulders," said Megan, pointing her nose toward a large rock outcrop. "I'm curious to see what they do."

As they watched, one of the men pointed into the park then stood his rifle against the rocks and crossed the boundary.

"I wonder what he saw?" Megan murmured. She scrambled along the edge of the outcrop for a better view, leaving the spotting scope for Kate and taking the binoculars with her. Slowly poking her head above the lip of rock, she watched the other hunter scramble down the slope into a small clump of bush.

"What's he doing?" said Kate.

"Can't tell. Sometimes hunters will split up to try and drive animals out of the park and across the boundary, but I'm not sure what this guy is up to. What about your guy?"

"I can't tell from here," said Kate. "He seemed pretty focused on something on the park side of the boundary, but now he's glassing this way again. She laughed, her eye pressed to the scope. "They'll shit their pants when they see us watching them."

"Speaking of which," said Megan, "I think that's why this guy disappeared into the park. He was just looking for a place to take a crap out of sight of his buddy."

This revelation almost brought Kate to tears, laughing as Megan slid back down the rocks toward her. In a few minutes, both hunters were reunited and continued to make their way along the ridgeline.

"I'm surprised they still don't see us," said Megan, stepping into the open a little more to improve her sightline. No sooner had Megan spoken than one of the men pointed toward them, handing his binoculars to his partner. The two men appeared to be discussing something, then started downslope toward the treeline.

"Sorry guys," Megan said under her breath. "Probably scared them off," she added, looking at Kate.

"Probably for the best anyway," said Kate. "Keeps them honest."

"Any chance they're the guys you saw this morning?"

"No way to tell. I could barely see anything. And I only saw one person. Or at least I think it was a person."

Megan looked at Kate quizzically. "Trust your instincts Kate. If you think you saw someone, you did."

"You're probably right," said Kate.

Megan nodded and turned her attention back to the boundary. "Well, it doesn't look like too much is happening here. Let's get the horses and make our way down to the campground.

Maybe we'll run into these two and see what we can learn from them."

Kate and Megan packed up their gear and made their way back to Ash and Whiskey, then headed down the trail leading out of the pass. In several places along the trail, provincial signs warning that ATV use was restricted in the area had been driven over and lay flattened in the mud.

"What's with that?" said Kate, pointing to the first sign they saw.

"The province is trying to control access voluntarily," said Megan, shaking her head. "It won't work until they actually put regulations in place. Even then, I'm not sure if people will abide by the rules. ATVs are just tearing the shit out of this place."

"Sad," said Kate as they continued down the side of the creek.

Before entering the campground, Megan pulled up on Ash's reins and turned to Kate. "This is all new to you, so maybe let me do the talking. Give me a signal if you see something suspicious."

As they walked their horses into Whitehorse Creek campground, Kate was surprised to see a collection of horses and ATVs scattered among the campsites. At one site, a steady column of smoke wafted out of the chimney of a massive wall tent that served as a communal cooking area.

Off to the side, a small group of hunters were gathered around an open fire, drinking coffee and eating sandwiches as their horses grazed nearby.

As they approached the hunters, Kate and Megan recognized the two men wearing hunter orange ball caps.

"G'day gentlemen," said Megan, directing her comment to the two men, but taking note of the other party of three hunters sitting with their backs to them.

"Why, good day, ladies," said one of the men, getting up and tipping his orange hat to them. "What brings you out to these parts?"

Out of the corner of her eye, Megan noticed the snarl on the face of one of the men in the other hunting party as he motioned to his partners whose back was to the two park wardens. Glancing at Kate she nodded her head toward them.

"Just a routine boundary patrol," said Megan as Kate nudged Whiskey alongside. "Making sure no one crosses the line when they're hunting."

"Wouldn't think of it," said the hunter, a nervous twitch in his face obvious as he looked at his partner. "Would we?"

His partner shook his head and looked up at Kate. "Wouldn't think of it," he said. "Not worth losing hunting privileges, not to mention our guns."

One of the hunters in the other party chuckled to his partners and the trio started to leave. All three wore camouflaged ball caps and while two were dressed in what seemed like European style hunting jackets, the largest of the men wore a tattered denim jacket, brandishing the logo for TruNorth Drilling across the back. He limped slightly, accentuating his heavy-footed gait as he started toward the cook tent.

"What about you three?" Kate asked, certain she recognized the largest man as Zane Ritter.

Her question stopped the men in their tracks.

"Who's asking?" said Ritter. He turned and glared at Kate from under his grease-stained ballcap.

"We are," said Megan, nudging Ash toward the men and blocking the path to the tent while Kate gave Whiskey's reins a slight pull and subtly walked the horse around the edge of the fire pit, positioning her horse at the edge of a muddy stretch of trail leading back to the cook tent. "We're Jasper wardens but have ex-officio status under the Alberta Wildlife Act."

Ritter turned to Megan and shrugged. "Hmphh. What the hell does that mean?"

"It means I want to see your hunting licences," said Megan. She slid off Ash and stood in their path.

Ritter was about to protest but one of the other men spoke up.

"Show the lady your licence."

"Hmph," Ritter muttered. "Sure, I'll show *the lady* my licence." He slurred the words then spit on the ground. "Oh, excuse me, I mean, the *warden*." He pulled out his licence and gripped it tightly as Megan tried to pull it from his hand. "What d'ya say?" He stared menacingly at Megan then grinned and loosened his grip.

"I say give me your licence if you know what's good for you." Megan pulled his licence away and peered at it.

"Zane Ritter." She looked at Kate, who nodded.

"Yeah," said Ritter. He pumped up his chest and smirked at his partners. "Maybe ya heard of me?"

Megan pursed her lips and shook her head. "Doesn't ring a bell," she lied. "You supposed to be famous or something?" She smiled as she handed the licence back.

Ritter glared at Megan. "You better watch yerself squaw, er, I mean, *warden*. Things can happen out here in the bush and no one would ever be the wiser."

"Are you threatening me?" Megan returned the glare. "Cause if you are, that's a criminal offence and you'll lose more than your hunting privileges."

Ritter was about to say something else, but one of his partners grabbed him by the shoulder and motioned for him to walk ahead.

"He doesn't mean anything," said one of the other men. "We'll be on our way."

"Not before I see your licences as well," said Megan, regaining her composure.

Both men pulled out their licences and passed them to Megan.

"You're from British Columbia?" she said, noting the details on the men's hunting permits.

"Yes. We're outfitters in B.C.," said one of the men. "Just here checking out opportunities to bring clients into Alberta."

"I see," said Megan, handing the permits back to the men. "Keep in mind that this hunting area borders on Jasper National Park." She stared at Zane Ritter. "I'd hate to see someone take you across the boundary without you knowing it. It would cost you dearly."

Ritter snarled as his partners nodded in unison.

"Will that be all," said one of the men.

"Yes, thank you," said Megan. "Have a good day gentlemen."

As she watched the men walk toward the cook tent, Kate sidled Whiskey alongside. "You okay?" she asked quietly.

Megan nodded, but her face was still flushed. When Ritter and the others were out of earshot, she pointed to his tracks in the mud. "Looks pretty similar to the ones on the trail by the cabin."

She looked at Kate who was watching the trio disappear into the cook tent.

"Huh?" said Kate, "Yeah, sorry, I wasn't paying attention." She looked down at the tracks and nodded. "I bet they're the same." She hesitated and swung her head toward the cook tent. "Ritter's walk reminds me of the guy I saw in the fog. And his profile fits to a T."

"I bet you're right," said Megan.

"We'll have to do a bit of homework on the other two," Kate added.

"Outfitters from B.C.," said Megan.

"Makes you wonder what they're up to," said Kate.

"Probably no good if they're with Ritter," said Megan.

"And interesting accents," said Kate, almost as an after-thought. "Seemed very European don't you think?"

"German, I'd say," said Megan. "Maybe just a coincidence?" She raised her eyebrows as she looked at Kate.

"I think not," said Kate.

CHAPTER 37

WITH HER JOURNALISM training, it didn't take Kallie long to figure out the letters M.P.D. stood for Mountain Park Design, and in no time she had made an appointment with the company's president.

Stepping out of the elevator at the top floor of the New Energee Building in Calgary, Kallie was immediately impressed with the décor of the bright and airy offices: modern and linear, but with strong traditional overtones.

Making her way slowly toward the reception desk, she scanned the series of images adorning the walls, a mix of backcountry shots showing mountain peaks and verdant valleys interspersed with photos of chalets and lodges, predominantly wooden structures but with hints of more contemporary building materials. She was particularly struck by a collage explaining the firm's mantra "designing with nature in mind," showing the integration of natural elements and lines with the architect's vision for achieving symmetry with the design.

"Do you like it?"

The attractive woman behind her bore a striking resemblance to photos of the company president Kallie had seen online. Although a little older than those images, the woman's wardrobe portrayed someone very fit and active.

"I do," said Kallie, her focus drawn back to the intense brown eyes. "I like it very much," she added, feeling slightly flushed by her own reaction and the sultry tone of her reply.

"Stephanie Landegard," said the woman, holding out a hand while running the other through her short, over the ears, dyed-brown hair. "President of M.P.D."

"Kalina Strong," said Kallie, noting the firm grip and muscle definition. She handed Stephanie her business card. "But you can call me Kallie."

"Strong Media," said Stephanie. "You're the young woman who called about the interview."

"Yes," said Kallie. "Outside of my regular work, I freelance for a few magazines and newspapers. That work often leads to connections I'm able to help professionally via Strong Media."

"Help do what exactly?" said Stephanie, sizing up Kallie from top to bottom.

"Communicate a vision," said Kallie. "Although you obviously do a nice job with that already." She pointed to the collage. "But so many times we lose people in the details, when all they really want to know, subconsciously at least, is whether or not a project aligns with their values. If it does, they're more likely to buy in, literally."

"So you're talking about investors?" said Stephanie, ushering Kallie down the hallway.

"I like to think we're all investors," said Kallie. She raised her eyebrows and smiled. "But not every investment is financial, is it? Sometimes, the financial investors are not as important as those with a vested interest."

"Go on," said Stephanie as she led Kallie past the reception desk and into her office. "Hold my calls," she said to the young receptionist before closing the door behind them. "It's Kallie, right?" she added, unbuttoning her leather vest and placing it on a chair while maintaining eye contact. She turned and walked past the large ornate desk. Leading Kallie to one end of a loveseat by the window she sat down next to her.

"Do you mind?" Kallie asked, as she pulled a small recorder from her purse and placed it on the seat cushion between them.

"No, it's quite alright. I'll let you know if we get into subject areas that are off the record."

"Of course," said Kallie, glancing out at the Calgary skyline. "Nice view."

Stephanie nodded, taking her eyes off Kallie for a moment to look out over the city.

"That's the real challenge with communications," said Kallie, turning back to Stephanie, "convincing people the view is nice. Well not this one, perhaps. This is an easy sell. I'm thinking of other situations where it's not as obvious."

"I'm intrigued," said Stephanie, relaxing into the soft leather.

"Well, I'm sure you must have been involved with projects that have had some opposition." Kallie continued. "From the public or neighbours or people that just didn't look at it the way you wanted them to?"

"Of course," said Stephanie. "It's inevitable."

"How have you dealt with that on other projects?"

Stephanie hesitated and looked out the window. "It's about managing expectations." She paused again and looked at the recorder. "Would you mind?"

Kallie turned off the recorder and Stephanie continued. "We help clients realize their vision, but we do it in a phased approach. We manage information and feed it out as we see fit."

"So you give the public a little bit at a time."

Stephanie nodded. "Yes. We don't like to overwhelm people. We counter potential opposition with a stepped-down version of the final product. In fact, we rarely show the final product, except to our clients of course. There's no point laying it all out there for public consumption if it's going to turn a lot of people off. As I said, we manage information flow."

"What kinds of projects are you involved with?" Kallie motioned to turn the recorder back on and Stephanie nodded.

"We focus on projects in the foothills and mountains. Our specialty is parks, both urban and wilderness. We have projects from California to British Columbia, but we're also expanding into Europe and South America."

"Are there projects you can share?" said Kallie. "The piece I'm writing is focused on western Canada."

"Well there is a project in Jasper ..." Stephanie caught herself. Kallie reached for the recorder and turned it off.

"But's it's especially sensitive," Stephanie continued. "I'm not at liberty to discuss the details."

"That's fine," said Kallie. "Tell me about some of your other projects. Ones you can discuss freely. Maybe we chat about Jasper another time."

"Over dinner perhaps?" said Stephanie.

"Perhaps," said Kallie. She sensed things might be progressing a little too fast for her liking and in a direction she wasn't interested in going, but seeing an in, she didn't want to throw water on the fire. "I do think the Jasper project might be more in line with what my editors are after."

"Yes, and I'm probably being overly cautious," said Stephanie. "I don't think it's really that big of a deal, just a lodge in the park ... although it needs to start out as something simpler. To get it over the first hurdles you know, the environmental community, the do-gooders." She smiled. "Some people react negatively to the first hints of development. They're such hypocrites."

"I know what you mean," said Kallie. "But they can be brought along if you manage the message. Massage them so to speak."

Stephanie smiled. "I like you." She slipped off her boots and crossed her legs, her toes brushing against Kallie's calf. "We obviously have some common interests."

Kallie returned the smile. "What strategies will you use to sell the Jasper project?"

CHAPTER 38

KATE HAD LOTS to tell Ben when she got back from the horse trip, not the least of which was the new wrinkle she and Megan figured had to be related to the mystery surrounding the proposed coalmine. It was definitely too much of a fluke for Ritter to show up in the Whitehorse Creek area with German outfitters, that was certain.

And although the discovery raised more questions than it answered, Ben felt Megan and Kate had at least been able to make some progress, where he was still spinning his wheels.

"No one you spoke with had any idea why that survey stake would be in the Maligne Valley?" Kate asked as she unloaded her pack and put things away.

"No one," said Ben. "And no one I talked with could figure why Ritter would be up there."

"Marion was the only one with a plausible explanation about the survey stake."

"You spoke with Marion? I thought Lou didn't want us to involve her if we could help it?"

"I know, but I figured it was worth a try. The old proposal to build a backcountry lodge at the lake is all she could think of."

"She still thinks the survey stake is a remnant from some previous work in the valley?" Kate shook her head. "No way. Besides, why would it be marked 'D.M.I.'?"

"I don't know," said Ben, rubbing his eyes. "But I'm bagged and you must be as well. Let's crash." He took Kate's hand and led her down the hallway to the bedroom, smiling to himself when she crawled in under the covers and immediately fell asleep.

Turning off the lights, he slid in next to her and closed his eyes, going over in his mind all of the possible linkages he and

Kate had discussed about the German connection with Ritter, the mine and the Maligne Valley.

Sometime in the wee hours of the morning he woke with a start and realized the phone was ringing.

Reaching to grab it before Kate woke up, Ben rolled out from under the covers and sat up on the side of the bed.

"Hello?"

"Hi there, sorry to bother you so late at night."

Ben recognized the voice and looked at the digital clock on the bed stand.

"It's two in the morning. Christ, Kallie, what's up? Are you okay?"

"Yes, yes, I'm okay. Just had to fight off an overzealous lesbian to get your information, that's all."

"You what?" Ben laughed into the phone. "What are you talking about?"

Kate stirred and looked bleary eyed at Ben.

"Kallie," he said, mouthing the words and pointing to the phone.

"I think I found what you're after," said Kallie. She went on to give Ben the details.

"Really?" he said, repeating the word several times as he listened to Kallie's version of events.

"Thanks so much. I owe you." Putting down the phone Ben looked at Kate, who was now leaning on one elbow, eagerly waiting to hear what Ben had to say.

"Things are starting to make more sense," Ben started.

"How so?"

"It seems Helmut Stenger's objective may not be a mine at all."

"No?"

Ben shook his head. "No. He's after a backcountry lodge in the park." Ben went on to tell Kate about Kallie's discoveries. "Marion's suspicions about the lodge were right on the mark."

"Stenger is trying to get his foot in the door with a *temporary* set-up?" said Kate.

"Yeah," said Ben. "Preferably by proposing minor additions to an existing operation in either the Tonquin or Maligne valleys. Then he'd build a proper lodge, maximizing the allowable build-out of the existing leasehold. Apparently the new DG is ready to agree to the full plan, Stenger will get his way, and grizzlies and caribou be damned."

"Well that sucks," said Kate.

"And there's more," said Ben. "Not only does Stenger own the company behind the mine, but he also has interests in other companies in Jasper, although Kallie couldn't confirm which ones, exactly. He's got his fingers into everything and he's politically connected right to the top. To the minister for sure, but probably even as far as the prime minister."

"No way."

"Way," said Ben. "Remember, the prime minister is from Alberta and has huge clout here."

"He tells the minister how it has to be," said Kate, "and the minister tells the director-general for Parks and so on down the line."

"Exactly," said Ben. "And senior management is complicit in this because they've been pushing Anne to have her staff focus on the mine."

"As a diversion?"

"Yeah, I think so. While Stenger's people do whatever they have to do to keep up the ruse."

"Stenger's people?" said Kate.

"Well, Ritter has got to be tied to this somehow. But Kallie referred to other people Stenger has on the ground in the Jasper area. In any event, Stenger's real objective is the lodge. He's got mines all over the world, but he doesn't have a lodge in Jasper. That's his goal. Apparently he's had his eye on this prize all of his life."

"How the hell did Kallie find all of this out?" said Kate, pulling herself up to sit next to Ben.

"She didn't get into the details," said Ben. "But she has her ways."

CHAPTER 39

FRUSTRATED TO BE summoned back to Ottawa, Anne Winters was certain it had something to do with the rumours starting to float around Jasper. Her curiosity had piqued when Lou Walker briefed her about the helicopter trip with Vincent-Blais and Helmut Stenger, as well as the information Ben, Kate and the others had uncovered. There was also something about her own first meeting with Helmut Stenger that had thrown her off about the man, but the encounter had been brief and she didn't want to jump to any conclusions.

The German businessman had seemed elusive when she questioned him about the mine. He knew few specifics, or at least that's how it seemed, almost as if the mine were secondary to something else. And it was *the something else* that nagged at Anne as she speculated what Stenger was up to. Vincent-Blais' presence didn't help console her fears but in the end, it was the comment from Marion that caused her the most concern.

She'd thought about confronting Konrad with her reservations about the German businessman, but felt it was better not to tip her hand to her new assistant. Still she wasn't quite sure what to make of things or who she could trust.

She did have the chance to meet briefly with Jeremy Large over drinks when she arrived in Ottawa, but even he seemed out of sorts and offered little advice for her meeting with Maxime Bolduc.

All he would say was that he wasn't in a position to say anything.

Not so helpful, Anne thought.

So when she saw Tom Erickson arrive at Parks Headquarters the following morning, she quickly cornered him in the entranceway.

"Ah, yes, Anne," said Tom. "Sorry you had to come back so soon."

"You and me both," she said, drawing Tom to the side. "What's this I'm hearing about a backcountry lodge?" she whispered. She put Marion's and her own suspicions out there before Tom could change the subject then watched his reaction.

"It's nothing to worry about," said Tom.

So it is true, she thought. *He's not even trying to deny it.*

Tom scratched his head and looked around the maze of open cubicles. He led Anne into an empty office and closed the door. "Maxime is considering allowing minor improvements ..." he paused, then added, "to the horse operation in the Tonquin Valley."

"The Tonquin?" Anne was completely thrown off guard. "I'm hearing the Maligne."

"Not going to happen," said Tom. "There may be some modest improvements in the Tonquin, but not the Maligne."

Anne was about to continue but Tom cut her off.

"Don't read so much into everything, Anne. I'm telling you nothing of consequence has been proposed, let alone approved."

Anne cringed. She'd been around long enough to be wary whenever weasel words like *nothing of consequence* started to creep into a discussion. But she held her tongue, sensing that pushing the issue right now might set Tom off. "That's good to hear," she said.

"Besides," said Tom. "You've got enough on your plate, with the mine and all. That's why Maxime wanted you back in Ottawa."

Right, because I can get so much work done on things that matter when I spend all my bloody time in pointless meetings in Ottawa. Anne fumed, but managed to calmly continue the conversation. "Speaking of which," she said, "What do you know about Helmut Stenger?"

Now it was Tom who was thrown off guard.

"Nothing," he said, avoiding Anne's stare. "Why do you ask?"

"No reason, just curious." Anne realized she should play her cards even closer to her chest.

Tom looked at his watch. "We should get going," he said, clearly irritated by Anne's questions. "Maxime is expecting you." Leading Anne out of the office, Tom nodded to the receptionist as they passed and showed Anne into the director-general's office.

"Good to see you again, Anne." For once, Maxime Bolduc seemed to be in a good mood. "Have a seat."

Anne sat down, suspicious about where this meeting was headed. Just then the door opened and Jeremy Large walked in.

"Of course you know Jeremy," said Bolduc. There was something about the change in his tone that raised other flags for Anne.

Anne nodded to Jeremy as he sat across from her.

"I've asked Jeremy to sit in to help with the transition."

"What transition?" Anne asked.

"Jeremy is in line for another posting. Tom will be taking over for him."

Anne wondered if there was something more to the matter but said nothing. When she looked at Jeremy his face appeared ashen.

"How has Vincent-Blais been doing?" the director-general asked.

"He's just getting settled," said Anne. "To be honest, I have so much on my plate, I haven't really had time to sit down with him and discuss priorities."

"I understand," said Bolduc. "But, the proposed mine is going to challenge your ability to deal with everything on your plate. You need to delegate some of your workload to Vincent-Blais. That's why he's there. You can't fight battles on a number of different fronts."

"I'm not comfortable with his abilities."

"Well get comfortable. You need to think about the big picture." The director-general's tone hardened, but the reference to the *big picture* infuriated Anne. She hesitated for a moment to consider her situation, but decided to put it all out there and see how Bolduc reacted.

"The big picture?" said Anne, her tone aggressive. "I've heard that my whole career from senior managers, suggesting the people actually working in our parks don't appreciate the big picture. Well what exactly is the *big picture* other than an excuse to satisfy your own conscience when you know you've deep-sixed a park and approved something that should never be allowed."

She paused to catch her breath before firing the next salvo.

"Maybe it would help if you kept the people on the ground in the loop, so they could appreciate the big picture," she challenged.

"What do you mean?" said Bolduc, his face flushed.

Anne looked at Tom Erickson and then at Jeremy Large. He shook his head slightly and looked at the director-general. "Just the roundabout way I've finally heard about plans for a backcountry lodge in *my* park," Anne continued.

Bolduc looked at Tom, who looked shocked but shrugged and raised his hands in front of him. Bolduc then turned his attention to Jeremy, who remained expressionless.

"Don't look at them," Anne offered. "They didn't say squat. You think living in Jasper I wouldn't hear things? Do you really think you could slide something like this through without me finding out?"

Bolduc turned back at Anne, pausing before he spoke. "Anne, you need to concern yourself with facts and not dwell on rumours. There is no provision in the park management plan for a backcountry lodge in the Maligne Valley."

"Who said anything about the Maligne Valley?" Anne looked at Tom with fire in her eyes. She turned to Jeremy Large, hoping he might say something, but he seemed to be sitting back with his eyes closed, lost in his thoughts. She turned back to Bolduc. "So it is the Maligne Valley."

Bolduc's face flushed as he and Tom looked at each other.

"Now I'm really disgusted," Anne continued. "When I hear rumblings in the community about the park, I am obliged to check them out. When were you going to tell me about the lodge, anyway?" She turned to Bolduc. "I'm concerned with anything outside the scope of the current park management plan. Why is this the first I've heard about this request? And when were you going to share the *big picture*?"

The director-general sighed and looked at Tom again before turning his attention back to Anne. "Anne, you may be the superintendent, but you are not the final decision-maker. You are there to manage the park, not chase ghosts."

"That doesn't answer my question about the lodge," Anne persisted.

"You're overreacting, Anne," said Tom.

"You know as well as I that these things tend to be incremental," said Anne, glowering at Tom Erickson. "You know a major addition to the park like a backcountry lodge would raise the ire of a lot of people."

"No one said anything about a lodge," said Maxime.

"Hear me out," said Anne. "A proponent puts forward a proposal for *modest improvements* to an existing operation *in the Tonquin Valley.*" She glared at Tom. "Your words. Then *he* starts talking about a lodge in the Maligne." Anne motioned toward Bolduc. "You two need to keep your stories straight before you start in on me about how to manage a park." Turning back to Bolduc she continued. "You think there will be soft opposition, but because the proponent is local and the improvements are *modest*, you think nobody will make a big fuss about it. And, once you get it through the approval process, you put out a press release, on a Friday or a holiday weekend, when there's less chance anyone will notice. When they do, they realize the proposal is actually for something much more complex.

"But you'll say the project's been approved, the public has had their chance to present their concerns, and before you know it we have a lodge in the park nobody wants, well, nobody that actually lives in Jasper or works in the park wants. But that's not the story you just told me. I don't know who to believe: Tonquin or Maligne, local proponent or someone else. It's a classic *bait* and *switch*. The mine is...," Anne paused, as she sensed the connection between the mine and the notion of a lodge was more real than imagined. "The mine is merely a distraction, to focus our attention away from the lodge, whatever lodge it ends up being. That's really the *big picture*, isn't it?"

Bolduc sighed heavily. "Anne, this is a very sensitive issue."

Anne looked at Tom who was biting his lip. "Clearly," she said, poised to go for broke with her suspicions. "And Helmut Stenger is behind it all. Isn't he?"

"Anne." Maxime Bolduc stood behind his desk. "You need to decide if you can follow direction or not."

"What am I being directed to do?" Anne was reluctant to back down.

"Focus on your job. We didn't say anything about approving a lodge. So stop charging after unfounded rumours started by selfish environmentalists who don't want to see anyone step foot in a park. It's that simple."

"To start with: *you each* said something about a lodge," said Anne. "And those environmentalists you speak of are actually doing the job we should be doing. If we said no to some of these development proposals right from the get-go, no one else would have to do our jobs for us."

Bolduc raised his hand and glared at Anne. "Enough. I've heard enough," he fumed. "You work for me and it's time you started doing your job."

"I *am* doing my job," Anne countered as she peered into his pinpoint pupils, momentarily thrown off by her recollection of Lou's reference to Bolduc's 'snake eyes'. "I'm following the direction in Jasper's park management plan," she added as she regained her fighting form. *"You know,* the public document that identifies our commitments to *all* Canadians on managing the park for the next ten years."

"Really Anne?" said Maxime. "You know as well as I do, there is always room for interpretation of those *commitments.* So start following orders, or else."

"Or else?"

"Or else I will have to remove you from the Jasper position and replace you with someone who can take direction."

"Like Vincent-Blais?"

"If necessary."

"No 'thanks, Anne, for all your hard work in Jasper, in help-ing preserve some of the most beautiful landscape in Canada, in helping to protect endangered wildlife populations.' You'd rather have someone who isn't invested in the park running the show? Someone like Konrad?" Anne was incredulous.

"If necessary, yes."

Anne stood up. "Thanks for your time. I'll see myself out. Oh and by the way Maxime, I don't work for you. I work for the taxpayers of this country."

"Anne," said Tom Erickson. "Please wait." He looked to Jeremy Large but there was no response. "Anne," he continued, following her to the door.

Anne opened the door and was about to leave but turned back to Maxime Bolduc.

"I want a transfer. My terms. Or I'll blow this thing out of the water."

Maxime Bolduc began to respond but Anne had already closed the door behind her. *I might anyway,* she thought as she stood outside his office, shaking uncontrollably. She was about to walk away, but not before a shouting match erupted in the director-general's office, seemingly between Tom Erickson and Jeremy Large.

She loitered momentarily, trying to catch the gist of the argument, which seemed to centre on trying to convince Jeremy Large to reason with her, but she didn't wait around for its conclusion. As she walked past the receptionist, the door crashed open and Jeremy Large suddenly emerged from the director-general's office. He slammed the door, looked at Anne then headed the other way as Anne and the receptionist watched wide-eyed.

*****

Returning to the hotel until her flight back to Edmonton left the following day, Anne was surprised to see the message light blinking on her room phone. Shedding her jacket and slipping out of her shoes, she sat on the edge of the bed and listened to the message.

It was from Tom Erickson, asking her to meet him for supper to discuss her future with Parks. The call didn't sound as ominous as Anne might have expected considering how she stormed out of Headquarters, and although one side of her wanted to blow off any idea of meeting with Tom, her survival instinct suggested she should at least hear him out.

But she also wanted a second opinion.

Her phone call caught John just as he was returning to the Pocahontas warden station after a day flying caribou surveys.

"Hey," she said, when he finally picked up the phone.

"Hey." John was surprised to hear from her. "How are things going in Ottawa?"

"Okay. Well, maybe not entirely okay. That's why I called. I think I just got myself fired."

CHAPTER 40

HELMUT STENGER ADJUSTED his glasses and regarded his reflection in the office tower window as the setting sun highlighted the Berlin skyline. Stooped and balding, he felt every bit of his sixty-five years and was ready for retirement.

Looking at the spectacular colour photo of Maligne Lake hanging above his desk, Helmut relished the notion of a back-country lodge in the Canadian Rockies, his dream ever since his early days climbing in Jasper. He laughed to himself at the irony of the words inscribed on the picture frame's small brass plaque:

in Wildheit ist die Erhaltung der Welt.

"In wildness is the preservation of the world." The words of Henry David Thoreau expressed an ideal Stenger bought into—but only if it didn't stand in the way of progress. Helmut Stenger was, after all, an advocate for wilderness. But it came second to his aspiration for wealth.

As the sun set on Berlin, Stenger looked at his Rolex and determined his contacts in Canada were now at work for the day. He poured himself a glass of his favourite pinot noir, a Konig spätburgunder, pressed the speed dial on his phone, and sat on the edge of his desk.

"Office of the superintendent." The woman's voice was raspy and curt.

"Ms. Winters please," said Stenger.

"May I ask who's calling?"

"Helmut Stenger."

"One moment please. I'll see if she's available."

After a short pause, another woman's voice came on the line sounding tired and distant.

"Good morning, Herr Stenger. Or should I say good afternoon?"

"Yes, yes, good afternoon, Ms. Winters. I was just checking in to see if you received your directions."

"I did." The voice sounded resigned.

"And what is the next step in your process?" said Stenger.

"Normally, we would be proceeding to a full environmental review."

"But in this case?"

"In this case, the minister is apparently waiving the requirement."

"And?"

"There is no and, Herr Stenger."

"Ms. Winters, please call me Helmut. Herr Stenger makes me feel like an old Kraut."

"Very well, Herr Stenger. But you should know that I am less than impressed with what you are trying to do here in Jasper. In fact I intend to look into the legality of this entire matter under our *National Parks Act*."

"I realize this situation puts you in an awkward position, Ms. Winters. But you must realize this direction is coming down from your own minister. You shouldn't feel compromised."

"Regardless of how you got this far with your pet project, I do have a responsibility as park superintendent. The law is the law."

"Is that a threat Ms. Winters?"

"Not at all. I merely intend to make certain the law is followed."

"I respect that."

"Do you?"

Helmut Stenger paused, irritated by the question. "Regardless, superintendent, I assure you that, if necessary, the law will be adjusted to accommodate this action. The lodge will be built. And I'm certain the new superintendent will do everything in his power to make the process as painless as possible."

There was an uneasy silence on the other end of the line.

"Whatever you say *Herr* Stenger."

Helmut Stenger could feel the vitriole in Anne Winter's tone.

"But the *new* superintendent has a lot to learn about this park and the people in this town," Anne added. "They won't be as forgiving as you might think."

"Yes, I understand there are some who might be opposed to this project. There always are. But I'm prepared to deal with them." Stenger's voice was caustic. "Good day, superintendent. And good luck with your new posting. I wish you the best. Guten tag."

Taking another sip of wine, Helmut Stenger pressed one button then another before he moved around the ornate desk and sat in the large leather chair. He took the phone off speaker and picked up the receiver.

"The minister, please," he said, pausing for a moment to scan the document in front of him. "Yes, tell him Helmut Stenger would like to speak with him on a matter of some importance."

CHAPTER 41

SNOWFLAKES FLOATED PAST the streetlights as Marion looked out her kitchen window toward the outline of Roche Bonhomme. Winter would soon be on its way and the town would be busy again with the hordes of skiers who descended on the ski hill at Marmot from Edmonton, and as far away as Europe. She liked this interim period when it seemed as if the park and its wildlife got a chance to catch their breath after the non-stop pace of summer in a national park.

After spring, fall was her favourite time of year.

Over the years, she had seen ever increasing numbers of people coming to the park, arriving earlier in the spring and staying later into the fall. The so-called 'shoulder seasons' were getting just as busy as summer, as the power of the Parks marketing machine pulled more people through the gates and more revenue into the government's coffers.

So much for wild places, she thought. *Wildlife doesn't have a chance.*

The seemingly unstoppable pace of development was a bad omen. In the end, it was their desire to try and slow things down that led Marion, Malcolm and the others to join forces and start Jasper Wild.

A reasoned voice, Marion thought, against the organized lobbyists that were constantly trying to get project after project approved. Taken individually, they didn't necessarily seem significant, but their combined impact on the park was undeniable.

It gave the expression *death by a thousand cuts* a whole new meaning.

Placing the dishes in the rack, Marion dried her hands and poured a cup of tea, then headed into the living room. Turning on the small light by the end of the sofa she settled into the matching chair and opened her laptop. Quickly scrolling through her messages, she was disappointed to see no response from her email to Environmental Justice, a pro bono organization that often worked for non-profits such as Jasper Wild.

Marion was once again hoping to enlist the help of Environmental Justice's lawyers to present Jasper Wild's arguments against the mine, and to fight the proposal of a new backcountry lodge. Although it wasn't yet public knowledge, Anne had confided in her and the others about the meeting in Ottawa with Maxime Bolduc, and the almost certain conclusion that plans for a backcountry lodge were indeed in the works.

Marion sighed heavily and was about to tackle another file when a barely audible *ping* notified her of an incoming email.

The message from Environmental Justice was flagged as urgent and had a short subject title: **Mine proponent linked to atrocities in D.R.C.**

She was about to dig into the details when she thought she heard footsteps outside. Closing her eyes and listening, Marion sensed someone was coming to her back door. She placed the laptop on the end table and got up to check.

A knock confirmed her gut instinct.

She turned on the porch light and opened the door to a smallish figure dressed in a navy blue pea jacket and woolen cap.

"Hello, Marion," said the man, his accent noticeable.

"Yes?" Marion was unable to put a name to the face.

"It is Helmut," said the man.

"Helmut?" said Marion. She rocked a little on her feet. "Helmut Stenger?"

"Ja. It is me." Stenger stood on the doorstep as light snow settled on his cap.

"I'm sorry," said Marion, momentarily taken aback then stepping to the side. "Come in, come in."

Helmut stepped inside and stamped his feet on the mat.

"Let me take your jacket." Marion reached for his coat as Helmut undid the buttons and handed it to her. As he stepped past her and slipped out of his boots, Marion shook the snow off the jacket and hung it on a hook. When she turned around to face her visitor, she hesitated for a split second, then wrapped her arms lightly around him.

"My goodness, it's been years," she offered, then stood back and looked at him, sizing him up. "I don't think I ever replied to your card after Malcolm's funeral."

"Not to worry. You know Malcolm and I didn't always see eye to eye. But I was sorry to hear the news."

Marion stalled for a moment and brought a clenched fist to her mouth. "I'm sorry," she said, as a single tear slid down her cheek. "I'm still not over it."

"I understand," Helmut said, almost apologetically. "Perhaps I should not have come."

"No, no," said Marion. "What's done is done. It's time to put the past behind. I'm too old to hold a grudge, especially one I had no part of. It's time to forgive."

"Thank you," said Helmut. He looked around the kitchen then back at Marion. "A comfortable house."

Marion smiled. "Yes. Not too large, but it worked for Malcolm and I. Now that our children are grown up and gone, it's actually a little too big to take care of. I'm thinking of downsizing." She led Helmut into the living room and offered a seat. "Would you like some tea?"

"No, no thank you. I can't stay for long." He sat at the end of the sofa next to Marion's chair.

"No?" said Marion, taking her seat. "What's your hurry?"

"I'm in town on business. I had a few minutes and really only dropped by to say hello."

"Business? What sort of business?"

"I think you know," said Helmut matter-of-factly. "The coalmine."

Marion looked at Helmut then pulled the computer onto her lap. She closed the latest email and opened her bookmark regarding the proposed mine.

"So you're part of D.M.I.?" she asked, sliding the computer around so he could see the screen.

There was a momentary pause as Helmut Stenger looked at the computer. "Yes. I own Deutsche Mining International," he said finally. "I suspect you already know everything." He smiled wryly and looked at Marion. "I recall Malcolm saying you, how do you say it, you don't miss a beat."

"I try not to," said Marion. "Especially when it comes to the park."

Helmut Stenger shook his head. "The mine has nothing to do with the park. It is outside, on provincial land."

Marion laughed. "I think you know better than that, Helmut." She continued to scan the computer. "It even says on your website 'D.M.I. has mining interests on the border of Jasper National Park in Alberta, Canada.' Why mention it if it has nothing to do with the park?"

"Merely to give potential investors a sense of where the property is." Helmut sighed and sat back in the chair. "Ever suspicious," he grunted. "You haven't changed in all these years."

"I'd hoped *you* would," said Marion, each word accentuated with a nod of her head.

Helmut Stenger stood and held his hands open, his palms facing the ceiling. "I'm sorry, Marion. I did not come here to fight with you."

"Why did you come then?" Marion remained seated.

"To pay my respects. Nothing more."

"I'm sorry," said Marion. She placed the laptop back on the end table and stood up. "I'm just tired. It seems to never end, one project after another." She walked Helmut to the porch and watched as he knelt down and pulled on his boots. He seemed such a diminutive figure, but she knew anyone presupposing him based on his size would be making a big mistake.

When he stood up she handed him his jacket.

He put it on along with the navy cap and stood for a moment, his head hung low, as if staring at the floor mat.

"Are you okay, Helmut?" There was genuine concern in Marion's voice.

"Ja." The old German looked up at her. "Yes." He hesitated. "I was just thinking, wishing really, that things would have been different between us. Malcolm and I, I mean. We were just kids, really, when we met. We shared many great moments and we became men together. We were *not* that different."

Marion thought for a moment before saying anything. She knew her husband and the man in front of her were polar opposites. At one time, perhaps, they shared some common interests. But Helmut Stenger had chosen a much different path. At any other time there would be no way Marion would give Helmut the consolation of suggesting he and Malcolm were cut from the same cloth but it wasn't worth getting into now.

Marion leaned forward and wrapped her arms around Helmut. "No you weren't," she lied.

Helmut stepped back from Marion's embrace and regarded her for a moment.

"Do you really mean that?" He grasped her hand and peered into her eyes.

Marion nodded.

"Thank you," he said. He slid his hand from Marion's and opened the door. "It was nice to see you again."

As he turned to make his way from the porch, Marion noticed Stenger's reflection in the window of the outside door. The look on his face was unsettling.

"Hmphh," she muttered under her breath as she closed the door and waited for Helmut's silhouette to disappear down the sidewalk. Turning off the outside light, she made her way back through the kitchen and settled into her chair. Pulling the computer back into her lap, she tapped the mouse pad and the screen lit up. Opening her email she returned to the most recent one from Environmental Justice.

It made for interesting, but somewhat disturbing reading as Marion read between the lines about the workings of a large multinational in countries where the bribery of officials and government corruption were almost second nature.

What she read reinforced the nagging feeling in the back of Marion's mind about the real purpose of Helmut's visit. For some reason, she felt it had more to do with his interests in the Jasper area than paying his respects to Malcolm. They had been good friends at one point, but had parted company many years ago. Why would he come back now?

Maybe he had had a change of heart, she thought, but his reflection in her door as he left suggested otherwise. She wondered what Malcolm would make of Helmut's appearance at her door.

Can a leopard change its spots?

Malcolm would have said no.

CHAPTER 42

1965

STANDING ON TOP of Pyramid Mountain, the two men pulled jackets from canvas packs and stood into the breeze, regarding the valley stretching out to the south then turning their attention north toward the town.

Below them, the Athabasca River scribed its way into the heart of Jasper National Park while its tributaries feathered off toward the south and west. Spreading out from the valley bottom, vast expanses of lodgepole pine and Douglas fir forest blanketed the benchlands and rolling terrain; the subtle changes in the many shades of green signaled the transition to subalpine forests of fir and spruce creeping skyward toward the alpine's rock and ice.

"Ahhh, wilderness," said the young German.

"Mmm," said the Englishman. "But it's changing."

"Change is natural," said the German. He pointed to several large patches of grey snags, the leftovers of past forest fires, now gradually succumbing to a succession of alder, willow and coniferous seedlings. "Those fires burnt almost fifty years ago, but the forest is taking back the land."

"Yes," said the Englishman. "Those are the inevitable changes of succession."

"And look," said the German, casting his arms about him. "So much land for wildlife."

"But it's a little misleading," said the Englishman. "Much of the park is actually rock and ice and not hospitable to most wildlife." He pointed to the valley bottom. "That," he said, "is the prime habitat, and it accounts for less than ten percent of the national park."

"Still," said his partner, "ten percent is good."

"If it were all of use to wildlife," said the Englishman. "But it isn't." He pointed to the small town of Jasper sitting above the Athabasca River. "The town, the golf course, the highway and railway, it all cuts into the best wildlife habitat in the park. And there seems to be no end to the number of developments proposed for the park."

"The price of progress," said his climbing partner.

"Maybe. But I don't think all of the trappings of progress belong in a national park. The development has to stop somewhere."

The young German laughed. "Always the same with you, Malcolm. You spend your life fighting the inevitable."

"Why is it inevitable, Helmut? I see it happening outside the park. But why should we allow it inside the park?"

"Because," Helmut Stenger put his arm around his partner, "Money talks. You should know that by now, my friend."

"True. But it shouldn't take priority in our parks."

"Hmphhh," Helmut muttered. "It does and it will. I wager it will win every time." He extended a hand.

"I'll take your wager." Malcolm Seawell gripped Helmut's hand forcefully, almost putting the two off balance.

"Whoa, whoa. Be careful what you wish for. One slip and we both could be on the wrong side of fate."

*****

Together, Malcolm Seawell and Helmut Stenger climbed peak after peak throughout the Rockies, with the German returning each year to conquer new heights. Over time, his trips became less frequent as the thin wedge of opposing viewpoints about the value of wilderness and the price of development gradually pushed their relationship to the point where their differences were greater than the interests they shared.

Malcolm's blossoming relationship with Marion Stonehouse, a comrade in arms when it came to matters of the environment, also widened the divide between Helmut and Malcolm. Though their parting wasn't a bitter one, it left little room for reconciliation as Helmut Stenger, now an aspiring mining engineer pursued more and more aggressive projects in third-world countries, taking advantage of corrupt governments and, sometimes, brutal regimes as his company stretched its tentacles around the globe.

Malcolm Seawell resented the approach and never hesitated to voice his opinion whenever his friend bragged of his conquests.

Malcolm never forgot the wager they made on the summit of Pyramid Mountain. He cringed whenever he saw another development project approved in Jasper National Park, or any national park for that matter.

Eventually Malcolm and Marion's passion for keeping Jasper as untrammelled as possible led to the creation of Jasper Wild. The pair became stalwarts of the newly founded group and almost ran it as their own before Malcolm's untimely death. Despite his years, Malcolm was a force to be reckoned with, second only to his indomitable wife, and each drew strength from their partner's conviction they were doing the right thing.

Whenever Malcolm toyed with the notion of moving to get away from the constant battles with developers and the very park managers hired to protect park interests, it was Marion who stood firm and shut the door on any notion he had that there were greener pastures elsewhere.

Still, Malcolm wasn't sure he could sustain the effort required to fight new development proposals. As he and Marion discovered ever more frequently, the battles seemed to be getting more vindictive. Nastier.

As development inside and outside of the park came under more scrutiny, there were fewer opportunities for those who wanted a piece of the pie. And the pie was getting more expensive, being offered only to those with the deepest pockets, or some political connection.

These were not people who gave up easily.

But as prospective developers pulled strings and greased palms, Malcolm and Marion's resolve tightened. Jasper Wild would not give up without a fight, no matter how hard the powers that be tried to wear them down.

Nil bastardo carborundum.

So when Malcolm became suspicious of what he'd found in the forest near Maligne Lake, he sprung into action, trying to get some answers. The notion of a long forgotten proposal to build a lodge at the lake was the first thing he thought of. But in Malcolm's mind, there was no way that was going to happen.

Over my dead body.

CHAPTER 43

ANNE WINTERS SAT motionless on the young Paint, looking across the valley at the Palisades as the horse nosed the dried grasses at its feet. Sliding off the horse and letting the reins fall to the ground, she walked around the old wooden structure, the sill logs deteriorating and the interior now filling in with buffalo berry and willow as the roof slowly caved in on itself.

She had hoped to have the site restored as a point of interest along the Overlander Trail, but that wasn't likely to happen now. It was one of those items of unfinished business that added to her regret at leaving Jasper, if that's what she chose to do.

Tom Erickson had been pretty clear about her options when they met for dinner before she left Ottawa. Although he'd been unforgiving in how he presented them to her, Anne knew Maxime Bolduc was behind it all.

The Snake hadn't got his nickname by chance.

He had a ruthless side and it showed in the offer to Anne: *take one for the team* (Tom's words) and help push the lodge through, resign, or be fired.

Tom had tried to soften the blow with a fourth option: say nothing to anyone and accept a transfer to the coast. Someone was needed to spearhead the proposal for a new national park in the Gulf Islands and it would give Anne the extra years she needed to retire with a full pension.

The last option was enticing.

But Anne couldn't get past how hurt she was. After all her years of loyal service, it had come to this.

She had so many other issues she wanted to tackle and had been methodically addressing each of her priorities, fully expecting to see them all through before she retired.

Jasper would have been a good place to end her career. The West coast would be good as well. But giving in would have made her no different than others who seemed to compromise their values to secure their position in the outfit. Could she live with herself if she did that?

During her career, Anne had been blessed with working with a diversity of people who all shared a commitment to the ideas behind parks. But that was changing and she was disappointed with the number of new hires, especially in middle management positions, that only seemed to want to get to the next level in the pecking order. Many came from outside the organization and had little interest in the types of activities she'd come to take for granted: hiking, backcountry skiing, camping.

Still she was encouraged when some of them embraced the chance to try new things and in doing so, became some of her staunchest allies. They'd seen the pressures building outside of parks and other protected areas and knew it was inevitable these same pressures could wreak havoc if they were allowed inside.

It gave her hope for the future that there were young people willing to fight for the same things she was fighting for, people like Megan Weaver, Ben Matthews and Kate Jones.

But this latest battle was taking its toll.

Anne felt she'd lost sway with the folks above her like Tom Erickson, while others, like Jeremy, were being let go. The only thing Anne could put her finger on was the change in government, even though in the past it seemed as if what party was in power made little difference to how well parks fared.

But now it seemed to relate more to an overarching sense that parks were a luxury the country could no longer afford, a lower priority for funding, which was leading to the gradual deterioration of the infrastructure meant to serve the people who visited the parks. And yet, for those who had money and influence, apparently you could get your own lodge built in the park.

Or at least that's what Marion was suggesting and she seemed to have proof.

For her own part, Anne had more or less written off Marion's conspiracy theories until Marion told her the story about the visit from Helmut Stenger. Anne had done a double take when Marion mentioned his name and said she was certain there was more to the visit than Helmut suggested.

Anne had learned not to question Marion's intuition. If Marion thought there was more to Stenger's interests in the park than he was letting on, she was probably right.

So she decided to go with her own gut and take a chance. *It might seal my fate,* she thought. *But if they're going to move me, I'm not going without a fight.*

Anne was about to turn back toward the barn just as John Haffcut emerged into the clearing riding his favourite mare.

"Jimmy said I'd find you here," he said as his horse sidled up alongside Anne's.

Leaning slightly the two kissed.

"Mmmm," Anne murmured. "Better not let anyone see that."

"Screw them," said John. He looked at her and frowned. "You okay?"

Anne nodded but said nothing.

"You sure?" He reached for her hand on the saddle horn and held it in his own, running his fingers along her palm.

"It's going to be tough to leave."

"Then stay. Get them to give you some kind of assignment. They do it for everyone else they want to keep around."

"Exactly," said Anne. "But they don't want to keep me around. They know my thoughts about development and some of the other plans they have for this park. And to try and slide something through like this, how did they think I'd react?" She took a deep breath. "So moving me gets me out of the picture. Removes a potential thorn from their side."

"There are other thorns," said John.

Anne gripped his hand tightly. "Yes there are and I love you for it, but …"

"But nothing," said John. "We can fight this."

Anne laughed half-heartedly.

"I'm serious," said John. "You and I both know their tactics. They intimidate and threaten to fire you. They do whatever it takes. And if we let them do it, they'll do it again and again."

"But you know my options?"

"I do. But if we let them divide and conquer us, these parks are lost." John pressed Anne's hand into his own.

"Who's the 'we'?" said Anne.

"You, me, Megan, Ben and Kate. I'm sure Lou would be willing to dig in his heels. Even Jimmy Rand."

"And Marion too, I assume." Anne chuckled. "I can only imagine Vincent-Blais's reaction when Marion sets into him. I wish I could be a fly on the wall."

John laughed. "He won't know whether to shit or go blind. But actually I don't think we should involve her anymore than we have to."

"Why would you say that?"

"Because we do it all the time. For years we've let Marion, Malcolm and Jasper Wild fight our battles. It's not fair. We're the ones taxpayers pay to fight for their parks and we shouldn't offload our responsibilities onto people like Marion."

"But Jasper Wild has the ability to make connections we can't. You know we can't go to Environmental Justice or anyone like that as government employees."

"Agreed," said John. "I didn't say we didn't need allies like Marion and the others. But this is our battle."

"So we put our jobs on the line?"

"They can't fire us all," said John

"Can't they, John? Things are different this time. There's something really disturbing about this notion of a backcountry lodge. None of the people I know in Ottawa seem to be able to do anything about it and a few of them have also been told to watch what they say. Jeremy Large has even been put out to pasture and I'm sure it's over this."

"Jeremy Large? I thought he wouldn't say shit if his mouth was full of it."

"That's more than a little unfair," said Anne. "He's politically savvy and knows how to work the system. His heart is definitely in the right place. I don't know where Parks would be if he hadn't been there to ride shotgun on a bunch of development proposals over the years."

"Yeah, to be fair, I'd heard the same thing from some of the folks across the country. He took some risks."

"More than a few," said Anne. "He was involved in a lot more than you'd know about. But he worked behind the scenes. He could be buddy-buddy with his political masters, but that doesn't mean he always saw eye to eye with them. This time around though, Maxime had it in for him. He was literally told to grab his stuff from his office and was escorted out of the building."

"Unbelievable," said John.

"There's something really shady about it but I haven't spoken to him yet so I only know what others are saying."

"And you think it's related to what's happening here in Jasper?"

"Not just Jasper. There are plans for a number of the parks. But obviously Jasper is what I'm most concerned about. Anyone who stands in the way might be at risk. And that includes Marion."

"Marion?" said John. "Seriously, what are some high-priced government bureaucrats going to do to with someone like Marion?"

"That's what worries me, John. I don't know. I don't like to think about it, but I can't seem to get it out of my head. And the more I learn about Helmut Stenger and this lodge proposal, the more I wonder about what really happened to Malcolm Seawell."

"What do you mean?"

"He was an accomplished climber, John."

"But he was getting close to seventy. He wasn't a kid."

"The autopsy showed he didn't have a heart attack or any other health issue that might have caused him to fall. With everything we're learning, Marion must be worried sick."

"Are we talking about the same Marion Seawell?" John asked with raised eyebrows.

Anne smiled. "You're right. She's the toughest person I know. Still I worry about her."

"If what you're suggesting is true," said John, "it's the people behind all this who'd better be worried."

CHAPTER 44

IT WAS LATE in the afternoon when Anne returned to the administration building, walking in as many were heading home for the day. As she made her way to the top floor and walked down the long hallway to her office, she was surprised to see Konrad Vincent-Blais heading in with an armload of files.

Following him, she closed the door quietly before he noticed her. "Well, well," she said, startling Konrad. "What exactly are you up to?"

Konrad turned around to face her. "Moving my things in."

"I can see that," said Anne. "But you know I haven't even made my decision yet."

"It's been made for you," said Konrad, placing the files on Anne's desk.

"You're lying," she said, although she suspected he wasn't.

"You've been given your options," said Konrad.

"But not much time to think about them."

"Tom Erickson's bought you some."

"Time, you mean?" Anne didn't know whether to believe Konrad or not.

"You're officially out of the superintendent's position," Konrad explained, "but Tom got Maxime to agree with giving you a few days to make up your mind about going to the coast, *or not*. A leave of absence if you will."

Anne was flabbergasted. "My chair isn't even cold and you're already moving in. That doesn't look suspicious at all, Konrad."

"Yes, well, there's no time like the present is there?"

"Apparently not," said Anne. She walked around her desk and sat down in the large leather chair. "Do you mind giving me a chance to clean out my things before you take over this space."

Konrad shrugged. "Fine. I can do it tomorrow, after you've left."

Stung by the tone of his voice, Anne sat upright as Konrad was about to open the door and leave.

"Konrad," she said curtly.

"Yes?" Konrad looked up sharply, as if responding to a command.

"What's your deal anyway? These parks are about protecting wild species like grizzlies and caribou and giving them the space they need to survive. Wild space, wilderness."

"Ah yes, the preservationist argument," said Konrad. "Wilderness, lock it up and throw away the key."

"I didn't say that," said Anne, trying to figure out what made Konrad tick. "There's lots of room here for people. God knows we get millions of visitors to the mountain national parks every year. We're hardly locking the parks up. But bears and other species need their space. They epitomize everything we stand for."

"What you stand for, perhaps," said Konrad. He opened the door to walk out.

"No, when I say 'we,' I mean what these parks stand for. And the public won't stand for anything less. I think you found that out in Wood Buffalo."

Anne's words hit the mark. Konrad turned back to face her, glaring. "We'll see about that when you're gone."

Anne smiled wryly. "I know that's what you're waiting for. But I haven't left yet. And even if I do, others will be keeping an eye on things."

Konrad smirked. "Others? Hmphh, should I be concerned?"

Anne shook her head and stared at Konrad. "Concerned? I don't know what you or Tom or Maxime have up your sleeves, but you should be careful. You might be skating on thin ice."

"Is that a threat?"

"You tell me. I'm not sure what's up with this supposed mine proposal, but if it's all a ruse for Helmut Stenger to get what he really wants, then all hell will break loose around here. You'd better be ready to deal with it."

Konrad smiled. "I'll deal with whatever I have to deal with," he said as he started out the door. He paused and stared at Anne. "And *whoever.*"

CHAPTER 45

THE EVENING GET-TOGETHER at Megan's had the feel of a clandestine gathering as John poured everyone a round of whiskey and made them swear to secrecy; the glint in his eye was the only hint he was having some fun with the moment.

"What exactly are we supposed to keep secret?" said Megan, wary of John's antics.

"If I tell you …"

"You'd have to kill me, yes I understand that, John." Megan shook her head and sighed.

John's mischievous smile disappeared and his tone hardened. "Alright, Megs," he said, needling her with the nickname he knew she despised, "I was just trying to bring some levity to the situation." He scratched his forehead and looked around the table at Ben, Kate and Lou just as Jimmy Rand walked in the door.

"Evenin', Jimmy." John motioned toward an empty chair, then turned to the rest of the group. "I guess now we're just waiting for Anne."

"What's up?" Jimmy asked, taking a seat as John poured him a shot of whiskey.

"Just drink that first," said John. "Your drink is an oath of secrecy."

"Sounds serious," Jimmy said. He tossed back the drink and pushed his glass toward John for a refill.

When Anne walked in, John was about to repeat the ritual but Lou intervened.

"For Christ's sake, John, give it a break before we're drunk and let's get on with whatever you wanted us here for. Besides, I'm starving." Lou looked around the table at the questioning stares. "Megan said there was going to be a barbeque so I didn't eat supper."

"It was the only way I could be sure he'd come," said Megan. She laughed as Lou pretended to hit her.

As Anne sat down, a feeling of seriousness settled over the room

"Someone shoot your dog?" said Lou, jokingly.

John and Anne shared a glance.

"What's up, Anne?" said John, sensing something wasn't right.

"I've been removed from the superintendent's position, effective immediately."

"What the ...?" Lou began. "What are you talking about Anne?"

"Well, I had an inkling it was imminent when I left Ottawa." Anne explained her latest trip to Ottawa and the options she'd been presented with. "And now, Konrad Vincent-Blais is your new boss," she finished.

"Unbelievable," said Lou.

"Is that why we're here?" said Jimmy, slightly stunned like the others.

"Well, it's related," said John. He turned to Anne. "Although I didn't realize it was quite so imminent?"

"Neither did I," she said.

John clasped his hands and cracked his knuckles. "Okay, here's what I propose. We can accept this, like so many times in the past ..."

"Or what?" said Lou. "Fight it?" He turned to Anne. "The hand of cards you've been dealt, just sucks, that's for sure. But what do you think you'll end up doing?"

"I don't know," said Anne. "If I were to leave, I'd feel like I was letting everyone down."

Lou waved off the comment. "Don't worry about the rest of us. You're a few years away from retirement and they've got you over a barrel. You can't throw away your career for something we aren't even sure is in the works."

"Oh, there's something up," said Anne. "On the surface they're making it look like Helmut Stenger is after a coalmine, but his real objective is a backcountry lodge in the park. Maybe he wants both. But I believe it's the lodge he's really after. And he's very connected if he can force the termination of a park superintendent."

"And it seems he'll stoop pretty low if people like Zane Ritter are somehow involved."

"Seems so unlikely," said Megan, "but there's got to be a connection. I mean, why would Marion have had a run-in with him in the Maligne Valley and then Kate and I encounter him with a couple of German outfitters down around the proposed mine area?"

"You're right," said John. "A German mining company, Ritter putting in survey posts for them, a similar survey stake found in the Maligne and Marion running into Ritter there as well, and you two meeting Ritter with two Germans in Whitehorse Creek. There's just too much for any of this to be coincidence."

"There's also the info Kallie dug up about Mountain Park Design," said Ben, explaining what Kallie had found out in Calgary about the design firm and the suggestion that information about the lodge was being carefully managed and would be fed to the public gradually to soften the notion of a lodge being built in a designated wilderness area.

"It's classic bait and switch," said Anne. "I told Maxime Bolduc as much. God, he and Tom Erickson couldn't even keep their own stories straight." She paused. "He still insists the mine is the focus, but from everything we're learning that doesn't seem to be the case. The mine is just a distraction."

"There's also Marion's revelation that she knows Helmut Stenger," said Megan.

"And what happened to Malcolm Seawell," said Anne.

"Do you really think that's related?" said Lou, scratching his head. He turned to Jimmy Rand. "Jimmy, you found Malcolm's body. The RCMP investigated it, but in the end, the coroner ruled the death accidental. Isn't that what you thought as well?"

"Well, yeah, I guess," said Jimmy. "I mean I found Malcolm lying in the bottom of that slot canyon, and it looked like he fell from pretty high up. But truthfully, how would anyone know if there had been someone on top of that cliff who might have helped make it happen."

"If that was the case," said Lou, "we're talking murder." He looked around the table. "Would someone really go to that extent to get a lodge built in the park?"

"Maybe not," said Anne. "But even so, everything else still points an incriminating finger at Helmut Stenger. I'm convinced it's all related to him trying to get what he wants."

There was a moment of silence as everyone pondered the situation.

"So what we do?" Lou asked. "I presume that's why we're here, to figure out next steps?" There was silence around the table as everyone looked at each other. "And I probably don't need to remind you," Lou continued, "if we take this matter into our own hands, we all might be facing the same 'option' Anne is facing." He stopped for a second. "Actually, we probably wouldn't have any options. We'd all be fired."

"What are you proposing?" said Ben.

"Nothing. I'm just stating a fact."

"But there has to be a way to fight this," said John. "We can't just throw in the towel."

"Can't we?" said Lou. "It seems we've done it before."

"C'mon, Lou. You know this is bullshit." John was getting angrier by the minute.

"I agree it's bullshit, but what are you proposing we do about it?"

"Just a second," said Kate. "Let's think about how we got to this point. Maxime Bolduc is intimidating Anne to force this lodge proposal through. And Konrad will use the same tactics, if history is any indication."

"And we all know none of this is above board," said Ben. "We saw similar tactics used in Wood Buffalo."

"So what?" said John.

"The so what," said Ben, "is that we can approach this in the same way we had to deal with things up North. We need to expose what's happening."

"To the media?" said Lou. "That'll bring a whole heap of shit down on us that you won't be able to deflect like you did in Wood Buffalo. Jasper isn't a northern park that gets a couple thousand visitors a year. This place is big business and the stakes for doing something like that here are whole lot higher. You might stop a lodge, for now, but you'd be gone, we'd all be gone, and before you know it, there'd be another lodge proposed. And built, if that's what the powers that be decreed."

"Are you saying do nothing?" said John. "After what they're doing to Anne?"

"I'm not saying that, John." Lou directed his next comment to Anne. "I'm just saying we think about the consequences of whatever we do."

"What *do* you think we should do?" Anne asked.

"I don't think we need to go to the media," said Lou. He turned to Ben. "You might want to talk to your friend Kallie and tell her to keep things to herself. At least for now." Turning back to the group he added, "And someone needs to talk to Marion to make sure she doesn't go to the media either. Actually, when it comes to Marion, we should keep her out of this altogether. We don't want to see her get hurt."

"I'll speak with her," said Megan.

"I'll come with you," said Anne.

"If we've got it right," Lou continued, "and if all the pieces line up like we think, we need to let Maxime Bolduc know we can expose this whole thing and probably expose his political masters as well. And *if*, and it may be a big if, but if Malcolm Seawell's death is tied to any of this, no director-general, government minister or anyone else would survive the kind of damage a story like that could do.

"And if Malcolm's death wasn't accidental," Lou continued, "we also know we're dealing with people who will stop at nothing to get their way."

"Marion's friends from Germany did say to be careful," said Kate.

There was a moment of quiet reflection around the room.

"What do you suggest we do?" said Jimmy.

"Well, first we need to know if we're all in?" said Lou. "If someone has reservations, I don't want them to feel like they have to get involved with this."

"Fair point," said John. He poured himself a shot of whiskey and looked around the table. As everyone pushed their glass forward, he poured them a shot.

No one spoke, but everyone raised their glass. "To whatever comes next," John said.

CHAPTER 46

KONRAD WAS CAUGHT off guard by the impromptu gathering in his new office, but he was unable to do anything before Jasper's chief park warden barred the door, standing in front of it in a way that implied Konrad wouldn't be able to leave without an altercation.

"I thought you should meet some of *the others* I was referring to." Anne leaned over the large desk as Megan, John, Ben and Kate stood in a semicircle behind her. "And there are more."

"Am I supposed to be intimidated?" Konrad glared at the group, focusing on Ben and Kate. "Matthews, Jones, here in Jasper you won't get away with the types of things you did in Wood Buffalo."

"So we've been told," said Ben. He looked around at Lou, who had joined the group. "But I would expect you won't either," he added under his breath.

"That's water under the bridge," said Anne. "Let bygones be bygones. We're here to give you an option before things become unstoppable."

Konrad started to interject, but Anne cut him off. "Hear us out. We'll only say this once."

Konrad sat back in the large leather chair with an air of smugness. "Go on."

"Here's what we know," said Anne, as she began to outline most, but not all, of the information the group had acquired, each revelation making Konrad sit up a little straighter and pay more attention to Jasper's former superintendent.

When she finished, Konrad sat forward, his elbows on the desk, his hands forming a steeple. "What am I supposed to say to that, Ms. Winters? It all sounds so preposterous."

"Does it?"

"Yes, and I don't have any more time to chase rumours than you did. Look at what that got you. My focus is the proposed mine along the park's border. That's the direction I was given and that's what I intend to do. And if I understand correctly," Konrad looked at everyone in the group, "that's the project you are all supposed to be working on."

Konrad nodded to Ben and Kate. "Matthews, Jones, isn't that what you were brought here specifically to deal with? And Chief," he added, turning to Lou, "isn't that your direction as well. My suggestion, unless all of you want to be disciplined for insubordination, is to get on with the jobs you were asked to do."

Lou scoffed at the last comment. "You plan on firing all of us, Konrad?"

"If necessary." He turned his attention to Megan. "I'm looking at some people that have very tenuous positions to start with. At the bottom of the ladder, you might say."

"You've got a lot to learn, son," said Lou. "And you'd probably have learnt it if *you* started at the bottom of the ladder. But as it is, you were catapulted to the top." Lou paused. "We aren't so stupid as to come here without prior knowledge of some other bits of this puzzle that could knock you off your high horse if they came to light. If they do, they might also take down some of your friends in high places."

"Is that a threat?"

"Not intended to be," said Lou. "We came here to offer you an out before this thing takes on a life of its own. If you don't at least consider it, you're kissing your ass goodbye. You might want to smarten up and listen."

"I've listened and I've heard all I need to hear. Now if you'll excuse me, I have work to do. I know you do as well."

Lou looked to Anne and motioned toward the door. Without another word, the group left Konrad's office and shut the door behind them.

Anne looked at Lou as they walked down the hallway. "Do you think he'll reconsider?"

"Nah," said Lou. "But at least you gave him a chance. In the end we'll be able to say 'told you so.'"

CHAPTER 47

FIGHT FIRE WITH fire, Konrad thought ... *two can play that game ... and if they think I'm the weak link in the chain, they better think again.*

Konrad didn't wait long to contact the two men Helmut Stenger had hired to do his bidding. Stenger had avoided calling the men his operatives, but sitting across from them in the small nondescript café on the outskirts of Hinton, Konrad now understood that's essentially what they were.

The largest, Gunter, was obviously ex-military based on his tattoos, while Jakob, who also seemed at ease with his partner's small talk about hunting all manner of wildlife, clearly had a similar fascination with guns and other weapons. When they asked Konrad what his outdoor interests were, he merely waved off the question and focused on some notes he had taken during his last talk with Helmut Stenger.

The German businessman had stressed he could not attend the gathering, impressing upon Konrad the need to minimize contact between himself and the other parties involved, but he wanted Konrad to make contact with his men in the event he required their services at some point in the future.

Based on the two urgent calls he got this morning from Maxime Bolduc and Stenger, Konrad was certain things were transpiring faster than anyone had anticipated. He was also certain he'd need the services of Stenger's men sooner rather than later.

The director-general had apparently been the recipient of a call from Anne Winters who, in so many words, threatened to expose the plan to build a backcountry lodge in the Maligne Valley, which wasn't news to Konrad after his confrontation with Anne and her loyal troupe of wardens. Bolduc intimated that Anne wasn't specific on details, but seemed to be toying with the notion of leaving Parks. If she did, Bolduc knew she had enough information to cause trouble. More than he originally thought, in fact, although he didn't know how she was getting her information.

The second call from Helmut Stenger amplified the concern.

Helmut was convinced Marion Seawell and her organization would get in the way of their plans and needed to be watched. He knew she'd been thoroughly researching his company and suspected she was also getting information from his nemesis in Germany, a conservation organization that had caused him no end of headaches with his mining ventures in Africa. Helmut had also been informed by Arnold Grimes that Marion was in contact with Environmental Justice, who were now making their own inquiries with Arnold's department about D.M.I.'s interests near Jasper.

The final straw was Stenger's comment about a freelance journalist, Kalina Strong, who was digging into details about the lodge with the design company Stenger had hired in Calgary to stickhandle the project through the various approval and regulatory processes. The mention of the young woman's name brought back a lot of memories about the Wood Buffalo fiasco, none of them good.

"You know her?" Helmut had asked.

"Only peripherally," said Konrad. He went on to explain how they had never met, but she and two park wardens had helped scuttle his plans in Wood Buffalo. When he told Stenger those same two park wardens were now in Jasper, Helmut's tone changed.

"I don't like this," said the German businessman. "We might need to adjust our tactics slightly. I propose increasing the activity along Jasper's eastern boundary. We need to maintain people's focus on the mine and divert attention away from any talk of a proposed lodge in the park."

"I don't know if that's the best tactic," said Konrad. "With everything they know about your proposal for the Maligne, we might have to deal with it instead."

"And do what?" Stenger asked.

"I'm not sure yet," said Konrad, acutely aware of the spot he was in, between his own boss and Stenger on one side and Anne Winters and her supporters on the other. As well as anyone, he understood the political sensitivity of what they were trying to accomplish, but he was also acutely aware of the need to stay at arm's length from Helmut's hired guns—unless it was absolutely necessary to make use of their services. Now in the superintendent's position, he didn't want to take the chance of compromising what he was working toward.

As Konrad sat thinking about everything he'd been told that morning, he wondered how Helmut's men might help him. Even Stenger had indicated that these two were not people he had first-hand experience with, but rather came recommended by a friend. Konrad's concern heightened when the two Germans informed him of the local they'd also hired to assist them. Although he didn't say anything, Konrad didn't like loose ends, or loose cannons. The more people in the mix, the greater the chance there was of something running afoul of their plans.

"Here is he now," said Jakob, as Zane Ritter walked in the door. He waved Ritter over to the corner table, motioned for him to sit down, and introduced Vincent-Blais.

Zane Ritter nodded and shook hands, then turned to the Germans. "What's up?" he said as he pulled out a chair and sat down.

"We just wanted you to be aware that Konrad is now involved," said Gunter.

"And he may have some work for you," said Jakob. "In Jasper."

"I didn't think there was much to do there," said Ritter. "Other than showing that guy from Calgary the location in the Maligne Valley."

"Konrad may have other things he needs dealt with. Some people who might not see things the same way as we do."

Ritter chuckled. "You must be talking about the freakin' park wardens we met." He glanced at both men but they avoided the comment. "Well don't worry about them. They're the least of our worries."

"What do you mean, 'park wardens you met'?" said Konrad.

"It was nothing," said Gunter.

"Just a couple of women wardens we met on a hunting trip around the mine," said Ritter. "A freakin' Indian and her blonde friend." He laughed. "I nearly scared the shit out of the blonde."

"A scouting trip," said Gunter. "Nothing more." He stared at Ritter and shook his head then turned back to Konrad. "Our main business is professional outfitting in British Columbia. Ritter has a background in outfitting around here. Jakob and I thought we would take advantage of our time in this part of Alberta to scope out future opportunities for our clients." He shrugged. "It's nothing to concern yourself with." Gunter looked at Ritter again. "The encounter with the wardens was routine. They were just checking permits. Nothing more."

"Whatever," said Ritter. "But if that's the type of people Konrad here is talking about, deal me in. I'd love nothing better than to give those fish cops what for. Hell, I'd even pop that little bear they're all so worked up over."

"You mean the grizzly that lives out around the mines?" said Konrad

"Yes," said Gunter, interjecting himself between Konrad and Ritter. "She's getting a lot of attention. But she's not our concern."

Ritter snickered. "Right. I'll concern myself with her if I feel like it. And screw the mines."

Konrad ignored Ritter's comment and turned back to Gunter. "When it comes to dealing with opposition to the mine, or whatever else your boss wants you to work on," said Konrad, looking around the café, "how far does he want you to go?"

Gunter hesitated.

"Or maybe I should ask how far you're willing to go?"

Gunter's expression turned serious.

"As far as we have to go to get the job done," he said as Zane Ritter sat grinning ear to ear.

"What about you?" Konrad asked Ritter, losing patience with the man.

"What they said," said Zane.

Konrad sat silently forming his own opinion as the Germans and Ritter talked around the idea of intimidating anyone who might be seen as a concern.

So this is how Stenger works, he thought as he watched the back and forth between the men.

His first impression was that he didn't care for the Germans, and cared even less for Ritter. He was concerned too many people were getting involved. Still, as much as Konrad preferred to do things alone, the trio might be useful if things got down and dirty. Ritter seemed capable of just about any kind of dirty work he could think of; his dislike of park wardens was a feeling Konrad shared. But Ritter's bragging about his antics suggested he was already well known to the authorities, a risk Konrad assumed Helmut understood, if Helmut even knew Gunter and Jakob had hired Ritter.

The Germans, on the other hand, seemed professional and more discreet. As long as they didn't draw attention to themselves, they would probably remain unknown entities and be valuable assets.

"Well, we're probably done here," said Konrad, motioning to Ritter. "If I need your help, I'll be in touch."

"Sure, whatever you say." Zane Ritter turned his attention to Jakob and Gunter. "I guess I'll see you two later if you want to do anymore scouting." Leaning on the table he turned back to Konrad. "If you want me to take care of your people problems or anything else, these guys know how to get a hold of me."

As they watched Ritter leave, Konrad looked at Gunter. "Does Stenger know you hired him?"

"He knows we hired a local outfitter to help us, but that's all. He doesn't need to know."

"Probably good that he doesn't find out," said Konrad. "He runs a pretty professional operation. He wouldn't want Ritter to screw it up. As for yourselves, it's probably best that you don't hang around with him anymore than you have to. Stenger wouldn't want you to draw any more attention to yourselves than necessary."

"We understand that," Gunter said, seeming to take offence to the comment.

Getting up from the table he motioned to Jakob. "Let us know if you need help," Gunter said to Konrad. "In the meantime, Stenger has given us leeway to do what we need to do regarding the mine. We know our jobs." Before he and Jakob walked away, Gunter tossed a business card on the table. "Call this number if you want to get in touch."

As they headed for the door, Konrad hung back to gauge whether or not they'd attracted any attention from the few people sitting around the café. Satisfied they hadn't, he nodded to the waitress and made his way to the door. He could see himself making use of Gunter and his partner as long as they kept to the script and followed Stenger's direction. He hoped their extracurricular activities with Ritter didn't change that.

CHAPTER 48

MARION FOUND HER way to the Parks administration building a few days after Anne vacated her office, quite out of sorts that Anne Winters had apparently lost her position. The visit from Megan and Anne did not go over well with her, especially their strong suggestion that Marion let them deal with whatever Maxime Bolduc and the others in Ottawa were scheming about.

"With all due respect, Anne," she'd said, "if Jasper Wild left all the serious issues to Parks management, there'd be fast food restaurants and rubber tomahawk shops from one end of town to the other. Jasper would be just like Banff. Besides," she added, "this is personal. My dislike of Maxime Bolduc and his cronies predates you and many of your staff. And I intend to let this new fellow, Konrad whatever his name is, have a piece of my mind."

Despite their best efforts, Megan and Anne made no headway with their older friend and left Marion with a simple request: at the first sign of trouble, let them know so they could help.

"Who are you?" Konrad asked Marion, who stood in front of his desk demanding his attention.

"I could ask you the same thing." Marion glared at Konrad.

"If you don't mind, I have work to do." Konrad tried to hasten Marion's exit, but she was unmoved and instead, sat down in the chair next to the large desk.

"So do I," she replied.

"What are you doing?" said Konrad.

"I'm going to brief you on issues the group I represent are monitoring. Jasper Wild is the name of the group, in case you didn't know."

"Yes, I've heard of you and your group, but I don't have time for this now."

"Is that so?" Marion raised an eyebrow at Konrad and settled further into her seat. She leafed through a bundle of papers and slid a single page across the desk.

"What is this, exactly?" said Konrad, scanning the document.

"Our list," Marion said emphatically.

"And what do you expect me to do with it?" said Konrad.

"Be prepared to address these issues when we bring them to your attention," said Marion. "That's all."

"Is this a list of all of the development proposals the park is considering?"

"Yes," said Marion. "More or less. An easy way to shorten it would be to just say no to some of them."

Konrad shook his head. "I don't have time for this." He got up and motioned to the door. "Sorry, Mrs. ...?

"Seawell, Marion Seawell."

"Well Mrs. Seawell, if you'll excuse me, I have important work to do."

"None as important as the items on that list."

"Really?" Konrad challenged.

"Really," said Marion. "By the way, how long have you worked for national parks? You seem much too young be to a park.superintendent."

Konrad waved off the comment.

"Have you even read the park management plan?" Marion demanded. "Everything on that list relates to the current management plan, which our group provided input on. If it's not in the plan, it shouldn't be taking any of your time away from what *is* in the plan. And I can assure you, backcountry lodges *are not* in the plan. Even *modest improvements* to existing operations are not in the plan." Marion looked proud of herself. "There, I wanted to get that in before you used it on me. Parks may think they can pull one over on us with a modest proposal, but we all know those soon turn into something much bigger, don't we?"

Konrad avoided commenting, but Marion knew she'd struck a nerve as his face reddened.

"Proponents use that strategy all the time," Marion continued. "Put forward something small with a local operator behind it. We protest, but not vigorously because we know the operator and they live in our community. A project gets approved, and the next thing we find out is the project has morphed into something bigger, a larger development. Then we learn our local operator has cashed out and a bigger company, often one with international interests, now owns the project. And their vision is nothing like the one presented in the proposal that was approved by Parks management."

Marion stared at Konrad. "Bait and switch is the oldest trick in the book."

"Mrs. Seawell, I'll ask you one more time to leave," he said, his voice rising.

"Or else?" Marion was steadfast.

Konrad opened the door to his office. "Leave."

Marion embedded herself in the chair. "Not until I get some answers. What do you know about this lodge that's being proposed for the Maligne Valley?"

Konrad walked back to Marion and took hold of her arm. "Mrs. Seawell, get out."

Marion resisted. "You need to consider that list."

Get out," Konrad shouted, startling Marion who sat stoically in the chair and catching the attention of Megan Weaver, who was walking past the superintendent's office.

"Everything okay in here?" Megan poked her head in the doorway and saw Marion.

"Who are you again?" said Konrad, forcefully.

"Megan Weaver. A park warden."

"Well, would you kindly escort this woman out of my office?"

As he spoke, Marion got up and made her way to the door with Konrad at her heels.

"I can," said Megan, reaching for Marion's arm, "but if you don't mind me saying, you should be more respectful. Marion's one of the park's biggest supporters."

"I don't care who *she* is. *I'm* the new superintendent. *And* your boss."

Megan was unperturbed. "Still, you should be more respectful. Anne Winters would never have dealt with anyone like that."

"Just get out," Konrad yelled. He reached behind Marion and shoved her through the doorway and into Megan, quickly slamming the door.

Stumbling backward, Megan held on tightly to Marion as the pair regained their balance. "Unbelievable," Megan said as she straightened out her clothes. "Are you okay?"

Marion nodded. "Hmphh, it will take more than some junior bureaucrat on an ego trip to knock me down."

CHAPTER 49

CONVINCED ANNE WINTERS had sicced Marion Seawell on him, Konrad told his executive assistant Anne was not to be allowed inside her former office under any circumstance. He didn't understand why Tom Erickson had given Anne more time to make a decision regarding her future, but he assumed Tom and Maxime Bolduc were concerned she could scuttle Stenger's lodge. Konrad knew the political fallout could take them down as well.

As for Marion Seawell, she was simply banned from the park's administration building. Konrad wanted to keep her as far from the heart of the park's decision-making as possible.

Konrad had other ideas for her bleeding-heart friend, Megan Weaver, especially once he realized she was the daughter of Gordie Weaver in Wood Buffalo National Park. Konrad figured she had probably played a role in the bison fiasco, like her father did, and was partly responsible for him being demoted and banished to Inuvik.

They're all cut from the same cloth: Marion Seawell, Megan Weaver, Kate Jones and Ben Matthews. Can't forget Jones and Matthews.

He had other plans for Kate Jones and Ben Matthews and was determined to show them who was boss. But right now his main concern was to stop anyone who might prevent him from accomplishing the assignment he'd been given by Maxime Bolduc. The director-general was adamant Konrad had to do whatever was necessary to prevent Anne and the others from throwing Stenger's project off the rails.

"You have my full support," said Bolduc. "Tom will deal with Anne, but you must deal with any other opposition at the park. Use Stenger's people if you have to. Do whatever it takes."

Konrad appreciated that he had access to Gunter and Jakob, even Ritter if necessary, but he was keen to prove to Maxime Bolduc and others that he didn't really need the Germans, or Ritter for that matter. In a way, he also had to prove it to himself that he was up to the task.

But first things first, he needed to learn more about the park. Even his executive assistant, who seemed nonchalant about the goings-on with Anne Winters and showed no outward malice toward Konrad, suggested he would need to get out and explore the park if he was going to deal with the myriad issues facing a park superintendent.

To do that, Konrad knew he needed at least one ally in the park, someone to show him around, in the Maligne Valley especially. Almost as if she was reading his mind, his executive assistant suggested the Maligne warden, Jimmy Rand, who knew the park better than anyone and obviously knew the Maligne like the back of his hand.

Konrad was hesitant about trusting his orientation to Jasper to a park warden, but at least Jimmy Rand had not been part of the gang of six who stormed his office. He also found out from his assistant that Jimmy was close to retirement, so Konrad pegged him as someone who wouldn't want to do anything that would jeopardize his last year or two of work.

Konrad's assistant arranged the time and the following morning Jimmy Rand met Jasper's new superintendent at the administration building.

"Anything in particular you want to see?" Jimmy asked as they drove out of town, pushing one knee against the steering wheel to keep the truck on the road while he pulled a tin of tobacco from his jacket pocket and popped some in his mouth.

"Well, you're the Maligne warden," said Konrad. "Maybe we should start there."

"Fine with me," said Jimmy, smiling. He turned onto the highway then took the exit for the Maligne Valley. "If you don't mind, I've got to make a quick stop at the horse range to check on Sarge. My horse," Jimmy added in response to Konrad's quizzical look. "Then we can drive to Maligne Lake."

As they pulled into the horse range, Jimmy parked the warden truck next to a large round bale sitting by the barn and jumped out. "Wait here, I'll be back in a minute." When he returned he tried to open the truck door to get in then looked across at Konrad, talking through the window. "Musta locked it by mistake," he called out.

Konrad moved across the bench seat and unlocked the door, surprised to hear his own door open as Jimmy jumped in. Before he could say anything, Konrad felt himself shoved into the middle of the seat as Ben Matthews pushed into the truck cab next to him.

"What the …?" Konrad blurted.

"We need to get this over with," said Ben, pushing his body tight against Konrad to prevent him from trying to escape, then slamming the passenger door shut.

"Matthews, you'll regret this," Konrad said, shaking with rage. "And you too," he added, turning to Jimmy.

Jimmy raised both hands in the air as Ben explained, "He has nothing to do with this Konrad, but I knew you'd never come out with me on your own. Jimmy is just trying to mediate things, if you know what I mean." Ben motioned for Jimmy to drive.

"Where are you taking me?" Konrad said as he sat wedged between the two park wardens.

"Where you wanted to go," said Ben. "Don't worry. We're not going to hurt you."

"Then what are you up to, Matthews?"

"I know we got off on the wrong foot in Wood Buffalo and wanted to make amends."

"Hmphh, right."

"And I know you weren't behind all of the shenanigans that happened up North, but I also know you paid a bit of a price. I don't want you to make the same mistakes here."

Konrad started to protest but Ben pushed into him a little harder. "Just be quiet and listen. When I'm done, Jimmy will drop me off and you two can continue the tour. This won't take long."

"I'll show you whatever you want," said Jimmy, "and get you back in one piece."

"Anyway," said Ben. "Like we told you the other day, we know the score." He pushed closer to Konrad, pinning him between himself and Jimmy.

"The mine you're asking us to work on is just a distraction. Kate and I have spent time out along the Eastern Slopes and there's not much to suggest any new mine is even being considered. But, like we told you in Anne's office, we did find some survey markers with Stenger's company markings and, interestingly enough, found another one just like them near Maligne Lake.

"A sloppy bit of work on the part of someone, don't you think?" Ben continued. "And we have reason to believe that 'someone' is a fellow by the name of Zane Ritter. But maybe you haven't met him yet. Or maybe you have?"

Damn Ritter, Konrad thought as he felt Ben's elbow dig into his side.

"Interestingly," Ben added, "two of our wardens also met Ritter with some German hunters close to the mine. Now what kind of a coincidence is that? Isn't the company proposing the new mine German as well? And isn't the owner of that company really more interested in a lodge in his old stomping grounds? Isn't that really the objective?"

Although Ben had backed off and given him more room, Konrad felt his chest tighten.

"Do I need to go on, Konrad? Or can you see that you might just be getting yourself in deep with some very sloppy operators. I can't imagine how it'll look to whoever's calling the shots when this pile of crap blows up, but I'm pretty sure you'll be covered in shit along with the rest of them."

Konrad silently took it all in. He wondered how much more Ben and the others knew. If push came to shove, he could throw Ritter and the Germans under the bus, but he had to wonder if Bolduc and Stenger might not be willing to do the same to him. He had no way of knowing who to trust, and Matthews was obviously using that to get to him.

"Anne Winters thinks Maxime Bolduc is just using you to satisfy his own aspirations," Ben continued. "Apparently there's a reason they call him 'the Snake.'" Once more Konrad felt Ben's elbow digging into his side. "Do you seriously think Bolduc is looking out for your future?" The pause was giving time for Konrad to reflect. "And Helmut Stenger?" said Ben. "What do you think he's after? Do you think he just wants to help a Parks bureaucrat get to the next rung on the ladder?"

Konrad had similar misgivings, but he wasn't about to give that up to Matthews.

"If that's what you think you better give your head a shake," Ben added. "You're expendable."

As they were about to turn back onto the Maligne Lake Road, Ben motioned for Jimmy to pull over onto the shoulder then turned to Konrad. "Just think about what I'm saying before someone else gets hurt. None of us want to see that happen." Ben opened the truck door and slid out, allowing Konrad to move back across the seat. "And by the way, if you physically assaulted Marion Seawell at the office yesterday like people are saying you did, there will be hell to pay for that too."

With that, Ben closed the door and walked toward another warden truck parked along the Maligne Lake Road.

As Konrad strained to recognize the driver, Jimmy Rand turned onto the road and drove off in the opposite direction toward Maligne Lake.

Konrad straightened out in the seat and ran a hand across his forehead, feeling slightly emboldened now that Matthews was no longer in the truck. He looked quietly at Jimmy as the older warden paid attention to the road ahead. He was willing to give him the benefit of the doubt for what just happened, but as for Matthews and the others, he wouldn't go that far. If they weren't worried about their own futures after making a stand in his office, they'd better be worried now.

As they drove along the road toward Maligne Lake, Konrad revisited everything Ben said, and everything he didn't. In some respects, they seemed to know more than he did, and that was concerning. He wondered how much more they knew and looked across at Jimmy who sat quietly through the whole exchange with Matthews.

Willing to break the impasse with Jimmy and cut through the silence, Konrad asked, "What's wrong with a lodge anyway?"

Jimmy looked at Konrad for a second before turning his eyes back on the road. "Bears don't use 'em."

"So *we* can't?" said Konrad. "Why does it always have to come down to the bears or some other animal?"

"Because these places were set aside to protect wild places."

"And lock out people?"

"Hardly," said Jimmy, screwing up his face and tossing a serious look at Konrad.

"You realize we are on a road put here by and for people? You know millions of people come through the park gates every year? People are hardly locked out."

"So what's one more development? What's a few more people?"

"Well, there's the rub, isn't it?" said Jimmy, opening his window and sending a long stream of tobacco juice off on a trajectory. "There's no end of people." He wiped his bottom lip with the back of his hand and looked back at Konrad. "But there's only so many bears and so many caribou and so on. If you look around, there aren't a lot of places outside of these parks where bears and caribou are doing well, at least, not in Alberta. Almost all of the Eastern Slopes are taken up with oil and gas sites, forestry cutblocks and mines. So if we start eating into what's left here inside the park, they don't stand a chance. Hell, we've already eaten into it enough, I'd say."

"It's the price of progress," said Konrad. "You really think people would rather have grizzly bears than a job for themselves working in a mine?"

Jimmy stared straight ahead. "But, some people want it all. Another mine outside the park and a new lodge inside. Both in bear habitat, both cutting into what's left. A little grizzly mother like Hope doesn't stand a chance. *Especially* with people like Zane Ritter out there." Jimmy looked hard at Konrad. "It's got to stop somewhere."

CHAPTER 50

MARION KNEW SHE'D struck a nerve during her encounter with Vincent-Blais and was somewhat perturbed by Anne and Megan's advice to let them deal with things. Unswayed by their argument, Marion continued researching Helmut Stenger and his company, trying to build as strong a case as possible to hand over to Environmental Justice when, and she knew it was a case of when and not if, the lodge proposal became public knowledge.

She was also still driven by the notion that Malcolm's death was somehow tied to the whole affair, and pored over her late husband's notebooks in search of clues. Malcolm was a meticulous note keeper, recording not only his climbing adventures and other explorations, but also embedding details of the myriad development projects Jasper Wild had provided input into over the years.

Now sitting in bed, scouring the notebooks for anything that might provide some insight about past development proposals in the Maligne Valley, she smiled as she read his accounts of climbing, hiking and other adventures mixed in with rants about the latest development proposal Jasper Wild was trying to fight.

Because it always seems like a fight, Marion thought. *Actually more like a battle. In a national park, it shouldn't be that way. Most of those developments just don't belong here. Period.*

Over the years, Jasper Wild had lost many of those battles, but they'd won some as well. And as Malcolm used to say, count your victories, no matter how small.

As Marion became absorbed in the details of the various projects, she noticed something odd in the chronology of entries, but couldn't quite put her finger on it. Flipping back and forth through many years of detailed notes, Marion realized what it was: compared to the older notebooks, the more recent ones included fewer and fewer details.

But if anything, Malcolm was more thorough over time. So why don't the notebooks reflect that?

Had Malcolm actually started a second set of books, as Marion had once suggested to him, dedicated solely to record-ing the extensive fieldwork they did to research those projects?

At the time Malcolm resisted. And as far as Marion knew, he only ever used this one set of notebooks.

But why the lack of detail?

She was missing something.

Sliding out of bed, she pulled opened the bedroom closet and looked at the stack of Malcolm's belongings she'd been unable to part with. Picking through the pile, she wondered if she'd passed over something that might lend a clue to the mystery. She'd started to go through the pile again many times trying to purge more and more of the clutter, but she rarely got far. Starting with the boxes on the top, emotion and memories soon took over and she found herself sitting on the bed in tears.

The pile represented everything she had left of Malcolm's belongings.

Looking at the heap again, she decided to try another approach. Methodically pulling everything out and piling it up next to the bed, Marion took the first box on top and inspected its contents, then placed it on the floor in the closet. Step by step she went through each box and added it to the pile in the closet.

She was barely into the process when she discovered a shoe-box inside one of the larger cartons. Opening it, she found a small collection of personal diaries she'd never seen before. Ignoring the rest of the boxes, Marion crawled back into bed and began reading.

These are very personal diaries, she thought as she read each entry, devouring the first book and starting on the next.

In them Malcolm expanded on the details of each of the development proposals Jasper Wild had dealt with in recent years. He also gave some insights as to why he started a second set of books in the first place.

Increasingly, the projects we ask ourselves to deal with beg the question, why? Why is this project even being considered for a national park? The proponent has no history of working in national parks and there seems to be no tangible benefit to allowing this development in the park, other than for the express purpose of feathering the proponent's nest. It's all about profit.

Malcolm went on to express concerns about who was behind many of the projects and noted his worries about the personal safety of Jasper Wild members as they investigated both the projects and the people putting them forward.

But it was Malcolm's journal entry referring to a previous proposal to build a backcountry lodge in Jasper that really caught Marion's attention, particularly the reference to Helmut Stenger.

'It is distressing to learn that my old friend Helmut Stenger seems to have turned an ethical corner," he wrote. "There is evidence he's engaged in inhumane projects in third world countries and benefitted from associations with corrupt governments. Now he seems to have turned his attention to his long sought goal: a backcountry lodge in Jasper. From what I've learned of his actions in Africa, and what I've been seeing recently in Jasper, I will have to take extra caution—both for my personal safety, and Marion's too. His suggestion Jasper Wild should turn a blind eye to the proposal was something I wouldn't previously have expected from Helmut. He should know I would never do that, but I now realize he is someone who will stop at nothing to get what he wants.'

Marion smiled as she read the last words in the entry, 'nil bastardo carborundum.'

But her expression turned serious again when she turned the page.

'Things are getting increasingly dangerous,' Malcolm had written.

'I must keep this from Marion. She is tenacious and would take matters into her own hands if she knew. And I don't want to see her hurt.

But if I have to name names, I will.'

So is that why he kept a separate set of diaries, Marion reflected on what she'd read. *And what did he mean that things were getting more dangerous? Did he know something he wasn't meant to know? Was he really going to name names? And if so, whose? Is that why he died? Was his fall really an accident?*

CHAPTER 51

KONRAD WAS MIFFED at the tactics Ben used to corner him, but the drive with Jimmy Rand and their pointed conversation had taken the edge off things for the moment. Still, Konrad wasn't about to let bygones be bygones as Matthews suggested, or forget everything that transpired after Wood Buffalo.

Inuvik had been a shock to his system and he would have pretty much made a deal with the devil to get out of there. With everything he was learning about Maxime Bolduc and Helmut Stenger's plans, perhaps he had.

But the opportunity they gave him was a no-brainer: help push Stenger's proposal through in Jasper without the wheels falling off and he would be in line for Jasper's top job, a pretty safe bet for rising further up the ladder. What could go wrong?

He still had aspirations to be a deputy minister someday, and although the demotion to Inuvik had temporarily sidelined that goal, he felt he was back on track. In his mid-thirties, he was still young after all.

In some ways he had leap-frogged his way into an even better place, positioning himself for a senior management role in Ottawa perhaps, although he questioned whether he wanted to work directly with Bolduc.

Perhaps another department, he thought. *Either way, Father would be proud.*

Anton Blais had aspirations of being a deputy minister himself until he made the mistake of being caught in a minor scandal with Cecilia Vincent, a parliamentary page. After that, his marriage fell apart and he lost sight of his career objectives. Anton and Cecilia moved to the outskirts of Ottawa and he never did regain the foothold he once had in the federal public service.

When Konrad was born, he was pulled in two directions, caught between one parent trying to relive his life vicariously though his son and the other who no longer wanted anything to do with the halls of Parliament. Despite having inherited all of Anton's swagger and bravado, it seemed Konrad could never satisfy his father's desire to restore the family name, always coming up short in Anton's eyes, and suffocated by Cecilia's mothering.

Over time, however, a door opened, and Konrad found himself in an entry level position in government, soaking up all he could about the workings of bureaucracy, watching how some people got ahead while others languished. The lesson he took home from it all was that good guys finish last. Konrad had no intention of being left at the back of the pack. He would do whatever it took to gain power and control, damn the torpedoes.

Now in Jasper, with a chance to redeem himself, Konrad had little time to consider his options. Bolduc wanted a quick vetting of Stenger's proposal and ordered Konrad to make it happen as painlessly as possible for Maxime and the minister. Anything less and he could kiss a government career goodbye.

Adding to the pressure were the human issues weighing on his mind: the cumulative effect of the visit from Anne and the others, his encounter with Marion, Ben's talk with him, and the veiled threat about what would happen if anything happened to Marion.

Lying in bed, thinking about how to deal with everyone and how to prove himself to his father and Bolduc, he realized none of them mattered. The only person he had to prove anything to was himself. And he didn't really need Gunter or Jakob, or Ritter for that matter. He could handle it.

The late night phone call caught him off guard.

"I'm hearing rumblings of a mini-revolt in Jasper," said the caller.

"It's nothing I can't handle," said Konrad.

"Like you handled Matthews and the others in Wood Buffalo?"

"Everything is under control," said Konrad.

George Mercer

"Is it?"

There was a long pause on the other end of the line.

"I'm hearing that Marion Seawell and Jasper Wild are making waves, trying to enlist Environmental Justice to make a case against the park. And Kalina Strong is apparently still poking her nose around the lodge designer's offices in Calgary.

"And by all accounts you have your own little gang of rogue park wardens in Jasper trying to kill this project. Including some of the same players from Wood Buffalo." There was another pause. "So help me, Konrad, if they do kill this project, you can say goodbye to any hopes of keeping the superintendent's position, or getting any other position in government for that matter. You better think of a way to steer them away from the Maligne Valley, or your career is over."

"And how do you propose I do that? It seems the mine is proving less of a distraction than Stenger thought it would be."

"Figure it out," said the caller. "It's all on you."

Konrad was about to reply but all he heard was dial tone.

Slamming down the phone, Konrad fumed.

Matthews was obviously only telling me part of the story, trying to get me to agree with him but screwing me behind my back by putting ideas into Marion Seawell's head and enlisting Kalina Strong to dig up more dirt for them.

The more he thought about it, the more he figured Ben and the others were merely using him, conspiring among themselves to shut down Stenger's project and screw his own aspirations in the process.

And then there were these calls.

He didn't need the added pressure.

He didn't like being told what to do, *by anyone.*

He'd figure it out; he was in charge now.

He needed to throw a curve ball at Matthews, Haffcut and the others to keep them preoccupied, something near and dear to their hearts.

But what?

CHAPTER 52

"WHOA, WHAT'S THE panic?" said Zane Ritter as Konrad slid into the pickup truck next to him and placed a small backpack between his legs. "I never expected you to call me."

"I need a job done." Konrad glared at Zane and motioned for him to start the truck. "I thought you were the best man for the job."

"Gotta like that," said Zane, as he pulled the truck onto the highway. "Where we goin'?"

"Head south toward the mine. I'll tell you when to stop."

As they approached the coalmine, Konrad pointed to a pull-off and Zane stopped in front of the guardrail.

"Watcha got there?" Zane asked as Konrad opened his pack and pulled out a small antenna, cable and leather case. Rolling down his window, he reached out and stuck the magnetic base of the antenna to the roof of the truck, then uncoiled the cable and plugged it into a device in the leather case.

"That a scanner?"

Konrad nodded.

"What're we lookin' for?"

"Bears."

"Bears?" Zane's head bounced up and down. "I like the sound of that."

"Hmph, I thought you would" Konrad muttered under his breath as he held the scanner between his legs and played with the dials. "Let's go." He smiled and pulled out a laminated list tucked between the scanner and the leather case.

"How'd you get the frequencies? They leave those layin' around?"

Konrad smirked but said nothing.

As they drove south along the highway, Zane pointed to a puff of grey smoke followed by a percussion-like sound in the distance. "They're blasting at the mine."

Konrad nodded and turned up the volume on the scanner, listening to the static while simultaneously scrolling through the series of six-digit numbers on the list.

Suddenly the scanner emitted a low pinging sound.

"Bingo." Konrad quickly adjusted knobs until the signal increased in strength.

"Which bear's that?"

"I think there's only one it can be," said Konrad. He pulled a small map from the pack and unfolded it across his lap.

"The little sow?"

Konrad nodded. "I think she's somewhere in here," he said, pointing to the map as the signal increased in strength.

"Let me see that," said Ritter, pulling over to the shoulder. He took the map from Konrad and laid it across the steering wheel. "I know where we'll find her." Zane shoved his foot to the floor and the pickup spun off the shoulder and shot down the highway.

"Take it easy," Konrad yelled as he gripped the scanner.

As the pickup wound its way southward, Konrad kept adjusting the volume until it was barely audible. They were driving parallel to a small river when Zane turned off the highway, slowly edging the truck along a pot-holed road until it opened up into an old borrow pit.

The scanner was now emitting a loud steady ping and Konrad turned it off.

"She's gotta be right here," said Zane.

Just then, the little sow grizzly strolled out of an alder patch followed by two small cubs. Eyeing the men, she stopped in her tracks and gave a quick snort that sent the cubs flying into the underbrush.

"This is too easy," said Konrad. "Get your gun."

Zane hesitated and shook his head. "Not a good place. A gunshot here will be heard right across the mine sites."

"Just get the gun," said Konrad. "For all anyone knows, it could be blasting." He opened his door slowly and slid out of the truck.

Zane followed suit and slowly pulled a gun case from behind the bench seat.

"Hurry up," said Konrad. "Or she'll be gone."

Zane glared across the cab at Konrad and slid the gun case toward him. "You want to do this?"

Konrad grabbed the case and pulled out the lever action .3030 Winchester. "Is it loaded?" He kept one eye on the bear as she ambled along the edge of the alders, staring at the two men.

"Course it is. But do you even know how to use that thing?"

Konrad ignored the question as he fumbled with the lever action, then aimed the gun at the bear. "How many bullets?"

"You only need one."

"How many goddamn bullets?" Konrad sighted down the barrel and fired.

"Five now," said Zane as the first shot crashed out of the rifle, sending the grizzly plowing though the vegetation toward a gravel embankment at the far end of the pit. "Jesus, you didn't even hit her."

Konrad scanned the far end of the pit, swinging the gun wildly as he sighted down the barrel once more. When Hope emerged from the bushes and started up the embankment, he squeezed off a second shot that seemed to ricochet off a rock just in front of her.

"I think I hit her," Konrad yelled as the bear turned and ran across the slope in the opposite direction.

"Christ," said Ritter as he scrambled around the truck and tried to grab the gun, but not before Konrad took aim and fired a third time.

The bear stumbled for a moment then started over the embankment.

Grabbing the rifle and pushing Konrad away, Zane took careful aim and fired, dropping Hope with a shot to the head. He lowered the gun and watched to see if she tried to rise, but there was no more movement from the female bear.

"What a clusterfuck," he said, tossing the gun into the cab of the truck and grabbing his pack from behind the seat. He pushed Konrad toward the alders. "Get goin'. We gotta take care of this right now."

Konrad stumbled forward. When he tried to turn around to speak, Zane pushed him harder. "Save your breath. You'll need it."

When they reached the bear, Zane pulled a skinning knife and a small hatchet from his pack. He turned to Konrad. "Go back to the truck and get the cooler in the back," he ordered.

"What are you going to do?" Konrad asked.

Zane shook his head. "Just get goin' and be quick about it."

When he returned with the cooler, Konrad saw that Zane had gutted the bear and cut off her paws. The radio collar lay on the ground beside her.

"What are you doing?" Konrad asked, picking up the collar.

"Making the most of a piss poor job." Zane tossed the paws and a small plastic bag into the cooler, then grabbed the collar from Konrad and threw it in on top."

"Why are you keeping the collar?" said Konrad.

"You'll see." Ritter motioned for Konrad to head back to the truck where Ritter dumped the bear parts into a green garbage bag and tossed them behind the seat. Leaving the collar in the Styrofoam cooler, he put on the lid and grabbed a roll of duct tape and ran several layers of tape around the rim of the lid.

"That should make it waterproof," he said, picking up the cooler and shaking it, then walking toward the river. When he realized Konrad wasn't following, he turned and nodded for him to come along.

At the edge of the river, Zane placed the cooler in the water then shoved it into the current. The two men watched as the small cooler was pulled downstream.

"That should keep them guessing," Zane said.

He reached into the water and cleaned the blood off his hands, then wiped them down the sides of his pants. "We better get outta here. One shot mighta sounded like they're blasting at the mine, but not four."

The two men walked back to the truck and stowed the gun back in its case. Zane started the truck and turned out of the pit, following the narrow gravel road back to the highway. Pressing the gas pedal to the floor, he spun the truck onto the paved highway and headed north.

"Is this the best way to go?" asked Konrad.

"Gonna have to be," said Ritter, slipping on a pair of mirrored sunglasses and looking across at Vincent-Blais with a toothy grin. "Hopefully we don't run into no fish cops. A man in your position wouldn't wanna be caught with the likes'a me. Especially with the cargo we're haulin'." He smirked and looked at Konrad. "Hold on tight."

CHAPTER 53

JOHN HAFFCUT WAS almost out of town, headed for a day in the field, when Dispatch called him back to the office.

What now?

John turned the warden truck around and made his way toward Jasper. Megan was waiting for him at Dispatch, along with Ben and Kate.

"What's up?" he said, noting the look of concern on their faces.

"It's Hope," said Megan.

"What about her?"

"Brent Rideout just called to say her collar was emitting a mortality signal during their last telemetry flight. They located her collar, but just the collar."

"What do you mean just her collar?"

"They found it in a Styrofoam cooler on the MacLeod River," said Ben. "Someone had removed it and sent it floating downstream to confuse anyone looking for it. It's hard to say how long it was in the current before it got caught up in some debris and stopped moving. That's when the mortality switch kicked in."

"Still, Hope could have dropped the collar somehow," John said.

Kate shook her head. "It had been cut off John."

"Damn."

"And they haven't found the body," said Ben.

"Well we have to," said John.

"The provincial guys have been looking all over for it," said Megan, "but have had no luck."

"It's got to be upstream of where they found the cooler," said John.

"Unless they killed her somewhere else and brought the cooler to the river."

"No," said John. "We all know what poachers are like. They're lazy sons-of-bitches. I can't imagine them doing that."

"Well," said Megan, "hopefully the provincial folks find her."

"I've got a better idea," said John.

"Which is?" said Ben.

"We find her ourselves."

"How?" said Kate.

"Let me worry about that," said John. "Trav, get in touch with Clay and tell him we need him here pronto. We'll head out to the MacLeod and help search. But before we go, I have to check out something else that's bugging me about this." Without further explanation, John motioned for the others to follow him. "Come on, let's get geared up."

Megan, Kate and Ben chased John down the hall to his office. Once they were all inside, John closed the door.

"What's going on?" said Megan.

John turned to the trio and caught his breath before speaking. "I didn't broadcast it when I did it," he said, "but Hope is a bear we collared in the park."

"Yeah," said Megan. "I remember you said you and Clay got her on your own. A chance shot at her somewhere in near Rocky Forks."

John nodded. "But what I didn't tell you is ... we put an abdominal implant in her."

"A what?" said Ben.

"A VHF transmitter sutured into the bear's peritoneal cavity," said Kate.

"Very good," said John, looking at Kate. "That's exactly what it is." He paused. "I didn't let people know because I figured Marion would go ballistic if she found out about it. God love her, but she kicks up enough of a fuss over collaring. And I swore Clay to secrecy."

"So would it still be working?" said Ben.

"*Hope*fully," said John. "No pun intended. It doesn't have great range, but if we go with the most logical assumption, Hope was killed somewhere along the MacLeod River or one of its tributaries upstream of where the collar was found, then we should have a pretty good chance of locating it."

"Sweet," Megan's concerned look morphed into a smile.

Before anyone could say anything else, there was a knock on the door and Trav walked in. "Clay is just lifting off from Hinton. He'll be here in twenty minutes or so. He said he'd call when he was landing, but wouldn't shut down. He's good for fuel so you guys can just hop in and go."

"Hey, thanks, Trav," said John as the dispatcher gave the group a thumbs-up and disappeared back down the hallway.

"Something bugs me about this," said John. "How did they find Hope?

"You think whoever did it was looking for her?" said Megan. John nodded.

"But how could they find her?"

"Maybe they just lucked out," said Kate. "People see her along Highway 40 all the time."

"I guess," said Megan. "It could just be a coincidence."

Kate grimaced and looked at Ben who was shaking his head.

"There's no such thing ..." he started to say.

"As coincidence," said Kate. She looked Megan in the eyes. "Please don't try to argue with him."

"Ben's right," said John. "At least in this case. Whoever killed her knew what they were after."

"We don't even know if she's dead for sure," said Megan.

John raised his eyebrows at his assistant. "We do. The collar was intact."

"But why would anyone target her?" said Kate. "They'd have to know it would draw the ire of a lot of people."

"I don't know," said John. "If we can find her, maybe that will help answer the question."

CHAPTER 54

JUST AS JOHN had predicted, they found Hope's decapitated body in the upper reaches of the MacLeod River, covered with a pile of willow and alder.

The abdominal implant emitted a faint signal, but Clay's tactic of flying as low as possible as he guided the helicopter upstream from where the cooler had been located worked, as he said, "like a hot damn."

The condition of her body and the location of the kill didn't provide a lot of insight to the untrained eye, but John and the others teased as much as they could from what they were given before John contacted the provincial officers and gave them directions to the site.

"Whoever did it made us want to think they were simply after paws and the gallbladder," said John.

"But you think there was more to it?" said Kate.

"I do," said John. "If there was an iconic bear in this area, Hope would be it. Her photos have been on the cover of every newspaper in the province. Whoever did this would have to know no stone would be left unturned to find them."

"So why do it?" said Ben. "Why take that risk?"

"To send a message?" said Kate.

"What kind of message is this?" said Megan.

"I don't know," said John. "And it's the last thing the mining companies want hanging over their heads."

"Do you think it's retaliation for something else?" said Ben.

"I don't know," John repeated. "I guess it could have just been a disgruntled hunter who stumbled on her. Or, it could have been someone who tracked her down."

"But they'd need a scanner for that," said Megan.

"Scanners are easy to get if you really want one."

"But they'd have to know the frequency," said Megan

"That's true," said John, sounding frustrated.

"How would they get that?

"I *don't* know. All I know is I'm really pissed."

"Do you have any idea who would do this?" said Kate.

John sighed. "Could have been anyone, even just someone with a hate on for bears. But I definitely have a few people that would be on the top of my list. And Brent Rideout probably would say the same thing."

"Someone like Ritter?" said Megan.

John nodded. "Yeah."

"But wouldn't he know he'd be one of the first people Fish and Wildlife would suspect."

"That's true," said John. "But I don't know if that's enough to stop him. And Brent said Zane was back into wildlife trafficking."

"Maybe it's just someone trying to throw us off," said Ben.

"Throw us off of what?"

"I don't know," said Ben. "Sticking our noses into the Maligne?"

"Hmphh," said John. "I wonder?"

CHAPTER 55

JOHN HAFFCUT WAS as mad as hell. One way or the other, he was going to get to the bottom of Hope's death and help bring whoever did it to justice. Strictly speaking, this was a provincial matter, having happened outside of the national park, but Hope had been collared in the park and these were shared bears. John knew his counterparts with the province would assist in whatever way they could if the shoe was on the other foot and the bear had been killed inside Jasper's boundary.

John wasn't sure who was responsible for killing Hope but he had an idea and returned to his office. Immediately, he sensed something was amiss, even though on first inspection, his shelves of reference books and journal articles appeared untouched. Something wasn't right.

Looking at the shelves of field equipment, John's eye was drawn to the telemetry scanner sitting by itself at one end of a long row of radio and GPS collars and antennae. Pulling the scanner off the shelf, he slid a finger down the inside of the leather case but felt nothing. Peering inside confirmed his worst suspicion.

The list of radio frequencies was gone.

"Goddammit."

John had a sinking feeling in his gut. He kept a laminated copy of the list with each scanner and only took it out when they were trying to locate animals. When he was done he always slipped it back inside the case.

"It has to be around here somewhere," he said, scouring his office for the list. Unlocking the bottom drawer of his desk, he checked his personal files. He often kept a spare copy of any sensitive information stashed with his private records, old medicals, pay stubs, T4s, and the like. Sure enough, his spare copy of the list was sitting in a file.

Returning to the shelves, he took another pass through their contents. He was certain the laminated list was with the scanner the last time he used it. Did he misplace it? No way. It wasn't in his nature. *Someone must have taken it. But who?*

Slowly a smile creased John's face as he turned back to the shelves of equipment.

He'd totally forgotten that several months ago, he'd set up one of the remote cameras to record any activity in his office after hours. He'd done it more as a prank than anything else, just to have some fun with the cleaners who came in during the night. He thought he'd kyboshed the failed experiment when the camera's flash nearly scared the shit out of the old cleaner, but he recalled now how he had simply deactivated the flash and left the camera in place to record anyone passing through the office door. If he was lucky, the batteries might even be working after all this time.

John pulled the unit down from the shelf and tried to take a picture but the camera was dead.

Just my luck, he thought.

He opened the side of the camera and pulled out the memory card. Sitting at his computer, he slid the card in the drive and downloaded the photos.

Quickly scrolling through the images he landed on the last two photos taken before the batteries had died. A smirk spread across John's face.

"Well would you look at that," he muttered to himself.

The first picture showed Konrad entering the office empty-handed.

The second showed him exiting with the scanner.

Gotcha, you bastard.

CHAPTER 56

JOHN DECIDED TO pick his spot to confront Konrad, but first he had to come up with a way to get Konrad to see him, not that he would want to, considering John was a member of the group who barged into his office on his first day of work.

If Konrad declined, John had an alternate plan. But he decided to keep it to himself to avoid drawing anyone else into another potential shit fight with the new boss. Well almost anyone. He might need a little help.

Kate and Ben will be pissed being left out, but this is how it's got to be.

After all, while the photos implicated Konrad, John didn't have any real proof Konrad was involved with Hope's death. Why jeopardize their careers with the outfit?

Getting into Konrad's office, to meet him on his own turf, so to speak, was an easy process, since John knew more about the superintendent's office than Konrad himself, especially the small, barely noticeable side door that led to a back stairwell and outside. And he knew where Anne kept the extra key in case she somehow got locked out.

Anne had relied on her escape route on frequent occasions to avoid particularly obnoxious members of the business community who wanted to see her, or just to get a break from the non-stop duties of being a park superintendent.

John knew it as a quick exit to avoid being caught with Anne in what some would consider awkward circumstances. Being in a relationship with the park superintendent, especially in a small close-knit community like Jasper, had its challenges, especially if you had a reputation as a hard ass warden.

*****

When Konrad walked in the following morning, he was taken aback to find John waiting in his office, despite the door having been locked.

"What the hell? How did you get in here?"

"It doesn't matter," said John. "This won't take long, if you tell me what I need to know."

"And what's that?" said Konrad.

"I was just wondering what you did with the scanner you took from my office?" said John. He walked back across the office and sat in the chair next to Konrad's desk.

"What are you talking about, Haffcut?" Konrad was unfazed.

"Let's not beat around the bush. Last week you scooped the scanner from my office, along with the list of frequencies for every collared animal in and around the park."

Konrad shook his head and looked down at the document on his desk. "Can you believe this?" he said, holding up the paperwork to John. "They plan to go ahead with a full review of the proposed mine along our boundary."

"I'm quite serious, Konrad," John ignored the attempt to change the topic. "You took the scanner from my office. I want to know why." He paused for a split second then slid copies of the two images across the desk.

Konrad's facial expressions stalled momentarily. "I have no idea what these are about."

"Really?" said John. "You walked into my office empty-handed and walked out with one of my scanners. The second image shows it as plain as day."

"So?" said Konrad. "I may have been in your office and I may have looked at your equipment. I found that flight Lou Walker took me on to be incredibly interesting. The technology fascinates me."

"Go on," said John.

"That's all there is to it," said Konrad. "I may have looked at the unit. But I put it back. It's back there in your office, right? There's nothing else to go on about."

"So what happened to the list of frequencies?"

Konrad stalled again, but this time John saw something different in his eyes, as if Konrad was searching his own memory for an answer. "What list?"

"The list you must have seen when you were flying with Lou. It was inside the scanner's leather case. Lou said you seemed interested in it."

Konrad shook his head. "I have no idea where it is."

John gauged from Konrad's reaction that he honestly didn't know where the list was, *Not now, anyway, but that doesn't mean he* didn't *know where it was before.* "What if I said we found it next to Hope's body?" John lied. "You recall Hope? The poster child for grizzly bear management in the province."

"Goddammit, Haffcut," Konrad said, jumping to his feet. "I have no idea what you're talking about. I only just heard the bear had been shot."

"You knew the bear was shot because *you* goddamn well shot her."

Suddenly a commotion outside of the office distracted the two men and Megan Weaver burst into the room.

"Did he admit it?" Megan yelled as the superintendent's executive assistant grabbed her by the arm and tried to dislodge her from the office. "Did he?"

Konrad's face was apoplectic as he stood and stumbled from behind his desk.

"Get her out of here," he yelled. He turned to John. "Both of you. Get out." John rose and turned to the door as Konrad grappled with Megan and pushed her out of his office. "You heard me, get out of here."

As he turned back to deal with John, Konrad's face was a writhing, scarlet mass of creases and folds. Grabbing John,

Konrad made another attempt to push him from the office, but John kicked the door closed and grabbed Konrad's wrists, holding them firmly as Konrad tried to struggle free.

"Let me go," Konrad yelped.

John snapped his arms and shook Konrad forcefully, pulling Konrad's face to within a whisker of his own.

"Never, ever lay a hand on me." John spoke in a whisper as he glared into Konrad's face. "Or anyone else for that matter." He paused. "Unless you want to get your ass kicked." He paused to let the words sink in. "I know you did it."

Konrad's eyes opened wide as he appeared to be searching for a way out of his dilemma.

John released his grip and without another word, opened the door and walked out, quietly closing the door behind him.

Catching up to Megan, they walked down the stairs of the administration building and out into the bright sunshine.

"That went well," he said to no one in particular as Megan looked away, smiling to herself. "Now we wait."

CHAPTER 57

KONRAD WINCED AND rubbed his wrists, cursing as his phone rang. He stumbled to the desk and leaned over, pushing the speaker button as he rolled his head to the side to alleviate the sharp pain in his neck.

"Not now. I can't take any calls now."

"You'll take the calls I tell you to take," said the caller.

Christ. Give me a break.

"Things sound like they've gone from bad to worse."

Tell me about it.

"Now I'm hearing that Marion Seawell is preparing a package of information for an environmental group in Edmonton." The caller paused. "A legal group. And naming names no less."

Konrad sprawled across the desk and rested his head in his arms.

"Did you hear what I said?"

"I'll deal with it," Konrad said finally. He reached for the phone and hung up on the caller. Rolling onto his back, he lay splayed across the desk, staring at the ceiling. *John Haffcut and the whole bloody works of them will regret this.*

I'll make them pay.

Thinking about his options, Konrad knew he needed help. He couldn't do it all alone. Then he recalled the scope of Helmut Stenger's offer.

Use them however you see fit, Helmut had said, referring to Gunter and Jakob. The unconditional offer had come with no strings attached. It gave Konrad some breathing room to avoid having to go back to Tom Erickson or, god forbid, Maxime Bolduc, for help. Konrad knew he had to take care of things himself or his future would be in jeopardy. He didn't need any other complications.

He had just recovered from the call when he heard Marion Seawell speaking with his executive assistant.

She's the last person I want to see right now, he said to himself as he bolted for his office door and turned the lock. Returning to his desk, he lifted the receiver and pressed the speed dial for his assistant.

"I have to see him," Konrad heard Marion say, her voice echoing in the hallway.

"Don't let her in here. I told you to keep her out of the building," Konrad spat into the phone. He slammed it down and then rifled through his desk, looking for Gunter's business card. He was still mulling over his options as he entered the number and waited, a bead of sweat trickling down the side of his face.

"I need you to help me with something."

CHAPTER 58

THE LAKE WATER flowed past the stern as Marion effort-lessly guided the cedar strip canoe through the reeds. Paddling around a small islet of tall grass and sedges, she was now out of sight of the highway and the steady stream of traffic speeding through the montane valley.

Working her way along the shoreline, she explored the lake's many nooks and crannies, stopping briefly at the mouth of a small indentation that fingered its way toward the slopes of the recent burn.

Suddenly, a flash of yellow attracted Marion's attention.

Raising her binoculars, she watched as a Western Kingbird voiced its disgust, drawing attention away from a well-camou-flaged nest. Marion followed the bird as it moved through the small knot of trees along the water's edge.

She didn't notice the approaching canoe until it was within a few metres of her own craft. There was something immedi-ately suspicious about the two men paddling toward her. They seemed completely out of place dressed in fishing vests and khaki pants, brandishing their wooden paddles with a lack of synchronicity that would frustrate any canoeist with even a modicum of experience.

Tightening her life jacket, Marion leaned forward and unclipped the dry bag from the canoe's centre thwart. She opened the bag as the two men pulled alongside. Looking unsteady in their boat, the man kneeling in the bow reached over and grabbed the gunwale of Marion's canoe, causing it to tip slightly toward them.

"Sorry about that," said the bearded man, steadying himself as his partner awkwardly grabbed both gunwales of their canoe.

"We don't get out a lot," said the man in the stern, clenching his teeth as if that would settle the rocking.

"So it would seem," said Marion, thinking she recognized a slight German accent. Marion forced a smile and tried to relax her grip on the paddle. "What brings you out here?"

"We heard there were some big bull trout in the lake," said the first man. "That's why we added this little baby to our arsenal." He reached down in front of him and brought up a small hardwood baton.

"I see," said Marion, generally unimpressed. "You brought a priest with you?"

"A priest?"

Marion pointed to the baton. "Those are referred to as priests because you use them to administer last rites to the fish."

"I never knew that."

"Me either," said the other man.

"What are you up to?" said the first fisherman.

"Exploring," said Marion. "I like to come out here to see how the loons are faring."

"Really?"

As if on cue, somewhere farther down the lake, a loon called. Its mournful message wavered for a few seconds.

"You must be from around here," said the first fisherman, pointing out the Jasper Wild logo on Marion's dry bag.

"Yes, I've lived here for a while," Marion acknowledged, not wanting to volunteer too much information.

The second man nodded and pushed his paddle into the silty bottom to steady the canoe. "What do you do?"

"Oh, nothing much," said Marion. "I'm retired now, so I spend my time enjoying the park."

"And raising a little hell," said the first fisherman.

"I'm sorry," said Marion, the man's comment confirming her first suspicions. "I don't know what you mean."

"I think you do," he said. He grabbed the gunwale of Marion's canoe and pulled the boats closer together.

"Please let go of my boat." Marion held her paddle tightly with one hand and tried to push the man's hands away with the other. As she floundered to regain her balance, she inadvertently stuck the second man with her paddle, raising a welt on his forehead.

"Verdammt!" he growled.

Absorbed with trying to right herself, Marion barely noticed the hardwood bat as the first fisherman struck her on the temple, causing her to fall forward. Conscious but stunned by the blow, Marion tried to gain a handhold as the two men rocked her canoe, tipping her into the water.

Flipping the boat over, the canoe smacked Marion on the chest, momentarily submerging her before the life jacket buoyed her back to the surface.

Laying face up in the water, Marion was motionless as the first fisherman pulled alongside and reached for her. Grabbing the shoulder of her lifejacket, he flipped her over in the water.

"That's better," he said, looking back at his partner who nodded his approval.

"Let's get out of here," said the second man.

Both men powered their paddles through the water as they laboured to turn the canoe back toward the highway and their vehicle. Finally aimed in the right direction, they paddled hard for the far shore.

CHAPTER 59

TRAV WAS OUT of breath by the time he'd run the length of the building and turned the corner into Jimmy's cubicle.

"We just got a call from Marion Seawell's daughter," he managed to say between gasps. "She's quite worried about her mom. Apparently Marion planned to go canoeing on Talbot Lake, but hasn't returned."

"Canoeing on her own again?" said Jimmy as Ben and Kate walked into the office.

Trav nodded. "Her daughter said she left in the morning and planned to be home long ago."

"Who?" said Ben.

"Marion Seawell," said Jimmy as he pulled his pack together. "Can you two come and give me a hand?" As they headed outside, Jimmy told Ben and Kate the few details he knew. While Ben and Jimmy loaded a canoe onto Jimmy's truck, Kate grabbed some extra blankets from the storeroom and they bee-lined it for Talbot Lake.

Marion's car was in the parking lot at the lake, the canoe's tie-down ropes hanging off the roof rack.

"She's obviously still out there somewhere," said Jimmy. He took a moment to advise Dispatch, then helped Ben and Kate put the Park's canoe in the water and grab paddles and lifejackets from a storage box on the trailer.

"I'm not much of a canoeist," Jimmy admitted sheepishly.

"That's okay, we've got this," said Ben as he and Kate put on lifejackets. "But we could probably use another set of eyes. Why don't you climb in the middle? We can paddle. You can try to spot her with the binos."

Donning a lifejacket, Jimmy stepped gingerly into the centre of the canoe and grabbed the gunwales to steady himself as he knelt down.

"Not too elegant," said Ben, as the trio pushed off from shore, "but it works."

Ben and Kate pulled their paddles through the water, taking direction from Jimmy as he guided them across the lake looking for something that might give them an idea of where Marion might be.

"Marion often likes to check out loon nests." Jimmy pointed them to a channel on the other side of the lake. "She told me there's usually a nest over there she likes to keep an eye on every year."

As they rounded the end of a small, grassy island, Kate pointed to an overturned canoe sitting motionless in a patch of reeds several hundred metres away.

"Doesn't look good," said Jimmy. He scanned the lake surface with the binoculars. "No sign of her."

"Maybe she's under the canoe," said Kate as they paddled furiously toward the craft and pulled up alongside.

Grabbing the gunwale of the partially submerged boat, Jimmy lifted the canoe and tried to flip it over. "She's not under it," said Jimmy, letting the canoe fall back into the water.

"But she must be somewhere close by," said Ben. "The water doesn't look too deep."

"It's deep enough to drown in," said Kate, scanning the lake. "But maybe she got to shore."

As the trio feverishly searched the shallow waters, they were startled by a familiar voice.

"What in the name of god's green earth took you so long?" said Marion, pulling herself to her feet as she stumbled out of the tall grass at the edge of the island, her long grey hair a tangled mass of knots, partially hiding a large purple welt on her temple.

Thrusting their paddles into the reeds, Ben and Kate pushed the canoe onto shore in front of Marion.

"Are you okay?" Kate asked, as she jumped out.

"I'm fine," Marion stammered, as Jimmy and Ben scrambled from the canoe. "Just very cold."

"Jesus, what happened?" said Jimmy as he quickly took off his jacket. He put it around Marion's shoulders then pulled a large first aid kit from his pack. "Let me take a look at that bruise."

As Marion submitted to Jimmy's assessment of her injuries, Kate wrapped the extra blankets around Marion.

"So what did happen?" Kate asked.

"I don't know." Marion shook her head and stared out at her canoe, still capsized in the water.

"Did you lose your balance and hit your head?" said Kate, hugging Marion to help her retain body heat.

"That must have been it," said Marion.

Ben stared across Marion's back and caught Kate's eye. He shook his head.

"But you don't remember?" said Kate.

"No," said Marion. She slid a finger across the massive bruise. "Do you think I have a concussion?"

"You probably do," said Jimmy. "We should get you out of here and back to town. You need to be checked out by a doctor."

"Kate and I'll get the canoe and bring it in to shore," said Ben. "Marion, do you think you're up to paddling back in your canoe with Kate? Jimmy and I will take this one but we'll stay close and give you a hand if you need it."

CHAPTER 60

HELMUT STENGER WAS in a fit when he heard the news about Marion Seawell.

Making a quick phone call to his two men before they did anything else to worsen the situation, he blasted them for the attack.

"Dummkopf," he screamed over the line, his voice echoing off the massive windows in his Berlin office. Berating the pair, he barely gave them a chance to speak, only catching their reference to Konrad at the end of his tirade.

"What do you mean Vincent-Blais ordered this? Since when do you take direction from him?" Helmut Stenger hadn't thought it was possible to get any angrier until Konrad's name came up and his fury deepened further. "Never mind," he said, bringing the call to a quick conclusion. "I will contact him myself."

Stenger barely hung up long enough for the call to disconnect before making his next call. As soon as Konrad's voice came on the line, Stenger launched into another tirade, this time in German, before catching himself and repeating his message in English.

Konrad was unrepentant. "I have been given clear direction by *my* superiors to leave no stone unturned in making sure this project proceeds. You told me as much yourself."

"Yes. But not at all costs, and certainly not using my people to attack Marion Seawell."

"Well, I didn't expect them to go that far. I just wanted to send a message. But circumstances have changed since we spoke."

"Not for me they haven't."

"Well they have for me," said Konrad. His voice took on an edge that concerned Stenger. "It's personal now," Konrad added.

Helmut Stenger shook his head in disbelief. "I should warn you, Konrad, you have now made it personal for me. It's no longer about business."

"What do you mean?" said Konrad.

Stenger heard the catch in Konrad's voice. "I mean you should tread carefully, very, very carefully. And never use my people or me again to further your own agenda. Do you understand?"

"But I thought you would condone my actions? You said as much yourself."

Helmut sat gob-smacked as he listened to a recording of the last phone conversation between he and Konrad.

"Can I use your men?"

"Use them however you see fit."

Helmut Stenger leaned into the speaker and spoke very slowly, his voice dripping with loathing, "You know very well what I meant Konrad. There is a difference between using my men for my work and using them for your own vendettas. I shouldn't have to say this again: tread very, very carefully."

Without waiting for a response, Helmut hung up the phone, staring at it for a few moments before picking it up again and dialing a number in Arusha.

He had hoped he would not have to bring Jackson Sironka into the mix. But the Tanzanian had proven invaluable to him in both the Congo and Mozambique. Now, more than ever, Helmut needed someone he could trust to accomplish what his operatives on the ground in Jasper had been unable to do.

There would always be opponents. But the only ones you had to be concerned with were the ones who had the connections or staying power to stop a project, those who added enough weight to give an argument a critical mass, a tipping point.

Marion Seawell and the small band of rogue employees had compromised his hopes for a lodge in Jasper. Helmut knew they had no plans of giving up. While most people would relent with their opposition as projects dragged on, people like Marion and her friends were the types to stick to their guns, right to the bitter end.

Martyrs, Helmut thought as he waited for his call to go through.

"National Parks Authority," said the voice on the other end of the line.

CHAPTER 61

MARION WASN'T EXPECTING the house call, but hoped she was right about things. There'd been non-stop visitors all week, but the person she really wanted to speak with hadn't shown up yet.

When he finally did, Marion wasn't certain how it might go.

"Meine Güte," Helmut exclaimed when Marion opened the door. "My goodness, Marion. Are you okay?" He stepped inside, his eyes riveted to the large welt on Marion's forehead. Hesitating just long enough to gauge Marion's reaction, Helmut Stenger stepped into her embrace. "Marion. I'm so sorry."

Marion held on loosely then stepped back and peered into Stenger's eyes. "Are you, Helmut? Are you really sorry?"

"God, yes, Marion. I had no idea, believe me."

"But they were your men?" said Marion.

Helmut's upper lip trembled and his eyes watered. "Ja. But this is not what I wanted. You must believe me."

"Then if not you, who?" said Marion as she stood tall in the back porch.

Helmut paused and looked past Marion toward the kitchen, but Marion was steadfast. "If not you, then who?" she repeated.

"I can't say," said Helmut, avoiding Marion's glare.

"Can't or won't?"

"I honestly don't know," said Helmut.

"But you don't deny they were your men?"

"No."

"You know I could have the police pursue them."

"There would be no point."

"Because?"

"Because the authorities wouldn't be able to do anything if they did locate them," said Helmut. "Even if they tried, nothing would come of it."

"But how can that be?" said Marion, somewhat baffled by Helmut's response.

"You don't want to know," said Helmut. "Or I should say, you don't need to know. It is complicated, Marion."

"Incredible," said Marion. "You'll stop at nothing to get what you're after. And I don't mean the coalmine. You were never after that. Your eye has always been on having a piece of this park for yourself."

"I do what I have to do."

"To what end? God knows you have enough money and power."

Helmut shrugged. "If I don't get the lodge, someone else will. That's the way the world works, Marion."

"In your world perhaps." Marion glared into Helmut eyes. "I know about your operations in Africa. They're shameful."

Helmut raised his eyes. "Perhaps, but Africa is different. Even more corrupt than Canada."

"Corrupt here? How do you mean?"

"Don't be naïve. It happens everywhere."

"So you grease some palms, pay off some politicians, and then what?"

"Generally, you get what you're after. Although not always." There was contempt in Helmut's face. "Sometimes, things and people stand in your way."

"And you deal with them?"

"Yes. I deal with them."

"Helmut, you have to know I will not stop fighting this."

Helmut smiled. "I expected as much. You and Malcolm never knew when to give up."

"No, we didn't give up," said Marion. "And I won't. It's something Malcolm instilled in me many years ago. Nil ..."

"… bastardo carborundum," Helmut completed the expression. "Yes, I recall Malcolm repeating his mantra time and time again." Helmut shook his head then placed the navy cap back on his head and turned to open the door. Before he did, he turned to Marion, holding out his arms. Instead of embracing him, Marion stepped back and looked away.

Stepping outside, Helmut stopped on the back deck and turned back to Marion once again, appearing to want to say something else. Instead, he turned and walked into the night.

"Don't let the bastards wear you down," Marion whispered, as she watched him go.

CHAPTER 62

JOHN HAFFCUT KNEW he had strong evidence to suggest Konrad had been involved with Hope's death, but he had nothing tying Konrad to Zane Ritter, and not enough for Fish and Wildlife to lay charges.

When Brent Rideout informed John that he and Dale Weychuck had conducted extensive interviews at the coalmines and had everything needed to get a search warrant, John was keen to accept Brent's offer to help out.

"We came away with signed statements confirming reports of shots fired and Ritter's truck being seen in the area on the day in question," said Brent. "With Zane's track record and what we found at the scene, it was enough to get the warrant."

John was ecstatic and appreciated Brent's offer to assist. In return John also offered to bring Kate, Megan, Ben and Jimmy to help search Ritter's property at Old Entrance.

"The more the merrier," said Brent. "The last time I was there we could have used a pack of search dogs to find our way around the mess. But let me do the talking, at least initially. There's no point yammering away at Ritter trying to interview him. He just won't bite."

As they drove up to Zane's hideaway, John gained a better appreciation of what Brent was referring to: a ramshackle collection of outbuildings surrounding an old pan abode style house that looked like it had been previously moved to the site and placed haphazardly on a series of blocks made from discarded railway ties.

"What a cluster," said John as the provincial officers and park wardens arrived at the property.

After exiting the vehicles, Brent led the group of searchers to the front door of the dilapidated house and knocked. Hearing nothing, he knocked again. "Looks like nobody's home."

He picked an old nail from a box of scrap metal at the top of the dilapidated steps and pinned a copy of the search warrant to the wooden door, stabbing it with the nail to hold it in place. "There. Now it's legal." Turning to Dale he added, "Why don't you work with Jimmy and Ben and check the outbuildings for anything suspicious. I'll search the house with John, Megan and Kate." He turned to John. "If Ritter shows up, the officer we posted near the Old Entrance road will warn us on the radio."

Turning back to the house Brent nudged the door open and walked inside.

The interior of the pan abode was consistent with the mess outside: a clutter of old furniture, cardboard cartons and wooden crates that would challenge the most nimble person to navigate.

"What a fucking mess," said Brent as he toed through the carnage. "He keeps his truck in better shape than his house. And his truck is disgusting."

"Pretty gross, that's for sure," Megan agreed. She and Kate worked their way through the front room and started to check the bedrooms at the end of the hall while Brent and John concentrated on the kitchen and dining room.

"Just as gross as the rest of the place," Megan said as they rejoined Brent and John in the kitchen.

"I can only imagine." Brent shuddered at the grime. He finished looking through the cupboards and pushed the doors closed. "Nothing worth seizing. Let's see how Dale and Jimmy are making out."

As they headed outside, Brent's radio came to life with a call from the third officer warning them Ritter was on his way back to the property.

"You guys done?" Brent asked as they regrouped with Dale, Ben and Jimmy.

"Pretty much," said Dale. "The buildings are full of junk. We found some old traps and skins and an old freezer that stunk to high heavens, but nothing incriminating."

"What about the house?" said Jimmy.

"Nothing much," Brent chuckled, "but there are enough building code violations to keep an inspector busy for a few weeks writing them up."

"I wonder where Zane is?" said Jimmy.

"We just got a call he's on the way here," said Brent.

The words were barely out of his mouth when a large pickup pulled up behind the Fish and Wildlife and warden trucks and Zane jumped out.

"What the fuck are you guys doin' on my property?" said Zane, slobbering deep brown tobacco juice down his stubbled chin as he sauntered up to Brent Rideout. "Ya got a warrant?"

Brent Rideout pointed to the piece of paper nailed to the front door. "Sure do. Go take a look if you want. But I'll explain it so you understand." He stepped forward and stabbed a finger into Zane's chest. "*You* are being investigated for poaching a grizzly bear down near the coalmines. And not just any bear."

"Hmphh." Zane muttered, seeming unfazed by the accusation. "They're all the same to me." He looked around the group but focused on Megan. "You brought a lotta help with you," he said turning back to Brent before nodding toward his house. "So whad'ya find?"

"In that shithole?" said Brent. "Nothing. I'd be surprised if anyone could find anything in there. I've seen doghouses in better shape."

"Do ya think if I poached a bear I'd be stupid enough to keep it here?" Zane glared at Rideout.

Brent didn't back down. "If you're stupid enough to poach a bear, yeah, I'm sure you're stupid enough to do just about anything." Keeping his eyes pinned on Zane, Brent held his hand just above his sidearm. "Remember what I told you before, Zane.

The next time we catch you with wildlife parts, bear paws, gallbladders, bison heads, whatever, you'll be doing hard time. You've already lost your job with the mine and they don't want you back. What else can you afford to lose?"

Motioning the others to their vehicles, Brent brushed past Ritter and was about to slide behind the wheel of his Fish and Wildlife truck when John spoke up. "Just a minute, Brent."

"What's up?" Brent asked.

"Did the search warrant include vehicles on the property?" John nodded toward Ritter's truck.

"Why, as a matter of fact it did." Brent smiled.

"What the hell are you two up to?" Zane yelled, rushing over when he saw Brent and John walk over to his truck and open the driver's door.

Brent turned to face Zane as John began to search the cab.

"Get the hell outta there," Zane shouted as he tried to move past Brent.

Dale Weychuck quickly came to Brent's assistance, preventing Ritter from interfering with John's search.

"I told you to get the hell outta there," Zane repeated as John climbed down from the truck. "There's nothin' in there that's of any concern to you."

"I wouldn't say that," said John, holding up a laminated card.

"What the ...?" said Zane.

"You know what this is, don't you Zane?" John caught a glance from Brent Rideout but didn't respond.

"I got no idea what that is," said Zane, unconvincingly.

"Sure, you do. It's a list of frequencies for all the radio-collared bears in these parts, including the little sow grizzly you and Konrad Vincent-Blais shot by the coalmines. I found it in the glove compartment of your truck."

"No freakin' way you did." Zane looked confused. "I never seen that before." He turned to Brent Rideout. "God's truth. I never seen that before."

"Sure you have," said John, as the others gathered around. "Konrad must've forgotten it." He glanced at Brent then back at Zane. "Or he left it there to set you up."

"You fuckers don't know what you're talking about."

"I think we do," said Brent, stepping forward and grasping the shoulder of Zane's jacket. "You're going to have to come back to the office with Dale and me for questioning."

"What the fuck, I have no idea where that came from," Zane yelled as Brent manhandled him up against the side of his truck, immobilizing him with an arm lock.

"Cuff him, Dale," he said as Zane screamed obscenities at the two officers.

When Dale had the handcuffs on, Brent helped put Zane in the back of the Fish and Wildlife truck and closed the door. Turning back to Ritter's truck he looked behind the seat and pulled out a rifle and box of ammunition.

"There's probably a pretty good chance this is the gun he used," he said to John and the others. "We'll take it with us and see what Ritter has to say. I'll let you know how it goes."

CHAPTER 63

AS THE GROUP of park wardens made their way back to Jasper, John Haffcut took some consolation in the reaction they got from Zane Ritter.

"That was a smart move to ask Brent about what was listed in the search warrant," said Kate. "And it's good that he'd listed vehicles on the property."

"Well, he was probably expecting Ritter to be there," said John

"Still," said Megan, "it's good that you jogged his memory to search Ritter's truck. We could have come away empty-handed."

"And a lucky break the list was in his glove compartment," said Jimmy. "I'm surprised he wouldn't have realized it was there."

"He didn't," said Ben.

"What?" Jimmy smirked at Ben and shook his head. "Of course he did."

"Actually, he didn't," said John, grinning from ear to ear.

"What do you mean?" said Megan.

"John didn't find the list in Ritter's truck," said Ben. "John had it on him the whole time." He looked at John. "Am I right?"

"I hate to say it, but you are."

"Jesus, John, you can't do that." Jimmy swore some oaths and stared at John.

"Sorry Jimmy, but I did. We all know Zane Ritter was involved with Hope's death, but our chances of finding anything would have been slim to none. This way he's going to get what he deserves and the best thing about it is we're going to be able to kill two birds with one stone."

"Konrad?" said Megan.

John nodded. "Yeah. I'm going to see him before Zane Ritter has a chance to call him. Brent said he would keep Zane occupied long enough to give us time to get back to Jasper."

"Was Brent in on this from the start?" Kate asked.

"No, but he picked up on it pretty quick when I asked him about Ritter's truck. He knew enough to go along with it."

"Gotta like that," said Ben.

"Huhuh," said John.

"How are you going to tackle Konrad," said Jimmy. "He's got a few more clues than Zane Ritter."

"Maybe too many. He might just be too smart for his own good."

*****

After dropping off the others at the warden office John went straight to the administration building. Ignoring Konrad's executive assistant, John walked into the superintendent's office and sat down next to Konrad's desk.

"You again," said Konrad, barely acknowledging John's presence.

"I knew you'd be happy to see me."

"Right. Make it quick. I've got work to do." Konrad sat back and peered at John. "What do you want?"

"I just thought you'd want to know that Fish and Wildlife arrested Zane Ritter today. They've got him in for questioning and he's going to spill the beans about your involvement in Hope's death."

"Still onto that, are we?"

"Seems they found that list of frequencies in his truck." Konrad started to object, but John kept going. "You know he has such a long rap sheet, another conviction will land him in the slammer, especially one for shooting a grizzly bear out of season. Unless Ritter gives them something they want."

Konrad leaned forward on his desk, paying rapt attention.

"Anyway that was enough to get him to admit you were there. And that you shot Hope."

"That's total bullshit," Konrad said when he had a chance to speak.

"We both know it isn't, Konrad. But I guess the litmus test will be waiting to see what your poaching buddy has to say. If he does what I expect he'll do, the Fish and Wildlife guys will be hot to trot to take you away. They just love catching big fish. And a federal park superintendent is probably as big as they could hope for."

John didn't wait around for more of Konrad's protests. He got up and walked out, smiling to himself.

A guy like Konrad will screw himself, he thought as he made his way back to the warden office. *They always do.*

CHAPTER 64

KONRAD WAS UNSURE of his next step, especially after threatening Helmut Stenger with the recording of him authorizing Konrad to use his men for the attack on Marion Seawell. Maybe he had taken that too far, or not thought it through enough, especially considering Helmut's connections.

If Zane Ritter did out him over Hope's death, Konrad risked losing everything: it would be game over for a national park superintendent charged with poaching an iconic grizzly bear.

But if Zane Ritter didn't talk, which Konrad figured was most likely considering Ritter's hate for authority, then Konrad was fine.

Just to reassure himself that he hadn't ruffled feathers further up the line, Konrad closed the door to his office and put a call through to Tom Erickson.

"What a surprise," Tom said when Konrad identified himself. "What gives us the pleasure?"

"Er, I assume you are alone, Tom?"

"Yes, of course. What is it, Konrad? How are things progressing in Jasper?"

"It has its challenges,"

"Doesn't everything?" Tom laughed.

Konrad hesitated for a moment, wondering how much he should or shouldn't say, giving Tom a chance to fill the void of silence. "Don't worry so much, Konrad. As long as Helmut Stenger is satisfied things are progressing, there should be no worries. You have our support."

There's the rub, thought Konrad. He wasn't sure what Helmut Stenger would do next. And to some extent it depended on what Zane Ritter did. Ritter could scuttle everything by saying too much and once the dominoes began to fall, there was no telling where they might stop. Everyone involved could implicate the next person and suddenly the poaching of a grizzly bear in Jasper could have ripple effects felt right up the line to Maxime Bolduc. Even further, if Helmut Stenger was as politically connected as was suggested.

Ending the call with Tom Erickson, Konrad stared at his phone. He had reservations about making his next call, but knew he had no choice. He had to find out how things stood between himself and Helmut Stenger in the event Zane Ritter spilled his guts.

"Helmut," he said, when the German came on the line. "My apologies. I realize now I took things too far earlier, but I honestly never intended for Marion Seawell to be hurt. I just wanted to scare her."

"Go on."

"But I *am* concerned about Zane Ritter. He was taken into custody this afternoon on poaching charges. If he says too much, he could start a chain reaction that goes to the very top of Parks."

"Zane Ritter only leads the authorities to you," said Stenger, sounding indifferent.

Konrad understood the implied message: Don't talk.

"Not entirely, Helmut. He's a direct link to Gunter and Jakob as well. As am I. As are you. We're all in this together." Konrad was feeling desperate. "You need me."

"I do?"

"Yes, Helmut, let's be practical. If you want your lodge to go through we need to work together."

"My, my, Konrad, you flatter yourself."

"Why do you say that?"

"Because I don't need you at all. In fact, you need me."

"What are you saying, Helmut?"

"It's an intricate puzzle Konrad. Actually it's more like a house of cards. While people like you focus on the top, catering

292

to people like Maxime Bolduc and me, it's really the bottom that's critical. You abhor people at the bottom, like Zane Ritter, for instance, but they are the people that can take you down. And when they do, the house of cards collapses."

"I don't understand," said Konrad, trying to gauge where Helmut was going.

"Of course you don't. Let me explain it to you." Helmut paused. "But first I have to ask you. You aren't doing anything so stupid as recording this call are you Konrad? That would be another huge mistake."

"No, I ... no, I wouldn't be so crazy." Konrad was caught off guard by the comment and slid the recorder back in his top drawer.

"Smart move," said Helmut. "As I was about to say, when I started down this road, I knew I had to start at the bottom. Well I should clarify. I worked the bottom and the top simultaneously." He laughed.

"Believe it or not, the top is actually easier."

"I'm not so sure about that."

"I know you're not," said Helmut. "That's because you underestimate people at the bottom. But they are the foundation, as I said. If they collapse, they bring the whole house down. You need to take care of those at the bottom, Konrad."

"You aren't worried about Gunter and Jakob being implicated in the attack on Marion?"

"Not at all. The authorities won't be able to touch them. I've made sure of that."

"But you must be concerned about them having hired Zane Ritter. Especially now that they've taken him in for questioning?"

"They didn't hire Ritter," said Helmut.

"What do you mean? If they didn't, then who did?"

"I did."

Konrad was a little stunned by the admission.

"Long before Gunter and Jakob came on the scene," Stenger added. "And now I'm told he's been released."

"He has?" Suddenly Konrad was distracted by a knock on the door. "I'm busy," he shouted. "Sorry, Helmut, excuse me a moment, I need to speak with my assistant." Konrad pressed the button for his assistant. "I'm busy," he blurted before she could say anything. "No interruptions."

"But there's someone here to see you. And it looks important."

"I'll be there in a moment." Konrad returned to his call. "Sorry Helmut, I have to go. But I'll get back to you."

"Very well, Konrad. But keep in mind what I said. You don't want the house falling down on *you*." Before Konrad could reply, the sound of a dial tone came over the line. At the same time the office door opened and two provincial Fish and Wildlife officers walked in.

"Are you Konrad Vincent-Blais?" Brent Rideout asked.

CHAPTER 65

THE EVENING SUN was dipping below the mountains, casting long shadows over the Maligne Valley as the group sat around the campfire at the Maligne Warden Station. Jimmy and Shirley Rand's departure from the lake had caught most of them off guard, as the couple opted to move to town with Jimmy edging closer to retirement, but Megan had obviously been in the loop and scooped the opportunity to become the Maligne Lake warden.

In fact, she hadn't been approved to take over the residence at the lake, but when Jimmy told her the news, they coordinated moving dates so the same horse trailer used to haul Jimmy and Shirley's belongings to town was used to haul Megan's furnishings back to the lake.

"No point sending it back empty," Jimmy said to Lou, who was about to blow a gasket when he heard about the unsanctioned move, but finally conceded a cowboy's practical sense won out over the park's policy for internal moves.

Freshly ensconced in her new digs, Megan wanted to reciprocate being given the opportunity to take over at the lake and for the help she got with her move. But her offer to host a housewarming party for Jimmy soon morphed into a larger affair to also say goodbye to Anne and John who were moving to the West Coast.

"I'm surprised they gave you the job," Lou told Anne as they reminisced about the past few months. "But I'm even more surprised they agreed to transfer John as well."

"It is a little bit surprising," said Anne. "I can only assume Maxime is doing this for his own reasons and not for our welfare."

"But we'll go with it," John piped in, raising his beer bottle. "To the coast. Literally."

"To the coast," the others replied amid the clinking of bottles and glasses.

"Well it's been a crazy few months," said John. "What with Konrad being given the boot and the whole mine thing seeming to have fallen off the table. Any talk of a lodge up here seems to have dried up for now."

"It's almost too good to be true," said Kate.

"Except for Hope," said John. "I'm not sure what Konrad was thinking but that was a miscalculation. It completely backfired on him."

"It's too bad Hope had to pay the price," said Kate.

"I still can't figure out the whole Zane Ritter and Konrad thing," said Ben. "Ritter walks free and Konrad ends up taking the rap for poaching Hope."

"Well, according to Brent Rideout, there were a few strings pulled on that one," said John. "Somehow, Zane Ritter and Helmut Stenger have a history together."

"They do," said Jimmy, drawing glances from the group. "It goes back many years when Ritter's father was an outfitter and Stenger was actively climbing in Jasper. When Zane started outfitting he and Stenger somehow connected. I don't know all the ins and outs of their relationship but obviously it was enough that Stenger used his influence with the province to get Zane off."

"But in the end, he implicated Konrad?" said Kate.

"Yeah," said John. "But once again, there's something behind that whole thing we just don't know."

"None of it sounds to be on the up and up," said Ben.

"Whatever," said Kate. "It's worked out in our favour."

"Yeah," said Ben. "That's what worries me."

Kate shook her head. "You're never satisfied."

"Well you know what they say when things seem too good to be true," he countered.

"I know." Kate sounded frustrated. "Let's just go with it for tonight and enjoy the party."

"Hear, hear," said Jimmy, looking down the lake as evening settled in around them, bringing a chill that pulled the circle of people closer to the fire.

"We'll miss this," said Anne as John put an arm around her waist.

"We'll miss you," said Lou. "Hopefully the bozo they've temporarily put in your position won't screw up."

"To Bozo," said John, raising his glass above the group's laughter. "I can say that now that I'm leaving."

"You aren't gone yet," said Lou, his frown quickly turning into a smile. "That might cost you."

CHAPTER 66

LOU WALKER ACTUALLY relished the opportunity to act in the superintendent's position while Parks' senior management sorted out the mess left after Konrad's exploits were uncovered. Lou would have been fine with Anne Winters taking back the reins, but she was already committed to moving to the West Coast. Still, Lou was surprised when Tom Erickson asked him to take over in Jasper and even more surprised when Maxime Bolduc agreed.

After the Jasper situation blew up, they obviously needed an experienced person to take care of park operations while they did damage control in Ottawa. Lou had been around long enough to know when push came to shove, it was the Warden Service that management leaned on to get the job done. It always was the case and as far as Lou was concerned, it always would be.

But he wasn't naïve enough to think he would be allowed to stay in the position longer than it took senior management to find a *suitable replacement* for Anne Winters. *Their words, not his.*

He was even more surprised, in fact, that senior management hadn't placed any conditions on his taking the acting position. They were obviously swamped with other challenges. All Tom Erickson asked of Lou was to keep Jasper out of the media in the near term.

Still, Lou wasn't about to let this opportunity slip by. Unlike others who held acting positions, Lou planned to make whatever changes he could while he was superintendent. And he had a long list of things he wanted to achieve in whatever time they gave him, starting with creating as many hurdles for any future development proposals as he could.

He wasn't entirely convinced the lodge proposal was dead and if he was right, he wanted to do whatever he could to lessen its chances of ever seeing the light of day. But while that was a longer term goal, he still had to deal with the day to day issues of running one of the largest national parks in the country. Things like the most recent request from none other than Maxime Bolduc himself to play host to a visiting representative of the Tanzanian National Parks Authority, the man sitting across from him right now.

According to Bolduc, Jackson Sironka was an experienced protected areas manager with a strong interest in wildlife populations. The situations weren't exactly comparable to those in Tanzania, but Sironka wanted to know how national parks in Canada dealt with conflicts between people living in and around the park and the wildlife the parks were meant to protect.

Lou had hoped to assign John Haffcut to show Sironka around, but when Anne Winters fast-tracked John's transfer to the coast, catching Lou off guard completely, Lou decided to give Ben and Kate a perk after their work on the mine file. Besides, they both had experience in Wood Buffalo, which Lou figured added to their value as useful contacts for Sironka, who had specifically mentioned that his tour in Canada might also include Wood Buffalo, a national park with large herds of wildlife not unlike those found in the Serengeti and other parks in Sironka's home country.

When Ben and Kate walked in, Lou did the introductions, but decided to duck out to let them get acquainted with Sironka. As he walked past his two park wardens, he nudged Ben and whispered, "This might be your chance to go to Africa."

CHAPTER 67
Weeks later

"READY FOR A girl's night out?" Kate asked Marion as they settled in for the drive to Maligne Lake.

"You and Megan flatter me," Marion chuckled. "Girl's night out, my foot. I'm old enough to be your grandmother."

"But still young at heart," said Kate. "So go with it. Megan's been pestering us to come to the lake so we might as well enjoy it."

"Yes. Enjoy it while we still can."

Kate shook her head and grinned at Marion as they slowly drove past the gate at the Maligne Hostel and headed toward the lake. "You don't think it's over do you?"

"Hmphhh," Marion muttered. "I'd like to think so, but you never know if it's over, or if they're just catching their breath."

"There's been no word," said Kate. "Hopefully the lodge idea is dead."

"As far as we know, a final decision hasn't been made." Marion raised her eyebrows at Kate.

Kate peered ahead as an early snow began to cover the road and wondered if a decision *had* been made, and in typical government fashion, management was waiting for an opportune time to let the news out. That was Ben's suspicion, suggesting senior management typically waited until the end of a week or just before a major holiday so they could put out unwelcome news without much fanfare, media coverage or opposition.

But then again, Ben was always suspicious, she thought. That was why he was still in touch with Kallie, asking her to stay on the trail of Helmut's company as well as the Calgary design firm Stenger had hired to work on the lodge proposal.

The lodge is definitely what they're after, Kallie had said. She'd seen the plan with her own eyes.

But when Kate and Ben asked if she could go back, Kallie had told them Stephanie Landegarde had closed things up so tight, she must have suspected Kallie was not what she was pretending to be.

But *you are* a freelance journalist, Ben had countered, asking her not to give up.

Kate had been less convinced and suggested Ben give it a rest now that Konrad was gone and the issue had died down.

But what if Ben's right this time? What if Bolduc and Stenger are just waiting to push the lodge through? God, I'm getting as cynical about government as Ben and Marion both, Kate thought as the road wound higher into the subalpine.

But lucky for Ben, he could forget about it for a while, now that he was in Tanzania.

As Lou had suspected when he talked to them after their meeting with Jackson Sironka, the Tanzanian had graciously offered an exchange opportunity to both Ben and Kate, and with Lou's blessing, they both jumped at the chance. But Lou had been unwilling to let them both leave at the same time. With John gone he still needed someone at Poco until things slowed down for winter. In the end, he agreed to let Ben go to scope things out while Kate would follow in a month or so.

In her heart, Kate knew she wanted the chance to go to Tanzania as well, but as she and Marion made their way to the lake, she wondered if it would ever happen.

Driving into a snow squall, she was suddenly bought back to reality as Marion pointed to a series of dark shapes making their way up the road in front of them. "Wolves," she said, sounding almost triumphant. "There's what we've been talking about all along. Wolves use the road to access caribou habitat. I can't believe people still contest the idea when you can see the proof of it almost any day of the week during winter."

"Some people just take longer to convince," said Kate.

They slowed down and watched as the wolves, obviously realizing they were being followed, weaved their way off the pavement and walked single file into the forest alongside the road.

"Or they refuse to believe it because they have other agendas." Marion countered.

While they drove past, the wolves edged farther into the forest, but were still visible from the road.

"Like a lodge at the lake?" said Kate.

"Exactly," said Marion, as Kate pressed on the gas pedal and drove past the wolves.

"Well, hopefully, that's not going to happen," said Kate as they drove into another snow squall.

Suddenly a large SUV, with the Mountain Park Designs logo emblazoned on the doors sped past and disappeared over the hill.

"You don't think so?" Marion shook her head and watched as the large snowflakes struck the windshield and melted. "After all that, you think Parks will reject the project?"

"It doesn't hurt to hope the right decision will be made."

"A faint hope." Marion sighed. "It seems to be all we can cling to anymore. The 'faint hope' clause. Like a prisoner on Death Row."

"It's not that bad," said Kate.

"No?" said Marion. "You think it's just a fluke that Anne, John and Ben are out of the picture? And you will be too in a few weeks?"

"Anne didn't have much choice. And John would have wanted to go wherever she went," said Kate. "And Ben and I have always been keen on an exchange. It's just a coincidence it happened now." She cringed as she realized what she'd said.

Marion laughed.

"You don't buy that?" said Kate. "You think it's some kind of conspiracy?"

"I don't think conspiracy is the right word," said Marion. "That would give them too much credit."

"What *do* you think?"

"I think they saw an opportunity to get John out of here and helped make it happen. Anne knew it wouldn't be healthy for him to stick around, so with the Snake's blessing, she offered him a chance to go to the Gulf Islands."

"And Ben and me?"

Marion's face drew tight and she pursed her lips.

"What?" said Kate.

"I'm not so sure going to Africa is a good idea."

Kate pulled her foot off the accelerator and looked over at Marion.

"What do you mean?"

Marion hesitated. "Well, you know I've always struggled with the idea that Malcolm's death was accidental, even though the RCMP took another look at Malcolm's file after my accident and came to the same conclusion."

"Yes, but what's that got to do with us going to Africa?" Kate pulled the truck over to side of the road and parked. "What are you saying, Marion?"

"It's complicated," said Marion. "Maybe it's just the ramblings of an old woman."

"Try me," said Kate.

"Well, it's just that Malcolm was more outspoken than me on development in the park. But in some ways, he was starting to accept that development in Jasper was unstoppable, that greed and money would win out every time. Now don't get me wrong, Malcolm was determined not to let that happen."

"And?" said Kate.

"And after what happened to me on the lake and after speaking with Helmut Stenger, I'm more convinced than ever Malcolm's death was no accident."

"You're scaring me Marion."

"I don't mean to, I'm sorry."

"But there's more isn't there?"

"It's just the German connection. And Helmut Stenger's connection to Africa and mining." She shrugged. "Maybe I'm putting too much into it."

"Stenger's companies have tentacles everywhere," said Kate. "Not just Africa."

"I know," said Marion. "It's probably nothing. It's probably just coincidence."

Kate cringed again. "Ben would say there is no such thing."

Marion's blank stare was unnerving.

"You think Ben was lured out of here? To Africa?"

Marion sighed. "I'm just getting you and me more upset. Forget what I said. I really don't know anymore."

After their day at the lake with Megan, the drive back to town was quiet as Marion nodded off for parts of the trip. Still Kate could hardly forget what Marion had said and worried about leaving Marion on her own.

"Are you going to be okay?" she asked when she dropped her off at her house that evening.

"I'll be fine." Marion smiled. "Thank you. It was a lovely day."

Kate watched her make her way to her front door and waved as Marion went inside. She lingered for a moment, watching through the house windows as Marion turned on lights and moved from room to room. Satisfied Marion was fine, Kate drove out of town and made her way back to the trailer at Pocahontas. If all went according to plan, she and Ben would be taking over the house when they returned from Africa, but for now, she was content to leave moving until she and Ben had time to do it together.

Driving past the empty house reminded Kate of their place in Cape Breton. Despite all the distance they'd travelled since those heady days working in the Cape Breton Highlands, she wondered how far they'd really come.

Different parks, on opposite ends of the country, but nothing is that different. Each has its challenges. And I expect Ben is finding out the same thing in Africa.

Pulling up in front of the trailer she sat and thought about their last hours together.

*****

"Here we go again," said Kate, as they stood in front of the security gate at Edmonton's airport.

"It won't be long before you'll be in Tanzania with me," said Ben. "And when we get back, we'll take care of that other business."

"You've got a date, Mister."

Ben smiled and hugged Kate. "That's a date I don't plan to miss."

"But you'd better get going or you'll miss your flight," said Kate, pushing out of Ben's arms. "Call me when you land in London." She kissed Ben and pushed him toward security. "Love you."

As Ben snaked his way through the line he looked back at Kate. "Love you," he said, talking over the heads of others in the line.

Kate smiled and waved as Ben disappeared through the doorway.

As she turned to leave, a Cape Breton lament played over the airport speaker system and she smiled.

*****

The music was in Kate's head again now as she got out of the truck at Pocahontas. Humming the tune, she made her way up the steps and opened the door just as the phone started to ring.

"Hello," she said, as she walked inside the trailer and laid her daypack on the kitchen table. "Kallie? I'm surprised to hear from you. Just a second, let me put you on speaker." Kate placed the receiver on the table and sat down. "What's up Kallie?" she asked as she unlaced her hiking boots.

"Has Ben left for Africa?"

"Yes," said Kate. "He was lucky enough to get fast tracked for the main vaccinations he needed and was out of here. He's been gone for a few days now. Why do you ask?"

There was a pause.

"Why, Kallie? What have you found out?"

"It's probably nothing."

"But?"

"Well, I was doing some more digging into Stenger's company and its activities in Africa."

"Yes?"

"Apparently Stenger's main operative was a senior manager with the Tanzanian authority responsible for its anti-poaching program and training of park rangers."

"TANAPA?" said Kate. "The Tanzanian National Parks Authority?"

"Yes." Kallie's voice wavered. "How'd you know that?"

"Lucky guess," Kate said, not liking where the conversation was headed. "Go on."

"Well, currently the guy is temporarily suspended from his position. He's under review because of a major poaching operation that took place on his watch. It's causing quite a bit of international criticism of the authority's rhino and elephant protection strategies."

"And?" Kate said.

"Well, there's some evidence the guy was taking bribes in exchange for diverting their anti-poaching units away from critical areas. So the poachers literally had free rein."

"I see," Kate said with a heavy sigh. "There's more isn't there?"

"Not much more. Just his name."

"It's Jackson Sironka, isn't it?" said Kate, sinking down on the chair.

"How the hell did you know that?"

"Coincidence," said Kate. She closed her eyes and took a deep breath as she thought about Ben being so far away in Africa.

It's just a coincidence.

Read the Prologue and First Chapter of Book Four in the
Dyed In The Green series.

Fat Cats
A novel by George Mercer
Copyright © 2017

PROLOGUE

LIGHT SNOW FLOATED down through the leafless branches of the large maple trees, obscuring the subtle signs John Haffcut needed to locate his quarry. On any other day it, might have been enough to turn him around, but having walked this part of the island many times before, he was fairly certain where he would end up and kept following his instincts toward a stand of Douglas fir at the edge of the maples. As he passed under the thick canopy of fir, he stopped for a moment to let his eyes adjust to the fading light.

The forest floor was a mass of dry twigs and fallen branches with very few signs he could use to continue his search. Opening the lid of the small metal box hanging from his neck, he turned the small plastic knob. Straining to hear the barely audible pulsing sound, he raised the H-shaped antenna over his head, turning it slowly until he found the direction where the signal was loudest. At this point he turned the dial down until the beeping was just a light murmur and began walking in the direction of the signal.

Haffcut placed each footstep carefully, avoiding twigs and branches that would crunch and crack under his weight, giving away his presence. At a small thicket, he crouched down to get under the lowest branches, keeping the antenna out in front of him to avoid ensnaring it in the underbrush. It was awkward going and the more he laboured to get through the thicket, the more he realized he'd dressed too warmly for this outing. Finally he made it through and was able to stand up, sweat beading on his face and running down the back of his neck.

The receiver's pulsing intensified and once again he swiveled the antenna in his hand until he found the loudest signal, then adjusted the knob again to turn it down. The signal was now about as low as it could go without turning the receiver off. He was close.

Thinking he heard a noise in the trees above him Haffcut stood stock still, held his breath and listened intently. Slowly he turned his head and gazed straight into the face of the large cougar suspended in the tree branches a few feet above him. The hair bristling on the back of his neck sent a wave of cold air down his spine as the cat's dark piercing eyes focused on him, contemplating its next move. Haffcut easily outweighed the feline by a hundred pounds or more, but had the large cat taken advantage of the element of surprise, she could have had him down on the ground in seconds.

He had come face to face with cougars many times before, but each time he stared into the eyes of one of them, it was entirely different from any previous encounter. He liked to think each episode was the result of his skillful tracking, his focused attention to detail in the subtle signs left behind as his quarry made its way through the forest. But in the back of his mind, he couldn't help thinking it was the other way around. The ending was becoming routine and this time was no different. He could never know for sure if it was *his* cat he was following, but in the final moments before he met his quarry, *he* was always the one looking over his shoulder.

Haffcut hesitated as the cat turned her head, allowing him a good look at her profile. For some reason, perhaps the fact he was uncharacteristically caught off guard, he didn't think the cougar was the one he was looking for, but the chance of another cougar being on the island was slim. As the cat turned, he could make out the thick leather belt of the GPS collar half hidden in the ruffled fur of her neck. Finally convinced this was his cat, he finally let out a sigh.

Slowly unzipping his fleece jacket, Haffcut pulled a small pistol from an inside pocket. Reaching into his chest pack, he removed a short metal cylinder with a barbless needle on one end and a feathered tailpiece at the other. He always kept his darts close to his chest, where his body heat kept them warm.

Opening the breach of the pistol, he shoved the dart down the barrel and pushed in the bolt. Taking careful aim, he waited for the cat to turn, giving him a clear shoulder shot before he fired. Although he was using the lowest charge possible, the impact of the dart was enough to set off a second charge in the rubber plunger at the base of the cylinder, forcing the Ketamine out through the needle and into the muscle tissue of the large cat.

For its part, the cougar just flinched at the noise of the powder charge going off and barely felt the needle penetrate and release its drug. She lay quietly in the branches for a moment then rolled slightly sideways as the drug took effect. Before she could fall from the perch Haffcut was underneath the tree and gently pulled the cat down. He cradled the cougar in his arms for a moment then laid her on the ground to remove the dart and retrieve the collar. The drug would easily last long enough for him to take off the old collar and put on a refurbished unit that would continue tracking the cat's movements and help him find it once again when it was time to take it off the island.

Until then, the cougar would be free to follow her instincts, searching the island for its plentiful bounty of introduced deer. From Haffcut's perspective it was an elegant solution to a man-made problem. People had decimated the wolves, bears and cougars that had naturally regulated the island's Blacktail deer populations and had added a menagerie of other species, including European Fallow Deer, brought to the island for sport hunting, creating a game reserve of sorts for the private land owners. In the absence of predators, the deer had over-grazed their habitat, out-competing the native deer and decimating the island's native vegetation and songbird communities. He was simply assisting Mother Nature, or whatever you wanted to call it, reverse the cascade of unwanted effects that were turning the southern Gulf Islands into an ecological hodge-podge.

The small fallow deer, weighing between twenty and thirty pounds for a young of the year and topping out at eighty pounds for a large male, would provide the cougar with a few days' food for each kill she made. Over the course of the winter, when the island was largely uninhabited, she could take between thirty and fifty deer, a substantial reduction thanks to the efforts of a single cougar. Over time, his cats would help turn things around. Salal, ocean spray and other native shrubs would become more prevalent, released from the intense browsing pressure of the deer. Eventually, sparrows, warblers and other songbirds would return to the forest.

It was a plan he had envisioned when he first began working on the island. It wasn't ideal, but it was a damn sight better than the alternative. At some point he might get caught or word might get out, but he hoped before anything like that happened, he would have made a noticeable difference and perhaps be able to convince enough of the right people what he was doing had more benefits than not. Only time would tell.

CHAPTER 1

THE OLD FOUR by four clawed its way up the frost covered woods road, spinning its wheels as it climbed out of the deep ruts left behind by skidders and logging trucks.

Peering out through the mud covered windshield, Vidar Gunvaldsson cursed as he manhandled the gear shift into low, cranking the steering wheel left and right to correct for the slipping and sliding. Resigned to the fact the truck's worn tires were no match for the greasy track, he pulled onto a siding and gunned the engine to spin the truck around, stalling it with a loud backfire.

This was as far as he could drive. From here he would be on foot. The rising sun would dry out the road for the return trip, and with any luck he would be able to find a cat and only have a few miles of tracking before he could catch it and get back to the truck. The dogs would help but first he needed to cut sign.

Sliding out of his cab he pulled an old canvas pack from behind the seat, checking its contents to make sure he had extra ammunition. He always kept a couple of tags handy just in case he ran into a Conservation Officer. Hopefully, he would be able to get the cat out of the bush and back home unnoticed, and save the tags for another day.

Reaching under the seat he pulled out a rifle, wrapped tightly in an old woolen blanket. Unwrapping the Winchester he checked the magazine to make sure it was fully loaded then laid it across the truck seat.

Walking to the back of the truck, his two dogs started to yelp as he opened the tailgate and unlatched the door of their wooden crate. Bursting out of the large box the two hounds toppled to the ground, sliding into the mud before turning their attention to Gunvaldsson and jumping up on him.

"Get down" he yelled, swiftly kicking the smallest dog in the ribs, sending it backwards with a yelp.

The larger dog sat down immediately, waiting obediently for the next command. The smaller dog returned sheepishly to his side, finally taking a cue from his brother and sitting down as well. Both animals had seen better days, their ragged coats and sunken rib cages providing evidence that life in the bush was taking its toll. To their owner they were merely tools of the trade and enjoyed none of the creature comforts *a pet* might realize.

Vidar Gunvaldsson was not a man of excess. He could make eight grand in a week guiding Americans on a cat hunt but was too stingy to spend hard earned cash on any of life's perks. A proficient hunter and trapper, he had honed his skills in northern British Columbia before moving to the Interior and finally to the Island, accepting a contract with the Wildlife Branch to help with the exploding cougar population on the coast. They needed trained cat trackers and he was one of the best in the province.

Grabbing his rifle and pack he locked the truck and began walking up the woods road, looking intently for any sign of cougar. Realizing his dogs were still at the truck he gave a loud whistle which sent them scrambling towards him.

"Heel", he said as the dogs caught up and fell in single file behind.

This was one of Gunvaldsson's favourite cougar territories. The old cutovers had lots of browse for deer and that in turn pulled in an abnormally high number of the big cats. The early morning frost and light dusting of snow also made for good tracking and would hold any recent cat scent for the dogs to follow.

A short distance from the truck Gunvaldsson found what he was looking for. Judging by the size and number of tracks, a small female with two young had followed a deer trail out to the road and picked it up again on the other side, heading east towards a large cutover.

Keeping the dogs close behind him, Gunvaldsson followed the deer trail into the bush, paying close attention to ensure the trio of cats didn't veer off and take another route. The cats were not far ahead but he wanted to make up some of the distance before putting the dogs on them. The kittens would slow the female down, giving his hunting party a slight advantage. They were of little use to him otherwise and would become collateral damage unless they were smart enough to abandon their mother, which was unlikely.

As they wound their way along the deer trail Gunvaldsson could tell that the cats were not moving quickly. Leaving the road, the female's stride length increased as she had likely heard his truck and quickly took cover with her kittens. But back in the trees, the stride length returned to normal. She had obviously not worried about being followed, focusing instead on her quarry somewhere out in the cutover. The maze of deer tracks and trails made it hard to single out any one animal but Gunvaldsson paid attention to ensure the cougar tracks were always on top of the deer tracks, confirming he was on the right trail.

His strategy was to get as close as possible before releasing the dogs, hoping the cougar had taken down a deer and was feeding on it with her young. Every distraction for the cat made his job a little easier and today luck was on his side.

Emerging from a thick stand of trees Gunvaldsson slowly raised a hand, signaling the dogs to stop and sit. The cats had moved off the trail and were obviously hunting. Scanning the clearing, a movement in the distance caught his attention.

Pulling binoculars from his pack he glassed the cutover. Just as he suspected, the cougar and her kittens had taken down a deer and were busy feeding, steam rising around them from the warm body of their prey. Raising her head periodically to check for signs of danger, the female was oblivious to Gunvaldsson's presence. Save for the chatter of chickadees in the nearby trees, silence reigned.

Gunvaldsson carefully picked his way through the tangle of alder bordering the forest. Waiting in the trees for his signal, the two dogs could barely contain their energy, sensing the impending chase. Determining he could go no further without alerting the cougar, he motioned for the dogs to come. He was not close enough for a clear shot and did not want to risk having to track an injured cat, opting instead to tree it with the dogs.

As the lead dog approached, Gunvaldsson wasted no time.

"Cat", he ordered, snapping his arm in the direction of the cougars and sending the hounds bounding off towards their target. The strategy worked well as the dogs were almost upon them before the female and kittens realized they were in danger.

Turning quickly, the cougars began their escape across the clearing, trying to gain the forest and lose the dogs in the rocky bluffs beyond the cutover. Gunvaldsson charged through the bush not wanting to be left too far behind. He had calculated correctly that the female would not make it past the few large fir trees remaining at the edge of the cutblock.

Sensing the dogs were closing in, the cougars quickly made their way up into the lower branches of a veteran Douglas fir, moving higher into its outstretched limbs as the hounds howled and yelped at the foot of the tree. Gunvaldsson did not have far to go. Knowing the dogs' barking meant the cats were treed, Gunvaldsson took his time covering the remaining distance, pulling the gun off his shoulder and levering a round into the barrel as he approached the big fir. The adult cougar was putting on quite a display, barring her teeth and hissing at the dogs ten feet below as the younger cats made their way higher into the canopy.

Calling off the hounds Gunvaldsson surveyed the situation, lining up for the clearest shot. This was the part he enjoyed the most. This was the payoff. Today's adventure had been short-lived compared to most chases but every once in a while he figured he was due. Everything didn't have to be so hard he thought to himself. He wasn't sure what he would do with the kittens but knew he was going home with at least one cat. The younger cougars would probably not survive on their own so he could knock them out of the tree and let the dogs have some fun or leave them to fend for themselves on the off chance one might make it and provide a future opportunity for him.

Either way it was a *win-win* for him.

Frothing at the mouth with anticipation, the two hounds sat shaking in the shadows of the large tree. Gunvaldsson pulled a short rope with two metal clips out of his pack, tied it to a nearby fir and called the dogs over, clipping each one into the line to keep them out of his way. He had already lost two dogs in the past year and didn't want a repeat performance. If the cougar came out of the tree on her own he would not have time to screw around. As he turned to walk back to the large fir the younger hound gave a sharp yelp as it tried to pull out of its collar and return to the action but the second swift kick of the day from Gunvaldsson put it back in its place.

"If you don't quit that you'll be cougar bait," he grunted. "You're not worth a bullet."

Returning to the cougar, Gunvaldsson shouldered the rifle and positioned himself for the clearest shot. He wanted to avoid the head as that would ruin the skin for his client, opting instead for a shoulder shot that he hoped would topple the female out of the tree. Lining the cat up in the gun sights he slowly squeezed the trigger.

The loud crack of the rifle reverberated across the clearing and the nearby bluffs as the cougar fell out of the tree to a chorus of yelps and howls. Gunvaldsson approached cautiously but the cat never moved. Turning her over he inspected for damage, pleased to see that the exit wound was relatively small. Looking into the tree, the two kittens had now climbed out of sight but he could hear their muffled cries as they perched precariously on the higher branches.

"Another day", he said out loud to himself, as he unhooked the dogs, coiled his rope and stowed it away. Putting on his pack he bent down and hoisted the cougar onto his shoulders, wrapping his arms around the cat's legs. Straining against the weight he stood up and grabbed the rifle. Signaling to the dogs he made his way slowly through the cutover, retracing his route back to the road.

ACKNOWLEDGEMENTS

AS WITH EACH book in the *Dyed In The Green* series, this novel was inspired by those men and women of Canada's national parks who share a "green" ethic and who truly are, in every sense of the expression, "dyed in the green". Many of these men and women nurtured my passion for parks and protected areas and were mentors who led by example and walked the talk.

But this story was also inspired by people who work 'on the outside', committed to our parks and protected areas and the wildlife and habitats they protect. Every park we've worked in has those people, willing to dedicate a big part of their lives to ensuring our parks and protected areas remain true to their purpose.

Whether they work inside or outside government, *Jasper Wild* is dedicated to those people who share a passion for our wild places and the species they support.

*****

Although writing is a very personal endeavour, this book has benefitted, from the input of numerous people. Once again I have to give special thanks to my editor, Kate Scallion, who took time from her pursuit of a law degree to edit the draft manuscript, and Iryna Spica, who made time in her busy schedule to prepare the manuscript for printing.

I would also like to thank Dan Stiles for his amazing cover designs for *Dyed In The Green, Wood Buffalo,* and now *Jasper Wild.* I look forward to working with him on the remaining books in the series and take my challenge as writing a story as good as the cover that holds it together.

Family is also a big part of the writing process and I am lucky to have supportive children, siblings and extended family, who encourage my efforts. A special thanks goes to my brother, Harry Mercer, for proofreading and providing feedback on the draft manuscript.

Finally, I want to thank Jan for her unwavering support and constructive feedback throughout the process of writing and revising this story. Besides being my partner in crime over these past three decades, these stories are as much hers as they are mine.

Ultimately though, writing *Jasper Wild* was my task, and whatever it lacks may be attributed solely to me. If you'd like to provide feedback, please check out the links to my websites and contact information on the next page. I'm always happy to hear from readers.

There are many ways to increase awareness and build appreciation and support for our parks and protected areas. I always expected I would be doing it through non-fiction, but after being exposed to fiction writing, I decided to use a fictional approach with the *Dyed In The Green* series.

My primary objective is to attract readers who might not otherwise be drawn to learn about our national parks, including the opportunities they present and the challenges they face.

If you enjoyed *Jasper Wild* or other books in the series, please help spread the word.

EGM
May 2017

ABOUT THE AUTHOR

FOR MORE THAN three decades George Mercer worked as a national park warden in Canada, including work in six national parks on both east and west coasts, the North and the Rocky Mountains. For ten of those years, George worked as a Park Warden and Wildlife Specialist in Jasper National Park in Alberta.

George continues to be passionate about parks and protected areas and this passion forms the backdrop for much of his fiction and non-fiction writing, which can be followed at www.george-mercer.com and www.writenature.com.

Originally from Gander, Newfoundland, George now lives with his wife and family in North Saanich, British Columbia.